Praise for

Heidi Swain

'Lose yourself in this heart-warming story of romance, community and secrets. The perfect story to read by the fire!' **Phillipa Ashley**

'Sweet and lovely. I guarantee you will fall in love with Heidi's wonderful world' **Milly Johnson**

'A little slice of joy' ***Heat***

'Sparkling and romantic' ***My Weekly***

'A true comfort read and the perfect treat to alleviate all the stress!' **Veronica Henry**

'The queen of feel-good' ***Woman & Home***

'The perfect read to relax and curl up at home with' **Caroline Roberts**

'A story that captures your heart' **Christie Barlow**

'Fans of Carole Matthews will enjoy this heartfelt novel' **Katie Oliver**

'A wonderfully uplifting story with a picturesque setting you'll wish you could visit' ***Culturefly***

Also by Heidi Swain

The Cherry Tree Café
Summer at Skylark Farm
Mince Pies and Mistletoe at the Christmas Market
Coming Home to Cuckoo Cottage
Sleigh Rides and Silver Bells at the Christmas Fair
Sunshine and Sweet Peas in Nightingale Square
Snowflakes and Cinnamon Swirls
at the Winter Wonderland
Poppy's Recipe for Life
The Christmas Wish List
The Secret Seaside Escape
The Winter Garden
A Taste of Home
Underneath the Christmas Tree
The Summer Fair
A Christmas Celebration
The Book-Lovers' Retreat
That Festive Feeling
The Holiday Escape
Home for Christmas
Best Summer Ever

Heidi Swain

All Wrapped Up

SIMON & SCHUSTER

London · New York · Amsterdam/Antwerp · Sydney/Melbourne · Toronto · New Delhi

First published in Great Britain by Simon & Schuster UK Ltd, 2025

1 3 5 7 9 10 8 6 4 2

Simon & Schuster UK Ltd, 1st Floor
222 Gray's Inn Road, London WC1X 8HB

Simon & Schuster Australia, Sydney
Simon & Schuster India, New Delhi

www.simonandschuster.co.uk
www.simonandschuster.com.au
www.simonandschuster.co.in

The authorised representative in the EEA is Simon & Schuster Netherlands BV, Herculesplein 96, 3584 AA Utrecht, Netherlands. info@simonandschuster.nl

A CIP catalogue record for this book is available from the British Library

Paperback ISBN: 978-1-3985-3870-2
eBook ISBN: 978-1-3985-3871-9
Audio ISBN: 978-1-3985-3872-6

Typeset in the UK by Palimpsest Book Production Limited, Falkirk, Stirlingshire
Printed and Bound in the UK using 100% Renewable Electricity
at CPI Group (UK) Ltd

FSC
www.fsc.org
MIX
Paper | Supporting responsible forestry
FSC® C013604

To

Rosie-Kate and Ian, a truly dynamic duo!

Chapter 1

When I woke, with the sun streaming through the bedroom curtains, on the Sunday of the August Bank Holiday weekend, feeling surprisingly light of heart and happier to be alive than I had in a long time, I had no inkling that now my grief was fading further into the background, it was about to be replaced with yet another emotion. And an unwelcome one at that.

However, by the time I had eaten breakfast, with the radio happily babbling, the back door wide open to let in the breeze, and posted something suitably sunny on my successful Insta account, AutumnEverything, I could sense a slow puncture in my previously buoyant mood and knew that I was destined to traverse yet more tricky emotional territory.

It took me a further few minutes of thinking as I plumped cushions, twitched curtains and tidied magazines to work out what I was feeling and it was the hollow echo of my feet on the scrubbed and sealed wooden floorboards that finally revealed the sensation I was experiencing.

All the while I had been renovating Rowan Cottage, my focus had been divided between coming further to terms with finding myself a widow before the age of thirty and creating myself the perfect solo sanctuary, but now the changes to the cottage were complete, now *I* was finally beginning to feel more complete, there was a vacancy in my life and it had been filled by a wholly unexpected sense of loneliness.

'Oh, my goodness.' I sighed, as I reluctantly accepted the sensation. 'And just when I thought I was finally getting somewhere.'

I had become quite the recluse since my move to the Fens and hadn't yet made a single friend in the area. I hadn't felt concerned about it before, but clearly it was time to find the courage to embrace yet further change in my life now that the spectre of loneliness was loitering.

'Best foot forward then, Clemmie,' I attempted to encourage myself. 'Because something will have to be done to remedy this.'

As the cottage renovation had neared completion, time spent working in the garden and learning about the local birdlife had stepped in to further help distract me from memories of what had happened to my husband, Callum, and I headed outside to immerse myself in the sunny morning in the hope that it would help dispel the impending sense of being utterly alone.

Three years since Callum's tragic death, I no longer plummeted headlong into the deep well of grief on a regular basis, but sometimes darker thoughts would creep up on me, and the garden and my feathered friends had become a welcome refuge when I needed to dig deep – no pun intended – and find the light again.

That morning however, and in spite of the sunshine, the clear blue sky and my best efforts to focus on the dead-heading and bird table propping up (I really needed to treat myself to a new one), it wasn't proving enough to shake the loneliness off. I took a breather and turned to look at my beloved sanctuary.

Set in the flat Fenland landscape, Rowan Cottage was picture perfect. Renovated, predominantly by my own fair hands, everything about it was idyllic. The wood and brick porch had a profusely flowering and highly scented old-fashioned rose clambering over it, the symmetrically set, freshly painted windows were dressed with pretty patterned curtains. The rooms were all filled with quirky and collectable treasures, and the façade and most of the garden was now every bit as pleasing as the inside.

With the finishing touches to the interior added just a few days before, the question of what I was going to do next had already started to raise its head. The last eighteen months had been a whirlwind of knocking down walls, replastering others, hanging wallpaper and picking out tiles. The work was finally complete, but I hadn't yet worked out what I was going to do now it was done.

I couldn't bear the thought of selling up and starting again, but suddenly, and shockingly, I knew with devastating clarity that Rowan Cottage alone wasn't enough. I quickly turned back around to look at the soothing view beyond the picket fence.

My parents had described the landscape as barren the first time they had visited and with barely a tree in sight across the Fens, they were right. However, whereas they had cited that as a fault, I had always adored the emptiness. With uninterrupted views to the horizon, there was nothing that could creep up on me here. No hidden nasty shocks waiting to pounce and that made the thought of trying to find somewhere new to live but with a similar outlook feel insurmountable.

Even though my happy home and its ideal setting suddenly didn't feel like the be all and end all, I knew beyond any doubt that it had become an essential part of who I was and I definitely wanted to keep it. Therefore, I would have to find something else, which didn't involve the services of an estate agent, to enthral me . . .

'Perhaps then it's finally time you rejoined the human race, Clemmie,' I mused aloud. 'Maybe it's time you stopped talking to yourself and found yourself an actual . . . friend.'

So immersed in my thoughts, I hadn't heard a car pull up on the drove road next to the cottage or the driver climb out.

'Hello!' the unexpected visitor called cheerily and I spun around, my heart hammering because they had made me jump. 'Hi!'

The woman, who I had seen stop by before, had a head of red curls and was wearing a vintage floral sundress. She had already opened and walked through the wooden gate and into the garden.

'I've caught you at last,' she laughed, unaware of how accurate her words were. 'I've stopped by at least half a dozen times before, but you're never in.'

That wasn't strictly true. I had been in, but I had chosen not to answer the door to her. Since the day I arrived, I had preferred to keep myself to myself. I had only ventured into the nearby town of Wynbridge, early in the morning or late in the afternoon when I knew it wouldn't be busy and, politely staving off any friendly overtures, I hadn't properly introduced myself to anyone local, aside from a few essential tradespeople and the postwoman.

However, having literally just acknowledged that my solitary existence needed shaking up, and finding someone in my garden at the exact moment I had uttered the words, felt almost like a wish come true, most certainly a timely nudge from the universe, and I felt duty bound to embrace it. Even if I was rather out of practice when it came to playing the host.

'Hello,' I therefore tentatively smiled. 'Hi.'

'I'm Lizzie,' the woman said confidently, walking further along the path, 'Lizzie Dixon.'

'Clementine,' I said back, brushing my grubby hands down my shorts, before I pushed my glasses up into my messily tied up sun-streaked blonde hair.

'Clementine,' the woman I now knew as Lizzie Dixon, repeated.

'Though everyone calls me Clemmie,' I amended.

I had almost said that my friends called me Clemmie, but given how I currently didn't have any, that would have been a stretch and a dishonest start to my first purely sociable interaction in months.

'Clemmie.' Lizzie beamed, as she clasped her hands to her heart. 'Oh, my goodness, that's the prettiest name.'

'Thank you.' I blushed.

'I don't think I've ever met a Clementine or a Clemmie before.'

'Me neither.' I smiled shyly. 'In my experience, there don't seem to be many of us about.'

Now names had been exchanged, I faltered.

'Well,' said Lizzie, looking over at Rowan Cottage, 'like I said, I hope you don't mind me stopping and announcing myself. I used to know the lady who lived here before you and I've been dying to find out what's happened to the place since she sold it. I know you've been renovating . . .'

'Yes, I have.' I nodded, eagerly latching on to the topic because I could wax lyrical about the cottage until the cows came home. 'It's undergone quite a transformation inside. Especially downstairs. The previous layout wasn't very practical.'

'And that bathroom was always glacial.' Lizzie shuddered, in spite of the warmth of the day.

Her description was entirely accurate, so I knew she really had known the place well. I had shivered myself every time I went into that room, especially during the winter, which was unfortunate given its purpose.

'The bathroom is upstairs now,' I told her. 'And wonderfully warm.'

Moving it had meant sacrificing one of the three bedrooms, but as it was just me living in the cottage, I hadn't minded that and I hadn't been concerned about the potential impact on the resale value either, because I'd never given the idea of moving on a thought. That was, until now when I'd realised how lonely I'd become. But that was still all it had been, I reminded myself. The possibility of moving again was just a fleeting thought.

'And have you kept the fireplace?' Lizzie asked eagerly.

'Yes,' I nodded, with a smile. 'That impressive oak mantel had to stay, but I've had a wood burner installed and exposed the brickwork around it.'

It was one of my favourite things in the entire cottage. Situated in the sitting room, right in the heart of the home, it was a comforting and welcoming feature, even when it wasn't lit in the height of summer. It was only the last week of August but already I couldn't wait to put a match to it again when the weather turned and autumn arrived.

'That sounds beautiful,' Lizzie said wistfully and I could tell she was dying to take a look. 'Anyway, I'd better let you get on. I just wanted to say hello really and I daresay you want to make the most of the day before the rain comes.'

Thunder was forecast and I had lived in the Fens long enough now to know that the summer storms could be spectacular. With an uninterrupted view from the upstairs windows, I could sometimes track the lightning moving across the landscape for hours.

'I've actually just finished what I needed to do out here,' I surprisingly plucked up the courage to say, 'so, you're more than welcome to come in and take a look around. Unless you're on your way somewhere.'

'I'm not,' Lizzie said happily, 'I'm a completely free agent today. We don't open the café on a Sunday. Or a Monday, come to that.'

'Café?'

'Yes, my friend Jemma and I run The Cherry Tree Café in Wynbridge and the gallery next door. Perhaps you've been in?'

'I can't say I have,' I confessed. 'But it sounds lovely.'

'It is,' she said proudly and looked at the cottage again. 'Are you sure you don't mind me coming in?'

'Of course not,' I said, taking a deep breath as I felt the parameters of my comfort zone stretch and change shape. 'You're very welcome.'

I left Lizzie looking around the sitting room and admiring the revamped fireplace while I washed my hands in the kitchen and made a jug of elderflower cordial. It had taken more than a few seconds for my heart rate to settle when we came in, but I wasn't surprised about that because I had never entertained a guest in Rowan Cottage before.

'I love how you've got your bookcase set up!' Lizzie called to me. 'All of the books on my shelves are just laid out in regimented rows.'

I had some books lined up but others were stacked in small piles and the interesting arrangement left spaces in between to showcase a few little treasures and tiny bud vases.

'Thanks!' I called back. 'I like it too, though it takes ages to dust.'

'And I have to say,' Lizzie further commented as I rejoined her in the sitting room, 'I absolutely adore the colour scheme you've gone for in here.'

'Thank you,' I said, carefully putting the tray on the coffee table.

'Does it feature in any of the other rooms?'

'It does,' I confirmed. 'It actually runs right through the entire cottage.'

Because I was obsessed with autumn, I had chosen an earthy, seasonal palette of muted matt orange, brown and mustard hues, with lighter touches of sage green and cream to decorate each of the rooms. Now it was finally finished, I could tell it was going to give the cottage a cosy, den-like feel throughout the whole of the year and I loved the thought of that.

'That sounds perfect,' said Lizzie as I poured and handed her a glass of cordial and the ice cubes chinked sociably together. 'Thank you. This is just what I need.'

'Me too.' I smiled. 'Would you like to see what I've done with the room that used to be the bathroom?'

'Oh, yes, please.'

I ended up giving Lizzie a tour of the whole of the ground floor and she gratifyingly loved it all. She admired the cushions I had found to adorn the Windsor chair in the kitchen, loved the set of vintage leaf-patterned mixing bowls on the wooden counter and the row of red geraniums in reclaimed terracotta pots in the utility cum boot room.

'You know, I'm certain I recognise those cushions in the kitchen from somewhere,' she said as we ended up back in the sitting room, drinking more of the cordial. 'Did you buy them ready-made or did you source the fabric and make them up yourself?'

Her question made my shoulders tense up and my heart start to skitter again. I knew I had featured the cushions on my Insta grid on more than one occasion and I would be devastated if by an incredible coincidence she had somehow seen that and the penny dropped because the account was entirely and purposefully anonymous.

'And that view from the utility room window seems familiar, too, now I think about it . . .' she further mused.

'I picked the cushions up online,' I said falteringly in the hope that I could throw her off the scent if she had indeed picked it up. 'Given that you're an accomplished sewer yourself, perhaps you've seen the same website.'

As I'd shown her around, she had told me that while Jemma ran the café and baked the most delicious cakes and other sweet treats, she taught sewing and ran all sorts of craft workshops both in the café and the gallery next door.

'Perhaps . . .'

'I thought the autumnal colours would work well with the rest of the décor,' I further said, but Lizzie didn't appear to have heard.

She clicked her fingers in what turned out to be a dreaded eureka moment. 'Of course!' she gasped. 'That's it! Autumn! It's your entire aesthetic, isn't it?'

'I suppose you could say that,' I nervously agreed.

'In fact,' she grinned, as she put down her glass and pulled out her phone, 'you could say autumn is your everything!'

She quickly showed me the screen on her phone which I was appalled to see featured my carefully curated and, until then, anonymous Insta grid. I felt my cheeks flush and my throat go dry.

I hadn't for one second, when I invited Lizzie over the cottage threshold, thought that I might be asking an AutumnEverything follower to join me. I had thought I was doing something positive for my mental health. Something to stop me feeling lonely!

'I knew I recognised that bookcase,' Lizzie carried on excitedly, completely unaware of my discomfiture as she looked at the shelves again. 'But it was the cushions that really gave the game away. I can't believe it.'

I was struggling to believe it, too.

'I love your account, Clemmie,' she gushed. 'I mean, I *really* love it. Your whole aesthetic is so beautiful and just focusing on one season is . . . inspired. You're a total genius and the cottage is stunning. Jemma and my assistant, Joanne, won't believe it when I tell them you're the person behind it and that Rowan Cottage is the setting! They're both *huge* fans.'

'Oh no,' I stammered, feeling panicked. 'You can't tell them. I don't want anyone to—'

Unfortunately, and frustratingly, she wasn't listening and didn't give me the chance to beg her to keep my secret.

'And this makes my stopping by today and finding you at home even more fortuitously timed,' she interrupted, as she continued to look around. 'Serendipitous, you could say. Yes, this is definitely fate.'

It felt more like bad luck to me. Very bad luck.

'But about my Insta account—' I tried again.

'That's the best bit!' she cut in. 'The proverbial cherry on the cake, in fact, because it makes you the perfect person!'

'The perfect person for what?' I frowned.

She looked so excited I thought she was going to burst.

'For taking it on, of course!' she further gushed, making no sense at all.

'Taking what on?' I asked.

'Oh, I'm sorry,' she said, shaking her head. 'I'm guessing you haven't heard about it. Let me fill you in and then I just know you won't be able to resist saying yes! You're the online queen of autumn, for pity's sake!'

I already had the impression that Lizzie Dixon was the sort of woman who could talk anyone into doing anything, but she was definitely barking up the wrong tree with me. I wouldn't be saying yes to anything, no matter how temptingly or cleverly she framed it.

'So,' she began, sounding only a trifle more together, 'simply put, the town is supposed to be hosting some events this year to celebrate the ber months.'

I hadn't expected her to snag my interest with any of what she was going to say, but she had managed it with just those few words.

'You mean, Wynbridge is going to have an autumn festival?' I gasped, immediately drawn in, even though I didn't want to be. 'There's going to be a specific festival to celebrate the season?'

'That's it.' Lizzie nodded, clearly delighted by my reaction. 'I guessed right then? You haven't heard about it?'

'No,' I confirmed. 'No, I haven't.'

Given that I barely left the cottage, that was no surprise, but Lizzie didn't know that.

'It was supposed to be a proper autumn festival,' she then further elaborated for my benefit, 'because thanks to the efforts of one farmer in particular, this area is fast becoming known as the pumpkin patch of East Anglia—'

'Well, of course it is,' I interrupted her, having momentarily forgotten that she now had the knowledge to send my world crashing down and that I was supposed to be resisting whatever she had to say. 'The fields were full of them last autumn and there seems to be even more given over to them this year.'

The orange orbs were growing by the day and I couldn't wait to see them at their peak ahead of harvesting. I had filled my grid with gourds last year and the response had been spectacular. I already had plans to post again as soon as they were ready.

'I've noticed there are more fields planted up this year, too.' Lizzie nodded. 'And, as a result, autumn in the region has the potential to be even more spectacular than usual.'

'You're right,' I agreed, knowing I couldn't deny that. 'But what's that got to do with me?'

'Everything!' she announced. 'Well, potentially everything, because I'm hoping you'll agree to help out!'

'With what?' I frowned.

'The festival, of course,' she said, rolling her eyes as if it was obvious while she glanced around my sitting room again. 'There isn't going to be anyone within a five-hundred-mile radius more qualified to get stuck in with it than you, Clemmie.'

Her kind words would have been flattering had she not unexpectedly just outed me as the face behind AutumnEverything, but now they, and the terrifying prospect of her sharing her discovery, were pushed to the forefront of my mind and filled me with a sense of panic and dread that made me want to rush to lock the cottage door again.

I might have just started thinking about the possibility of visiting the town and meeting some people, but I had no intention of revealing my online persona or throwing myself in at the deep end and getting involved in some huge community project. My reintroduction to living a more sociable life needed to happen slowly and be carefully managed if I was going to make a success of it.

'Well,' I hedged, in a desperate bid to put her off, 'I'm sorry but I don't actually have enough free time to help with the festival this time around, but I'll definitely visit it when it's happening.' Lizzie looked disappointed. 'Maybe I could sell some raffle tickets or something,' I conceded in the face of her faded enthusiasm, 'but only if you agree to—'

'But I'm not asking you for that sort of help!' she butted in again and with a fine disregard for what I'd just said about having no time. 'I'm asking if you'll actually run the thing, Clemmie! With your credentials and love of the season, there won't be anyone better. This is what I was getting at when I said my finding you at home today was meant to be.'

'You're asking me to run the festival?' I gasped, feeling slightly hysterical.

'That's it.'

'Even though we've literally just met?'

'A technicality.' She shrugged as if that was the most minor detail of all. 'Your love of the season is what counts.'

'But—'

'Are you working at the moment, Clemmie? Do you have a job?'

'Well, no, but—'

'So, you must have *some* spare time then, which is just as well, because you'd actually need to set it up and organise it pretty much from scratch,' she confessed. Her smile faded and her shoulders slumped. 'I do appreciate that it's a big ask . . .'

'It's an impossible ask,' I said firmly. When she'd first described it, I had assumed it was already in the offing, but clearly not. 'Who was it who came up with the idea in the first place?' I asked. 'Why can't they do it?'

Her former buoyancy completely deflated then.

'They can't do it,' she said, 'because they're sadly no longer with us. The guy who originally had the idea to do something pumpkin related in town was the farmer who championed the crop most and he died unexpectedly a couple of months ago.'

'Oh.' I swallowed. 'I'm sorry to hear that.'

'His name was Moses Talbot,' Lizzie continued. 'His family had farmed in the Fens for four generations. He was the last and it was his idea to make the most of the region's much-loved autumn crop by championing it with a specific seasonal celebration.'

'I see,' I sighed. 'Well, it was a lovely idea.'

'A fantastic idea,' Lizzie agreed. 'It still is. And though completely underdeveloped, a popular prospect, too. Everyone was keen to see it happen in some guise or other. Still are, in fact . . .'

'But there's no one else willing to take the vision on?'

'Jake and Amber from Skylark Farm, who have taken on some of the fields that Moses farmed, had hoped to do it,' she explained, 'but they've had to pull out because they just haven't got the time, and there's no one else come forward to step into the breach.'

'That's a shame,' I said sincerely, because the festival could have been wonderful.

'You would have loved Moses,' Lizzie told me, sounding wistful and a little brighter again. 'He had a passion for autumn that could almost rival yours. Hence turning over so much of his land to growing pumpkins . . .'

I found my heartstrings being tugged and myself wishing that I had met Moses, but I wasn't going to change my mind about me being the person to take the event on, on his behalf.

'And there's really no one else who can sort it?'

'Afraid not,' Lizzie sighed. 'Everyone else who has the organisational skills is gearing up for Christmas now. I know that probably sounds rather premature given that we're not even out of the summer yet, but there's so much to do. You might not have heard about the proposed autumn festival, but I daresay you know that Wynbridge is very big on the festive front and a lot of people are already committed to helping organise things for that.'

'I didn't know that either actually,' I corrected her and she was agog. 'I don't know much about the town at all, because since I've been living here all my time has been taken up with the cottage renovation rather than socialising.'

'But you've finished it now,' Lizzie then astutely pointed out, as she found her smile again. 'And you're not currently working on anything else, so, my coming here today was definitely meant to be.'

'You're reading too much into it, I'm afraid.'

'I don't think I am,' she nudged and wheedled. 'Now you've finished renovating, you must have literally oodles of time, rather than none. You can finally start socialising, get to know Wynbridge and more of the people who live there and all while you're organising the festival. We could do with some fresh blood to mix things up and I'm sure Moses would approve, given your love of autumn.'

She really had the bit between her teeth, but I wasn't in the least bit tempted. In fact, the responsibility of what she was suggesting was making me feel quite nauseous.

'You need to remember this festival is something a much-loved local had come up with, Lizzie,' I therefore pointed out. 'And as a result, I'm sure that the last thing anyone would want is a blow-in stepping in and taking over. I know how these things work,' I added, thinking back to the petty politics surrounding local events in my childhood hometown in the north of the country. 'You need someone who has lived here for at least three generations to take it on. Someone properly local who knew Moses and who can make his vision come to life. Someone who lives here.'

'You live here,' Lizzie said in exasperation.

'You know what I mean,' I tutted. 'And besides, there's no time to do it now, is there? It's September next week.'

Lizzie took a moment to consider that.

'Oh, I daresay you're right,' she eventually sighed. 'It is getting rather tight for time. Maybe we'll manage it next year.'

'Next year, for sure.' I nodded, feeling relieved that she was now finally willing to let the subject drop. 'Now,' I forged ahead, 'can we please get back to what I was trying to say about my Insta account?'

When I had set up AutumnEverything, I had purposefully kept my identity a secret and I had every intention of keeping it that way. Callum and I had made a *huge* success of sharing our whole first house renovation online. We'd had hundreds of thousands of followers, but I had shut all of the accounts down when he died because there had been so much publicity surrounding his accident, that the extra attention the accounts received, the reams of comments and messages, had been too much for me to cope with.

I didn't doubt that practically everyone who posted and messaged did so with the kindest of intentions, but it was way too much for me to process and individually try to respond to. I had absolutely no privacy or protection when I needed it most and was inundated with personal stories of grief from so many followers. Consequently, I felt even more emotionally exposed and it was utterly overwhelming.

After that, I had never intended to go online again, but when I moved to Rowan Cottage and started the work, I found I wanted to chronicle what I was doing and therefore created a new account, just the one on Instagram, but it didn't feature my name or photograph. I didn't want anyone knowing it was me behind it and I certainly didn't want Lizzie Dixon poking about and somehow stumbling upon my tragic past. My life in the Fens was all about a fresh start and I had no desire to see that scuppered.

'I hope you're not thinking I only asked you about the

festival because I thought the account would help promote it?' Lizzie frowned. 'Though it would, of course . . .'

'That hadn't even entered my head,' I was able to tell her with total honesty, because I hadn't had a moment to consider that. 'But what you need to understand, Lizzie, is that the account is entirely anonymous and it's essential to me that it stays that way.'

'But Jemma and Joanne won't saying anything,' Lizzie insisted, then added, 'Well, Joanne might, so how about I just tell Jemma?'

'No!' I waspishly snapped. 'I don't want anyone to know and if I'd realised you were an account follower when you arrived, I never would have invited you in.'

Lizzie looked taken aback by my outburst.

'I'm sorry,' I apologised, quickly modifying my tone. 'I didn't mean to snap, but this is really important to me, Lizzie. You might not think word would spread if you just tell Jemma, but it so easily could. She might know another follower and let it slip to them on the promise of not telling anyone and so it goes on until . . . well, the whole world knows.'

I knew my voice was getting louder again and Lizzie looked puzzled.

'And that would be a bad thing?' she asked.

'Yes, it would! Absolutely the worst. You have to promise me,' I forcefully, but more calmly said, 'that you won't say anything to anyone about me being the face behind the account.'

My parents knew about it, but that was different. They loved the account and seeing how many followers interacted with it served the handy purpose of making them believe that I had wholeheartedly immersed myself in my new life in the Fens. They had latched on to the idea that some of the people who commented on my posts were real life friends and I had no intention of disabusing them of that assumption. I had shared with them some of the difficulties I had faced last time around, but not the full extent because I knew they would spend time worrying that something similar could happen again.

'I honestly didn't mean to upset you,' Lizzie said, sounding less sure of herself in the face of my determination to make her promise to keep quiet. 'I was just excited to have worked out that Rowan Cottage is the setting of AutumnEverything.'

'And I really didn't mean to raise my voice,' I apologised again. 'but I can tell you that I have very good and very private reasons for not revealing my identity and I am begging you not to out me to a single person, so I can keep it that way.'

I couldn't put it more plainly than that.

'In that case,' she said, eyeing me with interest, 'of course I'll promise not to say a word.'

'Thank you.'

'It clearly means a lot to you.'

'It really does.' I nodded. 'It means everything to me.'

'Okay,' she said, thankfully not asking me why I kept the account anonymous. I wasn't sure how I would have fielded her enquiry had she been so direct. 'And I also promise that I won't try to further cajole you into taking the festival on,' she nudged, some of her previously breezy manner returning.

'Good,' I reminded her. 'Because there's genuinely no time to get it up and running now.'

Even though I hadn't known him, I felt sad that Moses Talbot's vision of an autumn festival of some sort wasn't going to be realised, but I definitely wasn't the person who could make it happen on his behalf.

'I know you're right really,' Lizzie sighed. 'And I suppose I'd better go.'

'I'll see you out.'

I quickly opened the door before the visit went further awry. There were dark clouds gathering on the horizon which felt entirely appropriate given what had just occurred.

'Thank you for showing me around and for the lovely cordial.'

'My pleasure.' I smiled, because until she'd recognised the cottage as being the main setting for AutumnEverything and then tried to pressgang me into organising the festival, it had been lovely. 'It's been great to meet you.'

'Come to the café,' she insisted as she stepped outside. 'Let me show you around my domain.'

'I'd like that.' I nodded.

'And if you leave it a few days,' she mischievously grinned, 'Jemma will be ready to launch her Autumn Delights menu.'

'I think we should give autumn a wide berth from now on,' I called after her as she walked back along the path.

'Whatever you say!' she called back as she climbed into her car and then quickly drove off, one hand waving out of the window.

I closed the door and leant against it wondering if all efforts to immerse myself in life in and around Wynbridge were going to be so complicated.

Chapter 2

My head was still buzzing long after Lizzie had left and as I thought over everything that had occurred in the brief time she had been with me. Not only had I decided it was time I rejoined the human race that day, I had also invited a stranger across the cottage threshold, been outed as the person behind AutumnEverything *and* been offered an unexpected opportunity. No wonder I was reeling!

Surprisingly, it didn't take me long to find Lizzie among my list of AutumnEverything followers because she turned out to be one of the people who commented the most consistently. Her declaration that she *really* loved the account was no exaggeration and having met the woman behind the many words she had posted, I could now read what she had typed with her voice in my head.

It was just a short leap from there to finding the account for The Cherry Tree Café. Just as I had known it would be, the grid was an absolutely gorgeous mix of cakes and makes and I hoped I could trust Lizzie to keep my secret because I would love to visit without fear of worrying that she'd shared more about me than I wanted anyone in the Fens to know.

In spite of my efforts not to worry about what Lizzie might or might not do, my sleep that night bore the brunt of my brooding and I spent much of the night tossing and turning and feeling hot and bothered as I got tangled in the sheets.

'So, what are you up to today?' Mum asked, when she video called rather too early the next morning. 'Did you get the storm? You don't look as if you've had much sleep.'

'Cleaning first, then some gardening, but only if it isn't too wet,' I said, wishing she hadn't alluded to the dark smudges under my eyes. 'And the storm did land. The thunder raged for hours, but it's feeling much cooler now, which I'm grateful for.'

I'd opened all of the cottage windows and the air blowing through and making the curtains billow was cool and fresh. I had been going to post a photograph of the spare room window with a jug of fresh flowers cut from the garden on the sill, but held back once I'd taken the shot.

I adored my online account, but currently had mixed emotions about posting so soon after Lizzie had recognised my things around the cottage. I would have to get over that, though, if I didn't want to fall out of favour with the algorithm.

'Your dad was watching the thunder tracker thingy,' Mum told me. 'He thought it looked as though you were clear of the worst of it by midnight.'

'Well, I had an early night,' I responded, unwilling to go into the real reason why my sleep had been disrupted, 'and it felt like it hung around for ages once it had woken me up.'

'Oh, I hate it when that happens,' Mum sympathised and I had to smile, because nothing short of a shot going off was able to wake her once she'd fallen asleep.

'So, how are you feeling?' she asked. 'Other than tired. Are you bored yet?'

'It's only been a few days,' I reminded her, knowing she was referring to the renovation work and decorating being finished and me having less to do. 'And there's still plenty to get on with in the garden.'

'Yes, but I know you, Clementine,' she commented cannily. 'You're at your happiest when you're up to your neck in brick dust and paint samples. Have you had any thoughts about moving to take another renovation project on?'

Both Mum and Dad had initially been devastated when I moved so far away but soon came to realise and appreciate the huge part the renovation had played in helping me come to terms with my grief.

As I had got to grips with the work, I had both the time and privacy to properly process my loss and I came to realise that just as I was changing the cottage, losing Callum had changed me. As the four walls accepted their new look, I accepted my grief. I didn't deny it, or try to paper over it, I made my peace with it and it was then that I was finally able to let the wound start to heal.

'I'm going nowhere, Mum. No more brick dust for me,' I replied sincerely. 'Rowan Cottage is my home now.'

'In that case,' she said, a frown etching her forehead, 'what are you going to do?'

The last thing I wanted was her and Dad worrying that I was going to be twiddling my thumbs and falling to brooding.

'It's looking likely that I'm going to be helping out with an event in town soon,' I fibbed, thinking of Lizzie's visit. 'And by the sounds of it, it's going to be pretty full-on.'

Mum looked thrilled. 'That sounds exciting,' she smiled. 'What is it?'

'I can't tell you the details,' I further blagged. 'My friend, Lizzie, has sworn me to secrecy.'

'I don't think I've heard you mention a Lizzie before,' Mum mused.

'You must have done,' I tutted, digging myself an even deeper hole to later climb out of. 'She runs a café in town, with her friend Jemma, and she called here yesterday to rope me into helping with this idea she's had.'

The festival idea might have come from Moses, but I wasn't about to get myself further into it and start attempting to explain that.

'Oh well, in that case,' Mum said happily, 'the garden will have to wait a bit longer, won't it?'

'I'm sure I can manage both,' I said confidently. 'What have you been up to?'

'Not much,' she shrugged. 'I had my hair done yesterday.' She turned her head from side to side so I could see the impact of the half-inch trim. 'Oh, hold on. I can hear your dad's back from picking up his paper and he's bound to want to say hello.'

'Is that Clemmie?' I heard Dad shout from the hall. 'Don't let her go. I've got something to tell her. I've just seen Jill and she said I could pass it on.'

Jill was Callum's mum and aside from birthday and Christmas cards, I'd completely lost touch with her and his dad, Colin.

Maintaining contact had been too painful after I'd made the decision to move away. I tried not to feel like I'd abandoned them, but I didn't always succeed.

'Did you hear that?' Mum asked.

'I did,' I said, with a sigh as I imagined Jill and Colin still buried in their grief *and* still living in the house that overlooked the river that had taken their son. 'I hope it's not bad news.'

Callum and I had only been married eighteen months when he drowned in the river that ran through the town while trying to save a child who had fallen in.

There had been days of rain ahead of the accident and the river was swollen to capacity as the extra volume of water squeezed its way down from the hills, through the town and under the bridge. The road either side had been filled with onlookers as it reached its peak early one evening and somehow a little girl had fallen in. Callum had been one of three people who stopped when he spotted the commotion as he drove by and then jumped into the swirling torrent to rescue her. He was the only one who had been swept away.

I hadn't known any of what had happened until there was a knock on the door and I found two police officers on the step looking grave. I remember I had been laughing as I skipped down the hall to open the door because I had assumed it was Callum, weighed down with the tins of paint I had asked him to pick up on his way home from work.

We were getting ready to decorate the last room in the house we had successfully bid on at auction, gutted and brought back to life. The whole place had been neglected for years and there were times during the three-year intense renovation when we had felt like giving up, but thanks to my love of social media, the project had accrued a huge and enthusiastic following online and with the extra support from our parents, we had rallied to see it through.

Or almost through. I had never got around to painting that last room and eighteen months after Callum's funeral, I had moved to Rowan Cottage with the walls I left behind in that one room still showing bare plaster.

'Hello, love,' said Dad as his face filled the screen and I slowly drifted up through the sea of painful memories that mention of Callum's parents always evoked.

'Hi, Dad.' I swallowed. 'Did you get your paper?'

'I did,' he said, holding it up, 'but not all the news is in print today.'

'Oh?'

'I bumped into Jill. And you'll never guess.'

'Go on.'

'They've put their house on the market.'

I felt my mouth fall open.

'They're selling up.'

'I don't believe it,' Mum said tearfully.

'Did you get that, Clemmie?' Dad frowned. 'I think the screen's just frozen.'

'No, it hasn't,' I said. 'And I did hear. I'm just in shock. I can't believe it. What absolutely wonderful news!'

Colin had barely left the house since Callum had died and the curtains were hardly ever opened at the back because the windows overlooked the river. I had hoped for so long that one day they would find the strength to leave and now they had. I was so relieved for them.

'I knew you'd be pleased.' Dad smiled and I could tell he had a lump in his throat.

'More than pleased.' I sniffed. 'A million times more than pleased.'

Mum looked as emotional as I felt and we were all still smiling when we signed off.

There wasn't much in the way of dust, but I set about cleaning right through the cottage, with my summer Spotify playlist blaring and the windows all still wide open. I was in an elated and celebratory mood as a result of Jill and Colin's decision and I hoped they'd be settled somewhere new in time for Christmas. It would be a push timewise, with autumn on the horizon but not completely beyond the bounds.

And talking of autumn . . .

Once the season had popped back into my head, it was impossible to shake off further thoughts of the festival that wasn't going to be happening in Wynbridge or the fact that I had told Mum that I was going to be involved in it. I might not have gone into the details but I knew she wouldn't forget I had mentioned something and, having looked again at what I had posted on AutumnEverything the previous year, it took no effort at all to imagine what could have been achieved if there had actually been some time to do something about it.

As I scrolled through my prettiest posts, I visualised exactly the sort of things a festival to celebrate the cosy season could include beyond the pumpkin fields Moses had loved and then without really meaning to, I started listing event ideas in my head. There were myriad opportunities to celebrate out of doors, along with art and craft workshops, whole community events – given what Lizzie had said about Christmas, I now knew

Wynbridge had a thriving community – delicious food to eat and seasonally spiced drinks, anything and everything to do with pumpkins of course, and all kinds of sweater weather fun.

My imaginings weren't ultimately going to come to anything, because there was no one available to make them happen, but it was fun to daydream. And, as long as Lizzie kept my secret, I would be able to enjoy sampling the autumn menu in The Cherry Tree Café, as well as admiring the fields full of pumpkins, which was some compensation.

'Oh no!' I yelped, as I realised that while I had been distracted, it had started to rain and the infamous Wynbridge wind was helping the downpour find its way inside. 'No gardening for me today, then.'

I rushed around and closed the windows and then spotted that the garden gate was swinging wildly in the wind. If I didn't secure it, it would probably be damaged.

'Damn,' I muttered, as I snatched up a jacket which was hanging above the shoe rack in the hall and pulled it over my head. 'Rain, rain, go away!'

By the time I'd dashed down the path and secured the gate, then rushed back into the porch, I was pretty soaked. I shook the jacket out, then held it to my nose. It was a battered, waxed garment that Callum and I used to share. It didn't smell of him now, but as I returned it to its peg and smoothed it down, I heard something crinkle in one of the inside pockets.

'No way.' I swallowed, as my hand reached in and came out with a crumpled piece of paper held tightly in its grasp. 'It can't be.'

One of Callum's most endearing qualities was that he used to leave me little, handwritten 'love-notes' where I least expected to find them. Some were romantic, others were funny or poignant, but they all touched my heart and made me smile. I had found a surprising number in the three years since he had been gone. The first one, most likely the last he'd written, had been tucked inside an already opened cereal box, another in a shoe I hadn't worn until the following summer and so it went on.

That said, I had worn the jacket dozens of times since he had passed, so I had no idea how I had missed the note I now clutched in my hand. There was no rhyme or reason for it being there, but it was definitely a note from Callum and I sat in my favourite armchair and carefully smoothed it out on my leg to read it.

Today you encouraged me to take a HUGE leap of faith, Clemmie, and boy, has it paid off!

This is just a little reminder that the best and loveliest things can happen when you take a risk!

Though you probably won't need reminding, because you already know it, don't you? Anyway, I hope this wasn't a waste of ink!

Love always, C x

Tears streamed down my face as I read Callum's words and fought hard not to wish he hadn't taken his very last risk. It briefly saddened me to think that I couldn't pinpoint what the leap of faith he referred to had been. I had pushed him out of his comfort zone many times during the house renovation with my ideas about decorating and design, so it could have been something as simple as painting the bedroom ceiling the same colour as the walls.

However, the details didn't really matter. It was the timing that truly counted. Had I been the sort of person who believed in portents, the timing of finding this particular note, just as I was poised to try my hand at socialising again, though not to the extent Lizzie had suggested, would have been entirely apt, wouldn't it?

Chapter 3

In spite of finding Callum's rallying and poignantly timed note and receiving three WhatsApp messages from Mum, in pretty quick succession, asking if I had more to share about the event in town yet, my jitteriness about heading out and exploring saw me putting off driving into Wynbridge by distracting myself at home for the whole of the next day.

I had been considering the possibility of adding a couple of hens to the cottage garden and immersed myself in so-called *essential* online research, however, when I woke extremely early on the Wednesday morning and padded downstairs to find I was still carrying the weight of being alone, I knew enough was enough.

I would do what Callum had suggested, I would take a leap of faith, I would trust that Lizzie had kept my secret and go in search of her and Jemma's café in town. That would be enough to begin with and who knows, perhaps some lovely things might end up happening as a result.

I took my time getting ready. I painted my toenails, picked out my prettiest patterned summer dress and sandals and tied my hair into a messy bun. I had never quite mastered the casual, tousled style, but ultimately, I was satisfied with the way I looked, felt a modicum more confident as a result and headed off in the Land Rover that Callum and I had invested in primarily to ferry building materials about.

'Absolutely not,' was the first thing I heard Lizzie say when I walked through the open door of The Cherry Tree Café. 'No, no, no, no, no.'

The artistically decorated café had been easy to find, set on one side of the busy market square, which I had taken a few minutes to properly look around. The market itself was bustling and there were a pleasing number of independent shops set around the edge.

I had known Wynbridge was a gem among small rural towns because the estate agents' details and an online search when I was looking to move had told me, but I hadn't before appreciated exactly how lovely it was when I had previously rushed in and out again. It was time I stopped missing out on what the place had to offer and The Cherry Tree Café was as good a place to start my more detailed explorations as any.

I knew I had audibly gasped as I crossed the threshold, but the inside smelt so enticing and was so perfectly pretty, dressed in late summer colours, it would have been impossible not to. The photographs online were appealing, but seeing it with my own eyes, and smelling it, too, was something else. This place was right up my street and I felt rather frustrated not to have called in before.

'I absolutely do not need a dog in my life,' Lizzie was now saying firmly to the man standing in front of her and with his back to me. 'And especially one that requires so much attention.

You know I'm here and next door far more than I'm at home, so I'm surprised you've even asked me. She wouldn't get what she needs from me at all.'

'Nor me,' said a younger woman, who was wearing a similar wraparound pinny to Lizzie's. 'I'll be leaving the UK to live overseas soon and with so much to sort out for myself, I won't have time to think about a pooch passport.'

I had wondered if she was Jemma, but Lizzie hadn't mentioned her friend was leaving the country, so it was more likely that she was Joanne, her assistant.

'And don't even think about asking me,' said a third woman who then appeared from what I guessed was the kitchen area, carrying a tray of drinks. 'I've got more than enough on my plate with this place, a husband *and* two kids to corral.'

She was most likely Jemma. I moved nimbly out of her way as she stepped around the heavenly looking packed cake counter and flashed me a smile.

'Take a seat,' she said. 'And I'll be with you in a minute.'

'Thank you,' I said, looking around again and thinking the table by the window would give me the loveliest view of the place.

There was a painted dresser with an impressive array of hand-sewn crafts to buy opposite it and I knew I would be hard pushed to resist heading home without something pretty to add to the cottage.

'Clemmie!' Lizzie then burst out. 'Well, hello you!'

My gaze swung back to her and the guy facing her turned around to look at me, too. His eyes widened as they met mine and I felt my cheeks flush. He was rather taller than me, not a stretch as I'm only five foot three, dark haired, blue eyed and wearing a polo shirt with something embroidered on the left-hand side. He opened his mouth and closed it again, which drew my attention to his full lips. He was sporting at least a few days' stubble, which also made rather more of his expressive mouth than I would have liked.

'This is who you want,' said Lizzie, giving him a sharp nudge and I felt my cheeks flame further as they both continued to stare.

'Is it?' he croaked, then cleared his throat, his eyes still fixed on mine as he also turned red.

'Yes.' Lizzie nodded. 'Try Clemmie. She could be just the person you're looking for.'

'You're Clemmie?' the woman, who had now served the drinks, asked. 'You're the person who has renovated Rowan Cottage?'

'Yes,' I tentatively said, turning to look at her. 'Yes, I am.'

'I'm Jemma,' she beamed. 'Lizzie has talked of nothing but you since you showed her around the cottage on Sunday.'

I felt my tummy twist when she said that and hoped Lizzie hadn't said too much.

'Has she not?' I nervously asked.

'She's gone on and on,' laughed the third woman. 'I'm Joanne, by the way.'

'The assistant I mentioned,' Lizzie elaborated for my benefit. 'Who, before long, I'm going to have to try and replace as she's moving overseas to join her partner.'

'Well, I'm sorry about that,' Joanne said with a smile that I didn't think quite reached her eyes. 'And I hope you won't forget me as soon as I've gone. I hope I've made as much of an impression on you as Clemmie already has.'

'Have I made an impression?' I swallowed, as my tummy knotted even tighter.

It suddenly felt like there were a lot more people in the café than there actually was and they all seemed to be staring at me.

'I'll say!' Joanne laughed.

'Lizzie has completely fallen in love with your place. She's said the inside is cottagecore perfection.' Jemma grinned. 'And now apparently, you're making the garden look just as lovely, too. I haven't been that way for a while, but I'm tempted to do a drive-by.'

Given that I knew she was also an AutumnEverything fan, I hoped she wouldn't ask to come in if she realised I was at home.

'You live on your own, Clemmie, don't you?' Lizzie then asked me to clarify.

'Er, yes.' I swallowed, as I started to flail under the bombardment of attention, but also felt grateful that Jemma hadn't mentioned my Insta account. 'Yes, I do.'

'There you are then, Ash,' Lizzie said, giving him another poke. 'You can ask Clemmie, can't you? She's probably a far more suitable candidate than any of us.'

My eyes flicked to the guy's face again. He was still staring and looked as red as I felt. He opened his mouth a second time, but no further words came out and I self-consciously shifted from one foot to the other. So much for my low-key trip into town.

'I'll take the table by the window,' I said to Jemma, then forced my legs to carry me towards it.

'Ash is the new vet in town,' Joanne said, immediately following me over.

'Not that new,' he corrected mildly.

Joanne ignored him.

'And he's got a homeless hound he's trying to find a place for,' she added.

'Oh,' I said, as I settled myself into the seat. 'I see. Well, I'm not really a dog person.'

'But this one is a very special case,' Lizzie carried on. 'Why don't you tell Clemmie about her, Ash?'

'No, it's okay,' he said, shoving his hands into his trouser pockets. 'She really needs to go to someone I know.'

I wasn't sure whether I felt offended by his refusal to share or not.

'She's grieving,' Lizzie then announced loudly, which stopped me wondering but made me feel light-headed.

'How . . .' I stammered. 'How did you—?'

'By which she means,' Joanne interrupted, 'the poor little dog is *actually* grieving. Her owner died a few weeks ago and no one in her family is willing to take her on.'

My lungs reinflated and the world righted itself a little on its axis again. They weren't talking about me. They were talking about the dog.

'Oh, my goodness.' I swallowed, thinking of the turmoil the poor thing must have been feeling. 'That's so sad.'

I felt my eyes fill with a rush of sympathetic tears and tried to blink them away. No one present was acquainted with my tragic history, so they might think my reaction over the top, especially as I didn't know the dog in question.

'She's staying with me at the moment,' Ash said croakily, his sad tone making me feel even more emotional. 'I couldn't bear to put her in kennels yet.'

'Why can't you just keep her full-time?' Jemma sensibly suggested. 'Then she won't have to go into kennels at all. I daresay she feels safest with you now, Ash.'

'Because she needs company,' he insisted. 'Proper, consistent company and someone who can give her all the attention she needs and deserves.'

'Which is why I can't take her,' said Lizzie. 'You know Ben and I are never at home and it would be far too chaotic to bring her in here and next door every day, rather than occasionally like Glynis did. Especially in the early days.'

'You're right,' said Ash, running a hand through his hair. 'And I don't know why I asked you, really, Lizzie. She needs somewhere peaceful with someone who can spend time with her to balance out any trips to town. Poor little Pixie.'

'Pixie,' I echoed.

'That's her name,' Ash clarified, pinning me again with his blue eyes. Eyes I didn't want to find beguiling, but was drawn to look back at regardless. 'And I'd better get back to her. She's home alone at Will's place and I don't like to leave her for long.'

'Still no joy finding a place of your own?' Lizzie asked him.

'Not yet,' he shrugged. 'But living in Will's barn for the time being is no hardship.'

'It's been converted,' Joanne said for my benefit. 'He's not stuck in a filthy byre with no hot and cold laid on and only a bucket to—'

'I think Clemmie gets the idea,' Ash cut in and I laughed.

It didn't strike me immediately, but it felt odd to hear a man, other than my dad, say my name.

'And now Will, that's my boss, has moved in permanently with his partner, Lottie, at Cuckoo Cottage,' Ash further explained to me, 'I do have the place to myself which doesn't give me much impetus to keep looking. But it's only until he puts it on the market.'

'Almost to yourself,' I corrected.

'Yes.' He nodded, with a slight smile which made the few lines around his eyes attractively crinkle. 'Almost to myself. I really had better get back. Do let me know if there's any further news about the Autumn Festival, Lizzie, won't you?'

And with that he was gone. Thankfully before she'd had a chance to tell him that she'd tried to strong-arm me into taking it on.

'Isn't he a dream?' Jemma wistfully sighed, looking after him as he crossed the square.

'Hey,' laughed Lizzie. 'You're a married woman, remember?'

'How can I forget?' Her friend grinned back while she fanned herself with a menu.

'And very happily married,' Joanne giggled. 'But what about you, Clemmie?'

'Me?' I squeaked.

'He's single. You're single,' she said, with a wink. 'At least, I think you're single.'

'I'm on my own,' was as much as I was willing to say on the subject of my relationship status. 'And definitely not looking for a partner. And even if I was, Ash is about as far away from my type as it's humanly possible to get.'

That wasn't entirely true, but I didn't want her getting any ideas and Jemma's next words were confirmation that I was right to put Joanne off from the outset.

'So, that's you told, Little Miss Matchmaker,' she laughed before heading back to the kitchen.

'Fair enough,' Joanne said, eyeing me astutely. 'Message received and understood. But I'm bored with Aiden – that's my partner – being on the other side of the world and I do love pairing people up. It's my favourite hobby.'

'Shouldn't your favourite pastime be getting yourself ready to leave?' Lizzie asked. 'I thought you had loads to do for that.'

'I've got three couples successfully together so far,' Joanne carried on telling me while ignoring her boss, 'and I've already decided that the happy ever afters are going to be my legacy to the town . . .'

Well, she certainly didn't need to get any ideas about amusing herself in that department where I was concerned, unless she was in the market for further boredom and a dose of disappointment.

'Never mind bugging Clemmie about all that,' Lizzie said dismissively and Joanne walked away without taking my order. 'What can we get you, Clemmie? And more to the point, *please* say you've come to tell me you've had a change of heart about taking on the festival idea?'

The autumnal additions to the menu weren't in place yet, so I ordered a coffee and toasted panini. I also told Lizzie that I hadn't changed my mind about offering to be in charge of organising and running the festival, but conceded that I would volunteer a little time to help out if, by some miracle, the idea that Moses had was realised.

With my mental mood board from the day before still floating about in my mind, it was impossible not to offer to do something, even though I'd been telling myself that slow and steady was the safest way forward on the social front.

'That's very kind,' Lizzie smiled sadly, 'but actually, we had a quick meeting about it in the pub on Monday and no one stepped forward. I did mention what you'd said about not wanting a newcomer to take up the cause, but just as I suspected, no one objected to that or the fact that you'd never met Moses, either.' I wasn't sure how I felt about her specifically discussing me. 'We truly don't mind who takes it on, just so long as someone does. Or did. It really is too late now.'

'In that case,' I said, purposefully pushing away thoughts of pumpkin carving competitions, 'fingers crossed for next year.'

It wasn't too busy in the café and I was mostly left alone to enjoy the panini and coffee, take in my surroundings and wonder what the poor grieving pooch, Pixie, looked like. She truly had my every sympathy.

I hadn't experienced a whole raft of lovely things as a result of my trip into town, but I'd met a few more people and felt both confident and relieved that Lizzie had kept her promise and hadn't told Jemma or Joanne that I was the person behind AutumnEverything. That alone was enough to make up for the awkwardness I'd felt on my arrival.

'So, what are your plans for the rest of the week?' Jemma asked, when she came to clear my table.

'Chicken research,' I told her. 'I'm thinking about having some, but I'm a total novice so I'm doing some studying first. I think it's too late in the year to get organised enough to take some now, but I can start planning for the spring.'

'You need to talk to Ash about all that,' Joanne said eagerly, as she popped a takeaway cakebox featuring the café logo on the table and Ash neatly back into the conversation. 'He knows his hens.'

'I think I can find everything I need to know online,' I told her as I pulled out my phone to pay. 'But thanks.'

A couple of days later, as I was bent over by the garden gate and pulling up a few weeds I'd previously missed, a truck pulled up with its windows down.

'Joanne mentioned that you were thinking about getting some hens,' came a voice from inside, which I instantly recognised as belonging to Ash.

'Did she?' I huffed, as I straightened, pushed my glasses back up and the legs of my shorts down so I wasn't exposing quite so much bare skin.

It was another hot day and it didn't feel any closer to autumn even though September was now just a few days away.

'Was she wrong?' Ash asked, clearly having noticed my irritated response.

'No, she was right,' I confirmed, amending my annoyance, because it wasn't his fault that she'd told him and he had then decided to call and bring it up. 'But I've decided to wait to do anything about it until the spring now.'

'Oh, that's a shame.'

'Why?' I asked, shielding my eyes from the glare of the sun.

'Because I was going to offer to get you set up. I'm helping rehome a flock of ex-battery girls next month and hoped you might be interested in taking a couple or even three.'

'I have been wondering about the rehoming option,' I pondered, thinking that for some reason he was easier to talk to when he was in shadow in the shade of his cab. 'That said, I couldn't cope with three eggs a day, so I'll probably only go for two.'

'Well,' he said, 'if you are interested in taking a pair on, let me know when you're ready for them and I'll give you some dates for future flock allocation.'

'Thanks. I'd appreciate that.'

There was a sudden noise in the cab that didn't come from Ash. It sounded like a canine sneeze.

'That was Pixie,' he said, with a nod to the passenger seat. 'She's supposed to be getting used to a harness, so I can transport her out of her crate, but she's not keen on it. She's not keen on anything at the moment.'

'With good reason,' I sighed.

'With very good reason,' Ash agreed.

I couldn't resist opening the gate so I could stand on tiptoe and peek in through the window to look at her.

'Oh,' I croaked, my heart melting at the sight of the scrappy little bundle of tightly curled up black and tan fur. 'She's tiny.'

She didn't make any effort to move, but I knew she was aware that I was there, because her little brows quirked as she moved her eyes.

'I think she tries to make herself invisible sometimes,' Ash said sadly. 'She thinks that if she can't see the world and doesn't engage with it, it won't exist.'

'Poor Pixie,' I empathised. I remembered a time when I had felt like that. How I wished I could communicate to her that one day the feeling would fade, if not disappear. 'Have you found a home for her yet?'

'Sadly not,' Ash sighed. 'And I haven't found anyone to run the autumn festival Lizzie is still obsessed with and I've said I'll support, either. Have you heard about it?'

'It might have come up in conversation,' I said, looking

across at him and then quickly back at Pixie, because he was closer now.

'Lizzie has still got her heart set on it happening,' he sighed. 'So, I've told her I'll deputise as and when, but only if someone else properly takes charge. She knows I'm time poor what with my work commitments and looking after Pixie, but she was fond of Moses and doesn't want to let the idea drop.'

He gave the dog a fuss, but she didn't react to his touch.

'But I thought it had been decided that the festival won't be happening now because of the lack of time?' I said, thinking back to my conversation with Lizzie in the café and what she had told me had been discussed in the pub. 'I thought the focus was now on getting it going next year.'

Ash shook his head and smiled. 'That's Lizzie for you,' he told me. 'She's still hoping for a miracle. And once she's got the bit between her teeth, she's one determined woman.' I'd already worked that out for myself. 'And Joanne's just as eager in some respects,' Ash then added with a disgruntled tut.

'She is?'

'Yes,' he sighed. 'But you don't need to know about that.'

'Judging by the look on your face,' I responded, 'I think I might. Forewarned and all that.'

'Actually, you're probably right,' he then conceded. 'Especially if you're single.'

'Go on,' I said, neither confirming nor denying my relationship status.

'Let's just say, Joanne sees herself as some sort of Cupid,' he elaborated. 'And when I first moved here, she made it her mission to try and set me up on dates with other Wynbridge singles every night I wasn't working.'

Given that Jemma had called her 'Little Miss Matchmaker' in my presence and Joanne herself had told me that she'd successfully matched three couples up and loved doing it, Ash's explanation didn't come as a surprise.

'That must have been annoying,' I tutted, thinking how stressful I would have found it. 'That is, assuming you didn't want to be set up.'

'I did not,' Ash vehemently said. 'And thankfully, she got the full message in the end.'

'Which was?'

'That right now, I'm absolutely not looking for love or anything like it,' he said with conviction. 'I'm still settling into my life here, and every minute I'm not on call, and I've got the energy for it, is spent trying to find myself somewhere permanent to live.'

'And somewhere permanent for Pixie to settle, too,' I pointed out.

'Yes,' he nodded. 'Finding somewhere extra special for her is a priority now, too. I haven't got time for a relationship, even if Joanne thinks I should be in one.'

He smiled and I found myself smiling back.

'You probably won't be surprised to know,' I told him because, having heard his view on romance, I now felt more relaxed around him, 'that I've already had to point out to her that I'm very happy on my own and I've only met her once.'

Ash laughed properly and my smile grew even wider.

'Well,' he grinned. 'You'll have to tell her a lot more than that before it sinks in, but it's a start and I suppose, if she's homed in on you now, that gets me off the hook.'

'Hey!' I objected.

'So, you're single, too, then, Clemmie?'

'Yes,' I further confirmed. 'And just like you, *very* contentedly so.'

I had felt unsettled when Ash's eyes had met and held mine in the café and I hadn't known why at the time, but now I realised it was because he was the first guy I'd looked at, as in *properly* looked at, and the first man who had properly looked at me, since Callum had died. However, having just heard him insist that a relationship wasn't on his radar had helped to diminish the impact of our first meeting considerably.

In fact, I got the feeling that, if we could keep Joanne out of the equation, Ash might become just the friend I needed to boot my sense of loneliness out of the door. We were both relative newcomers to the area and we were both content with our relationship lot. That sounded like an ideal friendship match to me. And, if he was going to potentially become a pal, perhaps, given that he'd already offered to deputise, he might be the perfect person to consider working on the autumn festival with, too . . .

Chapter 4

In the hope of getting to talk to Lizzie on her own, I waited until close to what I knew to be The Cherry Tree Café closing time to head back into town on Saturday afternoon. The weather had cooled considerably, the breeze had a definite chilly edge and, as a result, I pulled on a jumper and the waxed coat I had found Callum's note in ahead of setting off.

The extra outer layer felt like a good idea at the time, a sort of lucky talisman to support the monumental decision I had made, but by the time I had found a parking space, much further away from the café than I had hoped, and then walked at pace across the market square, I felt close to overheating, so I shrugged it off and draped it over my arm.

In spite of my soaring temperature and a fluttering accompaniment of nerves, I was happy to find I was feeling excited, too.

'Are you expecting rain?' asked Jemma, when I walked in carrying the rather cumbersome coat and found the place deserted.

I looked above the door and spotted the brass bell that had tinkled melodiously to announce my arrival. It was another sweet feature and one I hadn't noticed on my previous visit as the door had been propped open.

'Hey, Jemma.' I smiled. 'No, hopefully no rain today. Is Lizzie about?'

'She's still tidying up next door,' Jemma told me. 'Can I help?'

I had forgotten that I had read on their website that Lizzie was holding one of her crafting workshops in the gallery space next door that afternoon.

'No, I'll go and find her, but thank you.'

'No worries.'

'Is Joanne with her?' I asked as an afterthought.

'No.' Jemma smiled wryly. 'And please, don't worry about her matchmaking spiel from the other day. Lizzie and I have further put her off, so with any luck, she'll leave you in peace now.'

'Excellent.' I smiled back, but having heard what Ash had to say on the subject, I was still going to remain on guard. 'Thanks.'

The friendly bell tinkled again as I left and another rang out as I opened the gallery door. There was no one there, other than Lizzie, and that was perfect.

'All right,' I announced the moment she looked at me and before I became distracted by the stunning artwork on the walls or potentially lost my nerve. 'I'll do it.'

She looked confused for a moment, but then the penny dropped.

'The festival!' she gasped, her hands clasped, as she abandoned the squares of fabric she had been piling together. 'You'll run it?'

'I will,' I confirmed. 'But only if no one truly minds that I never knew Moses and if I've got some proper help to pull off whatever I turn his idea into, because obviously I won't be able to manage it entirely on my own, especially as we're now even more pressed for time.'

I was hoping that, with Ash onboard as a willing deputy, I wouldn't feel quite so overwhelmed by the extra-large leap of faith I was taking. It was just days ago that I had been reminding myself not to go all in, but the lure of an autumn celebration had ultimately proved impossible to resist.

'Oh wow!' Lizzie squealed as she clapped ecstatically.

'I know Ash has said he'll deputise if someone else oversees it, because he stopped by the cottage and mentioned it,' I stated, 'so as long as he's still keen . . . you're on. And so's the festival!'

'I don't believe it!' Lizzie laughed and clapped again. 'But are you sure you've got time? I know you aren't working at the moment, but you did nonetheless say that you were too busy before.'

'Let's just say that I've moved a few things around.' I shrugged, glossing over the excuse slash fib I'd previously cited without further explanation.

'In that case, thank you!' she gushed. 'Thank you. Thank you so much, Clemmie. Everyone is going to be thrilled.'

'I do hope so,' I said, biting my lip and feeling a twinge of apprehension.

I was delighted to already have plenty of autumn-based ideas to offer, but how the locals, who had never even met me, were going to receive them, was a concern. They might not think that what I had in mind was going to marry up with the initial idea Moses had dreamt up.

'Like I said the day we met,' Lizzie insisted, 'you're more than qualified to do it and everyone is going to be putty in your hands. Not that they'll know how capable you are,' she quickly added, 'because I haven't said a word to a soul about your Insta, but as soon as you start talking about autumn, they'll know you're the woman for the job.'

'Well,' I swallowed, hoping her knowledge of my ability to create a pretty grid online hadn't meant she'd overestimated my capabilities in the real world, 'let's hope you're right.'

'I am right,' she said emphatically, then chuckled. 'So,' she smiled, 'you and Ash.'

'Yes,' I said. 'Me and Ash. Two reasonably new locals stepping up to run the festival and potentially becoming *friends* in the process.'

She laughed at the emphasis I put on the platonic description.

'He's already told me how frustrated he got with Joanne trying to set him up,' I warned her, 'so I hope you haven't got any silly ideas about us, Lizzie.'

'Me?' she gasped as if butter wouldn't melt.

'Because you know, neither of us is looking for a partner.'

'But you are single?'

'I am,' I clarified. 'And I have absolutely no desire for that to change.'

'Well, don't panic,' she grinned. 'Jemma and I have already told Joanne to butt out and I'll be telling her again now because the last thing I want is her upsetting the autumn aficionado and her sidekick.'

'That's all right then.' I nodded graciously.

With any luck that would be the end of that.

'Now, come on,' Lizzie then suggested. 'Let's go to the pub to celebrate!'

I hadn't been to The Mermaid before and a trip to the pub

hadn't been on my radar when I left the cottage to tell Lizzie what I had decided, but in the spirit of embracing rejoining the human race and knowing I would be meeting lots of locals in the weeks to come, I decided to go with the flow and rather nervously walked with her across the square.

'What can I get you?' she asked, as we crossed the threshold of the surprisingly busy, traditional looking pub.

'A lemonade with ice, please,' I requested, as I took in more of the place and its customers. 'I've got to drive home in a bit.'

'I think I'll join you,' Lizzie agreed. 'The workshop this afternoon was really hard work and if I have a gin now, I'll be asleep by dinnertime.'

We walked over to the bar and Lizzie introduced me to the woman serving.

'Clemmie, this is Jeanie, Jeanie, this is town newcomer, Clemmie.'

'I'm pleased to meet you.' Jeanie smiled at me. 'Welcome to Wynbridge. How are you finding it so far?'

'So far, so good.' I smiled back. 'I haven't explored all that much of it yet, but what I've seen is lovely.'

'Clemmie has been renovating Rowan Cottage,' Lizzie elaborated.

'That's the place down Lark Drove, isn't it?' Jeanie frowned.

'That's right,' I confirmed.

'But that's been getting done up for ages,' Jeanie commented, looking quizzically at me. 'How come you're only just finding your way into the pub now?'

'Because she's been completely focused on doing it up,' Lizzie said on my behalf.

I wasn't surprised that Jeanie was curious. I had been locked in my self-imposed purdah for a year and a half, so my sudden appearance and people finding out where I lived, was bound to raise a few eyebrows. I needed to prepare myself for that.

'Fair enough,' said Jeanie, accepting Lizzie's answer while pouring our drinks.

'And now she's finished transforming the cottage,' Lizzie further explained, 'she's not quite so occupied and is going to have a think about whether there's enough time to help us put on the autumn festival that Moses had been so keen to develop.'

A gasp from further along the bar met my ears and I appreciated that Lizzie hadn't announced my decision as a fait accompli. I didn't know whether that was because she was waiting for Ash to confirm that he could still help or because she was offering me a get out of jail free card if I changed my mind, but I was happy to go along with how she'd put it.

'Are you really?' the woman who had gasped, breathlessly asked.

'This is Bella,' said Jeanie, with a nod. 'She's keen on the festival idea, too.'

Knowing Bella must also share my love of the season, I looked at her with interest.

'Lots of us are keen, Jeanie,' she said enthusiastically. 'There have been quite a few of us thinking about what Moses had in mind and how we might expand upon it. I'm guessing,' she added, turning properly to me again, 'that you must be the new addition to the area that Lizzie was alluding to the other night when she suggested some fresh blood could take the project on?'

'Got it in one,' Lizzie confirmed as I nodded.

'I'm very pleased to meet you, Bella,' I then responded as I realised Lizzie hadn't specified exactly who she had been talking to that night. 'I might ask to pick your brains if I get stuck for ideas while I'm mulling it all over.'

'Oh, you won't find much in there,' Jeanie teased and Bella gave her a look. 'Her head's too full of fairy folk in the run up to Christmas.'

'Yes,' laughed Lizzie. 'She's away with the fairies all right!'

'What they mean,' Bella explained for my benefit, 'is that I'm a fairy maker and my little enterprise is called Away With the Fairies. I'm just heading into my busiest time of the year, which is why I couldn't take on the festival planning myself.'

'It's not that *little* an enterprise,' Jeanie said.

'No,' frowned Bella. 'You're right. It isn't now, is it? I really do have to try harder to own the success I've made of it, don't I?'

'Yes!' Lizzie and Jeanie said together.

'Well, it looks absolutely wonderful,' I said, as Lizzie quickly showed me Bella's website on her phone and scrolled through the images of pretty fabric fairies. 'What a wonderful job you've got! I guess Christmas must be full-on for you.'

It was no wonder she hadn't volunteered to take on the role of festival coordinator with so many fairies to make.

'And for lots of other people around here, too,' she said, confirming what Lizzie had said about Wynbridge being big on Christmas the day we met.

If I made a success of the new venture, the town would hopefully be known going forward as being big on autumn, too. By this time next September, we could have almost a third of the year wrapped up in seasonal celebrations!

'Do you think you might possibly be able to spare just a little time to pitch in if it becomes certain that the festival will go ahead?' I asked Bella.

'I'll certainly try,' she evasively said. 'All along I've had my heart set on there being at least an autumn themed market day or two, so I could perhaps help out with that. I have this whole bolt of tiny leaf patterned fabric and I'm already turning it into fairy clothes. I'll be adding autumn fairies to my website, but selling them here in town would be great, too.'

I rather liked the sound of the fabric *and* the market. That gorgeous scene in *You've Got Mail* where Tom Hanks takes his young relatives around the autumn fair was one of my favourites in the entire film.

'Don't talk to Clemmie about autumn fabric,' Lizzie then laughed. 'Because she'll be pinching it to put up in Rowan Cottage.'

'You're a proper fan of the season then?' Bella asked and I watched Lizzie turn red.

'Well, of course she is,' said Jeanie as she moved our drinks across the bar, 'otherwise she wouldn't be thinking about taking the festival on, would she?'

'I'm sorry,' Lizzie groaned, once she'd paid and we had sat down. 'In my excitement, I let my mouth run away with me a bit there. I promise I won't let it happen again.'

'No harm done,' I charitably said, because I could see she was genuinely upset. I clinked my glass against hers. 'Let's forget about it. Here's to the festival.'

'To the festival,' Lizzie echoed, 'and to you and Ash making a huge success of it.'

'I'm pleased you've mentioned him,' I said, having taken a drink, 'because we really need to let him know that his offer to deputise is about to be taken up, don't we?'

'I'm going to leave that to you,' Lizzie said, reaching for her phone. 'I'll give you his number and you can call him. Consider that your first task as event organiser.'

'Don't you think it will be better coming from you?' I asked, even though it did appeal to my organised nature to be able to tick something off the to-do list so quickly.

'Your circus,' Lizzie said mischievously as she showed me her phone screen with Ash's number lit up. 'Your monkeys.'

'That sounds like chaos already,' I tutted and she laughed.

While I keyed his number into my mobile, Lizzie went back to the bar to talk to an older woman who had joined Jeanie.

'That's Evelyn,' Lizzie said, when she came back again and I had put my phone away with Ash's number added to my contacts list. 'Jeanie's aunt. She owns this place with her husband, Jim.' I looked over at her and she waved, so I waved back. 'She's said we can meet in here Wednesday night to rally the troops and officially launch the idea.'

I let out a long breath. The wheels were properly in motion now. It was really happening and not just in my head.

'That's just four days away,' I breathlessly said as I counted the days off on my fingers.

'It would have been sooner, but we wanted to give you some time to prepare,' Lizzie kindly said. 'And Evelyn knew that a few of the people who I'm hoping will come onboard aren't available to get together before then, either.'

'It'll already be the third of September on Wednesday,' I puffed, feeling slightly panicked.

'Don't worry,' she soothingly said. 'It'll be fine. You just come up with some ideas that will involve more than pumpkins and the general idea Moses had and I'll make sure this place is packed out to hear them. I have every faith in you, Clemmie, and I reckon by the end of the meeting you'll have more volunteers than you know what to do with and the festival schedule will be halfway complete.'

I hoped her faith in me was going to be proved right, because having now become more familiar with the market square I could easily imagine it decked out in autumn hues, with the smell of pumpkin spice filling the air. I was determined to take the idea that Moses had come up with and make it even grander.

'Not exclusively my circus then,' I smiled, feeling very appreciative of the fact that it didn't sound like Lizzie was going to leave me and Ash entirely alone to get on with it.

'I'll help crack the whip until you've met everyone and you're feeling ready to wear the ring-mistress outfit,' she winked.

'Great,' I laughed. 'I've always wondered how I'd look in a top hat.'

That evening, I lit one of my favourite autumn scented candles, draped a fleecy blanket over my lap and cracked the spine on a brand-new notebook. I had tried calling Ash, but he hadn't picked up, so I whiled away the time listing ideas because what I had to tell him felt far too important to send in a text. By the time I went to bed, I had a healthy-looking list of festival possibilities, but it was nowhere near enough to fill the whole of the season.

I had floated the idea of a long weekend of events set around the school half term and Halloween when I was in the pub, but Lizzie, Bella and Jeanie had all wrinkled their noses and said that wasn't what they envisaged for the festival at all. Like me, they'd clearly got bigger aspirations than what Moses initially had in mind, too.

It had been on the tip of my tongue to ask them to precisely describe what they had all imagined, but decided to save that question for the meeting the following week. I would doubtless be nervous, and opening the floor up for everyone to chip in would mean I'd hopefully have to talk less.

'Hello?'

The voice that answered the last of my many calls to Ash on Monday morning, sounded husky and thick with sleep, even though it was well after nine.

'Ash?'

'Yeah. Who's this?'

'It's Clemmie. Clemmie Bennett from Rowan Cottage.'

The line went quiet, aside from some rustling and I wondered if the call was about to be cut off. I had discovered that both Wi-Fi and phone signal could be a bit temperamental and patchy in certain parts of the windswept Fens if the mood took it.

'Clemmie,' Ash then said, sounding marginally more alert as he cleared his throat. 'Sorry, I didn't know this was your number, and I can see now that you've called loads. Is everything okay?'

'Yes,' I said, feeling embarrassed to have already rung so many times, but I had been keen to have him confirm his commitment before I got too carried away. 'I'm fine. Are you?'

'Yeah,' he sighed. 'Well, sort of. I was on call over the weekend and had an emergency to deal with both nights, so I'm a bit tired today.'

'And now I've rung and disturbed your sleep.' I grimaced, then imagined him in bed and went hot. 'I'm so sorry.'

'You're fine,' he kindly said. 'I needed to get up to see to Pixie anyway. She's patiently waiting to be let out and for me to get her breakfast.'

I imagined the little dog with crossed legs.

'In that case, I'll let you get on.'

As keen as I was to tell him about my involvement in the festival which would hopefully secure his, I didn't want to ruin his opportunity to catch up on some sleep, or keep Pixie waiting longer than she already had been.

'No, you're fine,' he insisted. 'You must have had a reason for ringing.'

'I did, I do, but honestly, it'll keep. I'll catch you later. Go and see to Pixie.'

'All right,' he said, sounding disappointed. 'I'll be in touch and I promise I'll be more awake when we talk again.'

We ended the call and I fell to wondering if Ash was really going to have any spare time to help out with the festival after all. His work was clearly full-on and then there was his house-hunting. And Pixie, of course.

'You might end up flying solo after all, Clemmie,' I sighed, as another event idea landed and I eagerly jotted it down.

Chapter 5

By the end of Monday afternoon, I had developed the festival ideas list even further and was feeling extremely pleased with what I had come up with. There were some very obvious suggestions it would have been ridiculous not to include, such as loads of things to do with the pumpkins that had inspired Moses to come up with the festival idea in the first place. Given the reputation the Wynbridge area of the Fens had for successfully growing them, they had to take centre stage, but there were also lots of other things that I'd now added to the plan, some of which were a little more unusual.

As I set about steaming some salmon and making a late summer salad for dinner, I hoped all of the ideas were going to be well-received as there wouldn't be much time to come up with more. Lizzie seemed resolute that I was going to be seen as a situation saver, rather than an interfering interloper, but time would tell and whatever folk thought, I really was going to need at least a little help to pull it all off. And talking of help . . .

'Just a sec!' I shouted, jumping almost as high as the kitchen ceiling as someone knocked loudly on the cottage front door and I quickly turned down the steamer on the hob.

As a result of Lizzie's visit, I felt rather tentative about welcoming anyone in, but when I saw who it was, I had a feeling my Insta secret would remain safe. Not that I was prone to making assumptions about my followers, but I didn't think my current visitor would be an AutumnEverything devotee.

'Ash,' I smiled, thinking his timing was impeccable. 'Hello.'

'Hi,' he smiled back. He looked rather tired, so I knew he still hadn't properly caught up on his sleep after the hectic nights on call. I hoped my earlier phone call hadn't completely put paid to his opportunity to rest. 'I know we didn't make a plan, but I happened to be passing and as you hadn't called back, I thought I'd stop. I hope that was okay. No problem if you're busy . . .'

'I didn't ring again because I was worried about waking you,' I told him. 'And I'm not busy. I was just making some dinner, but it's nothing that won't keep. Come in.'

I opened the door wider and stood back.

'I'd better not, if you don't mind,' he said, looking towards his truck. 'You see, I've got Pixie with me and I can't leave her for long.'

'I don't mind if you want to bring her in,' I offered. I really wanted to have the festival conversation sooner rather than later and this was too good an opportunity to waste. 'She's very welcome.'

'Are you sure?'

'Of course. I wouldn't have offered if I didn't mean it.'

'All right,' he said after a moment's hesitation. 'Hold on.'

While Ash collected Pixie, I checked the salmon, which was now perfectly cooked, turned the steamer off and covered the salad with a tea towel.

'Make yourself at home,' I called through to the sitting room when I heard him come in and close the door. 'I'll just be a sec. Would you like a drink?'

'Yes, please. If it isn't too much trouble.'

When I carried in a tray bearing a jug of my summer staple, chilled elderflower cordial, and two glasses, I found Ash sitting in one of the armchairs with Pixie on his lap. She had her head buried between his arm and his chest and her back to the room.

'Oh dear,' I said softly. 'She's really not happy, is she?'

I hoped coming into a different environment wasn't going to be too unsettling for her.

'Nope,' Ash sighed. 'She's been in full on invisible mode today.'

'I've put a bowl of water down for her in the kitchen, but I can't imagine she's going to go looking for it. Shall I bring it in here?'

'No, don't worry. She's only just had a drink, so she'll be fine.'

'Is there anything in particular that's triggered her today?' I asked, while Pixie slowly turned around so that her head was facing the room.

I wouldn't have thought it possible for a dog to express so much emotion, but she looked utterly forlorn.

'Earlier this afternoon, I took her to meet a potential new owner,' Ash explained. 'They were keen to take her, but it didn't work out. Pixie didn't respond to them at all and I need to know there's more than a spark of connection and some genuine affection on her side before I can let her go.'

'Of course.'

'The woman was so disappointed when I said she couldn't take her, but it just wasn't right.'

He sounded choked and stopped talking to take a drink. I knew how long it had taken for me to even consider trying to connect with anyone after losing Callum, but of course poor Pixie didn't have the benefit of being able to understand what was happening to her, let alone know that one day she might come through it. All she must have wanted was for her owner to walk back through the door and take her home. I felt choked myself as I imagined her feeling so abandoned and confused.

'She was with her owner when she died, you know,' Ash then told me as he gave Pixie's back a gentle rub. 'She was found sitting right next to her. She'd been there for hours.'

'Oh, Pixie,' I gasped. 'You poor darling girl. No wonder you're so traumatised.' Her lovely, dark eyes met mine. 'Losing the person you love most in the whole world is excruciatingly painful. Must be excruciatingly painful—' I corrected and blushed.

I quickly picked up my glass before I made more of a mess of what I was trying to express and ended up revealing too much.

'Clemmie,' Ash then started to say, his brow furrowed as the cogs in his brain began to turn in a direction that I would have preferred they didn't. 'Have you . . . ?'

Thankfully, what Pixie did next stopped him further developing that thought. She slowly stretched, then jumped off Ash's lap, timidly crossed the room and stared up at me.

'Hello, my darling.' I smiled down at her.

'I don't believe it,' Ash gasped as Pixie's tail slowly wagged. 'Have you come to say hello?'

She took a step closer and lifted her front paws on to my legs, with her tail still wagging.

'Well, I never,' Ash said in astonished wonder.

I put my hand out and she licked it, then tried to jump up.

'Can I pick her up?' I asked, my eyes flicking to Ash's face.

'I think you'd better.'

He looked even more astounded when I carefully lifted Pixie up, lowered her on to my lap and she made herself at home. She felt like she weighed nothing as she turned around on the spot, then snuggled cosily up as familiarly as if she'd done it every day of her life.

Ash and I looked at one another, but didn't speak, then sat silently for a while as I slowly ran my hands over Pixie's head and down her back and she relaxed further into my lap and then fell sound asleep.

'So,' Ash whispered, finally breaking the silence. 'Remind me what your thoughts are on dog adoption, Clemmie? The day we met, you didn't *really* say that you're not a dog person, did you?'

'I did,' I confirmed, as I continued to gently stroke Pixie. 'I'm not.'

'Well,' he chuckled, 'the evidence in front of me is suggesting otherwise.'

'That's as maybe,' I quickly but quietly said back, 'but as I recall also on that day, you were adamant that Pixie could only live with someone you knew.'

'Well,' he grinned. 'I know you now, don't I?'

'Hardly,' I pointed out.

'I know enough.'

'Such as?'

I was curious to know what he had gleaned and whether it was right or not.

'Well, I know you're single,' he started to reel off. 'That you have a beautiful home and garden, a passion for poultry and, given the number of feeders I've spotted hung up outside, a fondness for wild birds, too.'

'That's not all that much.' I smiled, but I was surprised by the amount he had managed to take onboard about me in the short time we'd known each other. And what he'd focused on noticing, too.

'And I also know,' he carried on, 'that Lizzie messaged me earlier saying I had to talk to you today though I've no idea why. Oh crikey.' He then puffed, 'I hope Joanne hasn't been thinking about my love life again. No offence . . .'

'No, don't panic.' I laughed and Pixie sleepily sighed at the disturbance. 'Lizzie wants us to talk about pumpkins, not passion.'

I had no idea why I'd put it like that and felt my face flush as a result. Ash looked rather warm, too.

'Pumpkins?' he frowned. 'Are you trying to put me off giving you my dog adoption spiel by talking about the Fens' favourite crop?'

'No.' I smiled, although getting off the dog topic was part of my desire to change the subject. 'Though it is connected.'

'So, what is it then?' he asked, his head endearingly cocked.

'Well,' I said, as I bit my lip to stop myself from laughing. 'It actually is about pumpkins.'

'Clemmie!' Ash scolded.

'I'm being serious!' I giggled, then took a deep breath. 'Pumpkins are going to feature heavily because I, by which I mean, we, are going to honour the idea Moses Talbot had and organise the first ever Wynbridge Autumn Festival.'

'What?' Ash gasped. 'Are you being serious?'

'I am,' I told him. 'The festival is now happening because we're going to set it up.'

'No way,' he blinked. 'I don't believe it. I can't believe you're taking it on!'

'*We're* taking it on,' I hastily corrected him. 'I've said I'll do it, but only if your offer to help out still stands.'

Ash ran his hands through his hair and sat back in his chair.

'Well?' I asked, when he didn't say anything. 'Please don't tell me you've changed your mind?'

'No,' he said. 'No, I haven't changed my mind.'

'What then?'

'It's nothing.'

'I don't believe you.'

He gave me a look I couldn't fathom.

'Come on,' I urged. 'Spit it out, because there's clearly something stopping you jumping for joy.'

'Well, it's just that, I'd hate for Joanne to use this as an opportunity to try and push us together when we're both so contentedly single. It would be awful if she meddled and caused some stress and tension between us.'

She'd clearly really done a number on him. The poor guy was paranoid, but her interference in my life was the last thing I wanted, too.

'You don't have to worry about that,' I reassured him. 'Lizzie and Jemma have had serious words with her and Joanne's properly got the message now that neither of us will tolerate being set up.'

'Really?'

'Truly.'

'So, we're safe then?' Ash asked, sounding hopeful.

'Safe as houses,' I confirmed. 'And Lizzie has said she's going to remind her yet again now that we're running the festival, just to be on the safe side, because the last thing she wants is us dropping it because Joanne has given us so much as a loaded look.'

'Oh, well, that's put my mind at rest.' Ash applauded, looking relieved. 'That really does sound sorted.'

'It is,' I said. 'No interference is allowed from Joanne, or anyone else, in any aspect of either of our lives.'

'Well, in that case,' he said happily, 'count me in!'

'You're sure?'

'One hundred per cent,' he pledged. 'Every spare minute I have, is yours, Clemmie. The festival's, I mean . . .'

'Well, that settles it then.' I smiled. 'We're kicking everything off with a planning meeting in the pub Wednesday night. I've only met a few people so far, so it would be great to have you there for some moral support. Will you be able to make it?'

'Of course.'

'Fantastic.'

'And, as that's so soon now, we'd better start coming up with some ideas. From what I can remember, Moses hadn't got any further than having pumpkins take centre stage but we're going to need more than that if we're going to make a success of it and have an entire season's worth of celebrating.'

'We're going to need *loads* more and don't worry, because I've already made a start,' I told him, pointing at the notebook on the table next to my chair. 'I've got a few suggestions to offer that I think should work.'

'Okay, let's hear them then,' said Ash, making himself comfier in the chair.

My tummy gave the loudest rumble as I reached to pick the notebook up and my mind flitted to the salmon and salad in the kitchen. I could easily double the salad and I'd steamed two salmon fillets to have one in a different dish the next day.

'Ash, I don't suppose you fancy staying for dinner, do you?' I offered, before I could overthink it. I couldn't remember the last time I'd shared a meal with someone and issuing the invitation felt like another leap forward. 'Unless you've already got plans?'

'No plans,' Ash smiled, 'and thank you, I'll happily stay, but on one condition.'

'Which is?' I cautiously asked.

'That you'll rethink your opinion about hound rehoming.'

He nodded at Pixie who was still fast asleep on my lap. It felt so comfortable with her there and she was the perfect fit.

'Well,' I said, as I looked down at her. 'I'm not sure—'

'Just think about it,' Ash said softly. 'Please, because I haven't seen her as content as this for a single second since she's been in my care.'

'Well, all right,' I relented, 'I'll think about it, but please don't go getting your hopes up. Or hers.'

'I'll try not to.' Ash smiled. 'But the two of you do look made for each other.'

If only he knew.

Chapter 6

By the time Ash and Pixie left that evening, I was shocked to discover that I was genuinely, and surprisingly, wavering about taking the little dog on. She had pottered about the cottage and out in the garden, finding the water bowl and making herself at home just as naturally as she'd settled on my lap and as if she'd always lived with me.

Ash said repeatedly that he hadn't seen her looking so relaxed in all of the time he'd known her and even though someone else might have assumed that he could have been saying that to try and influence me, I knew he wasn't. He loved Pixie too much to risk her future happiness on a whim.

For some reason, the little dog had felt comfortable around me and in return, I had been relaxed around her, too. However, in spite of the fact that I was fast falling for the little scruffy black and tan bundle, I told Ash that I wouldn't make a decision about potentially moving her in until after the first autumn festival meeting.

'If I find myself inundated with planning and prepping after that,' I pointed out, 'I won't have time to commit to settling her and that's not fair on her, is it?'

I ignored the fact that as I was saying the words, Pixie was cosily snuggled up in my favourite armchair and didn't look as though she'd need much, indeed any, coddling. I also tried not to be swayed by the words from Callum's last note. Pixie certainly had the potential to be a very lovely thing that could come as a result of taking a risk, but I needed to take her needs seriously and give them further consideration.

'And of course, I'd have to leave her here on her own while I'm setting things up in town sometimes,' I added, as much to convince myself as Ash that rushing a response would be the wrong thing to do, 'and she might not like that.'

'I think if you left her in that chair, she wouldn't budge.' Ash grinned. 'And I can tell you, her previous owner was a very sociable woman, so I'm sure Pixie would soon get used to going out and about with you. It's not like she doesn't know the town or the people in it and having the cottage to come back to with you after a trip out, would make all the difference.'

'That's not helpful,' I grumbled.

'Just giving you all the facts,' Ash laughed and gently picked Pixie up. 'I'll see you in the pub on Wednesday.'

'See you Wednesday,' I said as I opened the door to let him out.

'And thanks for dinner.'

'You're welcome,' I said, trying not to be further swayed by the sleepy but reproachful look Pixie gave me for allowing Ash to remove her from Rowan Cottage.

Ash had been keen on my autumn festival ideas and had come up with a couple of great ones of his own. Having chatted even more on the phone ahead of the meeting, by the time

Wednesday dawned, I felt as though we were as prepared as we could be.

I hadn't expected to feel quite so confident, but the spring in my step that day was a real bonus. I wasn't sure if the feeling would remain when faced with a pub full of people, but I endeavoured to keep the festival visual at the forefront of my mind, go with the flow and hold my nerve.

I spent much of the day in the garden and posted a selection of photos on AutumnEverything featuring the peachy-hued dahlias which were now flowering in abundance. It was the first image I'd shared that year to show how the garden was hinting at a sign of my favourite season being on the horizon and the likes and comments that rushed in suggested that my followers were as keen as I was to welcome in the scent of woodsmoke and get wrapped up in warm layers and big soft scarves again.

I was considering what to wear for the meeting that would set the right tone when Mum called.

'Hello, Mum.' I cheerfully smiled, as her face popped up and I carried on looking through my wardrobe.

'Hello, my darling,' she smiled back. 'How are you? You sound in a good mood.'

'I am.' I nodded, as I pulled out a Joe Browns autumn patterned dress and wondered if it would be too much or an aesthetically pleasing extra confidence boost. 'A really good mood as it happens, but I'm sorry I can't chat for long, because I've got to go out.'

Mum looked delighted about that.

'In that case, I won't keep you,' she promised. 'Going anywhere nice?'

'To the pub in town,' I told her. 'There's a meeting there tonight to discuss the event I told you about.'

'You didn't tell me much,' she wheedled, obviously hoping I'd share more now.

'Well,' I laughed, 'I'll tell you all about it tomorrow, because we're nailing down the details tonight.'

I was both surprised and excited to still feel so confident and I was practically itching to ring Lizzie and ask if we could move the meeting forward by an hour or two!

'I'll hold you to that.' Mum grinned. 'And you've got me thinking, as you're going to be involved with it, maybe your dad and I should come and visit while it's happening? It's been so long since we've seen you.'

'Oh, I'd love that,' I gasped.

Their presence at some point during the festival really would be the cherry on the cake. Though I'd have to prime them not to talk to anyone about the reason behind my move to the Fens. Or my Insta account. I felt my rush of excitement wane a little when faced with the prospect of that.

'That's settled then,' said Mum.

'Don't do anything until we've got the itinerary sorted,' I hedged, in spite of the fact there wasn't actually anything they could plan until the festival details were settled on, 'then I'll let you know the best dates.'

'It sounds like it's going to be a big deal, Clemmie.'

'It is,' I confirmed, with an eye on the clock. 'And I really had better start getting ready now, otherwise I'll be late. I'm sorry to cut your call short.'

'It's fine,' Mum insisted. 'I'm sorry for holding you up, but I will just quickly tell you why I was ringing in the first place.'

'Go on.'

'Jill and Colin have had an offer on the house.'

'Already?'

'Yep.' Mum nodded. 'Already and above the asking price, too.'

'That's amazing. Are they going to take it?'

'They are, and they're in a right flap now because they haven't started looking for anywhere to move to yet!'

'A time limited house hunt is just what they need,' I said seriously. 'They won't have a chance to think about anything else, while they're doing viewings, booking surveys and packing boxes.'

Mum agreed. 'This should really help them, shouldn't it?' she said thoughtfully. 'Of course, it will be hard when the day comes to hand the keys over, but it's the right thing to do.'

Knowing what a difference moving house, and indeed area, had made to me, I had every hope that my former in-laws would find the change as helpful and cathartic as I had.

'Totally the right thing to do,' I firmly said. 'And I'm sorry, Mum, but I really must go now.'

'Of course,' she said, waving my apology away. 'You get ready, my love. And let me know tomorrow what's going on.'

'Will do. Love you.'

'Love you, too.'

My phone went off again during the drive into town, but obviously I didn't check it until I had parked. A flurry of nerves had forced their way in as I had got dressed and, for the hundredth time at least, gone through my list of ideas back at the cottage. As a result of the jitters, I had set off earlier than planned in case they got the better of me and I was tempted to bail and retreat back into my previously reclusive habit.

I wasn't impressed that my earlier confidence had for some reason headed for the hills, no mean feat in the flat Fens, and was even less impressed when I listened to the voicemail Ash had left while I had been driving.

'Clemmie, I'm so sorry,' he apologised, even before I had a chance to say hello when I immediately called him back.

'You're absolutely certain you won't make it?'

His voicemail had explained that he was at a farm in the middle of nowhere and for some reason his truck wouldn't start. The farmer and his mechanically-minded daughter had both had a look at it, but it still wouldn't turn over.

'I've got to wait for recovery,' he told me, sounding genuinely upset. 'And the call centre said it could be at least a couple of hours until someone gets to me.'

'Could one of the farmers not drive you into town?' I suggested. 'And then I'll take you back for the truck later.'

'They can't leave the farm and I'm miles from Wynbridge, so you wouldn't make it back in time yourself if you came out to get me either,' he said, before I suggested the idea. 'I'm so sorry to let you down.'

I was sorry about that, too, but it wasn't his fault.

'It's okay.'

'It isn't though, is it?'

'Well, no, but these things happen and it can't be helped. I'm sure I'll manage, so don't stress about it. You're already having a bad enough day. But what about Pixie?' I then gasped. 'Is she with you?'

'No,' said Ash. 'She's at the barn and Will is going to check on her when he's finished at the practice.'

'But will that not upset her?' I frowned. 'Having someone other than you go in to see to her . . .'

'I love that you're so concerned,' said Ash, capitalising on my worry for the little dog. 'You are going to take her, aren't you?'

'Like I told you before,' I evasively said, 'I'll decide about that after the meeting tonight.'

'The meeting which is already off to a bad start,' Ash then sighed. 'I hope my absence won't influence your feelings about the festival or Pixie because I promise you, Clemmie, I'm committed to helping support both. And no, don't worry, she won't mind Will going in. She's used to him. He was her vet before I came along.'

'Thank you for saying that and I'm pleased Pixie will be okay. Now,' I said, taking a big breath, 'I'd better go and get set up before everyone arrives.'

I'd kept an eye on The Mermaid door and there hadn't been a stampede of early meeting attendees clamouring to get in yet. In my current state of depleted confidence, I wasn't sure if that was something I should feel relieved about or not.

'All right,' said Ash. 'And like I said before, I really am sorry not to be there.'

'I'll put you down for double duty next time,' I said sardonically. 'Let's catch up later.'

'Yes, let's do that. Good luck, Clemmie. Not that you're going to need it. You're going to do Moses and the town proud.'

'Thanks.' I tried to smile. 'I'll hopefully see you soon.'

As it turned out, I was going to need a miracle rather than a dose of luck to make the meeting a success.

'Where is everyone?' I heard Jemma hiss to Lizzie as the three of us stood and looked around the almost empty pub as the meeting start time ticked closer.

I glanced over at Jeanie who gave me an enthusiastic thumbs up from behind the bar, and as much as I appreciated it, it wasn't consolation for the lack of people. Yes, I'd been worried about facing a crowd, but the show of disinterest was embarrassing and not at all what Lizzie had prepared me to expect.

'I thought you said you were going to tell everyone about tonight and that more locals would be available if we waited until midweek?' I rather tersely said as we looked across at the many empty tables. 'I thought the autumn festival idea was a popular one around here and that folk were keen to see the idea Moses had actually come to something?'

'It was,' she said, looking around again and sounding confused. 'It is. They are.'

'Where's Joanne?' Jemma asked.

'On a video call with Aiden,' Lizzie told her. 'For once, she didn't seem all that excited about it, but she did say she'll try and come along later if she can.'

'I don't think we'll be here later,' I muttered.

Just at that moment, Bella came bustling in with a woman I didn't recognise. They had a dog each and I could see that the cute spaniel with a sparkly pink collar that Bella led in was far better behaved than the other woman's terrier.

'Jasper,' she scolded as he pulled at his tangled lead. 'Come on. Settle down.'

I hoped I wasn't poised to be heckled by a pooch, because he looked intent on creating mayhem.

'Let's give it a few more minutes,' Lizzie said with concern.

Fifteen minutes after the official start time, we decided that the few people who had bothered to turn up to hear what I had to say, were going to lose interest if we didn't kick things off, so Lizzie cleared her throat and made a start.

'So,' she finished up, having explained that the autumn festival had been miraculously saved and would now be going ahead, assuming there was more interest in it than was represented at the meeting. 'Without further ado, let me introduce you to Clemmie, who is going to be in charge of running the festival, with Ash working alongside her.'

I shakily got to my feet and looked at the few faces in front of me. Aside from Bella, her friend and Jeanie, there didn't look to be much in the way of enthusiasm or interest exuding from any of them.

'Where is Ash then?' a guy at the bar asked gruffly.

Sitting slightly away from the rest of us, I wasn't sure if he was part of the meeting or not.

'Good evening,' I said, hating the wobble in my voice that let everyone know how nervous I was. 'I'm Clemmie and, as Lizzie has just said, I'm going to be taking on the idea Moses had to celebrate autumn in the area and overseeing the Wynbridge Autumn Festival this year.' Lizzie let out a whoop which, mortifyingly, no one joined in with. 'And, as she also said, I will be running it with Ash but he has unfortunately been delayed this evening and can't now join us.'

'Along with everyone else, by the looks of it,' the guy then laughed.

'Oh, shut up, Jason,' Evelyn, the pub owner, snapped.

'With time being so short to get things up and running

now we're already into the ber months,' I pressed on, laying a hand on my notebook for a boost and looking to Lizzie for further support, 'we thought it would be a good idea to get going as soon as we can and gather as many people together here tonight to—'

'Not many people.'

'Are you going to pipe down, or am I going to have to throw you out?' Evelyn barked and we all winced.

The guy, Jason, shrugged and shut up, but still looked belligerent and given that he was right in my eyeline at the bar, the sight of him put me completely off my stroke. I had no idea what I had been going to say next.

'So, what have you got in mind?' Bella kindly asked, when I didn't say anything. 'Will it be a weekend of events or are you planning for things to happen right throughout the season?'

She could have guessed the answer, of course, because we'd discussed it during my first visit to the pub, but I appreciated the question as it pulled my focus away from the heckler and back to the ideas written in my notebook.

'If we can drum up enough interest,' I began, 'and before you say it,' I loudly said, looking directly at the jeerer, 'I know the number of you here tonight doesn't bode well,' that raised a bit of a laugh, 'I was thinking it would be great to have things running right through the season and with some whole community events scheduled for half term when all age groups could be more involved throughout the day. Ash and I have been working hard to come up with suggestions that will hopefully appeal to everyone.'

'But is that what Moses had in mind?' someone asked.

'As you well know, Moses didn't have time to come up with

more than the idea of piling some pumpkins up in the market square and auctioning them off,' Evelyn pointed out.

'But I'm certain his vision would have grown, just like Clemmie and Ash's already has, if he'd had the time to develop it,' Lizzie added.

'Fair enough,' sniffed the person who had asked.

'Can you give us some examples of what you have in mind, Clemmie?' the woman with Bella asked with a kind smile.

I opened my notebook and began working my way through our extensive list, explaining the details of some of the ideas if their purpose or connection to autumn wasn't immediately obvious.

'I love the craft workshop ideas,' Lizzie said keenly. 'I can take those on and run them in the gallery so long as the scheduling doesn't clash with what I've already got booked.'

'Thank you, Lizzie.' I nodded, practically wilting with relief that at least one thing was going to come off. 'That would be fantastic.'

'Wynbridge has no finer craft tutor,' Jemma chimed in.

'And the gallery, overlooking the square, will be the perfect space for the sessions,' I further said. 'We can definitely work around what you already have lined up, so we'll get together to discuss that.'

I could also imagine people making leaf garlands to hang around the square and knitting pumpkins in the café next door. That would make it a proper social occasion with an opportunity to chat and enjoy Jemma's bakes as well as contribute. I had seen posters on display around town from a local yarn bombing group so it would be great if they got involved.

'And I'll ask my husband, Tom, about the town hall availability for some of the other things,' said Jemma, typing notes into her phone. 'He works for the council, so he might have an idea as to where the spring bulb planting could take place, too.'

That was one of my favourite ideas and I hoped it would have a genuine whole community appeal if it could happen somewhere in the local park. Assuming enough people got behind it and I could talk someone into either donating the bulbs or convince everyone who wanted to plant some, to pay for them, of course. That was another issue to iron out . . .

'Well, I think this all sounds wonderful,' beamed Bella and the general nod of heads showed that most of the select gathering were at least considering it.

'Yes, yes, it's all very twee and wholesome, I'm sure,' Jason, who was still at the bar, nastily piped up, and it was obvious that he wasn't part of that group. 'But you're going to need hordes of volunteers to pull it off and as you can see,' he cast his eyes around and spread his hands wide, for dramatic effect, 'no one's really bothered about it after all.'

'Those of us who are here are bothered,' said Lizzie, rallying to the cause. 'And we can all contribute something.'

'But not enough to make it the great seasonal spectacular this newcomer is suggesting,' he huffed.

I looked at the scarce faces and as much as I hated to agree with him, I had a horrible feeling that he was right. I had been hoping to talk to business owners who might be willing to host food and drink nights, landowners who had known Moses and who might want to get involved with the all-important pumpkin picking and carving competitions, the knitters who loved yarn bombing opportunities and readers who might enjoy an autumn themed book club . . .

Disappointingly, none of those people had turned up, and even though a few names had been suggested regarding hosting events, if the people behind those names and venues weren't in attendance, then was there *really* any chance that they'd want to be involved?

In spite of Lizzie's insistence that the festival was wanted, practically no one had turned out to support its inception and that lack of eagerness and commitment didn't bode well for the future of the event. Perhaps the pumpkin auction Moses had initially envisaged and a couple of crafting workshops, would be all Ash and I would end up having to manage after all.

'It'll be a health and safety nightmare with this few of you,' Jason continued, hammering his point home.

'Right,' said Evelyn, opening the hatch in the bar that separated her from the customers, 'that's your lot. I think we've heard more than enough negativity from you.'

'And who even are you to the town?' Jason said angrily to me as he hopped down from his stool and fixed me with a glare I didn't think I had done anything to deserve. 'Half of us have never laid eyes on you before and yet here you are, swanning in and trying to take over as if you own the place. I daresay you never even met Moses, did you?'

I felt my eyes prickle with tears of embarrassment and my cheeks flame.

'Ignore him,' said Lizzie as he banged through the door and into the square with Evelyn in hot pursuit.

But how could I ignore him? My unknown status as a Wynbridge local had been one of the first things I'd flagged, when she'd asked me to take the festival on. Lizzie might not have acknowledged it, but why should anyone listen to me when they had no idea who I was or, come to that, knew how much I loved autumn? I should never have been seduced into saying yes as a result of Lizzie's honeyed words and my own vivid imagination.

'Take no notice, Clemmie,' Lizzie said more loudly when I didn't respond.

'He doesn't talk for the rest of us,' said Jemma.

'Though he does have a point,' said a woman who had been listening throughout the meeting, but hadn't spoken up before. 'I'm not saying you're not up to the job, my love, but I don't recognise you either.'

'I live in a cottage outside of town,' I told her, the words catching. 'I've been there about a year and a half, but have kept myself to myself while I was . . . renovating it.'

And I would be keeping myself to myself again after tonight.

'Do you mean the cottage on Lark Drove?' The woman frowned.

'Yes,' I said. 'Rowan Cottage. Do you know it?'

'Vaguely,' she shrugged.

'I've given him a piece of my mind,' Evelyn bristled as she marched back in. 'Don't pay any heed to anything he says, Clemmie. He's all bluster and no substance.'

'And I've yet to see him leave the pub without either you or Uncle Jim chasing him out,' said Jeanie, with a smile, but I couldn't see the funny side.

'Next time, I'm barring him on sight,' Evelyn declared, as everyone began to drift away or talk among themselves.

'You're not bothered by him, are you?' Jemma asked me as the meeting staggered to an unsatisfactory close without anyone announcing it was over.

'You've not really taken any notice?' Lizzie chipped in straight after.

'Of course, I'm bothered,' I told them both. 'And I have taken notice, because he's right, isn't he? Hardly anyone turned out tonight and it will be impossible to get the festival successfully off the ground with such little interest.'

'You're not giving up, Clemmie?' Lizzie asked, looking stricken.

'With a turnout like this,' I said, looking around, 'I can't see as I have any choice. I hate to say it, but you overestimated enthusiasm for this idea, Lizzie. I think you mistook your eagerness to bring Moses's idea to life for everyone else's.'

She, Jemma, Bella and her friend Holly, tried to convince me otherwise, but I wouldn't be swayed. Too few people wanted the festival to go ahead and a blow-in being in charge and attempting to turn it into something it hadn't started out as was most likely the reason no one had turned out to support it. I was better off keeping my head down, my own counsel and right out of town.

Chapter 7

With my first attempt to immerse myself in community life ending in such a disaster, my mood took a nosedive and I shrugged off Lizzie's promise to get to the bottom of the disastrous meeting, closed the cottage curtains and ignored both the knock on the front door that came the next day and the multiple messages stacking up on my phone.

The only person I had contact with, and that was via a WhatsApp message rather than a call, was Mum. I told her the meeting had gone ahead, there was loads to do as a result and I was saving the details until I could send her something official, like a poster advertising what was happening. I knew I was setting myself up for a further fall, but my current mood didn't offer up the right frame of mind in which to make a genuine explanation about what had embarrassingly occurred.

For two days, I lay low as the rain hammered down and the wind rattled the garden gate and made a determined effort to blow the end of summer out and the beginning of autumn in. Ordinarily, I would have been rejoicing about that, but not this time around. This year, I couldn't muster the enthusiasm to embrace the change or the energy to look again for hope and solace in Callum's encouraging and inspiring notes. I left the special treasure box I kept them in undisturbed on the wardrobe shelf in my bedroom.

'Clem! I know you're in there!'

It was Ash's voice that roused me from my Saturday lie-in with a magazine and pot of tea, but I still didn't feel inclined to respond to my new friend.

'I need your help! Please open the door.'

I didn't budge.

'I wouldn't ask you,' he continued to shout, 'if I wasn't desperate.'

With a long sigh, I carefully pushed back the duvet, to avoid upsetting the tray and peeped around the curtains. I couldn't see Ash because he was likely sheltering from the rain in the porch, but I did hear an indignant woof and felt annoyed that he had subjected Pixie, as well as himself, to a soaking.

I assumed his appeal for help was a ruse to get me to open the door, but with the pair of them in attendance, I supposed it was as good a time as any to explain what I had decided.

'Just a sec!' I shouted through the window that I opened only far enough for my voice to reach him. 'Hang on!'

I pulled on my cotton dressing gown and padded down the stairs, hoping that Pixie was going to forgive me for turning her away and that Ash wouldn't try to convince me that I would have more than enough time to look after her now the festival wasn't going ahead.

The failed meeting had plunged me into an emotional maelstrom and I had even found myself wavering about my former conviction to never sell Rowan Cottage during the long watches of the night. I hoped with the whole of my heart that the current upset would pass – my slow walk along life's path, with grief as my companion, had given me reason to believe that it would – but it didn't currently put me in prime position for being in the best headspace to take on and nurture a depressed pooch.

'At last!' Ash muttered, stepping straight in when I opened the door. 'I was beginning to think you'd left the county.'

'If this is about the festival or Pixie, or both,' I immediately began to say as I pulled back my shoulders and put on my bravest face, 'then please, just let me say—'

'It is about Pixie,' Ash interrupted, producing her like a magician with a rabbit in a hat, from the depths of the huge waxed coat he was wearing and thrusting her into my arms, 'and it would be about the festival too, given what Lizzie has told me about the meeting after I couldn't get you to answer your phone, but I haven't got time to get into it right now.'

Pixie started to wriggle and, not having the best hold on her, I put her down. She made a beeline for my armchair and jumped straight on to it, then looked at me with her head cutely cocked and her ears pricked.

'I know it's an imposition,' Ash carried on, 'but can you take her?'

'No,' I said, feeling cross. 'Ash, I can't. I'd already decided—'

'Not forever,' he cut in quickly. 'Just for the weekend.'

I looked from Pixie back to him and realised he didn't look like his usual sunny self and I got the impression that wasn't only because of what Lizzie must have told him about the meeting.

'What's happened?' I therefore asked. 'What's wrong?'

'My nan has had a stroke,' he told me, sounding distraught. 'And I need to go. The journey is too long for Pixie to manage and Will's working this weekend and so is Lottie and there's really no one else I'd trust her with.'

'Oh, my goodness,' I gasped.

'I know it's probably the last thing—'

'No, it's fine,' I told him, cutting off whatever plea he was going to make. 'Of course, I'll take her.'

I felt guilty for not noticing straightaway that something was wrong and for assuming the purpose of his visit was to convince me to rethink my decisions. Not everything was about me.

'You will?' Ash said, looking relieved. 'You're sure?'

'Yes,' I said. 'Just tell me what to feed her and go.'

Before I knew what was happening, he grasped the tops of my arms, pulled me close and planted a kiss on my cheek.

'You're a lifesaver,' he puffed, then let me go. 'I've thrown some bits in a bag. Hang on and I'll go and get them.'

I don't think it had even registered that he'd just kissed me, albeit in a fit of sheer relief, and I didn't have the bandwidth then to process it, either.

'Right, here you go,' he gabbled, rushing back along the wet path in record time. 'There's far more than she's going to need as I've got to be here ready for work on Monday. I'll collect her as soon as I'm back.'

'Okay,' I said. 'That's fine.'

'Now, I've written a note about how much she has to eat and when and I've put her bed in here, too. Though I have to admit, she's got into the habit of sleeping on the bed next to me, so you might want to . . .'

He ran a hand through his soaked hair and looked with concern over my shoulder at Pixie who didn't appear bothered by the unexpected change in her circumstances.

'I'm sure we'll figure it all out,' I told him, hoping Pixie wouldn't pine for him overnight. 'Now, go on. Get off, otherwise you'll never get to wherever it is you're going.'

'Okay,' he nodded. 'Okay. Thanks, Clemmie, and when I do get back, we'll talk about the festival. Yes? I'm not giving up on it yet.'

I didn't have the heart to tell him that I had. I knew that Lizzie had called at the cottage again the previous evening and that she and Ash had now talked about what had occurred, but it wasn't the time to get into all of that.

'Just drive safe,' I said, as I started to usher him out and didn't answer his question. 'I hope your nan is going to be all right.'

'Thanks, Clemmie,' he said again. 'I'll see you tomorrow night.'

Once he'd driven off, I closed the door and turned to look at Pixie. I'd never been in charge of a dog before. When I was growing up, we'd had a cat. An aloof creature who kept himself to himself, but I had the feeling that Pixie had the potential to demand far more of me than indifferent Mr Mittens ever had.

'Well,' I said, feeling a little ill at ease under her scrutiny. 'Let's just see how things go, shall we? What have we got in here?'

I took the bag Ash had given me into the kitchen and unpacked it. There was enough food for at least a week, according to the note of instructions that went with it, and a bowl as well as a lead, which matched Pixie's collar and her squishy bed. I put the food in a cupboard in the utility and hung her lead on one of the leaf-shaped wooden hooks next to the back door. It looked as if it had always been there, as did her bed – she chose to ignore it because she was comfortable in my chair – which I set down next to the log burner.

'Now, how about a drink?' I offered, only then remembering my tea, as I knelt next to the chair and gave Pixie a long fuss, which she lapped up. 'I'll go and get mine first.'

Pixie followed me up the stairs and had a nose in the bedrooms while I dressed and used the bathroom and then came down after me once she'd finished her inspection. I put down a bowl of water for her, then ate my usual breakfast of overnight oats, fresh fruit and chia seeds. Pixie looked at me appealingly while I chewed, but I didn't cave because Ash had written that she'd already had hers *and* underlined it, which made me wonder if she was a bit of a glutton. She certainly had the butter wouldn't melt look nailed, so I could see how a weaker mortal could have been taken in.

'Let's have a mooch around the garden, shall we?' I suggested, once I'd tidied away and noticed that the rain had finally stopped.

I'd avoided going outside during the previous couple of days. Not only because of the downturn in the weather, but in case either Lizzie or Jemma happened to drive by while I was out there, but now I needed to find a spot for Pixie to use, so I couldn't put it off any longer and actually, I found I didn't want to.

As my Insta grid showed, the garden was really starting to come into its own now and I didn't want to miss that for the sake of avoiding an awkward conversation. Not that I was in any rush to talk to anyone. If I heard a car approaching, I'd be ducking out of sight until it had gone, even though I knew Lizzie and Jemma were most likely then both at work.

'Come on, then,' I said, encouraging Pixie out of the door, once I'd pulled on my polka dot patterned wellies. 'Let's go and get some fresh air, shall we?'

Pixie had an eager root about, while I refilled the birdfeeders and cut a few of my favourite pompom dahlias that the rain hadn't ruined for displaying in the house. I had a fabulous Emma Bridgewater Black Toast jar which made the perfect vase for them and they'd look good on my grid. I stopped what I was doing to watch Pixie, who was drinking out of one of the birdbaths. She'd look great on my grid, too, but would be a dead giveaway about my Insta identity to anyone who knew her and me.

'Come on!' I called, when she started to show a rather too keen interest in the feeders hanging off the bird table and I felt a few heavy spots of rain. 'Time to go back in.'

The utility and kitchen floor was covered in wet little footprints within seconds of closing the back door and I quickly realised what the towels Ash had included in Pixie's bag were for.

'Stand still then,' I laughed, as I attempted to dry her feet and she scampered about and tried to lick my face.

Her tail was working like a rudder and I was relieved to find that she had accepted her unexpected sleepover with such good grace. That said, we hadn't tried to sleep yet . . . She wasn't keen on the mop I washed the floors with and retreated to my armchair, where we later whiled away the afternoon curled up under a fleecy blanket and watched both *Sleepless in Seattle* and *You've Got Mail.*

★

'Ash,' I yawned, when my phone woke me from a nap I hadn't expected to take, and I saw his number on the screen of my phone.

I'd got a stiff arm thanks to Pixie's dead weight laying on it but I didn't mind that, because it had been cosy to cuddle and I was very much enjoying her company. Had she not been visiting, I daresay I would have still been dug deep into the fug I'd fallen into as a result of the failed festival meeting, but having her to consider had pulled focus away from me and my woes and embarrassment, and I was both mindful and appreciative of that.

'Clemmie?'

'Sorry,' I apologised, stretching a bit as Pixie jumped down, then headed for the kitchen. 'I was asleep. How are you getting on? How's your nan?'

I heard Pixie bark and got up to see what she wanted. The pins and needles in my legs, which had been curled under me, made walking agony and I was pleased there was no one there to see me as I hobbled along.

'Was that Pixie?' Ash asked.

'Yes,' I said. 'I think she wants to go out.'

She was certainly looking very pointedly at the back door. I opened it for her and she dashed off.

'She'll always let you know,' Ash said. 'Are you getting on okay?'

'Yes, we're absolutely fine. We've just had a lovely nap. But what about you?' I asked again.

'Better than expected,' he happily said.

'Thank goodness.'

'Nan's definitely had a stroke, but it's quite a mild one.'

'That's a relief.'

'It really is. Mum was in a flap, not surprisingly, when she phoned, but the prognosis is looking good and as soon as Nan's up to it and her consultant is happy, she's going to move in with Mum and Dad. It's something they've been talking about for a while and they've got this little annexe at the side of the house, which is where I was living before I moved to Wynbridge, so that will be perfect for her.'

'Well,' I said, as I considered everything he'd shared. 'I'm sorry it's happened at all, obviously, but I'm pleased everything is going to work out and that you were able to get there so quickly.'

'It would have been a nightmare with Pixie,' he told me, 'so I really do appreciate you taking her at such short notice.'

'It was my pleasure and don't give us another thought,' I told him, as Pixie trotted back in with wet paws again and I realised I should have put the towel down for her to walk over. 'We're having a wonderful time.'

'That's a weight off my mind,' he said, then had to go.

I was pleased to have heard from him and even more pleased that the outcome for his nan was sounding so positive. I wasn't quite so pleased about the state of my floors, however, as Pixie chose that moment to skitter about and shake and made even more of a muddy mess.

That evening, I felt a little apprehensive as bedtime approached, but it all turned out fine. I had made a vague attempt to settle Pixie in her bed, but didn't stop her when she jumped out and followed me up the stairs to my room. She had soon snuggled down next to me and my only complaint was that she was a bit of a snorer, but she didn't hog the bed or scamper about in the night, so I soon forgave her that.

In fact, when I woke with sunlight streaming through the bedroom curtains, I realised I must have quickly tuned her snuffling out and that I'd enjoyed the best and longest night's sleep I'd had in years.

'Good morning, my friend,' I smiled, when I opened my eyes and found her looking intently at me. 'Are you all right?'

Her head dropped on to her paws and she let out a little whimper.

'Oh, Pixie.' I swallowed. 'It's okay.'

I had a horrible feeling that she had just experienced something I myself had been through many times before, though thankfully, not recently. In the time since Callum had died, I'd lost count of the number of mornings I'd woken and just for a second, I had forgotten that he was gone. The agony of then remembering what had happened was awful and it was my guess that Pixie had opened her eyes and recalled what had happened to her and her owner, too.

'It will get easier,' I said, leaning over and kissing her wiry head. 'You will feel better one day and for more than just a few minutes and then a few hours at a time. I promise.'

She huffed out a breath, but didn't move.

'Come on,' I said, sitting up. 'Let's go and greet the day.'

It was, in part, the little things that had saved my sanity. The dishes that had to be cleared, the laundry that had to be washed. The domestic tasks had given me routine and occupation and I hoped that letting Pixie into the garden and then giving her some breakfast might help distract her.

'Hello, Mum. Hey, Dad,' I said a while later, with Pixie

looking much happier and balanced on my lap, so she could clearly be seen on the screen.

I had decided to bite the bullet and tell my parents that there had been an unexpected change of plan and that the event I had said I was going to be involved with in town was now a non-starter. I was probably making more of the explanation than was necessary, but I knew they had both been worried about what I was going to do now the cottage renovation was complete and had therefore taken the opportunity to rope Pixie in to help.

'Oh, my goodness!' Mum gasped, the moment she saw her, which was exactly the reaction I had been hoping to elicit.

'Who's that little cutie?' Dad joined in, moving closer to the screen.

'This,' I said, kissing the top of Pixie's head and receiving a chin lick in return, 'is my pal, Pixie.'

'Hello, Pixie.' Mum beamed.

'Is she yours?' asked Dad.

'No,' I said. 'She's not mine. I'm dog-sitting for a friend. She'll be going home later.' That was something else I wasn't keen on. I was going to miss her padding about the place and muddying it up. 'I thought you might like to say hello before she gets picked up.'

'We like that very much,' said Dad.

'No wonder I haven't been able to get hold of you,' said Mum, assuming that I had been preoccupied with Pixie for the last few days.

I didn't correct her and it occurred to me that Pixie was providing both a distraction *and* confirmation that I had friends in the Fens. You'd have to know someone pretty well to ask them to look after your dog. Ash might have been desperate for help, rather than having been my friend for months, but Mum and Dad didn't know that and actually, I was pleased Ash had called on me in his hour of need. It was nice to feel trusted.

'She's certainly kept me on my toes.' I smiled, as I kissed her again.

'And what about this big town event?' Mum asked. 'Is that keeping you busy, too?'

Pixie chose that moment to jump down and wander off, but I didn't mind because she'd got the call off to a great start.

'Sadly not,' I sighed. 'It's now been decided that there's not enough people available to support it. Health and safety and all that, so it isn't going to happen.'

That was one way of putting it. Definitely a creative and positive spin on the truth.

'Oh, no,' said Mum. 'That's such a shame.'

'I'm really sorry about that, love,' added Dad.

'Yes.' I swallowed. 'I'm sorry, too. I was rather looking forward to it.'

I gave my ideas notebook a cursory look and realised that as well as still smarting over what Jason the jeerer had put me through, I was upset that what could have been a wonderful celebration of autumn, wasn't going to be happening, either.

'Will you still want us to come down?' asked Mum.

'Absolutely,' I said, without hesitation. 'I miss you guys and I can't wait to show you all of the finishing touches I've given to the cottage.'

They both looked delighted about that.

'And this time,' laughed Dad, 'because I won't be up to my ears in plasterboard and grout, there might be time and opportunity for you to introduce us to your friends.'

'And Pixie!' Mum added.

Pixie ran back over to me at the sound of her name and I scooped her up again and knocked over the phone.

'We'll get a date in the diary soon,' I promised, once I'd set it straight again. 'I'd love you to come before the pumpkins are all harvested. You won't believe what the fields around here look like when they're at their peak.'

'We got a bit of an idea from the photos you shared last year,' Mum reminded me, 'but it will be wonderful to see them for ourselves, won't it, Dave?'

'Trust you to focus on the most autumnal thing imaginable, Clem!' Dad laughed.

'You know me,' I laughed back, thinking of Moses again and wishing I had met him. 'Autumn is literally my everything!'

I ended the call before either of them asked what I was going to do now to fill my time and Pixie and I happily whiled away the rest of the day at the cottage.

Knowing that the full harvest moon was set to rise that evening and the sky had finally cleared again, I arranged cushions, blankets and snacks in the garden so we could be snugly settled in time to admire it as it crept golden, vast and glorious over the edge of the Fenland horizon. The appearance of the full moon was a spectacle I had regularly come to admire, with the dates noted on my phone calendar, and I was thrilled the weather hadn't scuppered my plan to view the glowing harvest spectacle as it had the previous September.

'Would you look at that, Pixie?' I gasped as the size and

colour intensified with every passing second. 'Isn't she magnificent?'

I took a few photos with a camera my parents had given me, but just like in the past when I went to concerts with Callum, I didn't allow myself to become preoccupied with snapping away and filming.

It never ceased to amaze me that so many people viewed so much of their lives second-hand, through the screen on their phone, rather than with their own eyes. It was lovely to have a record, but I preferred to stay in the moment as much as possible, even though I ran a successful online account where images were the focus.

As far as I was concerned, the secret to successful and comfortable stargazing, and indeed moon-watching, was entirely down to getting in the right position and I was in a semi-recumbent state when I heard Ash's truck pull up and Pixie started to bark.

My thoughts, as the moon rose, had drifted again to the autumn festival and I wondered if, rather than give up on it entirely, it might actually be worth considering running just an event or two over a couple of weekends, like I had originally suggested. It would be better than doing nothing at all and might inspire people to want to get further involved next year. And if that was the case, we could make it the spectacular then that Lizzie had been so certain it could be this first time around.

I sat up and stretched my neck from side to side, thinking I would run it by Ash now he was here. See if he thought that might be a feasible, rather than defeatist, option. Now the initial sting of the meeting had dulled a bit, and being preoccupied with Pixie had given me some distance from it, I found I really didn't want to give up on it completely after all. Like I'd earlier said to Dad, autumn really was my everything and it would be a shame to miss out on celebrating it in such a meaningful way.

'I was hoping you'd seen,' Ash nodded at the moon, as he climbed stiffly out of his truck and rolled his shoulders, while Pixie leapt up and down for his attention on my side of the gate. 'I've been watching it come up on the drive back.'

'That sounds safe.' I smiled wryly and then had to look away because the sight of him stretching his arms above his head and exposing a bit of his tummy made me feel a bit . . . funny.

'How could I not watch it?' he laughed.

He was right, of course. It must have been the ultimate distraction, just like Pixie had been for my parents earlier.

'She hasn't missed you at all, you know,' I pointedly said as he opened the gate and she ecstatically launched herself at him. 'To be honest, she hadn't even noticed you'd gone.'

'She's probably just relieved that I've come back,' he said, scooping her up.

'Oh yes,' I said, feeling chastened. 'I didn't think of that. How were things with your family when you set off? Is your nan really okay?'

He put Pixie down again and turned his full attention to me. I could see then how tired he looked and wondered how he was going to manage to be up in time for his stint in the practice the next day.

'As okay as she can be,' he said, sounding relieved. 'And I'm very grateful for that.'

'I can imagine,' I said, as I rubbed my hands together because the evening had turned chilly. 'Can I get you a drink or something to eat? You must be done in.'

'Thanks,' he said, picking Pixie, who was practically sitting on his feet, back up again. 'As appealing as that sounds, I'm going to pass. I'm afraid that if I stop for more than a minute, I'll be asleep on my feet and I really need to get back to the barn.'

'Of course.'

I had been about to offer to keep Pixie for another night, but seeing the way she nuzzled into his neck and the way some of the tension in his shoulders disappeared as a result, I decided he needed her company more than I did. Though it would be a wrench to say goodbye. Pixie had bought an extra something to Rowan Cottage and even if she didn't turn out to be the dog for me, I wondered if there would be another who might.

'I'll just get her stuff.'

Ash followed me inside, after commenting on how lovely my moon-watching set up looked. Had it been any other evening, I would have insisted he stayed and tried it out.

'Have you heard from Lizzie today?' he asked, as I bundled everything Pixie's visit had required back into its bag.

It felt like she had been with me for far longer than one night.

'To be honest,' I said, 'I haven't looked at my phone since calling my parents earlier, so I'm not sure.'

'I bet you haven't changed your mind about the festival, have you? As I mentioned before, Lizzie told me all about what happened at the meeting, because I was worried when I couldn't get hold of you, so I can understand why you went to ground.'

'Non meeting,' I muttered, feeling a little mortified that my withdrawal from the town had been so noticed.

'Oh, Clemmie.'

'I'm not feeling quite so bad about it now,' I sighed.

'Well, that's something. Do you maybe have an alternative idea in mind?'

When Ash had pulled up, I'd had every intention of discussing with him what I was now considering, but he looked so worn out, I put off telling him.

'I might, but it's the last thing you need to be thinking about right now,' I told him as he tried and failed to stifle a well-timed yawn. 'Are you sure you're going to be okay to drive back to the barn?'

'I daresay you're right,' he agreed. 'But we'll talk about it all soon. And yes, I'll be fine. It's not far. You'll have to come and visit. There's this magnificent hare who has practically made its home in the garden. I think you'd like to see that.'

'I'd *love* to see that,' I enthused. 'I often see them bounding across the fields and boxing in the spring, but I've never seen one up close. Can you get close?'

'If Pixie doesn't yap,' he smiled. 'Right, come on. Home and bed.'

'Yes,' I said. 'Time for bed for all of us.'

'Did Pixie make it into yours last night?' he asked, looking right at me.

'What do you think?' I smiled.

Chapter 8

In spite of the fact that I hadn't slept nearly as well without Pixie to keep me company, the next morning I woke feeling surprisingly, but pleasingly more determined than ever that the idea for the taster autumn festival I'd been considering the day before, was a good one. Consequently, I got ready, bright and early, to head into town, to run it by Lizzie, with nary a thought about what Jason had said playing havoc with my new-found, and almost completely restored, confidence.

Having the mini-festival idea to focus on helped me stop thinking quite so much about Pixie, or the lack of Pixie, and I was grateful for that. Considering she'd only been with me for one night and one full day, she'd made quite an impact and I was also wondering if, along with reigniting the festival flames, I should perhaps take her now after all. I had the feeling that we were a good fit and that the quality of my sleep would be much improved if I did offer her a home, but I wanted to be certain that she would benefit from the situation even more than me.

'One thing at a time, Clemmie,' I told myself as I picked out my favourite fox patterned scarf and draped it loosely around my neck. 'One thing at a time.'

My first thing was immediately thwarted because I had forgotten that both The Cherry Tree Café and the gallery next door, didn't open on a Monday, but I braced myself and instead ventured into the pub, the place of my humiliation, to try and get it back on track.

'Is it safe?' I joked, as I approached the bar to order a coffee. 'Or am I going to be made a fool of again?'

Evelyn shook her head.

'The only fool around here is Jason,' she tutted. 'I take it Lizzie has now told you what he did?'

'Aside from humiliate me, you mean?' I replied. 'No, she hasn't. I haven't seen her since the meeting and she hasn't mentioned it in any of her messages.'

I had felt guilty as I earlier listened to and read what Lizzie had sent. I really shouldn't have opted for total radio silence, because she was clearly concerned about me and yes, I knew I could have called or messaged her when I realised that, but I had decided, in the spirit of my renewed conviction to make meaningful connections, that talking face to face would be better.

'In that case,' Evelyn said intriguingly, 'I won't steal her thunder.'

'You don't happen to know where I might find her today, do you?' I asked.

'Most likely in the gallery,' Evelyn told me. 'She often works in the crafting space at the back when it's closed.'

'Of course,' I said. 'I hadn't thought that she might be there even though it's shut.'

'Do you still want a coffee?'

'I'll come back for one if I can't find her.'

'In that case,' Evelyn smiled, 'I hope I won't see you later.'

She was laughing at her own joke as I left and crossed the square to the gallery.

'I was starting to get really worried about you,' said Lizzie, as she immediately opened the door when she spotted me. 'I've been too busy to drive out to the cottage again, but I was planning to stop by as soon as I had finished up here later tonight if I hadn't heard from you by then.'

'I'm sorry,' I apologised, waiting while she locked the door behind me. 'I'm sorry I just sort of . . . disappeared.'

'No sort of about it,' she pointed out. 'You went completely AWOL and I couldn't even keep tabs on you on Insta because your posting seems to have slowed right down. I hope that isn't because I sussed out who you are.'

My lack of the usual regular posts had been a bit related to that, but I was over it now, so I wasn't going to tell her and make her feel even worse than she obviously already did.

'No, no,' I therefore said, airily dismissing her deduction. 'I've just been busy. Normal online service has been resumed from today and, if you agree with what I'm about to suggest, the festival might be back on, too.'

Her concerned expression transformed into one of excitement.

'Now about that—' she grinned.

'Me first,' I cut in. 'Please.'

'Go on then,' she laughed.

I explained about how I thought we could simply set up a couple of weekends of events and which workshops might work with the limited number of people we now knew wanted to be involved.

'It wouldn't take too much effort to sort it all out,' I finished up, feeling rather out of breath. Lizzie looked fit to burst, so I hoped that meant she was also keen. 'And this idea, on a much smaller scale than the original one, might be the perfect lead in for the full-blown festival next year. What do you think?'

'Well,' she laughed, 'for a start, I'm thrilled that Jason hasn't completely put you off.'

'He did for a while,' I admitted, 'but at the end of the day, I just can't seem to let this festival idea go, Lizzie. I really want to see it happen in some way. I might not have known Moses, as Jason was so keen to point out, but given his passion for the cosy season, I feel like we could have been kindred spirits.'

'Good,' she clapped.

'So, you think the mini festival idea *might* work then?'

'I actually think the original, grander idea will work—'

'No,' I cut in, trying not to sound frustrated. 'It really won't. You saw the turnout for the meeting and you heard the objection to me, the town stranger, being involved. It might have only been one voice, but I wouldn't want more to join it. With something smaller going on, I could keep a lower profile. Sort of direct the whole thing off stage. Make it more of a . . . side quest than an autumn extravaganza.'

Lizzie pulled out two chairs for us to sit on.

'Please, Clemmie,' she begged, as I flopped down. 'Please just listen. Yes, I did see the turnout and yes, I did hear the objection and I can tell you that Jason was entirely responsible for both.'

I frowned at that.

'How could he have been responsible for the turnout?'

Lizzie shook her head as if she still couldn't believe it.

'He got in touch with the woman who's the admin for the Wynbridge community online pages and told her to change the details,' she told me in a rush. 'He said, as bold as brass so she didn't question it, that there'd been a last-minute change of venue that needed announcing immediately or the meeting wouldn't come off.'

'I don't believe it,' I said indignantly.

'It's true,' Lizzie insisted. 'The admin was in such a panic, because the meeting time was so close, she made the changes and posted an alert to highlight it without checking the facts with anyone else. She feels absolutely awful now.'

'You're really being serious?'

'Deadly serious.'

'What a horrible position to put her in. The poor woman.'

'Jason is horrible.'

I didn't feel inclined to disagree. He'd certainly been horrible to me.

'He knew most people would check the page before heading out,' Lizzie said crossly, 'because it's always up to date and that meant his cunning tactic had maximum impact. The only people who made it to The Mermaid were the ones who hadn't seen the changed post, like us, because we were already nearby or on our way.'

'The *few* people who hadn't seen it,' I said bitterly.

'Exactly,' Lizzie agreed. 'I had no idea what had gone on until someone came in to the café and asked if Jemma and I knew why the woman who was supposed to be in charge of the meeting hadn't shown up. Once I'd set her straight, I then followed it up with the page admin and the trail led me straight to Jason and what he'd done.'

'So, was it about me then?' I swallowed. 'Had he somehow found out that I was the person in charge and for some reason taken a dislike to me?'

Lizzie shook her head.

'No,' she said firmly. 'No, Clemmie. Absolutely not. This is just Jason causing trouble and getting himself further agitated by the bee he keeps in his bonnet. If it had been Moses himself fronting the meeting, Jason still would have objected.'

'What bee might that be then?'

'The one he calls the Wynbridge gentrification project,' Lizzie told me.

She put sarcastic air quotes around the words and disparagingly rolled her eyes as she uttered them.

'The what?' I frowned.

'He's been a thorn in some of our sides for a few years now. Ever since we opened the café, we've heard him grumbling. According to him, all the new businesses in town and the Christmas market and festive events, have turned Wynbridge into, what he terms, a toffs' town.'

'A what?'

'The sort of place that's all style and no substance. Somewhere where you can buy bespoke crafts and artwork, but you can't find a post office or buy a pint of milk.'

'But that's ludicrous!' I objected.

'I know.' Lizzie shrugged.

'I might not know all that much about the town yet,' I forthrightly said, 'but I know there are plenty of places to buy groceries and I've seen the post office with my own eyes. Wynbridge has got the balance just right as far as I can tell.'

'Exactly. You'll struggle to find anywhere with a stronger

sense of community than Wynbridge, too,' Lizzie said proudly. 'There's a genuine generosity of spirit and neighbourliness here, but because some of us have a fondness for bunting and making the town look nice, Jason thinks it's turned into something—'

'Twee!' I butted in. 'I remember him saying the autumn festival would be twee and wholesome.'

'Oh yes.' Lizzie nodded. 'He did say that, didn't he? That should have alerted me to the fact that he'd climbed on to his usual soapbox, but I didn't twig . . .'

'So, what would he rather the town looked like? Somewhere that hasn't evolved at all or has become stagnant, with empty shops and neglected public spaces that no one cares about?'

'Most likely.'

'Well, I can tell you, I came across lots of those sad and dingy former market towns when I was looking to move a couple of years back and it was a blessed relief to drive through Wynbridge on my way to view Rowan Cottage and note the difference.'

'And yet,' Lizzie said astutely, 'you're only just now getting to know your way around the town and finding out how well it operates.'

'Better late than never,' I said, then quickly diverted the conversation away from the potentially personal deep dive I could feel it veering towards as a result of my admission. 'So, what happened at the other venue?'

'What other venue?'

'The one Jason sneakily said was really hosting the festival meeting.'

Lizzie looked at me and grinned.

'According to the person who came in here wondering why

you hadn't turned up to get everything going, it was packed out.'

'Really?' I gasped.

'Yep. A terrific turnout.'

I took a moment to digest that.

'I only wish a couple of the people who were at the wrong place had come along to the pub,' Lizzie huffed. 'That way, we could have sorted the muddle out on the night and not wasted more time.'

I wished that had happened too, but there was no point crying over it now.

'So, there actually was more interest in the idea than the few of us in The Mermaid suggested?' I asked, focusing on what was most important.

My heart rate quickened at the thought and increased tenfold with Lizzie's next words.

'There certainly was,' she said, with relish. 'There still is. And if you're still up for the challenge, they're all willing to turn out again and this time, *definitely* in the pub!'

Chapter 9

Of course, I was feeling terrified by the prospect of talking to everyone who had turned out for the first meeting at the wrong venue, because the weight of expectation to offer a fabulous festival weighed even heavier now, but I took a leap of faith and said a resounding 'yes' to Lizzie's request. And, having turned once again to Callum's words of wisdom, it wasn't the only thing I had decided to welcome in, either.

As soon as I'd got home from town that Monday, I had made myself a pot of tea and sat down in my armchair with the box containing all of Callum's notes resting on my lap. I took out and ran my fingers lightly over the words of his last one and acknowledged that *the best and loveliest things* really were on my horizon now. I was taking some risks and the rewards were starting to make their presence felt and when I picked out and read another note, I knew that, even with my nerves kicking in, everything was going to work out just fine.

I hadn't learnt to drive until Callum and I were engaged and the morning of my test, I had been absolutely terrified. However, Callum had sent me off with a few words, which he said I couldn't read until the time of my test and when I did, I found he'd cleverly turned my fear on its head.

You're feeling scared because you care, Clemmie. The fact that you're so nervous is proof of how much you want this and you always achieve everything you set your mind to, don't you? And that's because you go after it with the whole of your heart!

Callum was right about that, and this time around, what I wanted, along with making a success of the festival, was to give Pixie a safe and loving forever home.

'Clemmie.' Ash smiled, when he opened the barn door early that evening and found me on his doorstep. 'Hey. This is a surprise.'

'I asked Lizzie for your address,' I explained. 'I hope you don't mind that she gave it to me.'

He didn't have the chance to answer because the moment Pixie heard my voice, she'd skirted around his legs and bowled into mine.

'Hello, you,' I said, scooping her up. 'I was hoping to find you at home.'

'No,' Ash laughed, opening the door wider. 'I don't mind. Come in. I was just about to make a coffee. Would you like one?'

'Yes, please,' I said, practically tripping over the threshold because with Pixie wriggling in my arms and shoving her face in mine, it was difficult to see where I was going. 'Has she been like this all day?' I asked as she continued to squirm about. 'This is a vast improvement on her mood from before, isn't it?'

'No, she hasn't been like this all day,' Ash continued to laugh. 'And yes, it is a vast improvement. Her excitement seems to be solely reserved for when she sees you.'

'That's probably because we've got so much in common,' I unguardedly said, then felt relieved that Ash hadn't heard me over the noise of the boiling kettle.

'What was that?' he asked, moving closer.

'I said,' I amended, 'I'm honoured.'

'Good.'

'And she was pleased to see you the other night, too,' I pointed out.

'That's true,' he agreed. 'Now, how do you take your coffee?'

Once he'd made us drinks, Pixie had calmed down and I had admired the beautiful barn conversion Ash currently called home, we sat on the sofa with Pixie between us.

'So,' he said, as he passed me my mug. 'Is this a social call or . . .'

'It's partly a social call,' I told him. 'I wanted to see how you were feeling after the weekend.'

He looked touched that I had asked.

'Far better than I had expected I would be when I first got the call from Mum telling me what had happened,' he explained.

'Well, that's great. How's your nan doing now?'

'She's still in the hospital and will be for a little longer, but my parents are already getting the annexe organised and sorting things at Nan's house. Ideally, I'd like to be there to help, but obviously I need to be here for work. That said, I'll go up whenever I can.'

'You never did say where they lived, but I'm guessing it's quite a distance away.'

'Bakewell,' he said. 'In the Peak District.'

'Crikey, that's even further than I thought.'

'I can do it in under three hours, if the traffic is kind.'

'But not so easily with Pixie?' I surmised.

'I certainly couldn't do there and back in a day with her. She doesn't mind shorter distances, but her owner wasn't a driver, so Pixie isn't entirely au fait with the joys of being transported far on four wheels. It's all quite a challenge.'

'You really have got a lot on your plate now, Ash,' I said, biting my lip.

I had been going to tell him that the autumn festival was back on, and properly this time but I didn't want him to feel pressured into helping when he suddenly had trips to the Peak District to factor in to his already limited free time.

'That's life, isn't it?' He shrugged. 'There's always something waiting in the wings.'

'You're not wrong,' I sighed.

I had come to know that better than anyone.

'So, what else was your visit about?' he asked.

'What do you mean?'

'You said, your visit was partly a social call, so I take it there was something else?'

I thought then that I'd stick to discussing my decision about Pixie, rather than mention the festival, but Ash was one step ahead of me.

'I popped into The Cherry Tree for a takeaway lunch earlier,' he grinned, 'and Lizzie was looking very pleased with life. You wouldn't happen to know why, would you? She was tutoring a one-to-one crochet lesson so couldn't chat, but I could see she was bursting to say something.'

I had no choice but to mention the festival then.

'I daresay she was still buzzing about the festival,' I ventured.

'The festival,' Ash echoed. 'I did wonder if that might be it. What's happened now?'

'Well, for a start, we now know that the lack of attendees at the meeting last week, was down to a . . . technical hitch, so we're having another one tomorrow night to get it back on track.'

Saying it aloud made my tummy churn a bit, but in both a nervous *and* an excited sort of way. How often those two emotions got tangled up! Rereading Callum's note really had offered a timely reminder that my feeling jittery actually meant that I truly cared about whatever had caused the collywobbles (one of Dad's favourite words) and I clearly cared about the festival a lot.

'Well, that's great news!' Ash declared. 'And I know I'm going to be slightly more time pressured now than when I originally offered to step up, but I'll still help out.'

'You don't have to—'

'I know,' he said, cutting me off. 'But I promised I would, and I want to.'

'Well, only if you're absolutely sure.'

'I am. And I'll definitely be at the meeting tomorrow.'

'As long as your truck doesn't break down again,' I nudged.

'It won't and I'm not working tomorrow either, so why don't we go to town together? We could grab a bite to eat ahead of the meeting.'

'That's a lovely suggestion,' I said, puffing out my cheeks, 'but I'm not sure I'll be up to eating anything.'

'Of course you will,' he nudged back, with a laugh. 'Now tell me, what was the technical hitch that messed things up last week?'

Ash's eyes grew wider and wider as I told him about the

underhanded tactic Jason had employed in order to undermine the festival and why.

'What a horrible thing to do,' he stated, when I'd given him all of the details. 'And what a ridiculous attitude to have about the town. I had no idea he felt that way.'

'I agree.' I nodded. 'On both counts.'

'I feel very lucky to live near somewhere as lovely as Wynbridge.'

'Me too.'

'There aren't many places with the same depth of heart and soul that this place has.'

'That's pretty much what Lizzie said,' I happily sighed.

Now that I had spent a year and a half in the Fens, gently processing my grief, while vigorously renovating Rowan Cottage, and was ready to pull myself further out of my shell, I knew I was in the perfect place to nurture my progress and safely spread my wings.

'We're both very lucky,' said Ash.

When I looked up, I found he was looking at me intently and I felt my tummy take another tumble, but it was a rather different feeling to the one I'd experienced when thinking about the festival. I don't know what I would have said next, if anything, but Ash's gaze then moved to take in the view over my shoulder and the moment passed. I blinked it away, feeling . . . well, I wasn't sure how I felt, but my tummy was still a bit all over the place.

'Clem,' he then said, in a low voice. 'Turn around very slowly and look out of the window and whatever you do, don't disturb Pixie.'

The dog had curled up and fallen asleep while we were

chatting and I did as instructed, holding back the gasp that desperately wanted to escape when I saw why Ash had requested I remain calm and quiet.

'I don't believe it,' I whispered as I watched a huge hare, which was sitting on the path right outside the bifold windows, washing its face and ears. 'Look at that.'

'I am.'

'It's *huge*.' The hare didn't seem at all fazed by the fact that two sets of human eyes were tracking its progress as it set off along the path, but then perhaps it didn't know they were. 'Or at least, I think it's huge. Are they all that big? I've only ever seen them running across the fields and boxing at a distance so have nothing to compare this close up view to.'

'That's about average.' Ash nodded. 'They are pretty big.'

It was a magnificent creature, long eared and long limbed, designed for listening out and loping off at extreme speed. And its amber eyes were beautiful, too.

'And how are their numbers?' I asked. 'I know coursing in the Fens is an issue.'

'They're just about holding their own,' Ash sighed. 'And the farmers and local police are vigilant, which makes a big difference.'

Something else in the garden, which featured some beds of really wonderful looking roses, made the hare look up and, in a flash, it had gone.

'I was hoping I might strike lucky,' I said, in more than a whisper, now the beguiling creature had disappeared, 'and I did.'

'Indeed, you did.' Ash laughed and I realised then how close we had inched towards each other. He realised it too and quickly sat back. 'I haven't seen her since I got back from Bakewell. You're my lucky charm, Clemmie.'

I didn't immediately know what to say to that.

'How can you tell,' I started to ask, then had to stop and start again because my voice was a bit squeaky. 'How do you know that one's a doe? Or is it a jill? You said her.'

'Either works,' he shrugged. 'And I don't for certain. It's just a hunch.'

I shifted position and Pixie opened her eyes. I wasn't sure if she had been asleep after all or shamming.

'Would you like another coffee?' Ash offered.

It had been delicious, but strong and I didn't think I should have more.

'As lovely as this one was,' I therefore said, as I handed him back the empty mug, 'I'm going to say no, otherwise I'll never sleep tonight.'

'You're right,' Ash agreed, having looked at the clock on the wall. 'It is rather late to be having another. Can I get you something else?'

'No,' I said. 'I really should get back soon, but before I do, there is something else I'd like to discuss.'

I looked down at Pixie who had somehow stealthily moved to snuggle so close to my side that she was practically melded to me. Ash followed my line of sight.

'I'm about to lose my little companion, aren't I?' he asked, sounding endearingly emotional.

'If that's all right,' I said softly.

'It's more than all right,' he smiled. 'It's perfect in fact, because I'd already made up my mind, and so had Pixie, that she was going to go to no one else but you.'

'Really?'

'Really. Her heart is yours, Clemmie.'

'Oh, Ash.' I swallowed, feeling equally as emotional.

'You're going to be very happy together.'

'Do you really think so?' I whispered.

'Given that you said earlier that you've got so much in common,' he said, making my eyes snap up to meet his, 'I think your happiness is guaranteed.'

He didn't ask me to explain anything and I was very grateful for that. We agreed that he would drop Pixie off at mine the following morning because it was late in the day for me to take her and settle her in then.

Given that I was going to be in need of a distraction ahead of the festival meeting, I thought the timing was perfect. A day settling Pixie into her new home would stop me fretting and faffing and hopefully she'd be okay to be left home alone when Ash and I headed into town to meet my fate. Or fete . . . depending on your point of view.

I had been worried when I first started to seriously consider taking her on, that settling her in *and* running the festival would be too much, but knowing that she'd previously been a town regular and could sometimes join me, had helped me decide that I could cope and that she wouldn't find the busyness too stressful as she adapted to her new life.

'I'll see you tomorrow,' I happily sighed as I got ready to leave.

'We'll see you bright and early,' Ash said, sounding equally as happy, even though I knew he was going to miss having Pixie around.

'Bright and early it is, then,' I said, dropping a kiss on Pixie's head. 'And thank you, Ash.'

'No,' he said, 'thank you.'

Chapter 10

I was up bright and exceptionally early the following morning and as I wandered around the garden, with my first cup of tea of the day as was my usual habit, I could feel a definite change in the air as a result of the rain and wind from the few days before.

During the height of summer, there had been some occasions when this had been the only time I ventured out into the garden during the day because the August heat had soon turned oppressive, but now, in the second week of September, I needed a light cardigan to stave off the early chill and I enjoyed the sensation of that.

Having taken and posted a stunning photograph of the sunrise on AutumnEverything, I went back inside the cottage and turned my attention to making it Pixie ready, ahead of her stately arrival. Not that I needed to do anything much. Finding a few more towels to put in the utility room, which would be stored there with the sole purpose of drying her muddy paws when the weather turned inclement again, was the only real necessity.

By seven thirty, I was all set and when my phone pinged, I

snatched it up, but it wasn't a message from Ash, it was Lizzie. She wanted to check that I was ready for the meeting that evening and to say that she appreciated that I had commented on the post that had been added – and this time, not sabotaged – to the Wynbridge community page online. Given the number of responses the post had already received, I had a feeling that by the end of the evening, I might possibly be eating my former words about Lizzie overestimating the interest in the autumn festival!

The sound of Ash's truck horn on the drove had me typing a super speedy message in reply and then rushing to the door to welcome my new best friend. Or should that have been, friends?

'Here we are then,' announced Ash as he jumped out and walked around to the passenger side where Pixie was sitting on the seat, strapped into her travelling harness. 'Are you ready for her?'

'As ready as I'll ever be,' I said, feeling a sudden rush of nerves.

It was gratifying to see Pixie respond so positively to the sound of my voice and she practically leapt from Ash's arms into mine when he lifted her out. I hoped I was going to be able to look after her as well as her original owner had because she certainly seemed keen to be back with me at Rowan Cottage.

'Why don't you take her inside,' Ash suggested, 'and I'll bring in the rest of her stuff?'

'Is there much?'

'Um,' he grinned, looking sheepish. 'Perhaps a bit more than you might expect.'

It turned out that he'd treated Pixie to practically every toy on the pet market.

'I was trying to draw her out of herself,' he said defensively, as he carried in a huge rattan basket of brand-new looking things and caught the astonished look on my face.

'I never said a word,' I said, as I put up my hands and grinned and Pixie, with perfect timing, woofed and wagged her tail.

'Neither of you had to,' Ash laughed and I gave Pixie a further fuss. 'Shall we put her crate in the Land Rover?' he then suggested. 'She doesn't sleep in it and there's not going to be room to swing a cat if we put it in here with everything else.'

'That's a good idea,' I agreed. 'If I give you the keys, would you mind doing it? There's loads of room in the back and her harness can go straight in there, too.'

I was so preoccupied with Pixie that I forgot until later that Callum's work boots were still behind one of the seats in the Land Rover, but I didn't think Ash had noticed them anyway. Or, if he had, he hadn't commented on them.

Once I'd given Pixie her breakfast and while she further acquainted herself with the cottage, I ran through the list of questions I'd prepared the evening before to further ensure a smooth transition of ownership.

'Now,' I said seriously, addressing the first thing I'd thought of and added to my list, 'Pixie's jabs. Is she up to date? I'm guessing she is, but wanted to check.'

'She is,' Ash confirmed, 'and all of the paperwork and dates are in her folder, along with the practice details.'

'And what about flea and worm treatment?' I asked, having ticked off the immunisation question. 'What do you recommend I use for that?'

'Again,' Ash grinned, 'all in the pack.'

'Why are you grinning?' I asked, once I'd added more ticks to my list and noticed his expression. 'I'm a responsible dog owner and this is serious stuff.'

'Oh, I know it is,' he continued to smile. 'That's why I'm so happy. I love you for thinking to ask me all these things.'

I felt myself blush, more as a result of what he'd said than what he thought. He looked quite warm, too.

'So.' He then cleared his throat and carried on. 'What else have you got written down?'

Once we'd gone through everything, with the standard answer being that it was all covered in the pack Ash had put together, I offered him some coffee and toast.

'Thanks, Clemmie, but I won't stay,' he declined. 'I'm going to get off now actually.'

He sounded reluctant and I hoped he didn't feel obliged to go.

'Don't feel that you have to,' I said quickly. 'You said you're not working today, didn't you?'

'I'm not,' he explained, 'but I've got a flat to view and I think it would be best if I left you to settle Pixie in on your own.'

Just like before, she'd already made herself at home, so I wasn't sure what the time I'd set aside to settle her was going to involve now.

'Well, in that case,' I said, still showing Ash out because of his impending appointment, 'good luck with the viewing.'

'Thanks,' he said, wrinkling his nose. 'I'm not keen on its location because it's a bit of a drive from here and the rent seems optimistic given the size of the place, but we'll see.'

'You can tell me about it later,' I suggested. 'That is, if you're still up for the meeting tonight?'

'Of course, I am,' he confirmed adamantly. 'And like I suggested last night, a bite beforehand, too. I'll swing by about six, shall I?'

'That will be perfect.' I smiled, though I still wasn't sure I'd be able to eat anything.

Ash looked over my shoulder at Pixie.

'I'm not going to say goodbye.' He swallowed. 'With any luck, she won't even notice I've gone.'

She didn't either, but I decided I wouldn't tell him that when he came back later.

Pixie and I companionably whiled away the day together. I talked to her about what I had been through since losing Callum and told her that I hoped she really did feel an affinity with me as a result. She seemed to listen intently and I knew some of it must have sunk in, because she had run off to her toy basket once I'd finished explaining and then solemnly presented me with a toy which looked like a mallard duck. I didn't think there was any significance to what she had picked out, but it was a kind and heartfelt gesture.

While she napped after lunch, I sorted through her pack from Ash and then went back through my list of festival ideas and had a look at more of the comments that had been added to the meeting announcement post on Facebook. I could see quite a few businesses were going to be represented and if the owners really were as keen as their comments suggested, then finding hosts for the events was potentially going to be a doddle.

Ash arrived at six on the dot, looking handsome in a burgundy cord shirt and smelling wonderfully masculine. I felt my face flush as I closed the door behind him. Since losing Callum, I'd got out of the habit of noticing that sort of thing, so the observation, and the way it had felt so natural to take in Ash's clothes and aftershave, gave me a bit of a jolt. It had been on the tip of my tongue to say how the shirt colour suited him, but I decided not to. It made his eyes look even more intensely blue than usual, but that was another observation I kept to myself.

'How was the flat?' I asked instead.

'A total duffer.' He grimaced. 'Even worse than I expected.'

'Oh dear.'

'Um, back to the drawing board. But never mind about that, how's Pixie?'

'Perfect, of course,' I was delighted to tell him. 'It's not going to be five minutes before it feels like she moved in when I did.'

'Well, that's great.' Ash smiled. 'I'm certainly going to miss her, but knowing she's settled and happy here with you, Clemmie, is also a huge weight off my mind.'

'Good,' I said, feeling pleased. 'And now you can travel to see your family at the drop of a hat. Should you need to.'

'I can,' he agreed. 'And talking of traveling, are you ready?'

I still hadn't changed out of the comfy clothes I wore around the house, but that wasn't because I was running late for the meeting, rather that I was going to suggest a change to our plan.

'Not quite. I was actually wondering if you'd prefer to eat here, rather than in town?'

'You're not worried about Joanne getting the wrong idea if she sees us having a meal out together, are you?' Ash frowned.

'No,' I said, though I was a little then, because he'd jumped straight to that conclusion. 'Given that Lizzie and Jemma have set her straight on more than one occasion, that hadn't crossed my mind. I was thinking more about Pixie. I don't want to leave her for so long on her first proper evening here. I'm worried she might fret that I'm not coming back.'

Ash's comment when he'd arrived back from Bakewell, that he put some of her excitement at seeing him again down to her being relieved that he'd returned, had stuck with me, but he wasn't unduly concerned.

'She's used to being left alone at the barn,' he pointed out, 'so I don't think that will be a problem, but I'm happy to fall in with you.'

I was pleased he was willing to agree, but my mind was rather preoccupied then with what he'd said about Joanne.

'You don't *really* think Joanne has still got designs on pushing us together, do you?'

'No,' Ash said, as he bent to untie his bootlaces, but he was a little flushed when he stood back up. 'Of course not. I don't know why I said that. Now, what's on the menu?'

I'd made a classic quiche which was hearty enough to satisfy Ash's healthy appetite and I served it with a homegrown late summer salad and freshly made slaw which was full of apples, red cabbage and chopped walnuts and was a nod to the approach of autumn.

'Do you eat like this every day?' Ash asked, once he'd had his fill, having enjoyed an extra slice of the quiche.

'No,' I told him. 'Not anymore, but I do love to grow and cook with some of my own ingredients.'

'And you do it wonderfully,' he gratifyingly said. 'But why did you change?'

'Change?'

'Your eating habits. You suggested that you used to eat like this, but that you don't now.'

'Oh.' I blushed, as I gathered the dishes together. 'I just meant that what with the cottage renovation taking up so much of my time and being without a finished kitchen for so long, I just got out of the habit.'

'And now you're getting back into it?'

'I am,' I said, with a nod to his empty plate. 'And just in time by the looks of it!'

'I'm always willing to act as taste tester,' he grinned. 'Now, come on, I'll let Pixie out and then we'd really better get into town and try to nab a parking space.'

'There won't be so many people coming that we can't park,' I laughed, but it turned out he was right to be mindful about that.

We could hear how many people had packed out The Mermaid even before we'd fully opened the door and Ash threw me a knowing *I told you so* look before letting me cross the threshold ahead of him.

'Oh, crikey,' I gasped, as the noise of everyone chatting rushed to meet me and I tried to back out. 'Ash, I don't think—'

'It's fine,' he said softly behind me. 'You've got this. We've got this.'

In spite of his encouragement and the memory of Callum's wise words, I suddenly wasn't sure that either I, or we, had got anything. Being with Pixie all day and then with Ash for dinner, had served to stop me worrying, but now, faced with a properly packed pub, I felt overwhelmed and underprepared. This was as far from pacing my reintroduction to living a more social life as it was humanly possible to get.

'We've got this,' Ash said again, this time even more sincerely, while he discreetly reached for my hand and gave it a reassuring squeeze.

I turned to look at him and found him staring down at me. His striking blue eyes were full of kind encouragement and I nodded and took a deep breath, full of appreciation for his support and assuming the jolt that the feel of his hand in mine gave me was down to the emotion of the moment, rather than anything more meaningful.

'Yes.' I swallowed, squeezing his hand in return before letting it go and hoping Joanne wasn't somewhere watching and getting the wrong idea. 'You're right. We have. Let's go and find Lizzie and the others.'

Lizzie took no finding as she was on the lookout for us and within a minute, she had set us up in front of everyone and was joking with the assembled crowd about the disaster that Jason's interference had caused the previous week.

Everyone seemed to be in good humour and I attempted to use that to my advantage when Lizzie introduced me a second time and then offered me the floor.

'Good evening, everyone!' I loudly said, keeping a tight hold on my notebook to stop my hands from shaking. 'As Lizzie has just said, I'm Clemmie Bennett. And as someone else previously pointed out, I'm the blow-in the majority of you have never clapped eyes on, but have no doubt heard of after last week's cock up, and I'm also the person planning to push in and organise the autumn festival in honour of Moses Talbot this year.'

That raised a laugh and a cheer, most loudly from Bella and Jeanie, and I felt myself relax a little as a result.

'Well, thank goodness someone's willing to take it on!' shouted a woman I'd never seen before and who was at the front of the crowd.

Another cheer went up and I started to laugh.

'Well done!' Lizzie mouthed at me as Evelyn rang the bar bell which was everyone's cue to pipe down. 'I think we're off.'

We were well and truly launched after that. The next couple of hours flew by with me presenting what Ash and I had envisaged the autumn festival could include, and a show of hands used as the easiest way to decide what everyone thought would be the most popular events as I talked through them.

Nothing in my notebook was abandoned. In fact, the list had grown exponentially as the time went on and my head was a muddle of names as I struggled to make notes about who was willing to host what, what their businesses were and where they were located.

'Given that the first week of September has already passed us by, and thanks to Jason's meddling we've still not got a definite plan or announced anything yet, what do you think the odds are of getting something going by next week?' Bella asked hopefully, while holding up both hands with crossed fingers.

'As daunting as that timeframe is,' I responded, 'I think it's doable. Tomorrow I'll be going through everything we've discussed tonight and starting to put an event schedule together. I'd love to see the market square decorated and the shop windows dressed in time for the equinox on the twenty-second of the month, wouldn't you?'

Making the town centre and surrounding shops look seasonal had been a hugely popular idea and the enthusiastic show of hands was confirmation that everyone was in agreement that the equinox would be perfect timing.

'The equinox is on a Monday this year,' said Ash, who had pulled up the calendar on his phone. 'How about we aim to get everywhere decorated and prepared and then have an official festival launch, here in town the Saturday before, on the twentieth? It will be a much better day for attracting attention than a Monday.'

Again, everyone was in unanimous favour of that and the town dressing and official festival launch on Saturday, the twentieth, became our collective initial aim.

'Myself and the other yarn bombers are really keen to pitch in,' said a man at the back of the crowd. 'Are you happy for us to get together to start making things now? If we're going to help with the decorating in time for the twentieth, then we really need to.'

'Oh, yes please,' I enthused, feeling thrilled that the group was keen to offer some seasonally themed adornments. 'It would be lovely to have some autumn knits and crocheted pieces on display around the town, along with everything else.'

'I've found a fab pattern for crocheted leaf garlands,' he told me.

'They sound perfect,' I happily told him. 'I can already imagine them festooned around the market square. Thank you.'

'Count me in for helping with that, Bill!' shouted someone else.

'And me!' came another voice. 'And we'll need bunting, too.'

'There you go then, Bella; it looks like the town will be autumn ready for the big day.' Lizzie laughed and Bella gave us a thumbs up.

'Here's hoping the rest of us are!' I smiled.

'We will be,' Lizzie said quietly to me. 'I told you that you were the perfect person for the job, didn't I?'

'I'm not sure if this is anything like what Moses originally had in mind,' I smiled at her, 'but we're off and running now!'

Numerous sheets of paper for everyone to add their details and availability to were in circulation by the time the meeting came to a close. No one seemed keen to leave and I was delighted to see so many names, places and dates being scribbled down.

'We're going to come up with some autumn themed cocktails and mocktails,' the guy from Brambles Distillery told me, as he added his details to the food and drink list. 'We can sell them on the market as well as on site in the shop.'

'And Grandad and I will happily host an autumn feast night *and* a family gathering at Fenview Farm,' beamed a woman, who I think was called Fliss. 'So, you can promote your drinks there, too, Jack, if you like.'

As I stood there, trying to take it all in, my head was full of names, but I wasn't sure how many of them I could match to the right faces. Hopefully, having the next day to go through the lists would help me make sense of everything.

'I'm Hayley,' said another woman, who had been keen to share her ideas all evening. 'I'm the housekeeper at Wynthorpe Hall.'

'Wynthorpe,' I repeated, latching on to the name I had heard before. 'That's the hall owned by . . . the Connelly family, isn't it?'

'That's it.' Hayley nodded.

'I've seen some photos of it online,' I told her. 'It looks like a magnificent place.'

'It is,' she agreed. 'And the woods would have been perfect for hosting some events, but the site is currently out of bounds, I'm afraid.'

'Is everything okay?' asked Lizzie who was standing next to me and had heard what Hayley had said.

'Yes,' said Hayley. 'Everything's fine, but when the festival idea was originally shelved Angus and Catherine decided to forge ahead with their improvement plans for the Winter Wonderland because the woods weren't needed.'

'Oh, I see.' Lizzie nodded. 'I know they've been thinking about making some changes for a while. Are they having much done?'

'Tree work and path laying mostly,' Hayley explained. 'Hence the lack of access. They're gutted that they can't help out now.'

'Maybe next year,' Lizzie said and then rushed off because Jemma was beckoning to her.

'It is a shame,' I said to Hayley, thinking there could have been scope in the woods for a fungal foray. 'But please tell them not to worry. Like Lizzie said, it will be great to have them onboard next year. It always helps keep momentum going with this sort of thing if you're offering something new, so I daresay this was all meant to be.'

I knew Lizzie and I were getting ahead of ourselves,

suggesting the festival would be happening again, but I wasn't going to put off any potential future interest in it.

'You sound like Molly,' Hayley laughed, but I didn't know who that was. 'Next year for sure then. And the hall isn't a total loss in terms of help, because I think I might be able to do something.'

'Oh?'

'I'm an artist as well as a whizz with a vacuum cleaner,' she told me. 'So, if you want any posters drawing up to advertise the festival in general or even any individual events, I'd be happy to come up with some design ideas.'

'Oh, yes please,' I said, turning to a fresh page to jot her details down. 'That would be great. I'm going to set up online festival pages as soon as I can. Possibly even tomorrow, and if you could come up with something like a logo or banner to give the event an identity across every platform, that would be great. Though I appreciate it is very short notice . . .'

'No, it's fine,' she said helpfully. 'Leave it with me. I had already been doodling a couple of logos when the festival idea was first floated, so I can easily refine those. Are you settled on Wynbridge Autumn Festival as the name?'

'Yes,' I said. 'We'll stick with that. It's simple and shouldn't be hard to find as an online search because it's so specific.'

'In that case, give me your email address and I'll put my ideas together and send over what I've got in mind. Branding is key, right?'

'Absolutely,' I agreed. 'And that would be great. Thank you so much.'

Given that I loved an appealing aesthetic, I was thrilled that Hayley was willing to come up with a brand for the festival.

It might be something we could use year on year to build familiarity. Further down the line, we could even commission some merch!

I knew I was getting carried away again, but I was so excited. Yes, I had a huge task ahead of me, but I couldn't wait to get stuck in to organising it all and seeing it come to fruition now. And of course, after what had happened at the first meeting, it was a huge help that everyone was so kind and keen to let the blow-in take charge.

'Now,' said Lizzie, flopping down on to a chair as the crowd finally thinned, and once I had talked myself literally hoarse, 'I'm not usually the sort of person to say, I told you so—'

'You're *exactly* the sort of person to say that, Lizzie,' cut in Jemma's husband, Tom, who had just been telling me that the council were completely onboard with the festival but that there weren't any funds in the pot to support it.

Volunteers to support the events and ticket sales to fund them were going to be key, but I had a good feeling that both would be fine.

'Hey!' Lizzie yelped and pouted.

'But on this occasion,' I joined in, having gulped down the lemonade Ash had kindly handed me, 'you did tell me so and you were right.'

'So, you're definitely up for it then?' Lizzie asked, holding up crossed fingers which had become something of a theme of the evening.

'Of course I am,' I laughed, once I'd thanked Ash and as I started to gather up the many filled sheets of paper.

'Well, thank goodness for that,' Jemma chimed in, with a

nod to the growing pile. 'Because I don't think any of us have the head space to make sense of that lot.'

'I'm not sure I have now,' I joked as I flicked through them all. 'But I will by tomorrow. All I need to focus on for the moment, is getting the draft schedule drawn up and sending it out for the participants to check and hopefully confirm. And enlisting all of you,' I then carried on, 'to encourage the shop owners to dress their windows. And the yarn bombers to keep their needles clicking in time for the launch on the twentieth. And then get the events pages running online, of course . . .'

'*All* she needs to focus on!' Ash teased. 'That's all, is it, Clemmie?'

'Don't worry,' I grinned at him. 'I know how to delegate and with your help, Ash, we'll have it sorted in no time.'

'I'm sure you will,' Lizzie beamed. 'And you can leave the knitters and shopkeepers entirely to me and Joanne, if you like. We can go round the shops and make sure everyone knows how to join in, can't we?'

'Absolutely,' Joanne, who had been unusually quiet all evening, agreed. 'I think almost everyone who has a shop was here tonight anyway, but I'll go around the town tomorrow to double check.'

'That would be great,' I said. 'Thank you.'

'My pleasure,' she told me. 'I'm just pleased this is all happening before I leave.'

'Trust you not to want to miss out,' Lizzie laughed at her, but I wondered if there was more behind Joanne's comment than that.

'You know me so well,' was her response but I still wasn't

sure that a desire to take part was all that was behind her words.

I didn't know her well enough to ask, but I had the feeling there might be something going on with Joanne that she was keeping under her hat.

'And that much appreciated extra help will leave me more time for Pixie,' I said, having taken a quick look at the time. 'Though she already was right at the top of my priority list.'

'Have you taken her on?' Jemma gasped.

'I have,' I said, feeling thrilled with how my life was turning out now that I'd taken the leap of faith Callum's recently found note had encouraged. 'And right now, she's waiting for another cuddle, so I'm off.'

'We're off,' Ash laughingly corrected me. 'I drove us in, remember?'

'We're off.' I swallowed, feeling the words stick as I quickly looked to Joanne, but thankfully, she didn't seem to have heard him.

Chapter 11

I became worried on the not too lengthy drive back to Rowan Cottage that Pixie hadn't coped well with being left home alone for a few hours on her first evening. In fact, I was so preoccupied with my concerns about her that they completely knocked everything else I had to think about clean out of my head.

'Penny for them?' Ash asked, making me jump. 'You will be able to do it all, you know,' he carried on when I didn't answer. 'And I'll keep my promise. I'll help as much as I possibly can.'

'It's not the festival,' I said, willing the journey to go faster. 'Though there is an awful lot for us to get our heads around. Right now, I'm more concerned about Pixie.'

'Well, we're almost back now,' Ash sensibly pointed out. 'And I'm certain she's been fine. You know me well enough by now, Clemmie, to know that I wouldn't have suggested she could be left if I had thought she'd be upset.'

'Of course,' I sighed. 'I'm sorry.'

'Don't apologise,' he said kindly. 'It's truly wonderful that she has someone taking care of her who loves her so much.'

Thankfully, my concern that Pixie hadn't been happy home

alone turned out to be entirely unfounded. She was ecstatic to see us but didn't appear fazed about having been left.

'If anything,' said Ash, as he gave her a huge fuss, 'it's given her time to mooch about and get her tactic for making it up to your bedroom tonight settled in her mind.'

'Oh, she doesn't need a tactic,' I told him as I set down the paperwork I'd accrued throughout the evening. 'There was never any question that I'd make her sleep down here.'

Ash rolled his eyes at that. 'You're every bit as bad as I was,' he laughed.

'Well,' I said, looking at Pixie's perfect little face, 'she needs nurturing.'

'Don't we all.'

'Yes,' I said soberly. 'A little love goes a long way.'

Talk of love felt like risky territory to try and traverse after such a monumental evening, so I was happy when Ash didn't pursue the topic.

'I'm working tomorrow,' he told me, 'but if you need a hand on Friday and Saturday, just holler.'

'Won't you be driving back up to Bakewell again?'

'I wanted to, but Mum has insisted I don't need to. Nan has told her that she'd rather I visited when she's moved into the annexe, because she's still in hospital at the moment and visiting there is no fun.'

'In that case,' I said, 'if I do need you, I certainly will holler.'

'You can rest assured,' he said with a smile, 'I'll be listening out.'

I made the mistake that night of not leaving it long enough after the meeting before I went to bed. Consequently, I lay awake for ages with my recent dramatic life changes, festival ideas and thoughts of new friends circling interminably around in my head. It was all exciting, of course, but a lot to get my head around, too.

Pixie had no such qualms keeping her awake and softly snored away with barely a twitch which was a blessing and a relief. I eventually drifted off, but my few hours didn't feel anywhere near as restorative as they had been the first night she'd been my bedfellow.

'I have news,' I announced when Dad answered my WhatsApp call early the next morning.

'News that couldn't wait until a civil hour?' He yawned. 'Your mum's still in bed.'

'This is a civil hour,' I tutted, as I opened the back door to let Pixie back in and it was wrenched out of my hand and then banged shut.

It was a properly blustery day and I hoped the washing wasn't going to get blown off the line. With nothing blocking its path, the wind cut straight over the Fenland fields and across the garden, but its uninterrupted path did make for wonderfully fresh smelling laundry.

'You've got the windy weather then,' commented Dad, having heard the door.

'Yes,' I said. 'And it's chilly, too. I might be tempted to light the log burner later.'

'In September,' he said, sounding horrified. 'Whatever next.'

'It's cold,' I said, defensively, then smiled remembering the never-ending battle between him and Mum that occurred every winter over the heating thermostat. 'Go and wake Mum up, will you?'

'I am awake,' came her voice. 'What's going on?'

'Clemmie has news,' said Dad, propping the phone on the kitchen table so they could both sit and see it.

'Is everything all right?' Mum frowned.

'Everything is wonderful,' I said, bending to pick Pixie up.

After her trip to the garden, her paws felt cold through the thin cotton of my dressing gown and I thought I'd switch a few things about in my wardrobe and drawers when I could find two seconds together. Not that I minded not currently having two seconds together because the prospect of the festival was a more pleasant one than a winter spent alone.

'You've got Pixie again.' Mum smiled, as Pixie sniffed the screen and her damp nose left a mark.

'I've got Pixie for good,' I grinned, looking around her.

'For good?'

'I've adopted her,' I proudly announced.

'Adopted her?' Dad said. 'But when you had her before, you said you were looking after her for a friend.'

'I was,' I agreed, then explained Pixie's previously sad circumstances.

'Well,' sniffed Mum. 'She couldn't have ended up with anyone better than you, could she, love? You know what she's going through because you've been there yourself.'

Dad put his arm around Mum and I wished that I was there with them and could do the same. I wouldn't have minded a hug myself.

'Exactly,' I said briskly, giving Pixie a squeeze. 'I'm hopeful I can help her through her sadness. In fact,' I smiled, as she licked my chin, 'I think I already am.'

'Well, that's wonderful, my love,' said Dad. 'What lovely news to start the day with.'

'And that's not my only headline,' I added, as I put Pixie down and she wandered into the kitchen. 'You remember the town event I mentioned that was on, then off?'

'Yes,' my parents chorused.

'Well,' I said, taking a deep breath as I refused to feel daunted by the mountain of notes waiting for my attention, 'it's on again. Properly this time and I'm in charge of organising it.'

Dad was agog.

'What, the whole thing?' Mum gasped.

'Pretty much,' I laughed. 'I'm going to have a bit of help, but I'm responsible for the scheduling and advertising and the overall managing of it.'

'My goodness.' Dad grinned. 'And can you finally tell us what the event is?'

'I can,' I said, sitting up straighter. 'It's called the Wynbridge Autumn Festival and it's going to involve a whole series of events to celebrate the season.'

'In the heart of pumpkin country.' Mum clapped. 'How absolutely perfect.'

'It hopefully will be, Mum,' I agreed. 'The idea for it originally came from a local farmer who sadly died and didn't get the chance to see it come to fruition. This will be the first time it's happened.'

'And the woman taking it on just happens to be obsessed with autumn,' chimed in Dad. 'It's bound to be top notch with you in charge, my love. I know you'll do the farmer proud.'

That was what Lizzie had reckoned, too, so I hoped they were both right and I could pull it off successfully.

'Thanks, Dad. I'll email you the schedule as soon as I've got it sorted,' I promised. 'And then we can work out the best time for you to come.'

Mum and Dad loved the sound of that and after further cooing over Pixie who took their attention with good grace, I signed off and set to, working through the many pages of meeting notes. Once I'd arranged them into piles according to what everyone was offering, I then printed out blank calendar pages for September, October and November.

It was exciting to have things to immediately fill in, such as the launch date and times when the town would be decorated in readiness for it. After adding those, however, it was all a bit trickier to work out as I had to add events according to when the people offering to hold them were available to organise and run them.

I pencilled in any significant dates such as the equinox, the best time to see the Draconid meteor shower (weather permitting, of course), bonfire night, Halloween and half term and then further filled in as much as I could, making sure there was a balance of everything, with no long gaps anywhere and then, conversely, not too many things, especially if they were similar, clustered together.

The combination of practical craft workshops, outdoor nature events, reading opportunities, food and drink celebrations, special market days and pumpkin competitions, struck exactly the right chord with me and I hoped everyone who wanted to attend, though not Jason who had now been barred from The Mermaid, would be in agreement.

I also hoped all of the businesses I'd offered spots to would be able to stick to them as it would be tricky to change things around without having a knock-on effect.

'As long as everyone goes along with the dates they gave

me last night,' I said to Pixie, who was eagerly making her presence felt, 'then I don't think we'll have any issues. Now, what's up with you?'

As I went to stroke her, my tummy gave the loudest rumble and I realised exactly what was up with her.

'It's almost two o'clock, Pixie,' I gasped. 'We've missed lunch!'

I fed her first, then quickly scrambled some eggs, grilled some cherry tomatoes and toasted a slice of sourdough to stave off my own pangs. An email from Hayley, suggesting we could meet in the town library at ten thirty the next day so she could show me, rather than send me, what she'd come up with for the festival branding, landed while I was eating and I messaged Ash in the hope that he would be able to join us.

The branding and logo designs would become the online face of the festival, quite possibly for longer than just this year and I really wanted Ash's input when deciding on how it should look, as it was quite a responsibility.

'I'd love to help. Count me in. I'll pick you up around ten,' I read aloud, when Ash replied within a couple of minutes.

Excellent, I sent back. *See you tomorrow!*

My phone pinged again. *It's a date.* I stared at the three words and remembered Joanne's former determination to push us together. *Not a date, date!* came through immediately after and was accompanied by the grimacing emoji.

'I knew what you meant,' I whispered as I typed, after just a moment's hesitation, because I knew that Ash could see that I had read what he'd sent and I didn't want him to think I was pondering over it, even though I was.

See you tomorrow, I added, along with a smiley face and

then I put my phone down and decided it was time to get the washing in and take Pixie for a windy walk.

'Oh, wow,' said Ash, when I opened the cottage door to him the following day. 'Clemmie, you look amazing.'

'Do I?' I asked in surprise, as I looked down at the patterned dress and red patent Mary Janes I'd picked out. I didn't think it was anything particularly special but the compliment, coming straight after the 'it's a date' discomfiture of the day before, made my cheeks flush.

'Totally,' Ash huskily said, then cleared his throat. 'Very smart. No one's going to question your role as festival organiser looking like that. Not that anyone would . . . what I mean is . . .'

His words trailed off as Pixie wandered over to say hello and, with my attention then focused on her, I reasoned it was the text muddle that had got Ash a bit tongue-tied rather than anything else.

'Is she okay?' Ash asked, as the little hound sighed when he fussed her and then wandered over to her bed and flopped heavily into it.

She'd been a little subdued that morning and I had reminded myself that grief probably impacted on animals in much the same way as it did humans. I could now go for great stretches of time feeling fine, and then wallop, something would suddenly trigger me out of the blue and I'd feel its dreaded weight all over again. Or worse, nothing I could identify or pinpoint would occur, but I'd feel low anyway and without the benefit of knowing where the shift in emotion had sprung from.

I knew I was playing my part in Pixie's recovery, but it would have been foolish, and perhaps rather arrogant, to assume that I was the answer to her prayers. Just because she was apparently content living in Rowan Cottage, it didn't mean that her heart had healed.

'Sadly, I think she's having a low day.' I sighed in sympathy myself.

'In that case,' Ash suggested, 'we'd best take her with us.'

'To the library?' I frowned.

'Yes. Come on, Pixie.'

'Are you sure?' I asked, as Pixie climbed back out of her barely used bed.

'Yes, absolutely. Can you grab her harness out of your Land Rover?'

'You're really being serious?' I questioned. 'You did hear me when I reminded you that we're going to the library, didn't you? I don't think they allow dogs in there.'

'I take it you haven't visited the library then?' Ash smiled.

'Not yet. Why? What am I missing?'

'The manager, Kay, has an ancient golden lab who sleeps behind the counter all day,' Ash told me. 'Sandy and Pixie are great friends. He'll cheer her up no end.'

'Oh well, in that case,' I said, gathering up my notebook, bag and keys. 'As long as you're sure Sandy will be there, let's get going.'

Chapter 12

While I collected the harness, Ash telephoned the library to double check that both Kay and Sandy were going to be in residence and, having confirmed they were and that they'd love to see Pixie, we all set off. I sat in the back, while Pixie was secured in the front seat next to Ash, like the extra precious cargo that she was.

Unfortunately, we hadn't gone far before she started to crane her neck to see where I was leaning through the seats to look at her, and then started to fuss.

'Do you think we should stop?' I asked Ash. 'She's obviously not happy.'

'I think you should sit back so that she can't see you and then she'll be fine.'

'Are you telling me off?' I gasped, in almost mock outrage.

His eyes met mine in the rear-view mirror and I could tell he was grinning.

'A bit,' he laughed.

'Fine,' I huffed, sitting back and folding my arms.

'There,' he infuriatingly but justifiably said, when he'd driven a little further on and my traitorous friend had settled down completely. 'She's perfectly happy now.'

I stuck my tongue out at him and, catching sight of me in the mirror, he laughed again.

The library was towards the edge of town and Ash was lucky enough to secure a parking space right outside the door. In the spirit of not fussing, I let him lift Pixie out and attach her lead to walk her in.

'I hope we aren't going to disturb anyone while we're talking to Hayley,' I began to say, but then the automatic doors swung open and a cacophony of singing and clapping met our ears.

'I think we'll get away with saying a few words,' Ash said loudly, as he smiled down at me. 'If anything, we're going to struggle to make ourselves heard above what sounds like a very noisy Bounce and Rhyme session.'

'I think you're right,' I agreed, as we walked in and Pixie made a beeline straight towards the reception desk.

'Pixie!' The woman who had been working at a computer smiled in greeting. 'And you must be Clemmie,' she added, addressing me, 'her new owner?'

'I am,' I confirmed, thinking how cool the woman, who was probably about my mum's age, looked with cropped grey hair and lots of silver jewellery.

'And I'm Kay,' she told me. 'I'm delighted to meet you and equally delighted to learn that you've taken the festival on.'

'That's very kind,' I responded. 'And I'm pleased to meet you, too. I was already planning to call in to talk to you about the possibility of setting up some sort of autumn reads book club or reading group when Hayley from Wynthorpe Hall suggested we meet here to discuss something else.'

I looked around, but there was no sign of her yet, but then we were a few minutes early.

'I think a specific autumn book club is a wonderful idea,' said Kay. 'I already had lots of non-fiction books on order to make a wonderful seasonal display and, when I heard the festival was back on, I started to put a list of fiction titles together, too. Would you like to see it and let me know what you think people might like?'

I was thrilled that she was so keen and already a step ahead of me.

'I'd love to see it,' I therefore enthusiastically said, 'but I'm sure you're the better judge of what the local library members might like to read than I am. Would you be happy to pick the titles?'

'Of course,' she said, handing me a printed-out sheet. The action made her bangles melodiously chime together. 'And I'll take on the running of it, too, if that suits you? I have a couple of keen new volunteers who could help me. I haven't been the manager here all that long and I'm trying to shake things up a bit.'

'That suits me perfectly. Thank you, Kay.'

All the while I had been chatting to her, Ash had been bobbed down behind the desk and when I peered over the top, I found him stroking both Pixie and a golden Labrador who had an almost completely white face. The two dogs were happily settled together and Pixie was receiving a very thorough wash from her canine friend.

'I'm guessing this is Sandy?' I smiled.

The dog looked up at me with kind eyes and thumped his thick tail in response to his name.

'It is.' Ash nodded. 'He's the oldest member of Wynbridge library.'

'And the most popular member of staff!' Kay laughed, just as another bout of singing struck up, this time supported by a host of noisy instruments. 'He's also a bit deaf, which is a blessing on mornings like these.'

Pixie had no problems with her hearing, but didn't appear bothered by the noise.

'How's the new medication working out?' Ash asked Kay as he straightened up.

'I haven't seen any improvement in him yet, but you did say it might take a little while. Sandy's hips aren't what they were,' she added for my benefit.

'Keep me posted,' Ash sighed. 'I'm hoping you'll notice a change soon.'

'Will do,' she said. 'You can leave Pixie here with me while you talk to Hayley if you like? She seems settled back there.'

'Clemmie?' Ash said, looking at me.

'As long as you don't mind?' I said to Kay, feeling a little uncertain about leaving Pixie off the lead in a public building.

'Not at all,' smiled Kay. 'And don't worry. I won't let her out of my sight. Hayley and Molly are upstairs. I thought it would be easier for you to talk in the relative peace up there.'

'Thanks, Kay,' said Ash, moving off and with a quick glance at Pixie, who hadn't noticed me stepping away, I followed on behind.

'Do you know Molly?' I asked him as we climbed the stairs. 'Hayley mentioned her at the meeting in the pub, but I don't think she was there. Is she a member of the Connelly family?'

'She is.' Ash nodded. 'And she's also the Wynthorpe witch.'

I thought I must have misheard him, but there was no opportunity to check as we were then at the top of the stairs and I could see Hayley at the far side of the empty, open space with a laptop, sketchbook and lots of papers spread out on a large table.

'Hey, you two,' she smiled, when she looked up and saw us.

'I hope we haven't kept you waiting,' I apologised, because she looked as if she'd been there a while.

'Not at all,' she said. 'I was early. Molly decided to come in with me, so we arrived a while ago. You know she's not a fan of indoor crowds and the library has a tendency to get busy.'

I didn't know that, of course, but it didn't seem to be a surprise to Ash.

'And noisy, too,' he laughed, with a nod back to the stairs.

'Quite.' Hayley grinned. 'It can be too much for her.'

'But it's not been too hectic this morning,' said a soft voice behind me and I jumped. 'Though there's certainly a lot of energy coming out of the children's area now.'

I quickly turned around and found a very beautiful woman, wearing a dark green cloak and with an abundance of auburn hair looking right at me. She was the ultimate pre-Raphaelite muse and I had absolutely no idea where she'd sprung from because I hadn't seen her when we walked into the space which was completely open.

'I wish you wouldn't do that,' Ash puffed, with a hand on his chest.

'Do what?' she said, still looking at me.

'Manifest like that,' he complained. 'You almost scared me to death.'

Molly's eyes twinkled as she switched her attention to him.

'What a joy it would be if I could appear at will,' she smiled. 'If I could do that, I wouldn't have to endure Hayley's driving.'

'Hey!' Hayley objected and Ash laughed.

Molly returned her gaze to mine. I found it a little disconcerting.

'So,' she nodded. 'You're Clemmie.'

'Yes, sorry,' said Hayley, with a wave of her hand. 'Clemmie, Molly. Molly, Clemmie.'

'Hello,' I said, feeling scrutinised and, truth be told, a little vulnerable. 'Hi.'

'Hello,' Molly responded. 'I've been looking forward to meeting you.'

'As soon as I told her that you'd said Wynthorpe not being involved in the festival this year was *meant to be*,' Hayley told me, putting air quotes around the comment, 'her ears pricked right up.'

'It's always a joy to come across someone else who understands that everything in life is preordained and meant to be,' Molly wistfully said.

Given what had occurred in my life, I wasn't sure I did understand that, but without inferring that I'd experienced something to make me question, even resent, the idea, where enduring the traumatic bits were concerned anyway, I couldn't express it, so kept quiet.

'Right,' said Hayley, who was obviously used to her friend saying that sort of thing and took it in her stride. 'Come and tell me what you think of this lot, Clemmie.'

I went to move, but Molly stopped me by stepping close and lightly laying a hand on my arm.

'You're doing brilliantly,' she said, in a hushed tone. 'I know it's been hard, felt impossible at times, but you've taken the right step at every turn. You've given yourself time and there's little that's more precious than that. You've tuned in to what you've needed and allowed yourself to accept it . . .'

I was completely taken aback, and my initial reaction was to want to ask her if she was talking about how I had stepped in to manage the festival, but the quickest glance into her eyes, eyes that felt like they could see into the very depths of my soul, told me she wasn't referring to that at all.

'You're almost there, you know,' she whispered and the pressure of her hand increased a little. 'If you could just find it in your heart to—'

'Come on, Clemmie,' said Ash, and Molly let me go. 'Come and look at this.'

'Are you all right?' Hayley frowned at me as I walked over. 'You look a bit peaky.'

The truth was, I had been more than a little unsettled by Molly's words. It wasn't every day I encountered someone like her and her words of wisdom, for want of a better expression, had felt a little too personal for my liking. Especially given that I had kept my private life very private since my move to the Fens and that I'd never laid eyes on her before.

'Ohhh,' Hayley then said, drawing the word out as she glanced to the other side of the room where her friend was now looking out of the window towards town. 'It was Molly, wasn't it? What did she say to you? Something lovely, I hope. She doesn't always engage the old filter when she feels the need to share whatever it is she's . . . received.'

'Received?' Ash questioned. 'What are you talking about?'

'Nothing,' I said, with a quick glance at Molly myself. 'It was nothing.'

'She's already told me the autumn festival is going to be a

huge success.' Hayley grinned. 'So, I hope it was something along those lines.'

'Beautiful branding will help make it a success,' I said, as I tried to pull myself together and change the subject. 'So, come on, let's look at what you've so kindly designed.'

'Here you go then,' said Hayley, as she pulled some sheets from an A3 notepad towards us with a flourish. 'Take a look at these.'

'Wow!' I said as I made the hugest effort to forget Molly and focus on Hayley's art.

We loved everything she had come up with, but in the end, between us Ash and I settled on a banner featuring entwined autumn leaves and pumpkins and a simple, but bold font to go with it.

'That's it. That's perfect,' Ash said excitedly, as a few minutes later, Hayley expertly melded the two together via her laptop and then mocked up a poster so we could see the overall effect.

'And the colours?' Hayley prompted.

'Perfect,' I confirmed, admiring the red, orange, brown and mustard hues. 'Classy and classic, exactly the aesthetic I was hoping for.'

They were very similar to those I'd used to decorate the rooms at Rowan Cottage and the palette I favoured for AutumnEverything, but obviously, I kept that to myself.

'In that case, I'll mail them to you now,' Hayley said, suiting the action to the words. 'And once you've got all of the events confirmed, you can start advertising them using the designs you've settled on.'

It was all going to look beautiful.

'And not a moment too soon,' I said with a glance at the schedule I'd spread out on the table for us to refer to. 'We're launching in just over a week, so we need to keep pushing on now. Thank you so much, Hayley. You're incredibly talented and your design is perfect.'

'It was a pleasure to come up with it,' she smiled, while she also looked at the calendar of events I was hoping to soon confirm. 'But how are on earth are you going to oversee all of this lot, Clemmie? There's so much here.'

'I'm helping,' said Ash.

'And I'm not actually running the events myself,' I told her. 'I'm pulling it all together and keeping everyone up to date online, but the events, workshops, clubs etc are being completely overseen by the person or people hosting them. I'm just doing the admin stuff and running the calendar and, so far, it's under control . . .'

'So,' Ash nudged. 'Does that mean that you might end up not needing me after all?'

'Want you rather than need you, might be a better way of putting it,' said Molly as she joined us at the table. 'And she'll certainly do that.'

'She's off again,' said Hayley, rolling her eyes.

'Do you want me, Clemmie?' Ash asked.

'Of course I do,' I stoically said, ignoring the impossible implications of Molly's words. 'You're my right-hand man and I'm going to delegate all the trickiest stuff to you.'

'Great,' Ash snorted. 'I'll look forward to that.'

'That's not quite what I meant,' Molly whispered while Ash helped Hayley pack everything away.

I hadn't for one second really thought it was.

'What do you think of the schedule, Molly?' Hayley then asked her and I got the impression that Hayley knew I was feeling more than a little uncomfortable with her friend's presence and pronouncements.

Molly picked the sheet up and glanced down it.

'Absolutely perfect,' she said. 'Autumn is such a special season and it looks like you've thought of everything we could possibly wish for to celebrate it, Clemmie.'

'It's not all me,' I was quick to say. 'If people hadn't put themselves forward to take the ideas on, then lots of the things on the list wouldn't be happening.'

'Don't underestimate your hard work,' Ash said giving me a nudge. 'You've put hours into this already.'

'I just hope it's all a success,' I puffed. 'Then the time spent on it will be totally worth it.'

'There is one thing that might not work out,' Molly said, her gaze flicking up to mine. 'Do you mind if I mention it?'

'Of course not,' I told her. 'I'd rather know sooner than later. What is it?'

'The Draconid meteor shower suggestion.'

'The stargazing nights.' Ash frowned. 'Don't you think they're a good idea?'

'A wonderful idea,' she nodded. 'But—'

'I know cloud cover could be an issue,' I started to say, but she shook her head.

'It's not that,' she said.

'What then?' Hayley asked.

'It's going to be a full moon on the seventh,' Molly told us. 'Right at the peak of the meteor shower, the moon will be at its brightest.'

Ash and Hayley exchanged a blank look.

'Oh,' I said. 'I see. That's definitely not going to work then, is it?'

'Why not?' Ash asked.

'Because the brightness of the moon will impact on how many stars we can see,' I sighed. 'Okay, I'll take that off the schedule.'

It was disappointing, but couldn't be helped. Even if it wasn't cloudy, it would be hard to spot shooting stars with the moon lighting up the night sky.

'I had a feeling you'd understand.' Molly smiled at me.

'Oh, great,' tutted Hayley, but I could tell she was teasing. 'Another moon lover in our midst!'

'What's not to love?' I shrugged, returning Molly's smile for the first time, but given what she'd previously said, still feeling a little uncertain about her.

'Maybe next year,' she smiled back.

'Yes,' I agreed. 'Maybe next year.'

'What did Molly say to you?' Ash asked, once we'd collected a much sprightlier Pixie, said our goodbyes in the library and were back on the road. 'I know she said something to unsettle you because all of the colour had drained from your face when you came over to the table.'

'Do you think she really is a witch?' I asked, as I looked out of the truck window. 'Do you believe in that sort of thing?'

I felt Ash's eyes on me in the mirror for a moment.

'Absolutely,' he said seriously, taking me by surprise. 'She is and yes, I do. Don't you?'

'I can't say I've ever given it much thought,' I said, as we left the town behind. The view was soon a windswept expanse of fields which stretched as far as the horizon. 'Has she ever said anything to you to make the colour drain from your face?'

'Me?' Ash laughed.

'Yes.'

'No,' he said, with a chuckle. 'I'm not interesting enough.'

'Of course you are.'

'I'm really not.'

I looked at the mirror and then immediately away, because he was staring at me again.

'I wish you'd watch the road,' I rather tersely snapped.

'Are you telling me off?' he grinned.

'A bit,' I said, trying not to smile back.

'Thinking back,' he then ponderously said, 'Molly did say something when we first met.'

'Oh? Go on.'

'She said that I'm an open book,' he shrugged. 'What you see is what you get. I've got no baggage, nothing to hide and no skeletons in my cupboard.'

'I don't believe that,' I protested. 'Everyone has baggage of some sort or another.'

'Not me,' he said and I could tell he was still smiling. 'Do you?'

'Like I said, we all have something.'

'In that case,' he said teasingly, 'my guess is that Molly's winkled yours out of you already.'

'She has not,' I hotly protested.

'But there is . . . something?' he more gently asked.

'Nope,' I said, blinking hard. 'Just like you, I'm an open book, too.'

Chapter 13

The trip to the library had gone well, but it had given me a lot to think about and it had got me wondering whether I had perhaps taken rather too much on in too short a time. In my eagerness to rejoin the real world, had I rushed in, been swept along and bitten off more than I could reasonably chew? Was I trying to run before I'd mastered the art of walking again?

As I pondered over that, I knew I wasn't referring to the festival, because after the initial hiccup, the event had come wonderfully together. I was also enjoying getting to know more of the local area and I was delighted with how well Pixie was settling in. Those aspects of my life were fine, it was other niggles that were now popping up which I couldn't ignore.

Having got over (and hopefully completely cleared) the hurdle of Joanne's misguided desire to matchmake, I had thought Ash and I, and our freshly-minted friendship, were going to be okay, but Molly's hint about me *wanting* rather than *needing* him in a capacity that didn't involve our working together on the festival had got me in something of a spin.

Ash was kind, generous, clever and handsome. Perfect partner material, but I wasn't looking for a partner and that had to be what Molly had meant. After everything I'd been through, I knew I'd never have a romantic relationship again, but the so-called Wynthorpe Witch had hinted that in the future, my thoughts about Ash had the potential to change. I knew she was wrong, completely wrong, because my heart had been obliterated once and I would never put myself in a position where it could be destroyed again, but her prediction was still unsettling.

Therefore, in spite of my vehement resolution that I was right and Molly was wrong, I still took action, just to be on the safe side. In the days that followed, I put some distance between myself and Ash and made the trip to see Fliss at Fenview Farm to check out the setting for the Autumn Feasting and Family Food events alone, and I also opted to fly solo when it came to calling in to see Jack at Brambles Distillery.

As well as avoiding Ash, I also stayed out of town and immersed myself in things I could carry out at the cottage. That wasn't so much to do with what Molly had said, but rather the result of me still having plenty to organise and do.

I spent lots of time getting to know Pixie better, many hours promoting, organising and refining the festival's finer details online and via email and of course, posting on AutumnEverything. The account had attracted a flurry of new followers as the season switched from late summer to early autumn and I was back to sharing regularly again after my post-Lizzie recognition hiatus.

With the walls of Rowan Cottage wrapped comfortingly around me, it was a relief to find that I began to feel settled and content again. It had been the right decision to do what needed to be done in the way that worked best for me – I tried not to think how Molly had also pointed out that I had a talent for that – and towards the end of the week I was keen to head back to town and see everyone again, which was just as well as the festival launch and first autumn-themed market was then just a couple of days away!

The sudden drop in temperature, and consequently increased vibrant change in the colour of the leaves, had got practically everyone in the mood for what was to come and there wasn't now a spare stall to be had on the forthcoming market and tickets for the few events which were already available to buy were selling well, too.

'Oh, my goodness!' I laughed, when I arrived at The Cherry Tree Café in a very merry mood and found a table full of crafters determinedly focused on crocheting yet more autumn leaf shaped bunting to decorate the square with. 'It's beginning to look like a set from Stars Hollow out there! And in here, too!' I added, as Joanne held up a length of the vibrant red, yellow and orange leaves for me to admire.

'It really does,' she beamed, in agreement. 'Though Jemma is no Luke.'

I laughed all the more when she said that, because the Wynbridge café queen was absolutely nothing like the guy from Gilmore Girls who owned the diner there.

'I've just noticed that the majority of shopkeepers have now papered their windows so we can't see how they've decided to decorate,' I said excitedly, with a nod back out to the square. 'Is that something they do at Christmas, too?'

'It is,' Lizzie told me. 'And I'm over the moon that they're so willing to go all in for the autumn festival as well. The paper started going up earlier in the week as a result of the brilliant article in the local press.'

'You did well to secure that, Clemmie,' Joanne added, making me feel proud. 'It hit the right note and, having heard so many more people talking about the festival now, I know it's really helped spread the word.'

I had managed to keep myself and my role out of the limelight during the telephone interview and had focused solely on the businesses that were supporting and taking part in the festival and it had all come across in print wonderfully well. I hadn't enjoyed the best relationship with the press in the past. When Callum died, their interest in me bordered on intrusive, so this latest positive experience had restored my faith a little.

'Well,' I said, tapping the festival notebook which was now fit to burst with extra bits of paper and constantly within my sight, 'you know me, don't you? If I'm doing something, then I'm doing it right!'

I had meant the comment to be light-hearted, but the look it elicited from the two women suggested that it had provoked a train of thought that I hadn't intended. For the time being at least, I didn't want either of them thinking about me in any capacity other than that of festival organiser and I braced myself to field any awkward questions that my unguarded reference to them knowing me might subsequently evoke.

'Fliss from Fenview Farm was in earlier,' Jemma then said as she came out of the kitchen, spotted me and thankfully put us back on the festival track. 'She told me there's just one pair of tickets left for their Autumn Feast Night now *and* that the family event is going to be full to capacity soon, too. I think she's going to get in touch with you about the possibility of adding more dates, Clemmie.'

'She's already called,' I told her. 'I just need to update the schedule online and make an extra poster to advertise what else she's got planned.'

'That's fantastic.' Lizzie clapped.

'And I've just been to the library and Kay, the manager, told me the autumn book club is completely oversubscribed,' I carried on keenly, 'so they're having to order in more books from further afield to meet demand.'

'Oh, my goodness.' Jemma laughed. 'And there was you doubting the festival's appeal just a couple of weeks ago.'

'I know,' I said, shaking my head in disbelief, 'and now I'm really having to focus to keep up with the way it's all snowballing.'

'That's the wrong season.' Joanne winked. 'Brilliant though. And don't forget, you've got your lovely festival assistant, Ash, to help you. I hope he's pulling his weight.'

We'd barely been in touch since our trip to the library, but that was down to me rather than him and I chose my next words with care.

'Don't worry about Ash,' I said casually, as I walked over to the cake counter. 'I'm managing fine on my own so far, but I'll make good use of him once we're launched. I'm going to try and attend as many of the events as I can myself, but I'm hoping he'll be able to check out any that I can't make.'

I also hoped that would stop Joanne from thinking that we were joined at the hip and would be working the entire festival in tandem. Assuming that she was.

'But I thought you were already working on it all together?'

she pointedly said and I knew I had been right to emphasise that we'd each be doing our own thing.

'I'm managing fine,' I said firmly. 'And don't forget: Ash has extra family commitments to factor in now. His nan hadn't had her stroke when he promised to help, had she?' I knew he had shared the news, so I wasn't speaking out of turn. 'And as I can cope, there's no need to put him under more pressure at such a personally difficult time, is there?'

'I suppose not,' Joanne agreed after a moment's deliberation.

'I know I originally said I'd only take the festival on if I had help,' I continued, hoping to further hammer the message home, 'but so far there hasn't really been more work than one person can handle and Ash didn't know his time was going to be even further stretched than it was before, so we can't expect more of him now.'

'That's true.' Jemma nodded. 'And you really are managing everything, Clemmie?'

'Yes.' I smiled. 'It's a lot, but it's all fine.'

'Ash's nan is out of hospital now though, isn't she?' Joanne commented. 'And living with his mum and dad, so he'll probably have more time for you again soon.'

I ignored that.

'And what about your family, Clemmie?' asked Lizzie, switching to another topic I wasn't keen to expand on as Jemma headed back to the kitchen.

'Mine?'

'Yes,' said Joanne, picking it up. 'I know you said earlier that we know you, but we don't really, do we? Though we do know you're not originally from around here, so I'm guessing your relatives most likely live a bit of a distance away . . . ?'

'There's only Mum and Dad,' I reluctantly shared, 'and yes, they are quite a way off.'

'Do they visit often?' Lizzie asked curiously.

'And more importantly,' Joanne cut in, 'will they be coming to the festival?'

I was so looking forward to showing Mum and Dad what I had – hopefully – achieved once the festival was in full swing, but there was no way I'd be able to stop them talking to the likes of Joanne and potentially filling in some blanks about me. How much longer, I wondered, was I realistically going to be able to keep my reason for moving to Wynbridge under wraps?

My being a widow might not necessarily come up in general chit-chat, but it could. Would it be better to talk about it ahead of Mum and Dad's visit or risk leaving it to chance? I wasn't sure how I'd cope if it randomly cropped up in conversation without my being prepared for it, and given Joanne's now vaguely hinted-at continuing fondness for pairing people off, it might get a mention, because if she revealed some plan for me and Ash, then Mum and Dad could say something . . .

It would have been wonderful if my new life could have carried on without the sympathetic head tilts and sad looks sharing my history would doubtless provoke, but if I was committed to getting to know these people properly and building a full life for myself here, then sharing my past at some point had to happen, didn't it?

'I'm hoping they'll visit,' I said, mindful that my time to decide whether to share or not now potentially had an expiration date. 'We'll talk properly about it once the festival is underway.'

'And,' Joanne then asked, with a twinkle in her eye, 'will there be anyone else who might visit? By which I mean,' she then more bluntly added, 'might there be someone special left behind who will come with your mum and dad?'

'Joanne!' Lizzie tutted.

'Mum and Dad are pretty special in their own right.' I smiled tightly.

'Quite right,' said Lizzie as she tried to rescue me.

'But have you left your heart behind?' Joanne further probed, ignoring the warning look Lizzie threw her and which would have stopped most people in their tracks. 'Was it a matter of the heart that prompted a move such a long way from home?'

Callum was the largest and most important part of my past *and* my heart, but I wasn't about to drop him into the conversation – or should that have been, interrogation – until I had had the chance to further consider whether or not I was ready to.

'In a way,' I then, however, felt inspired to say, 'it was a matter of the heart.'

'Go on,' Joanne insisted.

'I fell in love with Rowan Cottage,' I said simply.

Joanne huffed and Lizzie laughed.

'And having seen it for myself,' Lizzie smiled, 'I'm not surprised.'

Joanne didn't look so amused. 'You blooming tease,' she tutted at me. 'I bet there was loads more to it than that!'

There most certainly was and what I then grasped I needed, was the listening ear of someone I had started to consider a close friend to hear what I had to share first. That was, someone I had started to consider a close friend until I had got the jitters because of what Molly had hinted at and, erring on the side of caution, backed off.

In a moment of much appreciated clarity I realised that talking to Ash might help me decide whether I was ready to go public about my past or not. And, whatever the outcome, it was high time I trusted my intuition about him, rather than be governed by Molly's ungrounded prediction, and reclaimed him as the closest friend I had in Wynbridge.

'I was beginning to think you didn't want me,' was the first thing Ash said, when I opened the cottage door to him that evening and he scooped an ecstatic Pixie up into his arms.

My thoughts shot back to Molly again, but I quickly cast them off. What I wanted was a friend and Ash had never given me any reason to believe he considered me as anything other than that. It wasn't his fault that Joanne had cast herself in the role of Cupid or that Molly had hinted that there might one day be something less platonic about my feelings for him and therefore, it was time to make amends for dropping him and I was going to hopefully do that by taking him into my confidence and making him my confidante as well as my friend.

'Of course I want you,' I therefore said, the word catching, as I closed the door and made light of my recent disappearance and silence. 'But given everything else you've had going on, I thought you probably needed a bit of space and the opportunity to get your head straight.'

'I did actually,' he said, as he put Pixie down, 'so, thank you, Clemmie. I'm pleased to say, Nan's now settled and Will and I have decided I should call off my house hunt until after the winter. He'll put the barn on the market in the spring rather than now.'

'So, you still haven't found anywhere then?'

'I haven't, but I'm happy, and relieved, to be able to stay where I am for a few more months and now I'm not trawling Rightmove every spare minute and worrying about what's happening in Bakewell, my head is in full-on festival mode and I'm completely at your disposal.'

'Well,' I swallowed, 'that's great. Perfect, in fact.'

'I'm guessing that means you've got loads for me to do?' he predicted, as he rubbed his hands together and looked keen to get stuck in. 'I know you've been going great guns with it all because everyone has been telling me. And, as much as I have appreciated you carrying everything yourself, I do want to make amends.'

'In that case,' I suggested, 'let's have some supper and I'll properly catch you up on it all.'

Fingers crossed, once we'd exhausted the topic of the festival, I would feel completely ready to embark upon the emotional deep dive that he had no idea was coming.

'Oh, my goodness, Clemmie,' Ash puffed, when I rejoined him in the kitchen having ducked out after I'd finished eating and telling him most of what was now happening with the festival, to check the log-burner. 'That was delicious. I couldn't manage another bite.'

It wasn't that chilly an evening, but I hadn't been able to resist lighting the fire and Pixie, currently laying with her nose practically on the hearth, obviously appreciated the cosiness as much as I did.

'I'm delighted you enjoyed it,' I told Ash. 'They turned out larger than I thought they would though, so I didn't expect you to finish it all.'

'I needed something hearty after the day I've had and that pasty was perfect.'

I'd made butternut squash pasties and served them with a tangy, green tomato chutney to cut through the sweetness of the squash. I hadn't been able to finish all of mine, but that was the result of nerves over what was still to come rather than a lack of gluttony.

'What did you think of the chutney?' I asked. 'It's freshly made, so the flavour could have probably done with a bit more time to develop.'

'You made it?'

'I did.'

'Well,' Ash said, 'I loved it *and* the pasty. The chutney was the perfect accompaniment.'

He certainly looked satisfied.

'In that case, you can take a jar away with you. Now, go through and give Pixie another fuss, while I make us some tea and then I'll run you through the last bits of the very packed festival schedule.'

I hoped that by the time I had done that, my courage wasn't going to fail me.

'You certainly seem to have thought of everything,' Ash later said, once I had shown him the printed schedule and the behind-the-scenes contingency that accompanied it. 'The only thing missing is the partridge in a pear tree.'

'That comes later in the year,' I laughed.

'Seriously though, Clemmie,' he said, sitting back on the sofa and taking Pixie with him, 'I don't think you're going to need me at all. Not that I'm about to duck out.'

'Well, that's good,' I said, 'because Joanne would be devastated if I didn't start to utilise you properly.'

I felt Ash's gaze switch from Pixie to me.

'Oh?' He frowned. 'What's she been saying now?'

'Nothing too incriminating,' I told him. 'But I'm not as convinced as I was before, after Lizzie had put her in her place, that she's permanently packed away her Cupid's bow.'

'In that case,' Ash tutted, as he rubbed Pixie's belly and she stretched out along the sofa next to him, 'we'd better be on guard.'

'Yes,' I said, biting my lip and feeling frustrated. 'You're right. Swords at the ready.'

Ash laughed at that.

'It's not funny,' I seriously said.

'It is a bit,' he smiled. 'The vision of us in full armour whenever we head to town, surely you have to be amused by the thought of that.'

'No, I don't,' I insisted, feeling further fed up with the situation and probably sounding it, too.

Ash stopped fussing Pixie and pinned me with his blue eyes, which made the room feel rather warmer than the fire allowed for. He leant forward and rested his elbows on his knees, with his whole focus trained solely on my face.

'Should I be offended?' He frowned. 'I know we said when we first met that neither of us were in the market for a relationship, but is the thought of being with me really so . . . repugnant, Clemmie?'

'No,' I hotly said. 'Don't be silly.'

'So, I'm not repulsive then?'

'Of course not.'

'Well, that's all right then,' he sighed, leaning back. 'I was beginning to get a complex.'

I shook my head at that. 'No, you weren't,' I tutted. 'And don't go getting all self-absorbed because now's not the time.'

'Why not?'

'Because,' I faltered, 'because . . . there's something I want to tell you and if you're being silly and huffy, I won't be able to.'

Sensing the mood had properly changed, he sat forward again. 'What is it?' he asked. 'Tell me.'

I took a deep breath.

'You do know that I consider us the best of friends, don't you?' Ash said seriously when I didn't launch forth. 'And that you can tell me anything in complete confidence.'

'Thank you for that.' I swallowed. 'It truly means a lot to hear you say that because I haven't actually made friends with anyone for a very long time. And I know I'm getting to know Lizzie, Jemma, and even Joanne, now, but I do feel that there's a different sort of connection with you, Ash.'

'Good,' he nodded. 'Because I feel that way, too.'

I relaxed a little as a result of his sincerely said words.

'I have been worried that Joanne's interference and her potentially continued meddling, actually might spoil things for us,' I admitted.

'Not a chance.'

'Well, that's good,' I said, as I geared myself up, 'because there's something in particular that I want to share with you and, for now at least, only you.'

'Go on,' he encouraged.

Having now said twice that I had something to tell him, I supposed then was the moment to get on with it.

'I want to tell you,' I finally began, clasping my hands tightly together on my lap, 'I want to tell you, the reason why until very recently, I've been living the life of a recluse here in Rowan Cottage.'

'Because you've been focused on the renovation.' Ash frowned.

'No,' I said, unclasping my hands again. 'No, that's a part of it, but nowhere near the whole of it.'

I let out a long breath and closed my eyes for a moment.

'Whatever it is,' Ash said softly, 'you can tell me, Clemmie. You can trust me.'

'I know that.' I smiled, when I opened my eyes again. 'I've never properly doubted that. But it's hard. Very hard. Even though I want to tell you.'

I'd never talked to anyone other than my parents, and Pixie, about what had happened and it was harder than I had expected it to be to try and push the words out, and in spite of the fact that it was Ash that I was talking to.

I didn't know what it was about him that had singled him out as confidante material. I'd been friends with guys before, but never felt such a close bond and so quickly and I was grateful for his patience now. Callum had been my best friend, of course, but he had been my husband too, which put him in an entirely different category of friend to Ash.

'There's a reason beyond ruining our friendship as to why I'm so resistant to, and upset by, Joanne's love of matchmaking, where I'm concerned, anyway,' I continued, coming at it from a slightly different direction. 'It's because . . . it's because, I'm a . . . widow.'

'A widow,' Ash gasped.

'Yes,' I said, letting out a juddering breath. 'The man I was married to, and utterly in love with, was killed in an accident in the town we grew up in.'

'Oh, Clemmie.'

'I moved here eighteen months after it happened,' I quickly carried on, 'with a view to processing my grief and coming to terms with it all and now that I have, now that I can properly breathe, I'm finally starting to join in with the world again.'

'I'm so sorry,' Ash said, running a hand through his hair and blinking hard. 'I had no idea. I'm so sorry this has happened to you.'

He sounded completely floored.

'Thank you,' I said, wiping away a tear and then taking a moment to collect myself. 'And besides you, Ash,' I then continued, realising that attempting this conversation with the other people I was getting to know, would still be too much, 'I'm not ready to tell—'

'Anyone,' Ash cut in accurately. 'You're not ready to tell anyone. I understand that. And you know I won't say a word, don't you? You know you can trust me completely.'

'I do know that,' I said, feeling grateful. 'I'm sure I'll be ready for it all to come out one day, but not for a while. I'm not there yet.'

'And no wonder you were so troubled by Joanne's preoccupation with pushing people together.' Ash then frowned. 'The last thing you want right now is someone trying to set you up.'

'That's the last thing I'll *ever* want,' I said, with emphasis. 'My heart was broken into a million fragments when Callum died, and even though I've somehow glued them back into some sort of shape, I'll never risk falling in love and suffering the pain of that catastrophic loss again.'

Chapter 14

Given that I had never actually said the words out loud to anyone before, when I later thought back over the conversation with Ash, I thought I had managed them well overall. I had been dreading the moment as the evening went on, but I knew I had ultimately coped because I had chosen the right person to confide in and also because I had previously allowed my grief free rein and myself the time to process it on a timescale that worked for me. Of course, it had been painful to talk about, but not unbearable.

Poor Ash, however, looked as though he'd had the stuffing completely knocked out of him. He had sympathised but not pried, and his manner had been both tender and kind, in spite of the shock. My hope of finding him a stalwart friend, even though we had only recently been introduced, had been confirmed. He was even more than I could have hoped for when I had made my brave decision to embrace a more sociable life again.

As I nudged my pillow into a more appealing shape that night and tried not to disturb Pixie who had no difficulty in falling asleep, I couldn't decide if my inability to nod off was the result of my conversation with Ash or if I was feeling nervous about the festival launch which was suddenly the next day.

It was long after midnight, when I settled on it most likely being a bit of both and finally nodded off.

Ash was back at Rowan Cottage, bright and early the following morning. I had wondered if there might be any awkwardness between us, but he didn't broach the subject again and we carried on as we always had. He arrived with an air of anxiety and excitement solely reserved for the day ahead. I was sure we would talk more about my past in the weeks to come, but on that particular Saturday, we were focused on nothing but the festival and getting it off to the best possible start.

'Come on!' Ash urged, as I pottered about in the kitchen and determinedly tried to stay calmer than he apparently was.

'I am coming on.' I smiled serenely.

The day was a huge undertaking for me and I was determined to remain tranquil in my approach to it, on the outside at least. I knew that if I succumbed to the jitters before I even got dressed, I most likely wouldn't go into town at all.

'I thought you'd be ready by now, Clemmie,' Ash scolded, as he pointed at my dressing gown. 'We're going to be late.'

'No, we're not,' I said firmly, in the face of his fussing. 'We've got plenty of time. Here,' I added, thrusting a honey covered crumpet into his hands. 'Eat this and calm down.'

He took a huge bite, chewed for nowhere near long enough and swallowed with a loud gulp.

'You'll give yourself indigestion, eating like that,' I tutted.

'Aren't you nervous?' he asked, as he licked the honey off his fingers. 'If I were you, I'd be terrified.'

'I am a bit nervous,' I confessed, 'but I'm trying to keep my head. Unlike you. Your increasingly Tiggerish behaviour isn't helping at all.'

'Sorry,' he apologised, looking chastened.

'Everything's organised,' I reminded him, 'so there's nothing to get worked up about, is there?'

'I suppose . . .'

'The extra market stalls went up yesterday and the stallholders know which ones they've been allocated,' I reeled off. 'And the shops are all responsible for their own window dressings and autumn themed stock. Aside from hanging a little more bunting around the square and arranging some seasonal veg, there's nothing left for me to do. It's just the market and a couple of other small things happening today and they're all set.'

Along with some of the stallholders selling their autumn themed wares, Jemma was going to be officially launching her Autumn Delights menu, which she'd held back, and Lizzie was offering a simple craft workshop for children in the gallery next door. Even the weather was behaving – cool and bright – and everything was poised to run like a well-oiled machine. Some nerves still required, but nothing to get in a flap about.

'That's as maybe,' Ash commented, as he noisily shoved another couple of crumpets into the toaster, 'but I'd be bricking it if I had to stand up in front of everyone and make a speech. Public speaking is definitely not my forte. And as for judging the shop windows. Geez! That's going to be a minefield.'

I had been about to pour tea from my favourite pot, but my hand froze in mid-air. 'What are you jabbering about?' I stammered.

'Well,' he said, with a shrug, 'everyone knows that the window dressing rivalry between the stationers and the—'

'No,' I cut in, as I shakily put the teapot down. 'I'm not talking about the best-dressed window competition. What do you mean about making a speech? Who's making a speech?'

He laughed, then realised I was being serious.

'You, of course,' he loudly announced. 'As organiser, you'll be the one talking about the festival and cutting the proverbial ribbon before it officially opens.'

'I don't think so.' I gulped. 'No one's mentioned anything about making a speech to me.'

'And the primary school choir is going to be singing "Autumn Days" on the stage.'

'What stage?' I screeched. 'You're having me on!' I felt a growing knot of pain in my tummy and a sense of panic descend. 'You're winding me up.'

'I am not,' he said, as the toaster popped and made me jump. 'I was treating a cat belonging to Hattie, a woman who works at the school, yesterday and she was on about it. The kids are really looking forward to it. They've been rehearsing all week.'

'I don't care about the choir!' I spluttered, as I grabbed my notebook and started frantically checking my notes. 'I mean, I do. Of course, I do. It's lovely of them to sing, and the song is perfect, but I didn't know anything about it and I'm definitely not making a speech. I've got nothing written down here to remind me that I've got to say anything to anyone.'

Surely, as the festival organiser, if this actually was in the offing, then I would have been informed about it, wouldn't I? So much for remaining calm and serene!

'Well,' Ash shrugged, 'it's obvious, isn't it? The festival can't launch without some sort of fanfare to mark the occasion.'

I put the notebook down again. 'The choir will provide that,' I desperately said. 'I won't need to chip in, too.'

'I think you will,' Ash said contradictorily, then put the crumpets on a plate and reached for the butter knife.

'Leave all that,' I said tetchily, as my nerves leapt to match those that he had turned up with but now seemed to have lost. Perhaps they were contagious jitters and he'd passed them on to me. 'Come on! We need to get ready! We're going to be late.'

'I am ready,' he tutted, as I rushed upstairs to get dressed. 'You're the one who's been dawdling.'

On the journey into town in Ash's truck, with me in the front this time and Pixie strapped in between us, I sent a frantic message to Lizzie asking if Ash had got it wrong about me having to make a speech *and* judge the shop windows. The pressure of that particular task had finally sunk in as I quickly brushed my teeth, piled my hair on top of my head and pulled on my favourite autumn outfit.

'No, Ash hasn't got it wrong,' were the unfortunate words Lizzie greeted me with, while he parked the truck and kept hold of Pixie and I rushed over to the café. 'Surely you realised that as official organiser, you'd have to give a speech to launch the thing.'

'No,' I hotly protested. 'I did not. Why can't you do it? Or someone else who knew Moses? Anyone but me! Please! As festival manager,' I added, drawing myself up, 'I'm delegating the task to you.'

Lizzie shook her head.

'I'm not doing it because you're the one who has turned the idea Moses had into reality,' she pointed out. 'You're entitled to take the credit, Clemmie, even if you don't want to.'

'I *really* don't want to,' I said, with emphasis. 'I really, really don't want to.'

'I take it you're not a fan of public speaking then?' Lizzie grinned. 'You were fine in the pub the night of the second meeting.'

'It's hardly on the same level, is it?' I cringed. 'That was a small, well, smallish, gathering, this is potentially going to be the entire town!'

'In that case,' she suggested as if it was no big deal at all, 'how about I come up on the stage with you and introduce you. Then, you can just say a few words after me?'

'How about you go on the stage on your own and you say all of the words?' I suggested again.

'Nope.'

She clearly had no intention of letting me off the hook.

'Fine,' I begrudgingly relented. I was still terrified, but I knew the battle had been lost. 'I'll say something after you. Something really, really brief.'

'Good,' Lizzie said. 'That's settled. But you're not getting out of judging the shop windows. That's definitely down to you.'

'I suppose that's fair,' I sighed. 'And I suppose I could rope Ash in to help with that.' He would be able to give me a heads up about the shop owners and the rivalry he had earlier alluded to that might cause ill feeling, depending on how the prizes were allocated. 'Yes, we'll complete that together.'

'Atta girl!' Joanne, who had been listening in, laughed. 'I knew you'd find a use for him in the end.'

By the time I'd spoken to the stallholders, and been distracted by more than one exquisitely crafted autumn themed item, helped the yarn bomb brigade hang more leafy bunting and assisted in the arrangement of some huge papier-mâché pumpkins (the real ones not yet being quite ready or large enough to make an impact) on the stage, I didn't have time to come up with a speech and hoped I would be able to wing it.

'Here goes!' said Ash, who bounded up to join me as the town clock moved to strike half ten.

I picked Pixie up and kissed the top of her head. She looked utterly transformed when I compared her to the dog I had met just a couple of weeks ago and I wondered if I looked different, too. I certainly felt it. Though not, in that moment, necessarily in a good way.

'Here goes, indeed.' I nodded, as perfectly in sync, the keepers in the shops around the market square began to peel away the paper to reveal the designs and artistic tableaus they'd each created in their windows to celebrate autumn and this first festival.

'Oh wow,' Ash gasped, as practically the entire square turned all the shades of autumn that I loved most.

Orange, yellow, brown and red appeared in abundance and I knew that my deputy and I were in for a tough time when it came to allocating the three awards because even from the distance we were at all of the windows looked spectacular.

'We'd better head over to the stage.' He nudged me and with shaking hands, I handed Pixie back into his care. 'Are you ready for this?'

'That's entirely irrelevant,' I said, with a wobbly smile, as I smoothed down the skirt of my leaf-patterned dress, 'because I've got to do it anyway, haven't I?'

'You're a wonder, Clemmie,' he sighed and when I looked up at him, I found he was gazing at me just as intently as he had the first day we met in the café and the evening before at Rowan Cottage. 'I think you're amazing.'

'Do you?' I swallowed, as Lizzie began to windmill and wave in our direction.

'Yes,' he said, lightly brushing my arm with his free hand and causing a shock, which I put down to my heightened nerves, to ripple through me. 'I do.'

Lizzie climbed on to the stage and was then right in my eyeline. I had no choice but to join her, but with Ash's words still ringing in my ears, the look in his eyes imprinted on my brain and the feel of his warm hand on my arm, I felt like I could conquer my fears. His support and kind words at such a daunting moment were perfectly timed and hugely appreciated. Another jolt landed as I acknowledged that Ash's presence and support felt almost as encouraging as Callum's notes back at the cottage.

'Break a leg!' Ash called after me and I took a deep breath.

By the time I turned around and looked across the square, quite a crowd had assembled and I hoped my nerves weren't about to spring back up and get the better of me. My palms felt hot and my tummy was doing somersaults, in spite of the confidence boosting moment Ash and I had just shared.

'How perfect is this?' Lizzie nudged me and I nervously nodded and again looked at the still growing sea of people in front of us.

It was then that I noticed that everyone seemed to have dressed with the season in mind and I could smell woodsmoke, nutmeg and cinnamon on the air. Had I dreamt up an autumn festival fantasy, this was exactly how I would have created it. It was truly idyllic.

I stoically told myself to forget the nerves which were trying to take over again and endeavoured to completely immerse myself in this very special moment. A moment that, even just a few weeks ago, I wouldn't have thought it possible for me to be a part of, let alone in many ways responsible for.

'Here we go,' said Lizzie. She fiddled with the microphone she had been given and her voice filled the square. 'Good morning, everyone!' she said loudly and the crowd cheered. 'And thank you for turning out this morning to celebrate the launch of the very first Wynbridge Autumn Festival!'

This evoked an even louder cheer and I began to feel genuinely excited. I knew the emotion would probably slip into reverse when it was my time to talk, but I hoped that Lizzie was going to say most of what was needed and leave me less than a sentence to struggle through.

'As some of you may know, there wouldn't be a festival happening if it wasn't for the wonderful person standing next to me,' Lizzie carried on and I realised my time to address the crowd, which was still growing, was going to come sooner than I had hoped. 'Lovely Clemmie here has stepped in to turn this idea that our dear friend, Moses Talbot, had into reality and for that I'm sure we're all very grateful. I know I am.'

'We are!' shouted Bella, which made the crowd laugh.

'Good morning,' I nervously said as Lizzie handed me the microphone. 'Of course, what Lizzie has failed to mention is that she actually strong-armed me into taking the festival on.' This evoked more laughs as Lizzie vehemently shook her head and pretended to look shocked. 'But I'm delighted that she did. I'm a relative newcomer to the town, but I already know that Wynbridge has a wonderful community and I'm thrilled to be a part of it now.'

I could hear a slight commotion happening behind me and turned to see a group of children being led on to the stage and arranged to stand in some sort of height order.

'We're very lucky to have the local primary school here to officially open the festival for us today,' I then gabbled to say, 'and so, without further ado, I'll wish you all a very happy autumn and lots of fun at the festival which will be running right into November. The Wynbridge primary choir, everyone!'

My words were met with an enthusiastic round of applause and then the opening bars of 'Autumn Days' rang out and the singing began. Everyone had joined in by the second verse and, encouraged by the crowd, the children sang even louder.

'Well done,' Lizzie said to me. 'That was brilliant.'

'I forgot to mention where the events are listed,' I groaned, as I shakily handed her back the microphone and she turned it off. 'I should have said about the social media pages, shouldn't I?'

Lizzie shook her head.

'Everyone knows where to look,' she said kindly. 'That's how half of them knew to be here today.'

'I suppose,' I said, biting my lip and wishing I'd had time to prepare a proper speech or at least a few notes.

'Honestly, hon,' Lizzie insisted, 'you were great.'

'I can't believe I've just spoken in front of all those people.' I gulped.

'Go and get yourself a drink.' Lizzie smiled. 'You deserve it.'

My legs were shaking as I edged around the stage and climbed down the steps.

'Good luck with the judging!' Lizzie called after me and I realised I'd also forgotten to mention that there was going to be a separate public vote on the shop windows, too.

I made a mental note to upload a promo post highlighting it later. I thought it was only fair that everyone else had the opportunity to vote for their favourites, too.

'You got your own way then,' said a gruff voice as I stepped on to the cobbled square.

'Excuse me?' I frowned.

I looked up to find Jason standing rather closer to me than I would have liked.

'All this,' he said with a dismissive nod to the stage and the packed market.

'Everyone who was in favour of the festival happening has *got their own way*, as you put it,' I corrected him. 'It's wonderful, isn't it?' I continued, refusing to show him that I felt intimidated. 'A truly great way to honour Moses and boost the town economy at the end of the summer season.'

'You didn't even know him,' Jason sniffed. 'And time will tell, won't it? I wouldn't count your chickens.'

'I haven't got any yet,' I said, refusing to back off. 'And I wouldn't try any more of your tricks about disrupting things if I were you. Everyone's on to you now, Jason, so you'd soon be found out.'

He went to say something else but sensed someone was behind him. It was Ash.

'Bloody incomer,' he muttered and strode off.

'Are you all right?' Ash frowned.

'Yes,' I said, though I wasn't really. The adrenaline from making my speech had only carried me so far and I hoped

Jason's opinion about me wasn't shared by everyone else. The crowd had seemed warm enough, but it might have been far cooler behind closed doors. 'Never mind him,' I further rallied.

'You did really well up there.'

'Did I?' I asked, as I picked Pixie up and took comfort in holding her little warm body close to mine again.

'Yes,' Ash said, firmly. 'You did. I know I haven't done anything to help with the festival yet, but I'm feeling properly proud to be a part of it after listening to you.'

'Well,' I nodded, as I determinedly shrugged off what Jason had said and the subsequent negative thoughts his meanness had evoked, 'that's just as well, because I have a very special festival job to do and it requires both of us.'

'Go on . . .'

'We're going to judge the shop windows . . . together.' I smiled.

'Oh, no,' said Ash, trying to take a step away, but I quickly put Pixie down and caught his jacket sleeve. 'You're not roping me into that.'

'Yes,' I said, keeping a tight hold on him, 'I am. And we're going to look at them all right now.'

'I'm sure you don't *really* need me for that—'

'Yes,' I cut in, 'I do. You've just said you're proud to be a part of the festival *and* you also said earlier that this was one task that was fraught with danger, so I insist on having my deputy's support to carry it out.'

He was wavering, but not entirely convinced.

'And I'll buy you lunch after we're done,' I added.

'Pub or café?'

'Your choice.' I shrugged, even though I wanted to go to the café and try Jemma's new additions.

'Oh well, in that case.' Ash caved, then reached for Pixie's lead. 'Show me the way.'

I made the right call in insisting that Ash accompanied me throughout the judging. He was the fount of all knowledge when it came to shop gossip and rivalry and, even though I wasn't going to really let any of that influence our final decision, it was fun to find out about.

I had decided early on which window I wanted to be the overall winner chosen by us and when we settled at a table in The Mermaid, because we couldn't get in at the café, I was delighted when Ash said that it was his favourite, too. We weren't going to announce our winners until the public had had the opportunity to vote for their favourites, via the box and ballot sheets set up in the town hall, but I felt like it was a weight off my mind to have it decided and I was now looking forward to the allocation of the two sets of awards.

'How many photos have you taken?' Ash asked, as I scrolled through the images on my phone after we'd finished the delicious and hearty stew and dumplings Evelyn had laid on exclusively for the first day of the festival.

'Quite a few.' I grinned.

'Dozens, by the looks of it. What on earth do you want them all for?'

I wanted some of them to post on AutumnEverything, but I wasn't going to explain about that and I hoped Lizzie wouldn't be tempted to add any cryptic comments on the posts I shared either. I had made sure the images were all autumnal (which wasn't hard given how beautifully the town was dressed) but didn't give any clue as to where they might have been taken. There were close ups of the pumpkins and some of the decorations, but nothing that screamed Wynbridge in either the general subjects or the background. They could have been taken in any other town or village celebrating the season.

'Well,' I said, 'it's a very special day and I just wanted to record it.'

'All of it,' Ash teased.

'Don't forget, I've been holed up in Rowan Cottage for the last eighteen months,' I reminded him, 'so it's only to be expected that I go a little overboard now I'm . . . out.'

'You make it sound like you were a prisoner.'

I took a moment to consider that.

'I suppose I was, in a way,' I said. 'I made myself a prisoner in my own home.'

'Sorry,' he apologised, looking remorseful. 'I didn't mean to upset you.'

'You didn't,' I told him. 'You were right and I stayed there, locked in my own world, with good reason. Had I not done it, I wouldn't be sitting here with you now.'

'It really helped?'

'It really did. Moving to Rowan Cottage and taking the time to do what I needed to, without anyone trying to convince me that my way was the wrong way, was the best decision I could have made. It wouldn't have been right for everyone, but it worked for me. I mean, can you imagine what Joanne and even Lizzie, would have been like if they'd met me as soon as I moved here,' I grimaced, 'and been privy to the circumstances surrounding my arrival?'

Ash let out a breath. 'They wouldn't have given you a moment's peace, would they?'

'Exactly,' I confirmed. 'Their attention would have been

kindly meant, I'm sure, but I wouldn't have wanted it and I wouldn't have achieved anything positive because of it. Staying home, on my own, was what I needed to do and I did it.'

My instinct about that being the right course for me had first come to light as a result of shutting down the online accounts Callum and I had. Once I was no longer being inundated with private messages and the harrowing details of other people's grief, I had felt such relief and, months later, the privacy the move to the Fens afforded me had added to that.

'Did your parents understand your need for isolation?' Ash asked. 'Do you have parents? I didn't even think to ask last night.'

'I do,' I confirmed. 'And they didn't, not in the beginning, but eventually they accepted it. When they could see I was focused on the renovation, and coping better as a result, they realised I was in the best place.'

I didn't mention that their faith in my eventual successful online 'social life' courtesy of AutumnEverything had helped to also convince them that I had a real-life social life and friends in the area to go with it, too.

'Well, like I said earlier,' Ash said quietly, 'I think you're amazing.'

'Just don't let Joanne hear you say that.' I smiled. 'Otherwise, we'll be back to square one. Now, I'm going to pay and then I want to explore the market before everything's sold.'

It wasn't an exaggeration to say that because the stalls had been doing a roaring trade all day. Clearly, the popularity of the cosy season was growing year on year and I was thrilled about that. Not only for my Insta account but for the appeal of the festival, too.

As long as all went smoothly, repeating it again next year really would be a no-brainer and it could be even bigger, because we'd have the whole year to prepare for it and with the Connelly family and Wynthorpe Hall on board, we'd have new events to offer, too.

'Have all of the autumn fairies gone?' I asked Bella, as I looked through the few handmade and characterful winged beauties she had left. 'I can't seem to find any.'

I'd had my eye on the fairies dressed in the autumn fabric she had mentioned before, but I hadn't had a chance to buy one earlier and now it looked like I'd missed my chance.

'They sold out hours ago,' Bella told me as she looked at Ash. 'Practically as soon as you'd launched the festival.'

'Oh no,' I groaned. 'Please tell me you'll be making more for the next market. The little crocheted acorn hats you'd fashioned for them were so perfect.'

'I'm going to be making lots more,' she told me. 'I've already sent off for more fabric because I've been taking orders since I sold out.'

'Well, you can add my name to the list,' I told her. 'I'm gutted to have missed out.'

Bella looked at Ash and they both smiled.

'You don't need to order one, Clemmie,' said Ash, as Bella reached under the stall. 'Unless you'd like two.'

Bella straightened up and in her hands was a fairy arranged in an acetate bag to protect it and which was tied up with an orange ribbon.

'This,' she said, with a grin, 'is for you, Clemmie.'

'Really?' I gasped.

'Really,' said Ash, who was smiling at me. 'I noticed you

admiring them this morning and asked Bella to put aside the one she thought you'd been most taken with.'

'I hope I got it right,' Bella commented.

I looked at the details of the fairy, my favourite of all the fairies I then realised. It was cosily nestled amid some leaf shaped confetti, which was the loveliest touch.

'You have,' I said, my voice thick in my throat. 'This was the one I really wanted.'

With her wild red hair and flowing dress, she reminded me a little of Molly from Wynthorpe Hall. She looked full of wisdom but had a mischievous smile, too. I wondered if the Wynthorpe Witch boasted both those traits? The wisdom was a pretty safe bet, but the mischief was yet to be decided upon.

'She's perfect.' I swallowed.

'Happy autumn, Clemmie,' said Ash. 'I think she's going to be the perfect addition to Rowan Cottage.'

'I think she is too,' I agreed. 'But you must let me pay for her.'

I had noted the price tag when I had been admiring her and knew she wasn't cheap.

'Absolutely not,' Ash insisted. 'She's a gift from me to you.'

'Really?' I blinked.

'Really,' he smiled.

'In that case,' I said, looking from the fairy to him and back again, 'thank you, Ash. Thank you very much indeed.'

Without thinking, I stepped up, stood on tiptoe and lightly kissed his cheek. His face felt cold beneath the warmth of my lips, but his complexion burned as brightly as my own when I stepped away again.

'You'll have to tell me what you decide to call her,' Bella

said, cutting through the post-kiss moment that felt like it meant more than it should. 'Naming your fairy is an important part of the ownership process. You can set an intention for her and she'll remind you to take action to manifest it.'

'Molly would tell you that would be best done under a new moon,' said a voice nearby and I turned around to find Hayley standing behind me.

'Which, as luck would have it,' I said a little breathlessly because I was still thinking about that kiss, 'happens to be occurring tomorrow.'

'What are the odds of that?' Ash smiled.

'What are the odds indeed?' I swallowed as I looked up at him again.

Chapter 15

I thought about how long Ash's blush had lasted after that spontaneous kiss on the cheek for a while after he had dropped us off and as I snuggled in my favourite armchair with Pixie and my beautiful, still to be named fairy. There wasn't a room the fairy didn't look right in and I imagined her visiting them all as she settled in with us and found her place.

She was the loveliest gift Ash could have given me and I hoped my spur-of-the-moment gesture of thanks hadn't upset or offended him because receiving her had been the perfect end to an incredibly successful day, both for the festival and myself. My life had been utterly transformed since Lizzie had arrived in my garden, and thoughts of her led me to also consider the final few minutes of my time in the town . . .

Ash, who was still looking a little flushed, and I had called into The Cherry Tree Café for some sweet treats to bring home and while I was looking at Lizzie's dresser of pretty things – all now arranged in autumn colours – and out of sight of the counter, I had overheard a conversation that made me feel even happier that I could call him my friend.

'You and Clemmie have turned out to be the perfect pairing

for getting this festival off the ground,' I listened to Lizzie brightly say.

'I can't take any of the credit,' Ash responded. 'It's literally all down to her. I haven't done a thing yet.'

'I thought you judged the shop windows together,' Joanne then joined in.

'Well, yes,' Ash conceded, 'we did that, but pulling it together and getting everyone organised behind the scenes, has been all Clemmie's work. It must have taken her hours and I know she's keeping everything online constantly up to date, too.'

That had been the moment my ears had really pricked up, but thankfully, Lizzie didn't make some crack about me being skilled in that department. However, Joanne's subsequent change in direction was more disconcerting than if Lizzie had.

'It's amazing to think that just a month ago none of us had ever even laid eyes on her, isn't it?' she said ponderously.

'And yet she'd been living in the area for a year and a half,' Lizzie joined in.

'Perhaps she had her reasons for keeping to herself,' Ash said, sounding guarded.

'Not now though,' laughed Joanne. 'She's a fully paid-up member of the Wynbridge community now.'

'More than fully paid-up since I roped her into organising the festival,' Lizzie pointed out with a laugh. 'I just need to pop to the kitchen for a quick word with Jemma.'

Clearly, she wasn't curious about the time I had spent alone since arriving in the Fens, but unfortunately, the same could not be said of Joanne.

'Lizzie's right about that,' she agreed. 'I suppose you've got to know Clemmie, better than any of us, haven't you, Ash?'

'What makes you say that?' he queried. 'I've already told you I've barely been involved with the festival yet.'

'But your relationship with her isn't only about the festival, is it?' Joanne pointed out. 'You gave her Pixie, didn't you? You wouldn't have done that if she was a stranger, would you?'

'Well, no,' he had no choice but to agree, 'I suppose not.'

Joanne was quiet for a moment, but then couldn't seem to resist carrying on.

'You know,' she said, in a confidential tone, 'I can't help thinking that Clemmie must have left her heart wherever she lived before.'

My mouth fell open.

'Ow!' Ash loudly said, which made me close it again with a snap.

'What?' Joanne tutted and I imagined he'd made her jump.

'You've just given me whiplash, Joanne,' he complained. 'You're totally transparent, do you know that?'

'I'm just curious, is all,' she said, sounding defensive. 'I don't like to think of Clemmie holed up all on her own with a broken heart—'

'You don't know that she has a broken heart.'

'Well, maybe not,' Joanne carried on, 'and I know you probably think I'm being nosey—'

'Aren't you?'

'No,' she insisted and given the sudden seriousness of her tone, I wasn't certain she was only saying it like that to try and get herself out of trouble, 'and I promise I'm not trying to interfere, either. I know you're both happily single, and even though I think you look really great together, I truly have set aside any former hopes I had of playing Cupid.'

'Well, that's a relief,' Ash puffed and I wondered if he'd given any thought as to how we looked together in the sense Joanne meant, because I hadn't.

'But I still hate the thought of her living alone for so long,' Joanne continued. 'We all know that's not what Wynbridge is about. No one who lives around here should be . . . excluded.'

'Even if they purposefully choose to exclude themselves?'

'Is that what Clemmie did?' Joanne gasped. 'Did she move here with the intention of hiding away?'

'Clearly not, given that she's got the festival up and running,' Ash pointed out mildly.

In spite of his faux pas, he sounded as cool as a cucumber, but my heart was racing.

'But she was here *ages* before Lizzie roped her into that—'

'Look,' Ash interrupted, finally losing patience. 'I know you think you mean well, Joanne, but not everyone's the same as you. Not everyone has to be involved in everything and know everyone else's business, and, if I were you, I'd keep out of Clemmie's.'

'Oh,' said Joanne. 'I see.'

She sounded genuinely hurt and even though I felt a tiny bit sorry for her because deep down I still had the impression that there was more going on with her than anyone else realised and that was probably why she was still using other people's lives as a distraction from whatever might have gone awry in hers, I was really more focused on feeling grateful that Ash was protecting me.

'I know you're feeling bored without Aiden and that you're just killing time here until you join him—'

'No, that's not it—' Joanne tried to interrupt, sounding even more upset, but Ash didn't give her the opportunity to elaborate.

'But if I were you,' he cut across her, 'I'd focus on your work with Lizzie or perhaps find someone who doesn't mind the attention and leave Clemmie to herself before your persistent prying makes her give up the festival for good.'

'She wouldn't give it up?' Joanne gasped. 'Would she?'

'She might.'

'Lizzie would kill me if that happened! And I genuinely only really want to know that Clemmie's all right.'

'As far as I know,' Ash said seriously, 'Clemmie is absolutely fine, but she won't be if she finds out you're still snooping on her. I mean it, Joanne, if you carry on like this, you can kiss the festival goodbye.'

Knowing the reason behind my move to the Fens, Ash was clearly worried that Joanne's intense inquisitiveness was going to deeply upset me and I felt truly touched to hear him further protect me so intently.

'I honestly never meant to cause trouble,' Joanne said, sounding genuinely contrite and upset again. 'I'm just curious as to why she's been a lone wolf for so long.'

I was again struck by the thought that there was something in her tone that suggested her interest in my circumstances originated from more than being nosey for the sake of it.

'Well,' Ash pressed home crossly, not picking up on what I had possibly deduced, 'don't be. If Clemmie has anything she wants to say about that, then I'm sure she'll tell us in her own time.'

I picked that as my moment to make my presence felt.

'Have you decided which cake you fancy, Ash?' I asked breezily, as I walked around the tables and into view.

'I think it's going to be cakes, plural, rather than just one,' he said, turning his attention to the counter. 'Because these all look amazing.'

I insisted on paying for the selection we picked out, citing it as a thank you for my fairy, but really it was a thank you for the forthright way he had looked out for me and, in the process, hopefully put a stop to Joanne's interest in my past, whatever her motive for wanting to know about it.

That said, if at some point the opportunity arose, I was definitely going to seize the chance to ask her about her future plans because I was becoming increasingly certain that they might have some bearing on her continuing curiosity.

I slept late the following morning and by the time I had seen to Pixie and made myself a mug of coffee, Mum had already called twice.

'I was all set to give up on you,' were the words she greeted me with, when I was eventually sorted and ready to call back. 'How did the festival launch go?'

'Well,' I said, picking up my coffee, 'you've seen the photos.'

I'd sent her and Dad reams and reams as I picked out those more general ones I'd taken of the town to share on the Wynbridge community and festival pages online, so they could see for themselves just how perfectly the square had been dressed to celebrate the changing season.

'We have,' Mum nodded, 'and it looked absolutely stunning. Was the launch well attended?'

I hadn't taken all that many photos with people in them, so that was a fair question.

'I think everyone within a fifty-mile radius of Wynbridge must have turned out,' I happily told her. 'It was heaving. And, as the person who had been responsible for putting it all together, I had to give a speech. If you can imagine such a thing!'

I was still struggling to get my head around that. Had I really stood up in front of all those people and talked and then put Jason in his place – or attempted to – straight after?

'My goodness,' said Mum, 'that must have been daunting. Did anyone record it? I would love to hear what you said.'

I felt myself go rather warm when she asked that.

'I don't think so,' I said, chewing my lip. 'I hope not, anyway.'

'Why?'

'Because it was really scary and I don't think I did the best job. I'd barely had time to prepare before I was holding a microphone.'

'I'm sure you did just fine,' Mum said kindly.

'Well,' I shrugged, 'either way, I had the best time after saying my brief bit and so did everyone else. Tills were ringing all day in the shops and on the market and the pub and café were packed out, too. It was a fabulous start to the festival and my new life here. I'm so happy now—'

I immediately stopped talking and hoped that Mum wasn't going to question why I'd said that.

'But you were happy before, weren't you?' She frowned.

It had been a vain hope.

'Of course,' I said quickly, feeling annoyed that I'd got so carried away when for the last eighteen months I had been so careful.

'And your new life in Wynbridge started a lot longer ago than yesterday, didn't it?'

She sounded justifiably confused.

'Of course it did.' I smiled. 'But yesterday felt like the cherry on the cake, I suppose. It isn't every day that you get asked to do something like organise an entire festival and then launch it, is it?'

'I suppose not,' she said, looking at me more closely than she had in a while.

'Don't go reading anything into what I just said, Mum,' I started to say, hoping to head her off before her thoughts spiralled.

'I'm trying not to, love,' she sighed, 'I really am, but I can't help thinking how different you are all of a sudden. How different you've been since you started talking about this friend of yours, Lizzie.'

'Well, that's because she's the one who roped me into sorting out the festival.'

'But before then, you'd never mentioned anyone in particular and you'd never shared any photos like the dozens that landed last night—'

'I thought you'd be pleased to see them,' I unfairly snapped.

I felt as cross with myself for opening this can of worms as I was with Mum for taking the bait I'd unwittingly dangled in front of her.

'You just seem to have changed all of a sudden, Clemmie,' Mum went on, 'and it's made your father and I worry that you weren't quite as involved in things as you made out before.'

'But what does that matter, if I'm involved now?'

'Of course it matters,' Mum responded. 'You've been living there almost two years!'

'And they've been two essential years in my recovery, Mum,' I said, going for broke because there was no point in carrying on pretending now she wouldn't let the topic drop. 'The truth is, I hadn't immersed myself in local life before, but now I am. I wanted to walk before I could run and I took the time to find my feet when I got here, so that when I started taking part, it would be in a way that worked for me.'

Mum looked shocked and I thought back to what I'd said about my time at the cottage alone to Ash. I had made out to him that my parents had supported the choice I had made to isolate myself, but in reality, they simply hadn't known the extent of it.

'Please don't make something out of this, Mum,' I said, starting to feel upset rather than annoyed. 'I'm the one who has walked this path for the last three years and I've taken the steps I needed to and at the pace that's been right for me.'

'Well,' she swallowed, 'judging by the photos, you've found your feet now, so I'll try not to fret over all the other months when I thought you were getting on with life—'

'I was getting on with life,' I butted in. 'I was living it *exactly* how I needed to.'

'In that case,' she said, with a small smile, 'we'll say no more about it.'

We looked at each other for a moment longer and I knew she wasn't going to hold my decision not to tell the truth against me.

'I take it Dad has seen through me, too?' I sighed.

Mum rolled her eyes at that. 'Since when have men ever noticed anything?'

I couldn't agree with that. Callum had always been pretty perceptive and Ash, though he was completely different to my husband in so many ways, was a guy with an eye for the finer details, too.

'In my experience, men notice things just fine,' I therefore replied.

'Yes, well,' Mum sighed. 'Not all men are like your Callum was.'

I decided then wasn't the moment to tell her about Ash. We'd covered enough new ground for one Sunday morning.

'Now,' she then said, 'where's Pixie? Let me see my favourite girl.'

'I thought I was your favourite girl,' I joked as I picked up Pixie, who was never far from my side, and sat her on my lap.

'Well, I've got two now,' Mum cooed. 'Aw, there she is!'

I wasn't really sure what it meant to set an intention, or how the lunar cycle could impact on it even though I did keep up with the waxing and waning of the moon, but after a quick search online, I soon had a little knowledge. Hayley had been right about a new moon being the perfect time to set what I interpreted as basically a goal or aim, and I decided that I'd give it a go.

I still didn't have a name for my fairy, but feeling a sudden desire to reread the note that Callum had written the day after we'd been treated to a stunning show of the Northern Lights from the comfort of our own back garden, and he'd romantically named me as his sun and moon, soon provided one.

'Aurora,' I said aloud, as I held the fairy up. 'That means dawn in Latin, Pixie,' I added, and she cocked her head as she listened. 'Our fairy friend has arrived right at the dawn of my new beginning, hasn't she? And yours, too. And therefore, Aurora feels like the perfect name for her.'

Pixie barked in agreement and then settled back down while I lit a candle and, following Callum's love of sharing notes, wrote, in the simplest of terms, what I hoped to achieve by the time the autumn festival came to a close in November.

In the grand scheme of things, it wasn't groundbreaking, but it meant a lot to me. My intention was to carry on along the new path I had already started to walk, but also continue to allow myself to take time out if I needed it.

Given that I had been home alone for a year and a half and had recently been thrust, quite literally, into a huge patch of limelight, I thought I had coped surprisingly well and my ability to take the changes in my stride, was a reminder that the fun-loving and gregarious young woman I had once been was still there.

Life might have knocked me about in the last few years, but at my core, the essence of who I was still existed and that was heartening. It was time to bring her out again and let her properly shine, but also look after myself while I did it.

I carefully pinned the intention to Aurora's skirt and then sat back in my armchair. My thoughts were initially all about Callum but they slowly drifted to include Ash and as if I had somehow conjured him, a few minutes later, he called.

'Hey, Clemmie,' he greeted me and I could tell he was smiling. 'How are you?'

'I'm good,' I happily responded, feeling relieved that my spontaneous kiss hadn't apparently done any lasting damage after all. 'How are you?'

'I'm great, but I wanted to check in to see if you'd recovered from yesterday.'

'What do you mean?' I asked, as I set Aurora aside.

'From the festival launch,' he elaborated. 'It was quite an intense start, wasn't it?'

'It was,' I agreed, and I realised how wonderful it was that Ash had the sensitivity to appreciate that it had been a lot for me, having gone from seeing literally no one to then addressing a huge crowd. 'But I loved every minute of it. And having you there with me made all the difference.'

'It did?'

He sounded touched.

'It really did.'

'Crikey,' he said, then went quiet.

'And now I can't wait for the feast at Fenview Farm,' I eventually said, when it was obvious that he, for some reason, was lost for words.

The feast was happening on Thursday evening and then Lizzie was running more craft workshops on Saturday. There were going to be a few autumn stalls set up on the market, too, but there was nothing really full-on happening. It was a slow lead in to October which I was grateful for because that was going to be an extremely busy month and hopefully by then I'd be well enough acclimatised to consistently keep up with it all.

'I'm looking forward to that, too,' Ash finally said. 'Events at the farm are always brilliant and I know you liked the venue when you visited.'

'I loved it and Fliss was great. And she promised to have the barn dressed for autumn by Thursday, so it's really going to look the part.'

The mention of dressing the barn made my heart skip. I was going to be decorating the cottage the next day, which was the equinox. It looked autumnal already, but with my many seasonal additions festooned and arranged about the place right up until Yule, it was going to look even better.

'Talking of autumn . . .'

'Do we ever talk of anything else?' I laughed.

'It's beginning to feel that way, isn't it?' Ash laughed, too. 'It's the equinox tomorrow.'

'I know.'

'Of course you do.'

'I'm going to be dressing the cottage and I can't wait.'

'Will it take you all day?'

'Probably, given the amount of stuff I've got, and into the evening, too.'

There were as many boxes of autumn decorations as Christmas things stowed in the loft. I wondered what Pixie was going to make of them all. I hoped she wasn't the sort of pooch who had a penchant for wrecking decs!

'Oh,' Ash then sighed, 'that's a shame.'

'Why?'

'Because I was going to suggest we take a walk. Jake and Amber at Skylark Farm have set up a nature trail around the farm and through the woods attached to the land that Moses used to own that abuts theirs and I wondered if you might fancy checking it out.'

I was tempted, but I had my plan for the day in place and really wanted to stick to it.

'On any other day,' I told him, 'I'd be there like a shot, but dressing the cottage for autumn is an equinox tradition with me now and I want to spend some quality time with Pixie, too.'

'Well,' said Ash, and I could hear his smile was back, 'I can hardly object to that, can I?'

'You don't mind?'

'Of course not. I still might go, but we can definitely do it together another time.'

'Okay.'

'You really are all right, aren't you?' Ash asked.

I could hear the concern in his tone and it made my heart melt a little.

'Yes,' I promised. 'I'm fine. And Pixie is, too. I'm just pacing myself a bit before October lands and the festival really gets underway. You've seen the schedule, so you know how busy it's going to be.'

'Well, that's all right then,' he said, sounding reassured. 'You're very sensible, Clemmie.'

I groaned at that.

'What?' he laughed.

'Does that mean boring?' I grimaced.

'Not in my book.'

'Well, that's all right then.' I swallowed as I repeated what he'd said to me and my cheeks grew hot.

'How's your fairy, by the way? Is she settling in?'

'She is,' I told him and I looked at her. 'Just like Pixie, she seems very content.'

'I'm sure she is, living with you and Pixie in wonderful Rowan Cottage. Have you got her name for her yet?'

'Aurora,' I softly said.

'That means dawn, doesn't it?'

'It does,' I confirmed, feeling impressed that he knew.

'Perfect.'

'Perfect,' I echoed.

I didn't need to explain why I'd called her that because he obviously already knew.

'Right,' he then said. 'I'd better let you go. I hope you have a wonderful time putting your autumn decs up tomorrow and chilling at home.'

'You really don't mind about the walk?' I asked one last time.

'Of course not, Clemmie. In fact, I admire you,' he said. 'All too often we know what we need to do to look after ourselves, but we seldom allow ourselves the time and opportunity to do it. Going forward, I'm going to try and take a leaf out of your book.'

'Well, that's made my day.' I beamed. 'I'll see you soon.'

'Yes,' he responded. 'We'll see each other soon.'

We ended the call on that happy note and I couldn't help thinking how wonderful it was to have a friend who accepted and understood my desire to hibernate when I needed to. It was beginning to feel very much like Ash had landed in my life at exactly the moment I needed him.

Chapter 16

The first few days of autumn arrived in a blaze of bright sunshine, which provided the perfect backdrop for some time at home. My priority for the equinox, which kicked the week off, was to dress the interior of the cottage. Then, in the days that followed, have a bit of a tidy up in the garden (but not to the detriment of the birds and wildlife) and stock the freezer with sustaining soups, pasties and stews which I could then look forward to after days spent at the festival, when I wouldn't have time to cook from scratch.

'Not that one, Pixie,' I laughed, as she stuck her inquisitive rather than destructive paws in and out of the decoration boxes and bags it had seemed to take me hours to single-handedly lug down from the loft. 'We'll start with these.'

Getting reacquainted with the autumn decorations felt nothing like as emotional as when I unpacked for Christmas. Practically all of what I had gathered together to celebrate the ber months had been found in the years after Callum had died, so there was little in the way of emotional attachment that inspired as much sadness as excitement as the tree decorations did and I was pleased about that.

My love of autumn was an obsession that was solely my own and I laughed as I opened each box and had 'ooh' and 'aah' moments over everything I rediscovered.

'Let's start upstairs, Pixie,' I said and she happily woofed in agreement. 'Then we can work our way down.'

The colours I had chosen for the cottage meant that the rooms always looked autumnal, but the bedding, cushions and fresh towels further transformed the bedrooms and bathroom and the metres of fairy light leaf garlands, which also lit up downstairs, too, draped over the headboards, around doors and along the banister, helped to enhance the look even more.

In the sitting room, the focus was the hearth and mantel and by mid-afternoon both were covered in pumpkin fairy lights, tiny fly agaric ornaments, more leaf garlands, woodland scented candles and pumpkins of all sizes, made from all kinds of fabric and materials.

'Good girl,' I praised Pixie, who had been keen to sniff everything, but so far, hadn't been bothered about pulling any of it apart. That boded well for when the potted Christmas tree was carried back inside, too. 'Now, let's get something to eat.'

Pixie had her usual meal, while I tucked into delicious squash soup which was velvety smooth and richly fragrant thanks to the addition of some smoky paprika. After that, we went for a long walk along the drove to stretch our legs ahead of adding cushions, throws and a rug to the sitting room and transforming the kitchen, utility cum boot room and porch.

I hadn't really been in the mood for a walk as I wanted to carry straight on, but we hadn't gone far before my effort to get some steps in, and give Pixie a decent run, was rewarded. Initially, I thought I had imagined it, but when I stopped and properly tuned in, there was no mistaking the sound of geese flying overhead.

I stepped on to the verge and shielded my eyes from the glare of the dipping sun and sure enough, there was a perfect V of pink-footed geese flying overhead and honking loudly. I would have loved to have known what they were saying to each other and I felt a prickle of tears as I remembered I had wondered the very same thing the year before.

My breath caught as I realised how utterly different my life was now. The dramatic changes hadn't even occurred over the last twelve months, or even weeks. It was all down to just one month and the arrival of new friends and my beloved autumn. How lucky was I?

'Come on then, Pixie!' I laughed. 'Let's get on. We've still got loads left to do!'

It was time for dinner when I'd finished dressing the cottage completely to my satisfaction and I spent the evening first fussing Pixie, then checking the festival pages online and finally, taking photographs of parts of the rooms which I would use on AutumnEverything over the coming months. I had been tempted to share a photograph of the geese, but feeling that spotting them that day had been such a special moment, I ultimately decided to keep it to myself.

I had barely finished posting an image of one of my autumn wreaths in lieu of the geese, when Lizzie commented on it and then sent me a photo of Ash and a few people I didn't recognise, standing on the edge of what looked like woods. My guess was that Ash had found some people to join him on his walk around the new nature trail at Skylark Farm.

I examined the image closer and thought he appeared a little out on a limb, but given how handsome he looked, all wrapped up in a knitted scarf and woolly hat, and the fact that there appeared to be a couple of women also there on their own, I didn't think he'd be alone for long.

'We wish you were here,' I read aloud as Lizzie's accompanying message loaded. 'We're heading to the pub in a bit if you fancy joining us?'

I glanced at the clock. I supposed I had time to get changed and join them in The Mermaid, but truth be told, what I had said to Ash still held. My heart belonged to Pixie and my cosy little home that evening and I was right where I needed to be. I no longer wanted to be holed up in Rowan Cottage forever, but a couple more days would completely restore my equilibrium after my intense bout of being sociable, and I had no desire to overrule that feeling.

Not tonight, but I'll see you all soon, I therefore messaged back. *Happy autumn!*

By Thursday, I had satisfied my need to mentally rest and reset, which was just as well as the Fenview Farm Autumn Feast was happening that evening. That week, I had spent as many hours outdoors as in, keen to take advantage of the dry weather, and the garden was looking much better as a result. I had also taken lots of walks and seen loads more geese which was a total treat and I'd taken a few decent long-range photos that I shared just with Mum and Dad and then filed away for myself.

It was mid-afternoon when Ash's truck pulled up and I realised, as he climbed out, that I had missed him every bit as much as Pixie who was greeting him with a cacophony of ecstatic barks and much tail wagging and jumping up at the gate. I hadn't purposefully avoided him, because I had just been getting on with things, but I realised with a jolt that the radio silence had been rather louder than I might have expected it to be.

'Hello, stranger,' I greeted him as he opened the gate and scooped Pixie up, though he couldn't keep proper hold of her for long because she was wriggling so much.

He was wearing the same berry coloured scarf he'd had on in the photo Lizzie had sent and I suddenly found myself wondering if there had been someone among the group who had thought he looked as handsome in it as I did. Irrationally, I hoped not, then quickly dismissed the thought because it wasn't any of my business.

'I know I haven't been in touch,' he said, almost apologetically. 'But we've been run off our feet at the practice and I've been immersed in a bit of a side quest, too. Also, I didn't want to disturb your peace and quiet.'

'Oh, Ash,' I said. 'You are kind, but I wouldn't have minded if you had called.'

'Really?' he sighed. 'Then I wish I had now. I'll bear it in mind next time.'

'You're always welcome,' I told him and meant it.

'So, what are you up to then?' he asked. 'I hope I'm not disturbing you now?'

'Not at all. In fact, I'm glad of the interruption, because I'm scrubbing out my bird feeders and it isn't the most glamorous of chores.'

'It's essential though,' he smiled. 'And perfectly timed.'

'Tis the season,' I joked.

'I didn't mean that,' he laughed, as Pixie continued to scamper about.

'What then?'

'I have some presents for you, courtesy of the side quest,' he grinned. 'Keep hold of Pixie and I'll get them out of the truck.'

'Oh, Ash,' I said, as I picked Pixie up. 'You've only just gifted me fairy Aurora, so you shouldn't be giving me anything else.'

'Where is she, by the way?' he asked, as he walked back through the gate.

'Currently sitting next to the fireplace,' I told him. 'I think she's found her spot.'

He unloaded a small cardboard box, then a wooden sort of base and finally a magnificent painted and decorated bird table which would sit perfectly on top of it.

'That's the lot,' he said, closing the gate so I could put Pixie down again.

'Is this really for me?' I gasped, as I looked at the details on the table.

'It is,' he smiled shyly. 'And there's this, too.'

Inside the box was a small feeding table, which matched the large one, but was designed to hang in a tree or under a ledge, by a metal chain.

'What do you think?' Ash asked nervously as he held it up. Everything was painted in a base coat of brown, but decorated with autumn motifs in orange, red and yellow. 'I don't think they turned out too bad for a first attempt and I only hammered my thumb instead of the wood a couple of hundred times.'

'You *made* these?' I swallowed.

'I did,' he said, sounding proud, but still a little shy. 'And the paint job is all my own work, too. Of course, I won't mind if you wanted to change that. It's not the best, but the woodwork is pretty sound. My old DT teacher would be impressed.'

'You made these for me?' I swallowed again.

'Yep,' he said, trying to make it sound as though it wasn't much, but to me it was everything. 'I noticed your other table was on its last legs, so I thought I'd buy you a new one. Then I thought I'd have a go at making one myself and got . . . well, a bit carried away.'

I was tempted to throw my arms around him and hug him, but mindful that I'd already spontaneously kissed his cheek just the week before, I didn't want to overstep.

'But whenever have you found the time?' I asked, feeling all kinds of emotional. 'You've just said you've been rushed off your feet at work this week.'

He looked at me and I looked at him.

'Well, I like to keep busy,' he said croakily. 'Especially if it helps out a . . . friend.'

I didn't know what else to say. The kind gesture and all the effort Ash had gone to felt above and way beyond what you'd do for your oldest friend, let alone a relatively new one. But then, I reasoned, it had been such a long time since I'd had a true friend, I had probably forgotten what went into nurturing this sort of relationship. I needed to up my game.

'More than helps me out,' I said, as a van pulled up behind Ash's truck and Pixie started to bark. 'Thank you, Ash. Thank you so much.'

'Is this Rowan Cottage?' the driver shouted.

'Yes,' I called back. 'Yes, it is.'

'I've got a delivery for you, love.'

I had no idea what it was, because I hadn't ordered anything.

'It's heavy. Where do you want it?'

'This will be the food I've ordered to go with the feeders,' Ash said to me. 'Some of it's come from a farm on the coast near Wynmouth. Hold on,' he called to the driver, 'and I'll give you a hand.'

It took a while to carry the boxes to the shed, decant the contents into plastic crates, set the tables up, finish cleaning and then filling the feeders, but the result was absolutely wonderful. The hanging feeder, gently swinging in the lowest branches of the rowan tree, after which the cottage was named, looked particularly lovely.

'Oh, Ash!' I said, clapping my hands in excitement once we'd finally finished and as I took it all in. 'They look so amazing.'

'Much better than that old thing,' he laughed, with a nod to where the old table was waiting to be chopped up for firewood because it was completely beyond repair.

'I'm totally in your debt now,' I told him.

'You can pay me in pasties,' he suggested.

'I've actually just finished stocking the freezer, so you're always welcome to drop in for a feed.'

'I'll hold you to that,' he laughed.

'Do you fancy something to eat now?'

'If it was any other day of the week, I would have said yes, but I'm saving myself for the feast tonight.'

'Oh yes, good plan,' I agreed. 'I think I'll do the same. Would you like me to pick you up later? I don't mind.'

'That's kind, but I need to take the truck. I'm on call and the chances are something will come up, so I won't offer to collect you either, otherwise you could end up stranded.'

'Fair enough.'

'I'll see you tonight.'

'See you later. And thank you, Ash.'

'It's really nothing,' he said, ducking his head.

'No,' I said, again resisting the urge to give him a hug, 'it's the very opposite of that.'

There were already a few cars parked at Fenview Farm when I arrived for the feast, but I couldn't see Ash's truck amongst them and I hoped he hadn't been called out already. While I had been getting organised for the evening, I had looked out of the cottage window to admire the bird tables and wondered what, other than food, I could offer him in return. He might have insisted that his gifts were no big deal, but they had made me feel thought of and cherished and I was keen to make him feel that way, too.

'Clemmie!' called Bella, as she climbed out of her little Fiat with a man I hadn't seen before. 'Have you been inside?'

'Not yet,' I said, feeling pleased that I wasn't going to have to walk in alone. 'I've only just got here.'

'This is my partner, Jude,' she told me, once she'd locked her car and they'd walked over. 'Jude, this is Clemmie.'

'The festival saviour.' Jude smiled at me. 'I saw you at the launch, but didn't have the chance to say hello.'

'Well, hello now.' I smiled back. 'It's lovely to meet you.'

'Come on,' said Bella, linking her arm through mine in a friendly gesture that settled my nerves more than she could have realised. 'Let's go in. I can't wait for you to see what Fliss has done with the barn.'

'And what you've contributed to it,' Jude laughed. 'Bella has helped with the decorating,' he added for my benefit.

'I've branched out,' she giggled. 'But only for tonight.'

As soon as we reached the barn door, Fliss, who owned the farm with her grandad, Bill, and regularly hosted supper club events showcasing local and seasonal food, rushed over with her partner, Eliot, to greet us.

The barn was the perfect setting for the festival's autumn feast and I could already see that she, and Bella, had gone all out to dress it to perfection.

'Come on in,' said Fliss, ushering me further inside. 'Come and look at what Bella has made.'

I could already see and her clever creations added perfectly to the rural ambience.

'Scarecrows!' I laughed. 'How clever, Bella! They're adorable.'

Every table had a couple, one sitting and one standing, and even though their outfits were all made from different fabrics, they all somehow matched, too. The poles on the standing ones had been used to secure them in the centre of floral table decorations which were a riot of autumn-coloured dahlias and chrysanthemums, gourds, grasses and seasonal greenery. There were fairy lights strung everywhere and the stacks of small pumpkins and sheaves of wheat gave the barn a wonderful harvest festival feel.

'The barn has never looked so good,' said Bill, who I had met when I came to talk to Fliss about their offer to host the festival's main food events. 'I think we're in for a good night.'

He wasn't wrong. Before long, all of the seats, bar one, had been taken and the feasting began. The tables were groaning with deliciously spiced platters of seasonal vegetables, slices and chunks of all kinds of bread, richly salted butter, hard and soft cheeses, charcuterie, hog roast and apple sauce. Everything had been locally sourced, the pork and apples, jugs of cider and juice coming from the Fenview neighbours at Skylark Farm, the cocktails and mocktails from Brambles, and I sampled practically everything.

'Where's Ash?' asked Jemma who was there with her husband, Tom.

Ash's seat was the empty one next to mine.

'I don't know,' I told her. 'He was planning to come, but he's also on call, so maybe he's working.'

'I was,' his voice piped up behind me. 'But I'm here now. What have I missed?'

He sounded out of breath and rather harassed. I knew how much he had been looking forward to the feast, and that he hadn't eaten ahead of it, so that was no surprise.

'Practically everything food wise,' Jemma tutted, as he sat down next to me and let out a huff of annoyance. 'You'll be lucky to get scraps now.'

'No, he won't,' said Fliss, magically appearing at his side with a huge and very packed plate. 'Because I've saved you a bit of everything, Ash.'

'Hey,' objected Eliot, from the other side of the table with mock outrage. 'He's got more than I had!'

'Yes, well,' said Fliss, giving Ash a wink and patting him on the shoulder, 'you didn't save Grandad's favourite hen, did you, Eliot? Ash did.'

Ash laughed at that and I was pleased to observe the upturn in his mood. I hated the thought of the evening being spoiled for him when he'd been looking forward to it.

'Did you really save Bill's favourite hen?' I asked him as everyone went back to their own seats and to no doubt refill their plates with the few bits of food that were left.

'No,' he confessed, in little more than a whisper, 'it was a total fluke that she recovered, but don't tell Fliss that otherwise she'll be cutting down on my portion sizes.'

I laughed at that, then turned to look at him and realised there was barely an inch of space between us at the packed table. He looked at me, too, and as friendly as we were, the close proximity felt a little too close for comfort.

'I'll let you eat in peace,' I said, pushing back my chair. 'You've got some catching up to do and there are a couple of people I need to thank.'

I'd pretty much said all of the thanks I needed to, but doing the rounds again gave me a moment, even though I didn't know why I needed one.

'Have you spoken to everyone now?' Ash later asked.

'I think so,' I told him, feeling fine again.

He'd long since finished eating and had helped move the tables and chairs to clear some space for dancing. I hadn't known that was going to be on the agenda. It had been a long time since I'd heard music played in a party atmosphere and my foot was tapping as I stood and watched everyone. Callum and I had loved to dance and I had forgotten how much I enjoyed it. I idly wondered if I still had the moves, as my dad was fond of saying.

'Would you look at them?' he would gasp in wonder when Mum tuned into *Strictly*. 'They've got the moves. And him a former politician, too. You wouldn't think it, would you?'

The memory of hearing that every Saturday on repeat for years made me laugh and Ash must have caught the sound.

'Would you like to dance?' he unexpectedly offered. 'Though before you answer, I have to warn you, I'm pretty rubbish.'

'No,' I laughed. 'But thank you.'

'I can tell you're itching to.'

I stilled my foot.

'I wouldn't want to put you through it, if it's not your thing,' I told him.

By the looks of the wild and varied shapes Jemma's Tom was throwing with abandon, Ash's alleged bad dancing wouldn't have been out of place, but I wasn't about to dance for the first time in a long time in such a public place. I'd save it for my kitchen. Pixie would love that.

'Hey! Come on!' Bella then called when she spotted us watching. 'No wallflowers allowed tonight!'

She grabbed hold of Ash's hand and pulled him into the crowd and the look he threw me was so desperate that I set aside my apprehension and thought my first thank you for the fairy and bird tables could be to support him on the dance floor.

'Just one dance then!' I shouted and joined the happy throng.

One dance turned into two, then two melded into three and by the time the opening bars of 'You and Me' by Shallou filled the barn, my heart was racing and I had let the music take me over completely, just like I used to. Ash was still enthusiastically dancing too, and not badly at all. He reached for my hand and spun me round and round while everyone moved around us.

It was the happiest and most relaxed I had felt in a very long time and when Ash pulled me close as the song headed towards its end, I was laughing and singing at the same time. Suddenly, our bodies were pressed together, his hands were on my back, my heart was racing and our lips were just an inch apart. It was very close proximity for . . . friends.

I'm not sure what would have happened next, if anything, but in the beat when time stood still, his jeans pocket began to buzz and I jumped away.

'You're vibrating!' I shouted.

'You're telling me,' he swallowed, his eyes trained on mine.

'No!' I laughed. 'It's your phone!'

He pulled it out of his pocket, then moved away so he could answer it in peace and I was left thinking we'd just had a very lucky escape and how fortunate we were that Joanne hadn't been around to witness it.

It was a shocking acknowledgement, but I knew I had been about to kiss Ash or Ash had been about to kiss me, but then I reasoned, it was only because we had been caught up in the moment. We had both been in an entirely uninhibited state, high on good food and fun music. It wouldn't have meant anything, but it could have made our purely platonic friendship awkward, so I was relieved it hadn't happened.

And of course, given that I was still in love with Callum, and had always been resolute that I would never so much as even look at another man in that way again, the guilt that kissing Ash would have doubtless triggered, would have been unbearable.

'Crikey,' I said to Bella, who was still dancing. 'I'm boiling. I need a drink.'

I poured myself a glass of apple juice and drank it slowly as I caught my breath.

'Hey,' I then said to Ash, who joined me. 'Let me get you a drink.'

The action gave me something to do and meant I didn't have to look at him for a few more seconds. I had almost recovered, but not quite.

'No time,' he said. 'But thanks. I need to get to the practice.'

'Oh no,' I said, though actually I felt a bit relieved as I glanced at him. 'You're not leaving?'

'Afraid so,' he nodded. 'And then,' he added, not quite looking at me, either, 'in the morning, I'm off to stay with Mum and Dad for a few days.'

'You didn't mention it before.'

'Did I not?' He frowned. 'I meant to.'

'Will you be gone long?' I asked.

'I'll be back in time for the start of the pumpkin picking,' he promised.

He still wasn't looking at me properly.

'You know, Ash,' I started to say. 'That dance just now—'

'Sorry, Clem,' he said, taking a step away, 'I really need to go. Say goodbye to Fliss and the others for me, will you?'

'Of course,' I said. 'But Ash . . .'

My words trailed off as he walked away. He didn't look back and I hoped our mad moment wasn't the reason behind his sudden departure from the county because I was certain it hadn't been in the offing before. But if that was the case, and I'd already managed to rationalise what had happened, why hadn't he?

Chapter 17

I didn't sleep soundly that night, but the next day I strengthened my resolve to further distance myself from what had happened at the Fenview Feast, because actually, nothing of worrying significance had happened. Ash and I had danced together. Full stop. We'd had a dance and a laugh and that was it.

I had nothing to feel guilty about and the more I thought about it, the more convinced I became that Ash *must* have made his plan to visit his parents before he thought to mention it to me because he didn't have the sort of job where you could just take off, did he? Ergo, all was right with the world.

'All hail the dancing queen,' Joanne greeted me, when I looked in at the gallery, with Pixie in tow on Saturday morning. 'I heard you had fun at the Fenview Feast and I've been hoping you'd come and tell us all about it.'

'I think that particular title belongs to Tom,' I said, thinking back to his extraordinary moves on the makeshift dancefloor. 'He was the one who really let himself go.'

'He does have that reputation,' Lizzie laughed. 'There's never a dull moment at a party if he's invited.'

'I can well believe that,' I laughed.

'How's everything going?' Lizzie then asked.

'Really well. I've been booking and scheduling some extra events and making sure the socials are all up to date with the details, too.'

'Brilliant.' Lizzie nodded.

'That's why I've not been around much,' I added for her assistant's benefit. 'I've been far too busy to come in here and gossip with you, Joanne.'

'That's you told,' Lizzie laughed and Joanne looked chastened. 'So, what are you up to today, Clemmie?'

I glanced at Joanne and felt a bit bad that I'd been so blunt with her in front of Lizzie. If there was something on her mind that she was masking through her apparent interest in other people's lives, then publicly telling her off was hardly the way to go about gaining her trust and getting her to confide, was it?

'Nothing in particular,' I replied to Lizzie. 'Now I've got everything sorted again, I'm going to be a free agent for a little while.'

The decision to still pace myself and balance the bouts of getting out and about with being back in the cottage with Pixie, was making all the difference to my confidence levels, but I was in no rush to tip the scales too far in either direction and sacrifice one for the other.

'In that case,' she said, putting her hands together in a pleading gesture, 'is there the slightest chance that you might consider helping me out in here today? Jemma really needs Joanne in the café because of staff illness, so I'm going to be trying to run two workshops back-to-back until late in the day and with no support.'

I might not have had a to-do list of my own to work through, but I wasn't sure I was up to helping Lizzie with hers and especially with no time to prepare myself to do it. My crafting skills weren't the best and I was still refining my social ones, too.

'But I've got Pixie,' I therefore quickly said, indicating my canine companion in the hope that she'd get me off the hook, even if I did feel bad about leaving Lizzie in the lurch.

'Well,' said Lizzie, bending to give Pixie a fuss, 'she wouldn't be the first four-legged visitor the gallery has had and there's a dog bed behind the counter, so she could take herself off to that if she needed some space. Maybe you could settle her there and see how she goes?'

The gallery bell rang out as the first workshop attendees arrived and Joanne got ready to head next door to help Jemma.

'You really would be saving the day,' Joanne said to me.

'And my sanity,' Lizzie added.

'Oh well,' I swallowed, 'if your sanity is on the line, Lizzie, then I really do have to stay, don't I?' I supposed as festival organiser it was inevitable that I would be asked to pitch in with this sort of thing at some point. 'I'll just follow Joanne next door and ask Jemma if I can borrow a water bowl for Pixie.'

'No need,' Lizzie smiled. 'Along with the dog bed, there's one of those behind the counter, too.'

'Perfect,' I said, letting out a breath. 'Come on then, Pixie.'

Pixie was a paragon of virtue the entire day. I hadn't initially committed to staying for both the morning and afternoon sessions, but she was so content, padding out for a fuss and some attention and then putting herself back to bed when she'd had enough, that the time flew by and I felt myself relax into it all as a result. The gallery was a wonderful place to work and Lizzie had the knack of putting everyone at ease.

A space in the afternoon session meant that I could both support her and take part and I ended up thoroughly enjoying myself. I was delighted that Lizzie had talked me into helping and grateful to Pixie for settling so well.

'I absolutely love these, Lizzie,' I said, holding up one of the three pumpkins I had selected to decoupage, after I had assisted her in making sure everyone else was sorted.

The other workshop, happening on a different table, involved sewing and stuffing a patchwork pumpkin. My sewing skills weren't all that hot, so the decoupage was perfect for me. Though if I did want to improve in the future, then I'd look no further than Lizzie for a teacher. She was patient, hugely experienced and full of tips and ideas. The ideal instructor.

My role for the day had been simple enough. I had handed out, tidied up, ferried food and drink orders to Jemma next door and taken lots of photos for the festival pages. I'd ended up enjoying myself far more than I had expected to and I'd coped well with the busyness of it all, too.

'They're cute, aren't they?' said a woman next to me as she looked at the trio she'd selected. 'I'm going to give these to my sister. She's mad on autumn.'

'It's a very popular time of year.' I smiled.

'Her obsession really started last year when she found this account on Instagram. All About Autumn, it's called. Or something like that.'

'Do you mean AutumnEverything?' Lizzie, who happened to be close by, asked.

'Yes, that's it!' said the woman. 'AutumnEverything. It's gorgeous. She's got me following it now, too.'

'That sounds lovely.' I swallowed.

My palms suddenly felt as sticky as the glue I was using to attach the pieces of paper to my three pumpkins and I could feel my cheeks were blazing.

'It's stunning,' said Lizzie, with not even a hint of a look in my direction which I appreciated. 'I love it myself.'

'I'm a follower, too,' said someone else.

'And me.'

'You know it?' the woman who had originally mentioned it laughed.

'Seems like we all know it,' said Lizzie. 'Now, does anyone need any help while I'm on my feet?'

Once I'd got my temperature back under control, I felt a swell of pride as they all carried on talking about the most recent photos I'd shared, but I had no desire to announce that I was the account owner. The last thing I wanted was anyone delving into my personal history online and messaging me like I'd experienced before, as a result.

I made a quick mental note not to post photos of the pumpkins I was currently decorating. It would only take one beady-eyed follower from around the gallery table to put two and two together!

'So,' said Lizzie once we'd finished tidying up at the end of the day. 'How was that?'

'Actually, I really enjoyed it,' I honestly told her.

'Well, you needn't sound so surprised!'

'You say that, but I am surprised. Publicly organising the festival and now helping out in here today, has been a huge leap from being home alone and focusing on nothing other than the cottage renovation for so long. I've really had fun, but I'm tired out from it all, too.'

'Oh, my goodness,' Lizzie responded with a gasp, 'I didn't even think of that. I'm so sorry, Clemmie. I really shouldn't have asked you to help today, should I?'

'No, honestly,' I told her, wishing I hadn't said anything because she looked so upset. 'It's fine. I've really loved it.'

'You're sure?'

'One hundred per cent. It's done me the world of good, but now I feel like I need a bit of a break.'

'Okay,' she said, letting out a relieved breath. 'You did look as though you were enjoying yourself and I have to say, you took to the role like a duck to water. You knew just what the customers needed, especially with a nod to styling, but then I already knew you had a great eye for detail, didn't I?'

'Yes,' I said, 'I suppose you did and thank you for not letting anything slip when AutumnEverything unexpectedly came up in conversation.'

'I promised you I wouldn't and I still stand by that. Now, can I tempt you to tea and cake?'

'That's kind,' I said, checking the time, 'but I'm feeling zonked now and my parking ticket is about to run out, so I'd better head off.'

I was relieved I'd remembered to extend it earlier in the day.

'You must let me pay for your parking,' Lizzie insisted. 'It's the least I can do.'

'Absolutely not,' I said, holding up the pumpkins I'd decorated and which she had said I could keep. 'You've already paid me in pumpkins.'

'You better not post those on your Insta,' she laughed, 'otherwise you won't have to worry about me outing you because you'll have done it yourself.'

'I'd already thought of that,' I smiled back.

'Right,' she said, looking around again while I attached Pixie's lead, 'you head off. And thank you again, Clemmie. After all this today, I hope you're going to assign your deputy to attend the library book club launch in your place tomorrow.'

'No, I'll be there,' I told her. 'I might not stay for the whole thing, but I'll be popping in for Kay's opening speech and I can't rope Ash in anyway, because he's in Bakewell visiting his family.'

'Is he?' Lizzie frowned. 'I didn't know that. I hope everything's okay.'

'He went yesterday and as far as I know, there's nothing wrong.'

'But that means you're flying the festival flag solo again,' she tutted.

'I am,' I smiled, 'but for now I can manage.'

On the drive back into town for the first book club meeting the next morning, I took a detour to admire some of the fields of pumpkins which looked to me like they were swelling by the hour. As I pulled on to a concrete pad on the edge of one of the fields, I thought about what had recently happened to Jake and Amber at Skylark Farm and hoped the festival would turn their pumpkin disaster into a helpful windfall.

They had only been able to offer the festival a field for pumpkin picking because the buyer who should have taken their crop had a last-minute change of heart regarding how many pumpkins they wanted. Not only had this left the farm with a whole field full of a crop that was no longer wanted, but it also left the couple out of pocket while they took legal action because the buyer was in breach of contract.

Hopefully, however, if all went well, and the newly created Skylark Farm Pumpkin Patch, which we'd discussed via a Zoom call when I was finalising the festival details, was a success, it might become an annual tradition with part of their crop being sold directly to the public on a pick your own basis, rather than to a third-party buyer.

I was fast learning that farming was a financially precarious business and I was also mindful that I needed to take care of my own financial future, too. As I had no intention of moving, I wouldn't be making a penny out of the Rowan Cottage renovation.

Callum and I had had big plans to buy, renovate, sell and move quickly up the property ladder, and we had been well on our way, but I had no interest in pursuing that path on my own and even though I had no current financial concerns, I knew I didn't have enough put by to live on forever. I would have to set my mind to properly planning my future now I was beginning to feel like I had a worthwhile one.

I took a few photos of the field, then set off to town with my new library card in my bag and wondering if the careers section had full shelves.

'Hello, you,' said Lizzie, who sidled up to me in the queue to take books out after Kay had told everyone what the plans for the autumn book club were. 'I see you've got some of the same titles as I have.'

Kay and her staff had distributed the recommended autumn

reading list and then arranged the meeting to discuss the first book. I had decided not to commit to reading a book in a fortnight, but opted instead to read some of the other titles I liked the sound of, at my own pace.

After a day of festival checking and organising, curled up with Pixie next to the fire with some cosy fiction felt like a wonderful way to spend autumn evenings as the nights started to draw in and it became too chilly to sit out. An accompanying milky drink, fleece blanket and soft lighting completed the image in my head and I couldn't wait to make a start.

'I couldn't resist these two,' I said, holding them up. 'They sound like perfect ber months reads to me.'

'And me,' Lizzie agreed. 'By the way, thank you again for yesterday.'

'It was my pleasure.'

'I hope you're not feeling too tired out today.'

'I didn't rush to get up this morning,' I explained, 'so I'm okay.'

My head was a bit fuzzy, but given how concerned she'd been the day before when I said my current life changes were full on, I kept that to myself.

'The photos you posted on the festival pages look amazing,' she praised, 'and I've had great feedback about you on the forms I got everyone to fill out at the end of the sessions.'

'Have you?' I blushed. 'I didn't expect anyone would have paid enough attention to me to warrant a comment.'

'Well, they did. You were friendly, helpful and had a great eye,' Lizzie reeled off. 'One woman also said you helped her put a palette together for her decoupage pumpkin that she never would have considered if you hadn't suggested it.'

'I know who that was.' I smiled, feeling pleased to have helped and delighted that she genuinely liked the striking choices I had encouraged her to make. 'And she was halfway there, really. Her selection just needed a little . . . tweaking to make it really sing.'

'Well, sing it did and Pixie was a popular addition to the day, too.'

'She was such a sweetheart, wasn't she? I think she took to it better than I did!'

'You were both brilliant,' said Lizzie as we moved forward in the queue and Joanne suddenly appeared next to us.

'So,' she said, giving Lizzie a nudge. 'Have you asked her yet?'

Lizzie looked at me and shook her head.

'Asked me what?' I frowned.

'Oh no, sorry,' Joanne winced.

'Sorry *again*,' Lizzie tutted.

'I've put my foot in it, haven't I?' Joanne sighed, sounding both fed up and frustrated. 'I'm going to head off.'

Lizzie puffed out her cheeks as Joanne walked out of the library. I couldn't help thinking that the spring in her step that I'd noticed when I first met her, was decidedly absent.

'Is she all right?' I frowned after her.

'Always,' Lizzie said with an accompanying eye roll, 'and it's exhausting. I'm fast approaching the point that I'm counting down the days until she leaves.'

I didn't quite know how to respond to that. Obviously, Lizzie knew her assistant a hundred times better than I did, so perhaps my take on Joanne's possible change of tone and body language was wrong.

'She's definitely leaving then?'

'Yep.'

'Well, I'm sure you'll miss her when she's gone.'

'Perhaps,' Lizzie dubiously said. 'But I won't miss her chatting to customers, when she's supposed to be helping them. I can't tell you the number of times things haven't got finished in the past and customers have had to complete them at home.'

I could appreciate Lizzie's frustration about that and I could imagine the customers weren't always thrilled about it either, even if they had doubtless been willing to talk at the time.

'In that case,' I suggested, 'if you have plans to replace her, you'll have to specify absolutely no matchmaking or casual chatting on the job description. Maybe take on someone quieter and calmer.'

'That's exactly what I've been thinking,' Lizzie then smiled. 'You're quiet and calm, aren't you, Clemmie?'

'In comparison with Joanne, I think you'll find most people are!'

I was now at the front of the queue and carried on listening to Lizzie bemoan her current assistant's incessant desire to talk, while I scanned my card and books, printed my receipt with the return date on and popped them into my tote bag.

'There must have been something about her that appealed to you when you took her on,' I tactfully said as Lizzie checked her own books out.

She looked thoughtful.

'Um,' she sighed, 'I suppose it was actually her bubbliness that secured her the job. Of course, I had no idea how tiring I was going to find her full-on personality when I had to work with it every day, though.'

'But not for much longer.'

'No,' she agreed. 'Not for much longer. She's leaving the country during the week between Christmas and New Year, because Aiden's next contract has been officially confirmed.'

'And is she excited about that?' I asked.

'What do you think?'

'I don't know.' I shrugged. 'That's why I'm asking.'

Lizzie was quiet for a minute as she gave Joanne's reaction to leaving some consideration.

'Do you know what?' she then frowned. 'Now I think about it, since Aiden's new role in the firm was confirmed and the moving arrangements made, she hasn't actually gone on about it all as much as I might have expected her to.'

I didn't say anything further as we walked out of the warm library and into the bracing October air, but I hoped that Lizzie might think more about Joanne's reaction to the prospect of heading off and perhaps ask her if everything was turning out how she had hoped it would.

'But however she's currently feeling about it all,' Lizzie said after we'd walked a few steps, 'I am still going to have to replace her.'

'Yes,' I agreed. 'I suppose you are.'

Lizzie rolled her eyes and groaned.

'What?'

'You're not very good at taking a hint, are you, Clemmie?' she tutted.

'What do you mean? What have I missed?'

'I want *you* to take the job,' she then shockingly announced.

'Me?' I squeaked, stopping dead. 'You're offering me Joanne's job?'

'Yes!' Lizzie laughed. 'I'm offering you Joanne's job. And after watching you yesterday, and reading the feedback I've had, I'm very much hoping you'll say yes.'

'You're really offering me the job?'

I couldn't believe it.

'Yes, I really am.'

We carried on walking along the pavement back towards where I'd parked. I didn't say anything because my head was spinning. Even though Lizzie had been singing my praises, I hadn't for one second thought that she might be about to offer me the vacancy she'd soon need to fill.

'You're not offended, are you?' Lizzie asked, when I didn't say anything. 'I know it wouldn't be everyone's cup of tea.'

'I couldn't be further from offended,' I promised her. 'I think I'm in shock.'

I had literally just a couple of hours ago been thinking about my financial future and without any form filling or email answering, a job offer had now landed out of the blue. Was this yet another moment proving that taking a risk, as Callum had suggested in his note, could lead to wonderful things? Organising the festival had meant taking a risk, as had helping out in the gallery the day before, and both had already paid dividends I could never possibly have predicted or hoped for.

'Good shocked?' Lizzie asked hopefully.

'Very good shocked.' I nodded, as the written intention to keep moving my life forward, which I'd pinned to Aurora's skirt, also came to mind. 'Can you tell me more about what the job involves?' I wanted to be in possession of all the facts before I committed to thinking properly about it and making a decision.

'Well, simply put,' Lizzie explained, 'I need someone creative, which I obviously already know you are.'

'Thank you.'

'And someone who I can rely on to work in the gallery,' she carried on. 'Help me with the exhibitions and, most importantly, take an active part in supporting the workshops.'

'Sort of like I did yesterday, you mean.'

'Exactly like you did yesterday,' she said, with emphasis. 'However, I'm adding some extras to the revised role, too, which I know Joanne wouldn't want to take on, even if she was staying in Wynbridge.'

'Okay.' I swallowed. 'So, what are those?'

'In time, I'd like you to occasionally be responsible for running the gallery when I can't be there and also coming up with and running your own workshops, too.'

'Crikey,' I said, thinking that sounded like rather a lot of responsibility when compared to what I'd done the day before.

'But the extras wouldn't happen until you were completely happy, confident and fully trained,' Lizzie stressed. 'There'd be no rush, but ultimately it would be wonderful to know that I could take a break or go on holiday, without having to close.'

'I see,' I said, as I slowly began to consider what was expected. 'And what about the café? Does the job involve working in there, too?'

The reason I had been roped into helping in the gallery was because Jemma had no extra staff in the café and Joanne was needed there.

'Only in extreme circumstances,' Lizzie explained. 'Like yesterday, for example. That sort of situation, where everyone is sick, rarely happens, but it's good to know the rest of the team are willing to pitch in if necessary.'

'Yes,' I said, taking that in. 'I can see it would be important to have a flexible approach.'

'Very important,' she nodded. 'It's time I loosened the reins a little and let someone else take on a bigger role.'

'I know that isn't easy though,' I empathised. 'I know when I've had work done on the cottage, I've quite often wished I was doing it myself.'

'We're not control freaks,' Lizzie grinned.

'Of course not,' I smiled.

'We just like things done properly.'

'Exactly.'

'And having the right person to work alongside me will make all the difference,' she said meaningfully. 'By which I mean . . .'

'Potentially working with me.' I swallowed.

'No potential about it,' she confirmed. 'Definitely you.'

I could appreciate how big a deal this was for her. Trusting someone else with something you had worked so hard to create was not something that was lightly done and I would need to be one hundred per cent certain that I was ready for the challenge before I decided whether to accept the offer of becoming a part of the Cherry Tree family.

As I further mulled over what she had said, I knew deep down that I was partway there already. I had absolutely no desire to leave the area and I was becoming more involved with the community each and every day thanks to Lizzie encouraging me to take on the autumn festival. That said, I still wasn't about to jump in feet first. Not when my life had already so suddenly become so full.

'I appreciate that it's a lot to take in,' Lizzie said kindly, 'and that it's come completely out of the blue.'

'You can say that again,' I smiled.

'And I can also tell, given what you said yesterday about going from being home alone to doing so much, that it would be a huge change for you too, but given how brilliantly you've organised the festival, I know you can do it. No pressure though!'

'Thank you for that.' I nodded, feeling a very heady mix of emotions.

'And if it helps your decision at all, I'd be more than happy for you to bring Pixie to work with you.'

'I was going to ask about her.' I smiled, feeling delighted that she could be involved. 'What would the hours be?'

'Part-time hours, around twenty to twenty-five. Maybe more at certain times of the year and when you were opening the gallery on my behalf.'

That didn't sound too onerous.

'And how would you feel if I came along to help with a couple more workshops while I think about it?' I asked. 'I'd really like to get more of a feel for what you offer and have a proper look around the gallery, of course.'

Lizzie looked thrilled. 'I would be delighted if you did that,' she agreed. 'It would give you a solid idea as to what you'd be letting yourself in for, wouldn't it?'

'It would. My only concern would be that if I ultimately decided that it wasn't the job for me, then you'd be left with no time to find someone else to take it on before you needed them.'

'Don't worry about that,' Lizzie insisted. 'I could easily find someone to fill in while I cast the net wider.'

I got the feeling that she truly had her heart set on me saying yes and although that was a little scary, it was also great to be wanted.

'All right,' I said, as I took a bracing breath and thought about what I'd earlier been considering when I stopped to look at the pumpkins. 'Leave it all with me and I'll come back to you as soon as I can.'

'I know you're swamped with the festival right now,' Lizzie said kindly, 'so there's no immediate rush.'

I appreciated that because even though I had the highest of hopes that it would all fall into place, I also needed some peace and quiet in which to think it through. What a wonderful autumn I was having and it had only just begun!

Chapter 18

Just as Lizzie and I had acknowledged, I now had plenty to think about and I spent much of the following week doing just that. My head was becoming increasingly insistent that the job Lizzie was offering me was exactly what I needed to make my future at Rowan Cottage even happier and also more financially secure. However, with so many changes happening and so much of the festival still to oversee, I didn't feel entirely ready to give her my answer just yet. I would wait until I had at least helped her in the gallery again before I completely decided.

I would have liked to talk about it with Mum and Dad, but I knew that they sometimes stressed about my financial security and didn't want them to nag me to jump at the chance of a regular pay check. In lieu of my parents, I also considered calling Ash, who had crept into my thoughts every time I dressed the bird tables, but then I worried that his continued silence might mean he had things happening elsewhere and I didn't want to be a nuisance.

It was a wonder to think that for so long I had kept things to myself and now, just a few weeks after walking back into the world, I wanted to discuss my plans and prospects with other people. It was quite a transformation and it felt a little frustrating that, for the time being at least, I couldn't do it.

'Oh well, Pixie,' I said, the night before the pick your own pumpkin patch at Skylark Farm was due to open. 'I think we should just put it a little further down the list of priorities for now, don't you?'

She yipped in response and licked my hand.

'I knew you'd agree.' I smiled, kissing the top of her head. 'All in good time.'

The pumpkin field was supposed to be open for business from ten a.m. that Saturday morning, but as I drove along the road towards it, it became obvious that we'd underestimated how many families would want to come along and take part. I felt certain that the weather, which was crisp, clear and bright, was playing its part in upping the popularity and novelty of the event and the visitor numbers were further bolstered as a result.

'Hey, Clemmie,' said Jake, after he'd flagged me down some distance away from the field entrance.

It would have been a job to spot where the field opening actually was because there were cars, trucks and vans parked on either side of the bumpy drove and in some places, they had turned it into a narrow single track with nowhere left to sensibly pass.

'What's going on?' I asked, as I checked there were no vehicles behind me. 'We did say a ten o'clock start, didn't we?'

'We did,' Jake nodded as he pulled off his hat and raked a hand through his hair, 'but there were so many people waiting by half nine, I thought we'd best make a start. I hope you don't mind.'

'Not at all,' I told him. 'I'm delighted the idea is proving such a popular one, but I'm not sure the police will agree if they come along and see the state of all this parking.'

'They wouldn't generally drive down here, but that's crossed my mind, too.' Jake grimaced. 'I've got plenty of help in the field now, so I can keep an eye out here and I'm trying to hurry folk along as much as I can without spoiling the experience for them.'

'Let's hope that after today, the novelty wears off a bit and then you'll get a steady stream of visitors rather than this mad rush.'

'That would definitely be better,' he agreed. 'But the field opening times will have to be limited because someone will always need to be here to monitor it.'

'Oh, yes,' I said, biting my lip. 'I didn't think of that.'

'Well, don't you worry about it.' Jake smiled, waving at a car that had just pulled up behind me. 'We'll sort something. Why don't you drive along to the farm, Clemmie? You can park there and walk back to the field if you'd like to take a closer look at it.'

I definitely wanted to take a closer look. I wanted to pick and buy some pumpkins to cook and decorate with, too.

'Will there be room for me at the farm?' I asked, as a car came to a halt right in front of me, close to where Jake was standing.

The driver honked the horn and my heart sank when I spotted who was in the driving seat. It was Jason.

'Yes,' said Jake, for the moment ignoring the irate new arrival. 'Amber has closed the gate to the yard to stop everyone piling in, but she'll open it for you. If anyone wants to visit the shop today, they're having to walk up from wherever they've parked along the drove.'

Mindful that there was also a car waiting behind me, I thought it best to quickly move along.

'Okay, thanks, Jake. I'll be back in a bit.'

I pulled my Land Rover as far over as I could, but Jason was determined to make the pass a tight and difficult one.

'What did I tell you?' he shouted up at me, as I tentatively drew level with him and almost touched his side mirror with my door. 'I told you this festival would be a health and safety nightmare!'

'A little bit of give and take and we'll be fine,' I shouted back, keeping my eye trained on the road and my mirrors to help me judge the gap between us. If he turned his wheel just the tiniest bit we were going to come to grief and I was sure he'd love that. 'If you don't move, I can get through easily.'

He gave another blast on his horn as I eased by and I could see Jake shaking his head.

'Thank you for your patience,' I shakily said and moved off, trying not to let his determination to further find fault rankle me. I bet he didn't even need to be driving down the drove and had only turned out to cause trouble. 'Well done, Clemmie,' I breathed.

Just as Jake had said she would, Amber found me a spot next to some other farm vehicles, and I felt even more mixed emotions as I parked my Land Rover next to Ash's truck. I was pleased he was about, but he hadn't let me know that he was back in Wynbridge, so I hadn't known whether to expect to see him or not. I felt as though I would have liked to have been more prepared, though heaven knows why.

'Hey, Clemmie,' Amber smiled. 'And hello, Pixie,' she added, as I freed her from her harness and lifted her off the seat while another stream of cars drove by.

'Hi, Amber,' I smiled back as I decided not to mention that Jason was making the parking situation even more difficult than it needed to be. 'Where do you reckon all these people have come from?'

I set Pixie down and the farm Labradors rushed over to say hello. I knew the three dogs were well acquainted so I was happy to leave Pixie to mix and mingle.

'Far and wide from what I can make out!' Amber laughed. 'We hoped the pick your own field would be a good idea, but we had no idea it was going to be quite so popular.'

'Me neither,' I commented. 'But then, with nothing else like it around here, I suppose it was bound to have a certain novelty value.'

'And make us some money to help cut our losses after our buyer moved the goalposts,' Amber tutted. 'If we turn a profit from this, we'll do it again next year over a longer time and with some proper parking arrangements in place.'

'I'm sure whoever organises the festival next year will be delighted to hear that,' I smiled. 'That is, assuming the festival happens again.'

Given that I'd already talked about the following year's possible event before, I didn't want people thinking I was making assumptions.

'Oh, I'm sure it will,' she nonetheless winked. 'And with you at the helm.'

'Do you really think so?'

'I do,' she said. 'You're doing our dear friend Moses proud

and the only way you'll lose the gig now is if something goes drastically wrong and I can't see that happening.'

'Well, I hope it won't,' I said and crossed my fingers as I tried not to think about Jason and his desire to cause issues when really there were none.

Had I not just had a run in with him, I might have felt as convinced as Amber then sounded.

'It definitely won't,' she insisted. 'Now, can I offer you a cup of something?'

'Thank you, but no. I'm going to head straight back to the field. I want to bag some pumpkins before you sell out, and help a bit, if I can.'

Obviously, as festival organiser, it was important that I put in an appearance, but on this occasion, I was as interested to see Ash as I was to play a part.

'I don't think we'll sell out just yet,' Amber laughed. 'But as you're going to be up there a while, you can leave Pixie here if you like. It's muddy in the field and she'll be fine with these two.'

'I had planned to keep her with me, but with so many cars on the drove, I'd have to carry her *and* the pumpkins, so I'll take you up on that. Thanks, Amber.'

With Pixie settled in the farmhouse kitchen, I tucked my jeans into my wellies, pulled on my hat, scarf and coat and walked back to the field. Thankfully, there was no sign of Jason, but I had to continually step on and off the road as some people left and others arrived. I chatted to a few of the families as I went along and loved seeing their rosy-cheeked children stoically carrying small, but still heavy pumpkins, while the adults with them staggered, bow-legged, towards their vehicles with much bigger ones.

'We've never done anything like this before,' one mum told me. 'The children were so excited to pick their pumpkin for Halloween fresh from the field, rather than out of a box in the supermarket. We won't carve it yet, though, and I've still no idea what to do with the flesh. I usually just bin it.'

'Don't do that this year,' I told her. 'I've got a great soup recipe at home. I'll post it on the festival online page later and you can give it a go if you fancy it.'

'Oh yes, please,' she said. 'I'm keeping up with the online chat and that would be great. You're Clemmie, aren't you? The festival organiser?'

'One of them,' I modestly said.

'Well,' she smiled, 'you're doing a brilliant job. We've loved everything so far.'

I had a spring in my step by the time I reached the gate and took in the sight before me. There were people swarming all over the field and next to the gate, there were a range of different sized pumpkins with prices painted on, along with a huge wooden bin full to the brim that customers could buy from direct if they didn't fancy doing any actual picking themselves.

Looking at the state of some of the people, I could see it was a bit of a mucky pursuit and I was pleased I wouldn't have to carry both Pixie and my pumpkins back to the farm.

'Clemmie!' Jake called and I headed over to him.

'How's it going?'

'Not bad. I've got someone else watching the road now and we've got enough volunteers to cut the pumpkins when the customers have settled on which ones they want.'

I hadn't thought about that aspect of it.

'And what about the parking situation?' I asked. 'Have you had any complaints? The drove is still heaving.'

'A very quick random visit from the local plod just now, who I have a feeling that Jason might have encouraged to come along, but I placated the officer with a huge pumpkin.'

'Well done you!' I laughed.

It felt good to get one over on Jason who was determined to ruin everyone's fun.

'He said he'd overlook the situation today, but going forward, we will need a better system in place.'

'Amber said you might consider doing this again next year if it's financially worthwhile.'

'It already is,' he grinned. 'So, yes, next year will definitely be going ahead and with proper planning in advance.'

'Jake!'

We both turned around and I felt my heart thump hard in my chest. It was Ash who had called him and he looked as taken aback to see me as I was thrown off guard to see him. Obviously, I had known he was about, because I'd parked next to his truck, but I hadn't spotted him in the field when I arrived and felt that my body's reaction to seeing him – my tummy had taken a bit of a tumble, along with my heart picking up the pace – was rather over the top.

'How much for this one?' he shouted to Jake and pointed at a massive pumpkin that was going to take some shifting.

'That one's not for sale!' Jake called back. 'It should have a sticker on it.'

Ash shook his head, having not caught the tail end of what Jake said.

'Jake!' called someone else.

'I'll tell Ash what you said,' I offered and walked off towards him, thinking it would be easier to start a conversation on the back of what Jake had said, as opposed to from scratch. 'Hi.' I swallowed when I reached him.

'Hey,' he said, looking at me, but only for the briefest moment.

'So, how much is it then?' asked the man standing next to him.

'I'm sorry,' I told him, 'but Jake said this one isn't for sale. It's supposed to have a sticker on it somewhere.'

Ash looked on the ground around it.

'Oh, here it is,' he said, picking it up. 'It must have fallen off. Any pumpkins with these stickers on aren't for sale. Sorry, folks.'

The couple walked away looking disgruntled.

'You pulled that sticker off,' tutted the woman to the guy as she plucked at his sleeve. 'I saw you do it.'

'Oh dear,' I said. 'He's in trouble.' Ash focused his attention on trying to get the sticker back on. 'They never would have been able to carry it anyway.'

'You're right. It's a bit of a monster, this one.'

He was still fiddling with the label.

'I didn't know you were back,' I said casually.

'I told you I'd be here in time for today,' he mumbled, as he finally finished faffing. 'I said I'd be here.'

'Oh yes,' I said, thinking back to our last conversation and then wishing I hadn't. 'You did, didn't you? How were things in Bakewell? How's your nan?'

'She's doing well,' he said, shoving his hands in his pockets. 'I helped make a couple of adjustments to the annexe for her, which has helped.'

'Time well spent then,' I said, shifting from one foot to the other as I wondered if his standoffish manner was the result of still feeling the impact of our silly near miss at the Fenview Feast.

It was the only thing that I could think of that might account for his unusually detached behaviour. I'd pretty much parked it the night it had happened, so why hadn't he?

'I think so,' he said, finally looking at me. 'Or I had thought so.' He swallowed and looked away again.

I had no idea what he meant by that.

'The bird tables are proving popular,' I told him and I hated the slightly desperate edge I could hear in my tone. 'Now the birds are getting the measure of them, there's always something on them. The goldfinches are the biggest gluttons, but that could be because there seem to be more of them than anything else.'

'It was a good time of year to get it all set up.'

'Yes,' I said. 'I suppose it was. The birds will be completely used to feeding from them before the weather really changes, won't they?'

'Exactly.'

'I've missed you this week,' I then blurted out. If he wasn't going to say it, then I would.

'Have you?'

'Yes,' I said. 'I have. Loads has happened since you've been gone and I wanted to talk to you about it.'

'To do with the festival?'

'No,' I said, feeling exasperated. 'To do with me.'

'Right,' he said.

'If my memory serves,' I said, starting to feel hot and fed up to be the one doing all of the running, 'we're friends, aren't we? And friends discuss things?'

'Yes,' he grimaced. 'Of course.'

'So, can we talk?'

I could see a family heading in our direction, weighed down with a variety of pumpkins.

'Can we pay you for these?' the man asked. He sounded out of puff. 'I've got cash.'

'Yes,' said Ash, in a completely different tone to the one he'd just addressed me in. 'Let's add up what you've got.'

'We've got loads!' boasted the youngest child, who was wrapped up as if it was the depths of winter they'd ventured out in.

Ash totted up a total and then offered to help carry the haul back to the field entrance while the woman went ahead to get their car.

'No, you're all right, lad,' the man said and staggered off. 'I can manage.'

'Jake could do with some wheelbarrows or trolleys,' Ash said, looking after him. 'Someone's going to slip a disc at this rate.'

'I can see you're preoccupied,' I sighed and went to walk off. 'Perhaps I'll catch you later.'

'I don't think we'll get a chance to talk today,' he said, as he pulled off his hat. 'I'm going to be on deputy duty all day.'

'Another time then.' I shrugged and then I did walk away.

'You're all right though, aren't you?' he called after me.

'Yep,' I said, turning to face him and giving him a thumbs up. 'Never been better.'

I didn't much feel like hanging around, but I didn't want Ash thinking his sudden unfriendliness had driven me away either, so I stuck it out and actually, by lunchtime, I had almost forgotten about him and was happy helping Jake. There were patches of the field that already looked barren compared to when I'd arrived and Jake was wondering if he was going to need to expand the pick your own patch to a larger site the following year.

'I better head off,' I told him, when there was a brief lull. 'I can't leave Pixie with Amber all day and I need to check the details for tomorrow's spring bulb planting event.'

'I hope you have a good turnout for that,' Jake said kindly.

'The interest has been so great that everyone who wants to plant has had to register,' I was proud to tell him.

'That was a good idea,' he said. 'Perhaps timed entry would have worked better here . . .'

'To be honest,' I said, thinking of the bulb planting, 'I didn't expect so many people would want to do it, so I'm pleased we've gone down the preregistered route. It would have been chaos otherwise.'

'Um,' he said thoughtfully, obviously still thinking about what had occurred in the pumpkin field that day. 'And it was good of Harriet and Rachel at the garden centre to offer so many bags of bulbs, wasn't it?' he then added.

I had forgotten that they were all such close friends, so Jake and Amber would know all about that.

'It really was,' I agreed. Harriet, and her partner, Rachel, had been very generous with their donation and they had agreed to come along with their bulb planters for anyone who didn't have their own trowels, too. 'And it was great that Tom got the council to agree to a site to plant in so quickly, too,' I added. 'I can't wait to see it in full bloom next spring.'

We were, under the supervision of the council parks department, going to be allowed to plant the bulbs in an area of the town park that usually didn't attract much attention. There had been talk of installing a couple of benches there the following year too, so I hoped that would also come off.

'You'll be as stiff as a board on Monday,' Jake laughed. 'What with all the carrying today and the bending tomorrow.'

'It's all good exercise,' I laughed.

'In that case,' he nudged, 'as you're feeling fit, why don't you take a walk around our new nature trail before you head off?'

'As wonderful as it sounds,' I told him, 'and I've been hearing good things all day, I'm going to save it for another time. What time are you closing up here today?'

'Fair enough,' he smiled and checked the time on his phone. 'You're always welcome. Officially we're finishing at half two, but if there are a few stragglers, I won't mind hanging on.'

'Well,' I said, 'I hope the idea continues to be a popular one.'

'Me too,' he agreed, as another customer came along to pay. 'It's got us out of a right fix. I'll see you soon, Clemmie.'

'Yes, see you again soon.'

I looked around the field ahead of walking back to the farm with three small, but heavy pumpkins of my own in a couple of string bags, but there was no sign of Ash. I hadn't meant to look for him and gave myself a bit of a telling off as I marched back, then an even more severe one when I caught sight of him next to his truck and my heart kicked again.

I had been about to call out to him, when I realised he was talking to someone. It was a young woman. She had been sitting in his cab, but climbed out and carried on what looked like an intense conversation which ended with a long hug. Clearly, Ash wasn't averse to talking to all of his female friends. Assuming she was a friend . . .

Stupidly, I hid out of sight, behind a tree which was conveniently next to the gate and waited until Ash had driven off and the woman had walked to the bottom of the yard. Then I ducked into the farmhouse, thanked Amber for looking after Pixie and headed back to Rowan Cottage feeling frustratingly far less happy than I had when I left it that morning.

Chapter 19

That evening, with the support of a couple of large glasses of wine, I did a great job of convincing myself that as I now had more friends than I could shake a stick at, the loss of one wasn't really any loss at all. However, when I woke late the next morning, thick-headed and unusually roused by an alarm I'd somehow had the foresight to set, I wasn't quite so convinced.

'Blimey,' commented Joanne, when I arrived at the park, feeling unsettled and rushed, to help get everything set up ahead of the bulb planting. 'What's happened to you?'

'Nothing's happened to me,' I said tersely, as I shielded my eyes from the glare of the sun and wished I'd taken a couple of painkillers. 'I've just got a bit of a headache, is all.'

'Where did you find it?' she smiled. 'At the bottom of a bottle?'

'I had two glasses of wine last night,' I said defensively, even though I wasn't accountable to her or anyone else for that matter. 'Just two.'

'Lightweight.'

'I think I'm coming down with something,' I said, which made her laugh far too loudly for my sensitive scalp.

My phone vibrated in my pocket, cutting off her chance to further tease me. It was a text message and not a very long one.

'No sign of Ash,' said Joanne, as she looked around while I read the message. 'I thought he'd be here by now.'

'He's not coming,' I told her as I tucked my phone away again. 'That was a message from him, saying he can't make it because Will is off sick and he's got to cover his on-call shift for him today and already has someone to see.'

Given our strained and somewhat one-sided conversation the day before, and my current fragile state, I felt relieved not to have to see him again so soon and go to the effort of having another potentially stilted exchange. Especially with Joanne in attendance.

'That's a shame,' she sighed, sounding disappointed.

'It can't be helped.' I shrugged, as if it didn't matter, though I couldn't then help wondering if Will *really* was sick, even if the thought did do Ash a disservice. 'And if there is something going about,' I further said, before walking off, 'I really might be coming down with it, mightn't I?'

Thankfully, given the state of my thumping head, I was in attendance at the bulb planting as a setting up volunteer and participant rather than part of the event management team, and once everyone had been ticked off the registration list and been issued with bulbs and tools (if they didn't have their own) by Harriet and Rachel and told where and how to plant by the park staff, I headed to my designated space and set to.

It didn't take me long to make a slit with my sharp trowel, pop a miniature daffodil bulb in and cover it over and, given the tight band still wrapped around my head, the pressure of which increased tenfold every time I bent over, I was relieved about that.

I knew that come the spring this part of the park was going to be a riot of welcome colours and scents, but on a chilly October day, and when I wasn't feeling at my best, that felt rather a long way off and not all that easy to imagine.

'Are you done?' Joanne asked, and I showed her my empty bag and the spot where I'd clustered my bulbs together for maximum impact. 'Me too.'

'I wouldn't have had you down as a gardener, Joanne,' I commented.

'I'm not really,' she said, inspecting her nails, 'but I thought it would be nice to leave something positive behind when I leave.'

'That's really lovely.' I smiled, feeling surprised that she'd considered that.

Perhaps my thoughts that all might not be well in her world weren't wide of the mark, after all.

'A reputation for being a chatterbox isn't the thing I want to be solely remembered for,' she then said, making me feel even more convinced that something was amiss.

'But you have such a talent for it.' I nudged her, thinking this could potentially turn into the moment to ask her how she was really feeling about her move abroad. 'And you've also had success with your matchmaking which is nice and will be fondly remembered, too.'

'And I'll tell you what else is nice,' she then said, before I had a chance to work my way up to the more sensitive side of things, 'working in the gallery. I know Lizzie has now asked you to consider working with her once I've gone and I really hope you are.'

'She has,' I confirmed, 'and yes, I am.'

Whatever was bothering her, she clearly wasn't wavering about actually leaving, which was a relief because the evening before, I had fallen to thinking that if I accepted the job and she then stayed, that could be awkward. I knew Lizzie had said Joanne wouldn't want the increased responsibility she was offering, but even so . . .

'Good,' Joanne said firmly. 'I mean it. I know I'm not perfect for the role, but I couldn't have worked for a lovelier team. If I were in your position, I wouldn't think twice about taking it. Unless you're thinking about moving on again, in which case you shouldn't join her, because that wouldn't be fair to Lizzie.'

'I'm not planning on going anywhere,' I told her.

'Does that mean that knocking the cottage about has helped rebuild your heart?'

I took a breath, but it didn't abate the unusual subsequent flash of temper.

'You just can't resist the urge to say the wrong thing, can you, Joanne?' I snapped, feeling cross with her again and just when I had thought how lovely it was that she cared about Lizzie. 'There's nothing wrong with my heart but if there was, you'd be the last person I'd tell.'

'Oh,' she said, sounding shocked to have been so harshly told off. 'Right.'

'I know for a fact that Ash has told you to stop poking your nose into my life,' I said even more sharply as I screwed the empty brown paper bulb bag up with some force, 'so if I were you, I'd take his advice to *your* heart and leave mine alone.'

I didn't hang around to find out how she was going to react to that. I very rarely lost my temper, but my head was still thumping and if I was being honest, I was still smarting over Ash's frosty return. None of that was Joanne's fault, of course, but she did have a knack for winding me up and this time, I'd let her know it. So much for seizing the moment and becoming a shoulder for her to lean on should she need it!

Early the next morning, and with thoughts of Ash's lukewarm return and the ticking off I'd given Joanne firmly banished, I called Mum and Dad to talk about when would be best for them to visit and with a view to delaying them a little. I wasn't exactly regretting my former eagerness to show them what I had set in motion, but with everything other than the festival feeling in a muddle, I wasn't sure I could cope with them descending and staying with me just yet.

'But isn't that when it's all over and done with?' Mum frowned, in response to my suggestion that they should come in November.

'Not at all,' I said, guessing that she'd been perusing the festival events pages. 'The weekend I'm suggesting is actually the *grand* finale and there's going to be all sorts of celebrations happening in the town along with a party in the pub. And,' I added, hoping it would be the clincher to delay them driving down and as a result, give me a little more time to get my ducks back in a row, 'it will be the best chance I have of introducing you to everyone.'

Assuming I still had friends left to introduce them to by then . . .

'But we rather fancied being with you for Halloween,' Dad chipped in. 'We could come for an even longer weekend then.'

'Yes.' Mum nodded keenly. 'There looks to be loads organised for that.'

'But it's mostly kids' stuff,' I explained, which was true. 'Films in the town hall, followed by a procession around the square. The finale events will be more up your street.'

'I think Clemmie's right,' Dad said to Mum, after having mulled it over. 'We want to get to know her friends, don't we? And if the last weekend of the festival will be the best time to do that, then I think we should go then.'

Mum looked at me and smiled. 'All right,' she relented. 'We'll come then.'

'In that case—' I started to say, but then someone knocked on the cottage door and Pixie began to bark. 'Oh, sorry,' I apologised. 'Someone's at the door.'

'We'll talk later in the week,' Mum said as I blew her a kiss and ended the call.

'Just a sec!' I shouted as whoever was visiting knocked again.

In spite of our former awkwardness, I rather hoped it was going to be Ash, but it wasn't.

'Can I come in?' asked the gargantuan floral bouquet I found on the doorstep. 'This weighs a tonne and my arms are about to give out.'

'Joanne,' I said, failing to keep the sigh out of my greeting. 'Yes, come in.'

'I hope these are okay?' she asked, as she transferred the flowers from her arms to mine and I almost buckled under their weight. 'I hope they're the sort of thing you like.'

Given that they were an autumnal extravaganza of dahlias, chrysanthemums and grasses in my favourite colour palette, they were perfect.

'They're beautiful, thank you,' I said, staggering to carry them into the kitchen with Pixie trying to jump up to see if there was anything hidden among them for her. 'But what have I done to warrant them?'

I propped them in the sink and turned around.

'Put me in my place, of course.' Joanne blushed. 'Given me the talking to that my mum then carried on with when I got home and told her why you'd snapped my head off.'

'I see.'

I rather pitied Joanne's mum. She must have needed the patience of a saint to cope with a full-on daughter like Joanne.

'And you did it with good reason, Mum said.' Joanne grimaced, puffing out her cheeks. 'And I know she was right. I know you were right, too. I've had a think back over all of our conversations and I'm really sorry that every time we've talked, I've done little other than try to dig into your past.'

'Well,' I said, 'you do sound sorry.'

'I am,' she said, sounding sincere. 'I really am. It's just that you and Ash would make such a lovely couple.' She wouldn't have said that if she'd seen us at the pumpkin picking. 'No,' she then said crossly, shaking her head and wringing her hands. 'Never mind. None of my business. I'm butting out.'

'I really do hope you mean that,' I said sternly.

'I do,' she said passionately. 'I really do. I know I got on Ash's nerves when he first moved here and now, I've wound you up too. I've no desire to leave Wynbridge under a cloud, so I'm committing to taking care of my own business from this moment on and only my business.'

'Well.' I smiled, hoping she'd be able to stick to that declaration and wondering if this was finally the opportunity to ask her what she was really feeling about leaving. 'That's music to my ears and the flowers are the perfect apology. One of my absolute favourite things, in fact.'

I endeavoured to always have a fresh vase or jug of flowers in the cottage, but since I'd become involved with the festival, I'd let the tradition slip a bit. Joanne's fabulous peace offering would more than kick it off again. In fact, I wasn't sure if I had enough jugs, vases, pots and jars to hold them all. What a wonderful issue to have!

'Finally, I've got something right.' Joanne smiled.

'Would you like a coffee while I make a start on arranging them?' I offered.

She considered her answer.

'No,' she finally said. 'Best not. I'm only just getting the hang of this not being a pain in the backside behaviour and I don't want to bugger it up on my first day.'

'In that case,' I then suggested, thinking this really was too good an opportunity to miss, 'how about we switch that scenario around? You stay and *I* potentially make a hash of saying something wrong to you, rather than the other way around?'

She looked wary, but agreed.

'So,' I said, as I began deconstructing the elaborate bouquet and filling the containers I'd gathered together and half filled with water, 'Lizzie tells me you're definitely leaving Wynbridge at the end of the year.'

That was common knowledge, but I had to start somewhere.

'Yes,' she said, passing me one of the dahlias. 'That's right.'

'And heading off to . . .'

'Germany,' she said on an out breath, which I for one hadn't known. 'Aiden and I are moving to Germany.'

I waited for her to carry on because she usually had so much to say for herself, but she didn't and when I considered it, I realised she hadn't sounded all that keen on her and Aiden's destination.

'And how are you feeling about that?' I therefore asked.

'Not good!' she burst out after a brief pause. 'I don't know anyone there. Or a word of the language. I've been trying to learn, but I just can't get to grips with it. I had thought I was going to be joining Aiden in Australia, which is where he is now and where I know a few people, and the language of course, but he's taken up the offer to be relocated to Germany!'

'I see, well—' I started to say, but the dam was breached and the words that poured out of her were determined to keep flowing now they'd been given the chance.

'I've actually been trying not to think about it,' she rushed on. 'Which is why I've stayed so focused on you and Ash, even though I said I wouldn't.' That certainly explained her continued preoccupation with us. 'And then, when I realised that you'd been living on your own for so long, I started to wonder if I could do it, too . . .'

And that accounted for the questions about my current lifestyle and her 'lone wolf' comment to Ash in the café.

'But you don't really want to break up with Aiden and live on your own, do you?'

'No!' she gasped. 'But maybe I could get my own place and we could do long distance, long-term, because I don't want to move to Germany with him, either. I was rubbish at languages at school and the thought of having no one to talk to . . .'

'I can see how that might be an issue for you,' I quipped,

in an attempt to make her laugh, but her eyes filled with tears and I realised I'd said the wrong thing. 'Sorry,' I apologised.

'I suppose I deserved that.' She sniffed, handing me another stem.

'Perhaps.' I nodded. 'But I am truly sorry that you're feeling this way. We all thought you were super excited about going. Everyone thought you were really keen.'

'When I thought I was going to Australia, I was super excited,' she explained. 'Really, really keen, but I don't want to live in Germany. Not that I've got anything against the country, but how am I going to find work there or make friends if I don't speak the language?'

It was certainly a conundrum and not one I had an answer for.

'Anyway,' she then nudged me, 'not everyone thought I was keen, did they? You'd obviously worked out I'd had a change of heart about my big departure, even if Lizzie and Jemma hadn't.'

'Well,' I said. 'I was privy to a conversation they didn't hear and I've picked up on a couple of things while you've been talking to them, too.'

'I think I've been getting on their nerves too much for them to take any real notice of me,' she said. I wasn't sure that was entirely true because they were simply so busy, but I didn't interrupt. 'And I know that's my own fault, because in my effort to distract myself from what's to come, I've gone into meddling overdrive and rubbed practically everyone I love up the wrong way. It's little wonder my boss hasn't seen anything's amiss, is it?'

She sounded utterly forlorn and I put down the flowers and gave her a hug which she willingly accepted.

'What does Aiden have to say about it all?' I asked her, when we broke apart.

'Oh, I haven't told him,' she said, with a wave of her hand. 'The move to the German office is a good promotion and I can't take the shine off that for him. He'd be devastated if he thought I was unhappy, so I'm just going along with it all.'

'As selfless as you think keeping quiet is, Joanne,' I seriously said, 'it's not going to help in the long run, is it? You absolutely have to tell him how you feel.'

'Do I?' She swallowed, looking tearful again.

'You know you do,' I said more softly. 'Because it will all come out in the end and he'll be so upset when it does. Please, talk to him sooner rather than later, because the clock is ticking.'

She let out a breath.

'I suppose you're right,' she said. 'The countdown is definitely on, but how can I tell him that I don't want to go?'

'I bet,' I said, 'if you put half as much energy into trying to find the words as you have into your matchmaking, you'll have a speech prepared in a heartbeat.'

She did smile at that.

'I daresay that's true,' she said. 'Thanks, Clemmie. It's been good to offload. I haven't even told my mum how I'm really feeling.'

'Well, you should,' I told her. 'Now, let's have a coffee and you can have a minute to gather your thoughts before you head home and start putting this situation right.'

I gave Joanne a few minutes' peace and once she'd left and I had congratulated myself on picking up on and addressing her discontent, I took my time arranging the rest of the flowers to my satisfaction. I then spent even more time photographing them. It didn't matter where I put them, they looked perfect and I knew I'd be moving the arrangements around the entire time they were at their best.

As well as arranging Joanne's floral apology and hoping that she would be able to both solve her own predicament and stick to her vow not to meddle, I also posted the soup recipe I'd mentioned to the woman I'd met at Skylark Farm because I'd forgotten about it before.

As I pottered about, I did my best not to become preoccupied thinking about the frostiness Ash had come back from Bakewell with and how I might be able to thaw it. I really did try not to dwell, but I can't say I succeeded for the whole of the time, and what occurred the next day put him very firmly at the forefront of my mind again.

'You'll be seeing Will today, Pixie,' said the cheerful receptionist in the vets when we arrived a few minutes ahead of the appointment time for Pixie's vaccination and check-up on Tuesday afternoon.

'Not Ash?' I frowned. 'I thought the appointment was scheduled so Pixie would see Ash.'

The receptionist checked her screen and shook her head. 'No,' she said. 'It's definitely Will.'

'Oh,' I said. 'Right. I must have got it wrong, then.' I knew I hadn't, but there was nothing to be gained from arguing the point, even if I had hoped that with Pixie between us, we might have taken the opportunity to get back on an even keel. 'I take it Will's recovered?'

'Yes,' said the receptionist, without any hesitation which

suggested his illness had been genuine. 'He's fighting fit now. Take a seat and he'll call you through when he's ready.'

I sat as instructed and shortly after, Will came out and introduced himself. Pixie, who had been rather cowed since we arrived at the practice – obviously having an idea of what she was in for – suddenly perked up no end and I liked Will as a result.

'How's she settling in?' he asked, once the vaccination had been administered and Pixie had been weighed and given a general once over amid a lot of fussing.

'Like she's been with me forever,' I was very happy to tell him. 'She had a couple of melancholic moments when she first arrived, but she seems consistently happy now.'

'Well,' said Will, ruffling Pixie's coat, 'she's certainly the picture of health. Though that said, you should never underestimate grief in animals or humans. It can come back—'

'Yes,' I cut in. 'I know how grief operates.' I hadn't meant to sound so blunt. 'And don't worry,' I added in a softer tone, 'I'll keep a close eye on her.'

'Ash was very lucky to find you,' he then smiled at me.

'Was he?' I swallowed.

I wasn't sure either Ash or I would agree with those words now.

'Yes,' Will said, looking slightly pink as he gave a nod to my furry friend. 'To take Pixie, I mean.'

'Oh, yes,' I agreed, as I lifted her off the treatment table. 'I was perfect for taking Pixie.'

I couldn't wait to get out of the building after that, but I wasn't even halfway across the car park when I realised I'd have to go back in again because I'd forgotten Pixie's prescription.

I'd paid for her wormer but, in my haste to rush off, I'd left the bag on the counter.

'Damn,' I muttered, as I turned us around. 'Come on, Pixie.'

'You can come out now!' I heard Will say loudly as I opened the door again. 'She's gone.'

He had his back to me and was flicking through a drawer of one of the filing cabinets behind the reception desk.

'I forgot to take this,' I said, feeling mortified as I snatched up the bag which was still on the counter. He could only have been talking about me and it was obvious who he must have been talking to. 'I'm properly going now.'

Will spun around to look at me, just as a door at the far end of the practice opened. I didn't hang around to see who came out of it and I didn't look back as I strode out.

'Bye,' I stammered and rushed off again.

I didn't think I could have felt more of a fool if I'd tried. Not only did it seem that Ash didn't want to talk to me, he didn't want to see me, either. I had no idea what it was that I'd done to provoke such a sudden and dramatic turnaround, but it didn't bode well for our friendship and it wasn't going to do much for us running the festival together, either!

Chapter 20

The next evening, the cloud cover was too dense to catch even a glimpse of the full moon, so I didn't bother sitting out, but I did feel grateful that Molly, the so-called Wynthorpe Witch, had alerted me to the lunar cycle before I'd checked it myself and I hadn't gone to the trouble of setting up Draconid meteor shower stargazing events as a result.

Even though the forecast predicted clear skies going forward, the brightness of the only just waning moon would have made it hard for attendees to spot much and with my friendship with Ash in ruins, a night out with him under the dimmed constellations trying to keep everyone entertained was the last thing I would have wanted. Assuming he turned up.

Before I'd taken Pixie to the vets I had felt resolved to clear the air between us, but the fact that he'd changed the appointment and then gone in to hiding to ensure he wouldn't have to see me, spoke volumes and I began to realise I'd put my faith in the wrong friend.

Consequently, I spent some time coming up with excuses I could make and situations I could conjure to avoid running into him for the next few weeks. It would be easier once the festival was finished, as long as I remembered to book Pixie's future appointments at the vets to specifically see Will, but in the meantime, I'd just have to remain in stealth mode and on guard whenever I thought it likely that our paths were going to cross.

Ash was the only person I'd talked to about Callum since my move to the Fens and, even though I hadn't shared much, I regretted telling him that I was a widow and that I'd closed my heart to any prospect of love in the future. Ash hadn't turned out to be the friend I'd hoped for and knowing that I'd shared such intimate details after knowing him for such a short time only served to make me feel even more of a fool.

'Never again,' I said vehemently, as I went around the cottage and pulled the curtains closed to shut out the night. 'I'll learn the lesson and never share that part of myself with anyone I don't know again.'

They were harsh words, fiercely spoken, and, in that moment, they were most sincerely meant.

When I got up the following morning, there was a message on my phone sent from Amber at Skylark Farm, asking me if I might have the time that evening to walk around the nature trail and give my opinion on the lighting they'd installed and whether I thought a couple of autumnal moonlight walks might be a suitable addition to the festival schedule.

Personally, I thought the idea had the potential to be another health and safety nightmare for Jason to flag, and it was that concern which prompted me to say that yes, I would be happy to call in and take a quick tour. There were still some dates on the festival calendar that coincided with the next lunar cycle that might work out, so it was paramount that the idea was given careful public participation consideration. Not that I was going to be liable for any potential mishaps, such as trips over tree roots – that would be Jake and Amber's responsibility – but I was nonetheless eager to eliminate any further grumblings from Jason.

'Come on, Pixie,' I said, as she wrestled with the pretty plaid coat I'd bundled her into. 'Best feet forward and all that.'

The yarn bombers, now they'd finished decorating the square, were knitting a variety of autumn themed outfits for dogs with a view to having a 'best dressed' competition at some point. I had been rather taken with the pumpkin outfit and wanted to enter Pixie for judging wearing that, but if she objected this much to a bog-standard coat, then I didn't reckon much for my chances of wrapping her up in an orange orb!

'If you stop worrying at it,' I told her as she gave me a martyred look, 'you'll soon forget you're even wearing it.'

There were a couple of vehicles parked up when I arrived at the farm, but with Amber already waiting for me in the yard, I didn't have a chance to work out if they belonged to the family or notice if Ash's truck was amongst them.

'Clemmie,' she said warmly. 'Thank you so much for turning out to do this tonight. We really appreciate it.'

'I'm happy to,' I told her. 'It's a wonderful idea and, as long as the path is safe to walk in the dark, it will be an interesting addition to the schedule.'

'That's what we thought, too,' she smiled. 'And with you having such a wonderful grasp of everything, we thought you'd be the best person to ask.'

'That's exactly what you said to me just five minutes ago, Amber,' said a voice behind me and I spun around.

'Ash,' I gasped, as I felt my tummy tumble. 'I didn't know you were going to be here.'

'Likewise,' he responded and turned bright red.

Given his behaviour over Pixie's appointment, I hoped he felt as mortified as he deserved to. I wasn't sure how I felt.

'As you're *both* so involved with the festival,' commented Jake who then joined us, 'we thought we'd ask the pair of you to walk the trail.'

'That's fair enough,' I breezily said, taking the high ground. 'In the interests of the festival and the safety of its attendees, I think that's a great idea.'

'Me too,' said Ash, but he didn't sound as convinced as I did.

'Right then, let's go,' I said, and tried to get Pixie to move, but she was still so preoccupied with tugging at her coat that she missed my cue for her to budge and I nearly tripped over her.

'What on earth is she wearing?' Ash frowned.

She then realised he was there and gave him a welcome that pierced my heart. I bet she wouldn't have bothered with him had she known he'd hidden from the pair of us just the day before.

'A coat,' I bluntly said. 'It's cold.'

'It is cold,' Jake then said. 'So, why don't you two head straight off and then we'll have a bite and something to drink when you're done?'

I didn't much like the thought of walking the trail with just Ash for company and I was certain he wasn't going to want to be alone with me, either.

'You two aren't coming?' he asked, with a nod to Amber and Jake, confirming that thought.

'No,' said Amber, 'we need to check on the kids and if we come around, we might influence you. You need to experience it for yourselves, really.'

'In that case,' I said, 'Ash needn't come at all because he's walked it already.'

'Not in the dark,' Jake pointed out.

'Right,' I tightly said. 'Let's go then.'

'See you in a bit,' said Amber as she and Jake headed over to the farmhouse and I followed Ash down the yard, through a gate a little way into a field and then to the start of the trail.

We didn't speak until we were at the start, when it became obvious that you could take the path in either direction.

'Right, I think I'll go around this way,' I pointed, when I could see he was going to head the other way. 'We can meet back in the yard when we're done.'

'You don't want to go around together?' He frowned and I shook my head.

'Given your behaviour in the vets, on the back of the frosty welcome I received in the pumpkin field, I hardly think you're going to want us spending any more time together than we have to, are you?' I huffed.

'Oh god, Clemmie,' he groaned. 'I'm so sorry about what happened in the practice. You must think I'm a total idiot.'

'To tell you the truth,' I sniffed, 'I've been far too busy feeling embarrassed for myself to consider what my thoughts are about you. Apart from the fact that I keep wishing that I hadn't ever got to know you in the first place, of course.'

Apparently, my sharp tongue wasn't exclusively reserved for challenging conversations with Joanne. Though I hoped, now she'd bared her soul and we'd got to the bottom of her frustrating behaviour, I'd had the last of those.

'I suppose I deserved that.' Ash swallowed and he looked so heartbreakingly upset that I almost forgave him. Almost. 'Will you let me explain?'

'Another time, perhaps—'

'I wish you would,' he pleaded. 'Please walk with me, Clemmie, because I really want to tell you why I've been such an idiot.'

He began to walk away and my head told me it was time to cut my losses, apologise to Amber and Jake and head home. I could still see where my Land Rover was parked in the yard and it would be easy enough to leave, but my heart was having none of it. There was some internal conflict playing off inside me and it kept me rooted to the spot until my heart finally won out and I followed Ash on to the path.

We walked some of the way in silence, and in single file, each of us focused on keeping our feet, especially along the stretches that weren't specifically lit and where the brightness of the moon didn't pierce the tree canopy. It might have been autumn, but there were still plenty of leaves on the trees and I couldn't help thinking that even though it was doubtless a beautiful walk, it wasn't a particularly practical, or safe one in the dark.

'There's some seating among the trees about halfway round,' Ash said, over his shoulder, 'we can talk properly there.'

'Rather than walk and talk?'

'If you don't mind.'

I didn't reply and a short while later, the path opened out and we found ourselves in a clearing which was lit by fairy lights and looked to be the prettiest part of the trail so far. In the dark, anyway.

'This is nice,' I said, looking around.

'The lights look great, don't they? Jake said he was setting something up here.'

'Really great.'

'They're not solar because it's quite shady here, so I'm not sure how he's running them.'

The small talk was fine, but my heart hadn't won the battle with my head to discuss the aesthetics of outdoor illumination.

'Ash—'

'I know,' he said, pulling off his hat and pushing a hand through his hair. 'I know. I'm sorry. I thought I'd have worked out what to say by now, but I'm still not sure where to start.'

'How about,' I suggested, 'you get straight to the point and tell me why you've suddenly turned from new friend and trusted confidante into someone who makes me feel awkward and embarrassed?'

'I wish you hadn't put it like that,' he said hoarsely.

I risked a look at his face and could see his eyes were bright as if they were shining with tears, but that couldn't possibly be the case, could it? Given that he was the one who had initiated the distance between us, first with his trip to Bakewell and then through his cold and odd behaviour since his return, I couldn't imagine he was feeling that emotionally moved.

'But it's the truth.' I shrugged, determined to be honest. If we were going to salvage anything, honesty had to be the way to go. 'Awkward and embarrassed is exactly how you've made me feel. And regretful, too,' I added, for good measure.

'But those are the last emotions I want you to associate with me.'

I looked at him again.

'How can I believe that when you've barely spoken to me since you've been back from your parents' and you hid from me in your place of work. You actually hid, Ash. And you've obviously talked to the people you work with about whatever it is that I've done wrong, rather than talk to—'

'You haven't done anything wrong,' he cut in, wringing his hat in his hands.

'Well, forgive me for thinking I hadn't done anything right!' I laughed without humour as my annoyance with him began to properly prickle.

Pixie whined and I picked her up and kissed the top of her head.

'You know, I think I should go,' I said, the words catching. 'The last thing I want is Pixie feeling upset, too.'

'I don't want either of you feeling upset.'

'Well,' I said, as I turned away, 'you've got a funny way of showing it.' I took a couple of steps back to where the path carried on. 'Please make my apologies to Amber and Jake and tell them I'll call them tomorrow.'

'It was the Fenview Feast!' Ash then blurted out and I turned around again. 'It was what happened that night, when we were dancing. I—'

'Nothing happened,' I interrupted.

I had known that had been the start of it.

'But it *almost* did,' he said, then shouldered all of the responsibility for our not-quite post-dance kiss. 'And I've hated myself for it ever since.'

As cross as I was with him, I couldn't allow that.

'Well, if you're so keen to apportion blame, then you have to allow me a slice of it, too,' I insisted, but Ash shook his head and wouldn't hear of it. 'I got just as *almost* carried away as you did,' I reminded him.

'No,' he said. 'No.'

'But why not?'

'Because I should have backed off sooner. Because you had told me that when your husband died, you had closed your heart and that you were never going to fall in love again and I therefore should have behaved better. That's why I object to you being at fault.'

'But I wasn't falling in love with you at Fenview,' I pointed out. 'I was dancing with you, Ash. And enjoying it. I hadn't done it in a very long time.'

He took a minute to process that.

'So, you're saying that you honestly felt that there was nothing deeper to what happened than that?'

'Nothing deeper at all,' I insisted as I firmly pushed away the memory of our bodies pressed together and the feel of Ash's warm hands on my back. 'You know there wasn't. It was just dancing.'

'Just dancing . . .'

'And I'm sorry,' I added, with a small smile, as I tried to inject a little humour into the situation now it had finally been broached, 'but I have to tell you, your moves aren't *that* good. They didn't even earn you a kiss in the end, did they?'

'Only because my phone started to ring and cut the moment off,' he said croakily. 'It could have happened otherwise; you can't deny that.'

'Well,' I said, unwilling to further consider the possibility, 'we'll never know now, will we? And besides, I'm grateful that we didn't kiss because we're friends, or supposed to be, not friends with benefits, and an adrenaline fuelled kiss could have really confused the situation and killed off our relationship.'

'I see,' he puffed, as he shoved his hat back on his head. 'Well, I'm the one feeling mortified now.'

'Why?'

'Because you've clearly not given it another thought,' he muttered. I wasn't about to refute that, even though it wasn't true and bent my desire for honesty right out of shape. 'Not in the same way I have, anyway. And I've gone and made too much of it and ruined everything between us in the process, haven't I?'

'You haven't ruined everything,' I insisted, feeling relieved that we seemed to be getting back on track, 'but you've definitely made too much of it. I barely gave the moment headspace once you'd left,' I blagged, 'but you've gone into hiding over something that didn't even happen. You've been acting like a nine-year-old.'

'Hey!'

'Well, honestly,' I couldn't help but laugh at his put-out expression. 'You have. You know you have.'

'I suppose,' he confessed begrudgingly. 'But can we say it's done with now we've finally talked about it?'

'Yes.'

'And you really mean it when you say that I haven't ruined our relationship?'

'I do. But—'

'No but.'

'But,' I carried on, 'should something like this come up again, not that we're ever likely to almost kiss in the future, but if something occurs that you're not sure about, please talk to me before you run off.'

'Now, I really do feel nine and like I've had a telling off.'

'Well, perhaps you deserve it.'

'I know. I'm sorry,' he apologised. 'Truly sorry. Friends again?'

'Definitely friends again.'

He held out his hand for me to take and seal our bond and I swear that when our fingers touched, there was more than one meteor that shot across the night sky. I had to fight the urge to snatch my singed fingers back from his grasp and I spent the rest of the evening in something of a daze.

Chapter 21

I had hoped my dazed demeanour had gone unnoticed but I knew it hadn't, because Ash telephoned early the next morning to ask if I was feeling okay and it was more than disconcerting, the way my heart skittered when his name flashed up on my phone.

I strove to put my physical response, and my out of character reaction to his hand holding mine, down to feeling relieved that we had cleared the air and that I hadn't lost the closest friend I had made in the Fens so far.

It was either that, or I'd caught the bug that seemed to be doing the rounds and it had muddled my head. Both were entirely feasible explanations as far as I was concerned and I clung to them to keep me afloat.

'Hey, Clemmie,' Ash said brightly when I answered his call and I could hear the smile in his tone. 'How are you feeling this morning?'

'I'm not sure.' I frowned. 'Why do you ask?'

'I don't know really,' he laughed. 'You just seemed a bit . . . odd after the walk last night.'

'Odd?' I squeaked.

'Perhaps that's not the right word.' He chuckled at my reaction. 'Sorry. Just not quite yourself, I suppose is what I really mean.'

'That's probably because I felt a bit bad about telling Amber and Jake that we didn't really think the trail worked in the dark,' I suggested, thinking his description of how I'd been wasn't actually all that wide of the mark.

'But they didn't seem to mind and Jake said he was happy to make further improvements ahead of the festival next year, didn't he?'

'I suppose. Perhaps you're right. I am actually feeling a bit . . . strange. Maybe I'm coming down with the bug that's doing the rounds. Or perhaps it was the influence of being out under the just waning moon . . . or something.'

Even I rolled my eyes at that, but there was something going on with me that I couldn't account for. I'd ended the trail with Ash feeling like a completely different person to the one who had started it.

'I think it must be the bug,' Ash responded teasingly. 'Perhaps you've got a temperature because you sounded almost delirious then.'

'Hey!' I objected.

'You sounded more like Molly than Clemmie. That's the sort of thing that she'd come out with.'

'Well,' I said. 'Perhaps it's time I embraced my . . . inner witch.'

'Definitely delirious,' Ash laughed. 'Shall I call round?'

'No,' I said, perhaps a little too quickly. 'Thank you,' I then more calmly added. 'I'll be fine. If the bug does strike, I have all the meds, blankets and fluids I need to see myself through it. You don't want to risk catching it. You were lucky not to pick it up from Will.'

I still couldn't think about his boss without a flush of embarrassment and felt my cheeks turning pink.

'Well, as long as you're sure?' Ash asked, sounding serious at last.

'I am.'

'In that case, I'll leave you to it. Let me know if you're not up to announcing the window display winners on Saturday and I'll do it on my own.'

'Oh, I'm sure I'll be fine for that.' I really hoped I wasn't going to have to miss playing my part in the announcement because I was delighted with our choices. 'But perhaps you could pick up the box from the town hall with the public votes in and take care of those?'

'Consider it done,' Ash promised. 'I'll pick them up and count them and I mean it, Clemmie, if you need anything in the meantime, anything at all, just call.'

'I will,' I said. 'Thanks, Ash.'

'My pleasure.'

I flopped back in the chair when he'd hung up and stared at my phone as if it might contain the answer to something. When I looked up, Pixie was watching me curiously, with her head cocked and wearing the same puzzled expression I imagined I was.

'I don't know either.' I shrugged. 'Perhaps I need a tonic or something.'

I managed without the tonic and the bug didn't land, so I was able to potter about the cottage, update AutumnEverything and even have another quick tidy up in the garden ahead of the weekend. By the time I set off to Wynbridge late Saturday morning, I was feeling excited about the prospect of going around and letting the shop winners know where they'd been placed.

There were autumn stalls set up on the market and I could see the yarn bombers had been out in force again. Every bollard, post box and sign now had something adorning it and the square looked utterly idyllic. Someone had even added some real pumpkins to the central display and it was with an almost happy heart and feeling almost full of the joys of autumn, that I made for The Mermaid to meet Ash.

I say almost, because there was something that was stopping my buoyant mood from being completely pumped up. I couldn't put my finger on what it was and tried my best to brush the feeling off, but the confusion slash apprehension was determined to linger and ensure my utterly blissed out state didn't quite scale the heights that the sight of Wynbridge decked out in autumn colours should have reached.

'Hey, Ash.' I smiled, when I spotted him waiting for us in the pub and Pixie and I headed over to his table, thankfully with no silly reaction occurring within the confines of my ribcage.

My heart was already skipping along after my walk around the chilly square, so its increased pace was doubtless the result of that.

'Hey,' he said, looking up and taking me in. 'How are you feeling?'

I settled Pixie under the table, then unwound my scarf and took off my coat. Jim and Evelyn had a fire roaring and Ash's choice of table was quite close to it which explained the sudden rush of warmth I was experiencing. Coming in from the cold and into the heat of the pub was bound to make me feel hot.

'I'm good,' I said, sitting down and looking at him. 'Really good.'

Was it my imagination, or were his eyes even bluer than usual? Perhaps it was the fact that I was looking directly into them, rather than up at them?

'Not still feeling out of sorts?' he asked, his brows pushed together.

'Not really,' I said, looking around, 'though . . .'

'Though what?'

'Oh, I don't know.' I frowned, as I tried to put my finger on exactly what it was that was bothering me. 'I don't feel unwell exactly, but . . .'

'Perhaps it's nerves?' Ash suggested.

'Nerves?'

'Yes,' he said. 'Perhaps you're feeling jittery about handing out the awards.'

'Oh yes,' I said, latching on to the idea, because nerves would explain the apprehension, if not the confusion, 'you might be on to something there.'

'Everyone knows it's happening today,' Ash carried on, further strengthening his suggestion, 'so it's bound to draw quite a crowd and given your aversion to being the centre of attention, Clemmie—'

'Yes,' I cut in, 'that's it. Of course, that's it. Phew! I'm feeling better already. Thank you, Ash.'

'Hey,' he shrugged self-deprecatingly. 'That's what friends are for.'

'Quite,' I said, as Pixie circled around my feet. 'And we all need a friend, don't we? I think Pixie has the jitters, too.' I tutted.

'I think Pixie is protesting to that coat you've made her wear again,' Ash laughed back.

'It's a lovely coat.' I pouted, pleased to have changed the subject. 'She just needs to get used to it.'

Neither Ash nor Pixie looked inclined to agree.

'Anyway,' he said, 'let me get you a drink and then we'll get down to business.'

'Is there business?' I frowned.

'Yes,' he sighed. 'There is a bit. What can I get you?'

'Just a coffee, please,' I requested as it felt too early for beer or wine.

He came back with my drink and a bowl of water for Pixie, which she noisily lapped at.

'I hope there isn't an issue with the public vote,' I said, as Ash sat back down and finished the coffee he'd been drinking when Pixie and I came in. 'It isn't a tie, is it?'

I had been mulling over what he could possibly want to talk business about while I watched him at the bar and it was the only thing I could think of.

'There is an issue with the public vote,' he told me and I felt my shoulders tense up. 'Though I have no idea whether it was a tie or not.'

'Oh crikey,' I said. 'Go on. What's happened?'

'The ballot box has been stolen.'

'What?'

'The ballot box has gone. Someone must have taken it.'

'What, the whole thing?' I gasped and he gave me a look.

'Sorry,' I said, shaking my head. 'Of course, you mean the whole thing.'

'I went to pick it up from the town hall and it was gone,' he explained. 'And no one else has moved it, because I've checked. It was literally there one day and gone the next.'

'Why didn't you tell me before?'

'Because I knew there was nothing you'd be able to do about it and I didn't want to disturb you unnecessarily in case the bug had landed.'

I could hardly object to his kindness and he was right, given that the box had disappeared into thin air, there wouldn't have been anything I could do to make it magically reappear. There were limits to my powers as festival organiser.

'According to Tom,' Ash further said, 'who was possibly the last person to see it, before the person who took it, of course, it was almost full to the brim with voting slips.'

'That makes it even worse, doesn't it?' I groaned. I was starting to feel angry now the initial shock had worn off. 'It was such a lovely way to make everyone feel involved and some mean-spirited sod has gone and spoilt it. Who would do something like that?'

'I can think of one person,' said Ash, with a nod to the far end of the bar.

I followed his gaze and was shocked to see Jason nursing a pint and looking comfortably at home.

'I thought he'd been barred,' I said in a low voice.

'Me too.'

'You know, I bet it was him,' I grumbled. 'He insinuated at the launch that I might not find the festival all plain sailing.'

'Oh, did he now?' said Ash, sitting up straighter and puffing out his chest as he pinned Jason with a look of pure loathing. 'Well, we'll see about that.'

'It's fine,' I said, laying a hand on his arm, because he had been about to stand up. 'There's no need for heroics, though your gallantry is appreciated.'

'I just don't want everyone missing out,' he said and I took my hand away now he'd stood down. 'Not after so many people bothered to vote.'

'They won't miss out,' I said, as a possible solution fortuitously sprang to mind. 'I've got an idea that will mean it can still happen.'

'What are you thinking?'

'How about,' I suggested, 'we award our winners today as planned, then make an announcement about the ballot box being stolen and set up a new one somewhere else for safekeeping—'

'Like in here or in the café, you mean?'

'Yes.' I nodded. 'That's it. The café would probably be best as so many families go in there and maybe we could change the vote slightly,' I carried on, feeling further inspired to make the most of the horrible situation. 'We could ask people to only vote for windows that haven't been placed by us and that way, the rest of the shops will get another chance.'

'That's a great idea,' Ash agreed. 'Everyone's bound to be disappointed about what's happened, but this is a brilliant solution, Clemmie.'

'As long as Jemma is happy to look after the ballot box.'

'I'm sure she will be.'

'In that case,' I said, as my stomach growled, 'let's quickly grab some lunch and then get the new plan underway.'

'I'm up for that,' Ash said, picking Pixie up and readjusting her coat while I quickly finished my coffee and then put my own coat back on. 'There's a wood-fired pizza stand set up on the market today. Can I tempt you to something from that?'

'You certainly can,' I confirmed keenly. 'It's ages since I've had one of those.'

We both picked the same toppings and the pizzas were delicious. Generous amounts of mushrooms, pancetta, Gruyere and caramelised onions covered the thin, crisp bases and we ate them on one of the benches that had been arranged where the stage had been on the day of the launch.

It was the perfect spot to people-watch from and we were on the lookout for any shady characters who might know something about the case of the disappearing ballot box. Being Wynbridge though, of course, and with Jason still in the pub, there were none.

'I didn't expect you to eat all of that,' said Ash, when I handed him my empty box.

'You sound disappointed,' I laughed.

'I am,' he said. 'I was hoping for a nibbled edge at least.'

'I'm not sure that's the sort of thing you say to a friend,' I pointed out and then wished I hadn't because it caused a blush to bloom.

'Oh crikey,' said Ash, also turning rosy. 'Not friendly territory at all. While I go and recycle these boxes, you can completely forget I said that.'

I was more than happy to oblige.

We'd printed certificates and had them framed for the winning shop owners to either add to their window displays or hang in the shops. Second and third place had been awarded to the delicatessen and jewellers respectively, and the overall winner was Hardy's, the art supplies and stationery shop which had used Keats's poem, 'To Autumn', as its inspiration.

All of the windows were beautiful, but that one was especially lovely with a wonderful display of many of the seasonal treasures Keats described and the poem copied out on a piece of parchment in the most exquisite calligraphy, and suspended amid flying paper swallows, at its centre.

Quite a crowd had gathered to follow Ash and I about as we did the rounds and unbeknown to me, Jemma's husband, Tom, had called the local press and a photographer turned up to listen to what was being said and take photographs.

Again, I hoped I wouldn't get a mention, but as festival organiser I supposed it was inevitable that my name was going to feature more at some point. The photographer certainly seemed to being taking a lot of photographs in my direction, but perhaps I was just being paranoid. Given the invasive media interest following Callum's death, I still wasn't much of a fan of the press and was very aware of him as a result.

Between us, when we had finished in Hardy's, Ash and I took the opportunity to explain to everyone who had gathered about why the public vote couldn't also be announced. In the face of my reprised anger and frustration over the ballot box, I forgot about the photographer and wasn't nervous about addressing everyone either.

'But who would do that?' someone at the front of the crowd asked angrily and lots of other people joined in. 'Who would be that mean?'

'That's what we'd like to know,' Ash sighed. 'So, if you have any information at all, do please let either myself or Clemmie know.'

Happy smiles had been replaced with furrowed brows and, as furious as I still was about what had happened, I quickly moved the announcement on in the hope that it wouldn't bring down everyone's mood and spoil the day.

'But not to worry,' I said robustly, 'because we're having another vote to make up for it and today's winners have agreed to not be included, so all of the other shops are in the running for this one.'

'And we'll be keeping the ballot box somewhere else,' Ash added. 'We'll let you know where as soon as we can.'

'Jemma has said you can put it in the Cherry Tree!' Tom shouted from the back.

'Fantastic!' Ash called in response, giving him a thumbs up. 'Thank you.'

We hadn't had a chance to talk to her yet, but Tom obviously had and she had kindly stepped up.

'Let's not let one naysayer spoil everyone else's fun!' someone else piped up.

'Hear! Hear!' was the rousing reply and I felt delighted to see everyone coming together to make the most of the horrible situation.

Once the crowd had dispersed, Ash insisted he was hungry again, so we headed over to the café to fill him up on cake and thank Jemma personally for offering to keep the ballot box.

'Can we come in with Pixie?' Ash asked, as we lingered on the threshold.

'Of course you can,' Jemma insisted. 'Get in quick. It's freezing out there today. How did announcing the winners go?'

Both the café and the gallery hadn't been included in mine and Ash's deliberations. They both had stunning seasonal displays set up, but Jemma and Lizzie had asked not to be considered as they had both been involved with the festival's inception and felt they had a vested interest.

'Really well,' I told her. 'Though, as you know, we couldn't announce the public vote.'

'Yes,' she said, with a shake of her head. 'Fancy stealing a ballot box! I told Tom it should be reported to the police. You won't have to worry about me losing sight of it in here, because I'm chaining it to the counter!'

'Thank you, Jemma,' I gratefully said.

'How long is the vote going to be running for?' she then asked.

'How about a week?' Ash and I said together, then smiled.

We hadn't discussed it, but both had the same timeframe in mind. It felt good to be on the same wavelength as my deputy and now we were back on a proper footing, I wouldn't feel awkward if I needed to call on him for support. With so much of the festival still to take place, that would be more of a possibility than ever.

'That should be long enough,' said Ash. 'We can't really leave it any longer, because the winners won't have time to make the most of it.'

'I'll have to quickly get more ballot papers printed . . .' I said, pulling out my phone to make a note. 'If we find out who the culprit is for stealing the first lot, we'll bill them for ink, paper and wasted time.'

'I'll sort the forms,' said Ash. 'That sounds like a deputy's job to me.'

'Are you sure?'

'Absolutely.'

'Thank you, Ash.'

'And I'll sort another box, too.'

'Oh crikey,' I huffed. 'I hadn't even thought of that.'

'Have a word with Tom, Ash,' said Jemma. 'He'll be able to source another box.'

'Great,' I said, making a note of that, too.

Jemma then gave me a look I couldn't fathom.

'What?' I awkwardly laughed, feeling taken aback by the change in her, now the business of the day had been organised and discussed.

'You need to talk to Joanne,' she said, after a moment had passed. She sounded nothing like she had before, which was disconcerting. 'She thinks she might have put her foot in it about something.'

'Oh, crikey,' groaned Ash. 'What's she done now?'

'It won't be anything horrendous,' I told him. 'Because I know for a fact that she's turned over a new leaf.'

Jemma said nothing.

'Nonetheless, I think I'll wait for my cake,' Ash sighed reluctantly. He obviously didn't have the same faith in Joanne that I did. 'I've suddenly lost my appetite.'

'In that case, why don't you go to the gallery?' Jemma then suggested. 'It'll be quieter in there and I'll send Joanne round.'

'Hello, you three,' Lizzie greeted us when we walked in. 'I was hoping to see you, Clemmie, because I was going to ask if you fancied volunteering to help with the lantern-making workshop next weekend?'

'Oh, yes, please,' I said, still feeling unperturbed by whatever it was Joanne thought she'd slipped up and done because I didn't think it could be anything that bad. 'I'd love to.'

'I thought it might help you make up your mind about my offer,' Lizzie smiled. 'Not, as you know, that I'm trying to rush you.'

'Offer?' Ash asked.

I then realised that I still hadn't shared with him what it was that Lizzie had suggested.

'I'll fill you in later,' I told him.

'I'm intrigued,' he smiled.

The shop bell rang out before I could give him a clue and Joanne walked in looking red eyed and awful.

'Whatever's happened?' Ash gasped, the moment he looked at her.

'It was the flowers.' She swallowed, looking at me. 'It was the photo of the flowers.'

'Flowers?' Lizzie frowned, as she rushed to lock the door. 'What are you talking about, Joanne?'

'I was in the café,' she carried on, still looking at me, 'and it was my break, so I thought I'd have a quick look online.'

I felt the cogs in my brain start to turn.

'And I saw this photo of the *exact* flowers I'd given you, Clemmie, posted on my favourite Insta account, Autumn Everything.'

'Ah,' I said and Lizzie groaned. 'I see.'

'On the what?' frowned Ash, pulling his phone out of his pocket.

'Then, I realised I recognised the kitchen they were in, too,' Joanne continued, with a sniff, and Lizzie handed her a tissue. 'It was the kitchen at Rowan Cottage.'

'It was.' I nodded, because I couldn't deny it, but I did wonder why her working it out had prompted her to be so upset. 'It is.'

'So, I have guessed right then?' She swallowed. 'You are the person behind the account, Clemmie?'

'You have and I am.'

Ever since Lizzie's visit I had known there was an inevitability that if I invited someone into the cottage and they happened to be an AutumnEverything follower, they were probably going to recognise the backdrop to some of the images because it had happened with her.

However, I hadn't given that scenario a thought when Joanne had unexpectedly turned up, but I supposed that as long as it was close friends only and they kept their deductions to themselves, then I could live with that. I would have to if I was going to truly settle in the Fens as more than a home-loving hermit. That said, I might not be able to accept the situation quite so bravely if Joanne now said she hadn't kept her discovery to herself and her upset did hint that that might be the case.

'I knew it,' she winced, rather than crowed. 'But when I showed Jemma, she said I couldn't be right because Lizzie had been inside the cottage and never said a word.'

'That's because I can keep a secret,' Lizzie was quick to say. 'Even from my best friend, if I'm asked.'

'So,' I surmised, 'you, Lizzie and sort of Jemma now know . . .'

'And so does the customer who was in the café,' Joanne continued, making me feel less stoic by the second. 'He'd been listening to our conversation and as a follower of the account himself, he was keen to know why you hadn't used it to promote the festival.'

'Who was the other customer?' Ash, who was now scrolling on his phone, asked. 'My god, Clemmie! Are you an influencer?'

He turned the phone around and I saw my grid.

'Yes,' said Joanne, before I could say otherwise. 'She is.'

'I recognise that bookcase,' he commented, then carried on scrolling. 'And those cushions . . . '

'The other customer?' I asked Joanne. 'Who was it?'

'I guess you must have a good reason for keeping the account anonymous, don't you?' she perceptively asked me, rather than name them, as she distractedly shredded the tissue.

'Yes,' I said. 'I do. A very good reason and a very private one, too.'

'Oh no,' she then sobbed and let out a shuddering breath.

'I had a big social media following before on a different account,' I further said. 'But I had to shut it down, after . . .'

'Oh crikey,' said Ash, who looked up as my words trailed off.

It was the emotional vulnerability that I had experienced after Callum's death and the endless influx of messages and comments that landed, that had strengthened my resolve to keep both my face and my name away from AutumnEverything. A few local friends now knowing I was the person behind it was one thing, but Joanne seemed to be working her way up to saying that her revelation to the customer in the café had the potential to let *everyone* know.

And if that was the case, it could mean that my darling Callum was about to be dragged into the limelight again and, if his story did come to light, I was possibly going to be bombarded with more well-meaning but unwanted attention, too.

I realised then that Ash, Joanne and Lizzie were all looking at me.

'What's the reason?' Lizzie asked.

'Never mind.' I swallowed. 'You still haven't said who the customer was, Joanne. It wasn't Jason, was it?'

That would have been the worst, but I couldn't really imagine him being on Insta.

'No,' Joanne finally said. 'It was the photographer from the paper and he said he's going to tell the journalist writing the feature who you are. I'm so sorry.'

She started to properly cry then and Lizzie looked torn between ticking her off and comforting me.

'Well,' she huffed, rather than doing either, 'that will certainly spread the word, won't it?'

'Oh, Joanne,' I sighed, as I scooped Pixie up for a cuddle.

'What are you going to do?' Ash asked me.

I took my time to rationally consider that. As unsettled as I was by the thought of having to manage a situation similar to the one I had experienced before, I knew nothing would be gained from breaking down or flying off the handle or wishing I could turn back time. I'd attempted all three in the past and with mixed, but mostly, unsatisfactory results. It was done now and I had to face the outcome, whatever that turned out to be.

'Wait until the paper comes out and see what's written, I suppose,' I said as I buried my face in the comforting warmth of Pixie's fur.

Joanne might have been the one to let the cat out of the bag, but as I had recently immersed myself in local life, I think I had known, somewhere deep in the back of my mind, that this was going to happen one day. I was amazed that I could sound so calm about it now the time had come far sooner than I might have hoped, but of course my attitude might change if the journalist did go ahead and mention more than AutumnEverything. . .

'We could talk to the guy,' Ash suggested. Out of everyone, he was the only person who knew my backstory and was now obviously, and kindly, concerned, even though I was resigned to it potentially being exposed. 'Ask him not to tell the journalist who'll be writing the story up.'

I shook my head. 'No,' I said. 'We're not going to do that, because in my experience, word has a habit of spreading no matter what you try and do to stop it.' Lizzie looked at me and I wondered if she was thinking back to the day we'd met when I'd said something similar. 'And don't worry, Joanne. I know you didn't mean for this to happen.'

'I really didn't,' she sniffed. 'By the time I'd realised that if you'd wanted everyone to know about it, you would have said something by now, it was too late. Is there anything I can do to make it less of a mess?'

'No,' I said, putting Pixie down again. 'I don't think so and you never know, in the long run, it might not end up being as much of a mess as you think.'

'But I mean it.' She swallowed, clearly not comforted by my words. 'I'll do anything.'

'Well, in that case,' I requested, because she obviously felt the need to do something, 'go and ask Jemma for some cake. I have a sudden need for a huge slice of something sweet.'

Chapter 22

Left to my own devices that week I daresay I might not have remained quite as relaxed about Joanne's Greatest Gaff – as Lizzie had named it – but I had Pixie to cuddle at night and Ash was so kind and often on hand by day, that my thoughts never took the darker turn they might have succumbed to had I been entirely alone. While the countdown to the newspaper being published ticked down, Ash and I delved deeper into what I might decide to do before it did, in private.

'I got your message,' he said, on the Tuesday morning when he just happened to be passing – *just happened to be passing* was becoming a bit of a standing joke between us as it was happening on a more and more regular basis and I was never sorry to see him. 'You've definitely decided that you're going to give Lizzie, Jemma and Joanne the go ahead to start spreading the news that you're the person behind AutumnEverything before the paper comes out?'

'Yep,' I said, as I unhooked two of my favourite Emma Bridgewater mugs from the dresser top and spooned coffee into each of them. 'It feels inevitable that the account is going to be named in the paper now, so I want us to get in first and explain to as many people as possible that I haven't promoted the festival on my grid because that's not what Autumn Everything is about.'

'I agree that's the right way to go,' Ash supportively nodded. 'If you make that clear, then no one can say you should have used it, can they?'

'Some people still might.' I shrugged. 'I learnt long ago that you can't please everyone, but I'll feel better knowing that we've stated my case before Friday when everyone might assume that I'm only talking about it then because my hand has been forced.'

To a certain extent that would have been true, but I wasn't going to make a thing of it.

'That's fair enough,' Ash carried on, 'and if the journalist has the audacity to print anything beyond the account name, then let's hope folk won't be impressed with them and leave it at that.'

'That's the dream,' I said, holding up crossed fingers. 'My biggest fear is that people will want to seek me out and start telling me about their own tragedies again. I hope that doesn't make me sound heartless . . .'

'Given what you've now told me about the messages you received after Callum died,' Ash compassionately said, 'it doesn't make you sound heartless at all. You're still coming to terms with your own grief, so the last thing you need is to take on other people's.'

'It feels so good to have someone in my life who gets that,' I smiled.

I knew my parents would also understand, but I couldn't possibly worry them with this. Thank goodness for Ash.

'Good,' Ash smiled back. 'I'm pleased you feel that way. You know you can always lean on me.'

'I do know that. Thank you, Ash. And you know what,' I carried on, feeling confident, in that moment at least, 'I doubt the article will feature more than the account name. After all, this story isn't about me, is it? It's about the shop window winners, so really there's no need to mention me in any more detail than they need to discuss you. We were simply the people handing out the awards, weren't we?'

'That's true,' Ash agreed. 'And this is a small local paper we're talking about, not a raging red top. The photographer might have been interested in you, but the journalist might not think your history is newsworthy at all.'

'Let's hope we're both right,' I said, as I took the milk he handed me from the fridge and poured a little into each of the mugs, 'and we'll know soon enough.'

'I'm sorry you've been put in this situation though.'

'Me too.' I swallowed, feeling briefly less buoyant. 'It's the last thing I need to have to contend with when there's so much still to do for the festival.'

'Oh, Clem,' Ash softly said, 'come here.'

I put the milk down and he stepped nearer and pulled me to him. He wrapped me in his arms and held me close to his chest. I relaxed and laid my cheek against his firm body, feeling so safe that I didn't think I'd ever want to move away again. Pixie, however, had other ideas and barked until we broke apart and he picked her up in place of hugging me.

'Thank you for that,' I smiled. 'I really needed it.'

'Anytime,' he said, his cheeks turning warm and pink. 'Now, I hope you're not jealous, madam,' he then said sternly to Pixie as she licked his nose. 'There's room for more than one wonderful woman in my life, you know.'

Having seen him hug someone at Skylark Farm on the day the pumpkin field opened, I already knew that, but it didn't diminish my appreciation of the embrace he had just, with perfect timing, bestowed upon me.

I watched as he put Pixie down again and then I handed him back the milk to return to the fridge, in a move that felt well-practiced and familiar given the number of times he'd called in recently.

'I don't think you will have done, Ash,' I then unexpectedly heard myself say, 'because I'm sure I'd sense a change in you, but have you looked up online what happened to Callum?'

'Absolutely not,' he hastily told me, sounding a little offended.

'I'm sorry,' I quickly said. 'I don't know why I asked you that.'

'I have more respect for you than to do that.'

'I know you do,' I apologised again. 'I know. I'm sorry.'

'It's okay,' he then said. 'I suppose you were bound to wonder and there are probably plenty of people in my position who would have done. That said, before you start thinking it too, I'm sure Lizzie and the others won't have looked either.'

I nodded and poured the boiled water into the mugs, then thoughtfully stirred them both.

'What is it?' Ash asked, picking up that I was pondering something else.

'I can't seem to stop thinking,' I slowly said, now his hug had staved off the brief overwhelm and allowed more rational thoughts to return, 'and not only because of Joanne's Greatest Gaff, that it might be time I told a few people that I'm a widow.'

Ash's eyes widened and I wasn't surprised, because I was amazed myself. I had fleetingly considered the possibility before, but then put it on the backburner when faced with the busyness of organising the festival. I realised I hadn't been ready then; however, since Saturday, things now felt as if they were gathering steam and coming to a head.

'I've made some genuine connections here now,' I said aloud, to further explain my change of heart, 'and put down some roots that reach way beyond the cottage boundary. So, I think it might be time. What do you think?'

'I think,' Ash seriously said, 'that sounds wonderful and you're absolutely right.'

'Really?'

'Really,' he carried on eagerly. 'You've made wonderful friends here, Clemmie, and friends talk, don't they? They share things, secret things that might otherwise become a burden, they talk about their past—'

'They do,' I cut in. 'They do all those things.'

'You love Rowan Cottage,' he forged on, encouraged by my enthusiasm, 'and you love Wynbridge now too, and I think you want to settle here *properly*, but you won't be able to do that if you're constantly looking over your shoulder and worrying that someone might find something out about you that you've left unsaid, will you?'

'I won't,' I acknowledged. 'And I'd always be scared that if my story did come out and I hadn't said anything, then my friends would be hurt because they hadn't known one of the biggest things about me. Being widowed, at such a young age, is a huge thing to keep from those you care for, isn't it?'

'It is,' Ash agreed. 'And you know as well as I do, that friends, true friends—'

'Share.'

'Exactly,' he smiled kindly and I handed him one of the mugs. 'Obviously, you don't have to tell everyone, but I do think that telling those closest to you will help you live a much fuller life here. It will help your friends build up a picture of you as they get to know you better, too. I know that I understand you more as a result of what you've shared with me.'

'You do?'

He looked at me for a long moment.

'Yes,' he said, then looked away. 'Knowing that you've loved and lost, that you've lived through this immense tragedy in your young life, explains a lot.'

I let out a long breath. Ash had a knack of making me feel seen. Seen, heard and understood and I valued that immensely. I could imagine he and Callum would have been friends, but I wasn't sure how the thought of that made me feel . . .

'What has it explained?' I asked and Ash pulled his gaze back to mine.

'We'll get into that another day,' he said, scooping Pixie up again with his free hand. 'Right now, we need to think about how we can quickly spread the word about AutumnEverything.'

'Oh, that will be a breeze,' I smiled. 'I'll just give Joanne the go-ahead to gossip.'

'Fair enough.' Ash nodded. 'And that will leave you free to talk to Lizzie and Jemma about Callum, won't it?'

'Yes,' I agreed. 'Though that doesn't feel like it's going to be anywhere near as easy.'

*

Early Wednesday evening, Ash and I drove into town separately as he was on call, so I could talk to Lizzie and Jemma in the café once they'd both closed up for the day. Joanne had a conveniently scheduled call with Aiden, so it would be just the three of us. I wondered if she had yet broached the subject of not wanting to move to Germany with him, but that was something I could ask her another day.

I had the conversation with Lizzie and Jemma all planned out and, as well as sharing some of my past, I was going to let them know that they could give Joanne permission to talk about me being the person behind AutumnEverything, and that they could also share my identity, too.

'Are you sure you don't want me to hang around?' Ash asked, once we'd parked up. 'I don't mind.'

'No,' I told him. 'I'd rather do this on my own, but I appreciate you offering. I'll walk over to the pub and meet you there when we've finished talking.'

'All right,' he said, taking my hand and giving it a squeeze. 'I'll see you there. And remember, Clemmie, this is your rodeo.' I smiled at that. 'You can say as much or as little as you want to.'

'As long as I say something, now that I've made up my mind to.'

'Exactly.'

Lizzie and Jemma were waiting for me as previously arranged and Jemma had set out almost a complete afternoon tea for us to feast on while we talked. It was a pity I had no appetite.

'Are you sure you wouldn't like one of these little apple and cinnamon pastries?' she offered, while Lizzie poured us all tea.

'They're so moreish,' Lizzie confessed. 'I can eat at least a dozen in a single sitting.'

'She can,' Jemma agreed, popping one in her own mouth and picking up another.

She'd clearly forgiven Lizzie for not saying anything about Rowan Cottage being the backdrop for AutumnEverything and that I was the face behind it, which was a relief.

'They do look wonderful,' I said as my tummy turned over. 'Perhaps I'll have one in a minute.'

'If there's any left,' Lizzie laughed, picking up three. 'Now come on, have you, by any chance, come to tell us that we can share the news that you're the person behind Autumn Everything ahead of Friday?'

I picked up a paper napkin and laid it on my lap.

'I have actually,' I told her. 'And so can Joanne. I know you've got some customers who follow the account because it came up in the workshop I helped you with, didn't it?'

'Yes.' Lizzie nodded. 'It did and I was already thinking they'd be the perfect people to find out first. We've still got a couple of days before the paper is published, so we can easily get the word out by then.'

'And this way,' Jemma grinned, 'we can have our say on your behalf and justify why you haven't used the account to promote the festival and what's printed in the paper after that won't come as a surprise to anyone.'

'Oh,' I said, with a rueful smile. 'Some of it might.'

'What do you mean?' Lizzie asked, between mouthfuls.

I screwed the napkin up and held it tight in my hands. 'Well,' I began, 'I know there's a chance that this won't be mentioned in the paper because it isn't relevant, at least I'm hoping that's the case, but I've decided that I'd like you both, as my friends, to know anyway.'

'Go on,' Lizzie said softly.

The change in her tone suggested that she'd picked up that I was poised to share something deep and meaningful, rather than something frivolous.

'I was once married,' I quickly carried on, getting straight down to it as I tried to ignore the painful lump which had already formed in my throat, 'and my husband, Callum, was killed in a freak accident in the town we grew up in and still lived in.'

In perfect tandem the two friends gasped and their hands flew to cover their mouths. They didn't say anything, but the sudden injection of deep shock into the room felt almost tangible.

'It was all covered very widely in the media,' I continued shakily, 'and eighteen months after his death, I moved to Rowan Cottage with the intention of privately processing my grief and trying to move my life on away from the shadow of public interest which dogged my steps, my thoughts, my everything really . . .'

'Oh, my darling girl,' Jemma sobbed.

'That's the reason why I've kept myself to myself for so long,' I carried on. 'There was an overwhelming amount of public interest in what happened and strangers used the house renovation account Callum and I previously had to constantly message me and share their own tragedies. I know it was all well-meant, or most of it was anyway, but it became too much for me to deal with in the end—'

'Oh, Clemmie,' Jemma further cried. 'That would have been too much for anyone to handle, wouldn't it, Lizzie? No wonder you shut yourself away.'

'We had no idea,' Lizzie said.

She looked and sounded absolutely shellshocked.

'I did wonder if you might have looked me up online when you recognised the cottage,' I confessed to her. 'But I realised you hadn't the first day I visited the café and I can tell you haven't since, either.'

'I had no reason to Google you, but if I had, and found this out, there's no way I would have been able to pretend I didn't know,' she confirmed.

'I'm even sorrier that your name has come to that journalist's attention now,' Jemma said, sounding deeply upset.

'And so was I when Joanne told us what had occurred on Saturday, but I've been thinking about it since then and talking to Ash—'

'Good old Ash,' Lizzie smiled, sounding a little more like herself again.

'And I'm not anywhere near as concerned now,' I carried on forthrightly. 'The focus of the story will be about the shop window winners, not my past. AutumnEverything might get a passing mention but that will be it.'

'Should be it,' Lizzie corrected.

'Yes,' I said. 'Fingers crossed.' And I held mine up to stress the point.

Jemma let out a ragged breath. 'You must have been so young when it happened, Clemmie,' she sniffed and I realised she hadn't heard any of what I'd said about the paper, because she was still trying to absorb my heartbreak.

'I was,' I confirmed. 'Callum and I were both very young. And we'd only been married a year and a half.'

'That's the most terrible tragedy.'

'It is,' Lizzie agreed, then added, 'And no wonder you didn't want Joanne playing Cupid and trying to shove you and Ash together.'

'Though you sound very close now,' Jemma pointed out as she wiped her eyes.

'We are,' I confirmed. 'He's a wonderful friend and a truly trustworthy confidante. I'm blessed to have him and I should go really, because he's waiting for me in the pub.'

Lizzie and Jemma both gave me a hug and I felt like a weight had been lifted from my shoulders. I had known my decision to talk to my new friends had been the right one and I was grateful for Ash's encouragement to do it sooner rather than later. I might have a tricky few days to come, but with friends by my side, I'd get through it. Friends who knew the whole of me now. There was nothing hidden.

'I can't even begin to express how sorry we are that you've been through this, Clemmie,' Lizzie said, as she kissed my cheek. 'And I'm even more sorry that Joanne has been the person responsible for the mess.'

'I mean it, please don't worry about Joanne,' I told her. 'Because this truly doesn't feel like the mess I once thought it would be. I'd already started thinking about sharing my past in my present, so Joanne's indiscretion has just sped things along a bit.'

'But you must be worried about AutumnEverything,' Jemma sighed. 'It's not going to be anonymous anymore, is it?'

'Probably not,' I resignedly said, 'but I'll think more about it after Friday. There's no point prophesising and worrying before the paper is even published. Whatever occurs, it will doubtless be a flash in the pan anyway.' That was the hope I was hanging on to. 'How is Joanne, by the way?'

Lizzie gave the question some thought. 'I'm not actually sure,' she frowned. 'She's certainly not been her usual self since the weekend but I get the feeling there's more going on than her stressing over talking to the photographer when she shouldn't have done. Why do you ask?'

'I just wondered,' I shrugged. 'Because I could tell how truly upset she was.'

Joanne's worries about her move weren't mine to discuss and I felt no inclination to return the favour she'd done me by saying more than I should. I was certain it would all come out at a time of her choosing, rather than mine.

'I do admire you, Clemmie,' said Jemma, who still looked close to tears. 'You're so kind to be thinking of Joanne and so brave, too.'

'I'm not always brave,' I swallowed, then added, 'and I do appreciate that you haven't asked me what happened to Callum. If you look online for Clemmie and Callum Bennett, you'll find everything you need to know. I still struggle to say the words . . .'

'Of course you do,' said Lizzie, pulling me in for another hug, which Jemma immediately joined in with.

I took my time crossing the square. I wanted a few seconds in which to collect myself and my legs were shaking so badly I didn't think they'd carry me if I tried to walk at pace. The cat was completely out of the bag now, but at least I'd been the one to release it.

'Clemmie!' I turned around and discovered it was Jason of all people who had called my name.

'Not now, Jason,' I said, and hurried through the pub door.

As it was early, the bar was quiet but I couldn't see Ash. I pulled my phone out of my bag to find he'd sent me a message, apologising that he'd had to leave because of an emergency. He hoped I was all right and would check in with me later.

'Damn,' I muttered, feeling shaky all over again.

'Hey,' said someone behind me as they caught the top of my arm and I leant into them. 'Are you all right?'

'Jason,' I said, as I levered myself away from him. 'I'm fine. I just need to go home.'

'You don't look in a fit state to go anywhere,' he frowned. 'Go and sit down and I'll get you a drink.' I opened my mouth to object, but he shook his head. 'Please.'

He neither looked nor sounded like his usual belligerent self so, hoping I wasn't going to regret it and feeling too unsteady to resist, I went to sit at a table.

'Here,' he said, a minute later as he put a glass in front of me and sat in the chair opposite. 'Drink that. It's only Coke, fully loaded mind, because you look like you need some sugar. I saw your Land Rover parked up earlier, so I knew you wouldn't want a brandy in it.'

The drink was cool and refreshing and I did start to feel better once I'd guzzled most of it down.

'Thank you,' I said. 'What do I owe you?'

'Just five minutes of your time,' he requested.

'You aren't going to have a go at me, are you?' I said, pushing my chair away from the table again. 'Because I'm in no mood for that. Or are you going to confess to being the person who stole the window dressing public ballot box?'

'No, I'm not going to have a go at you,' he hastily said. 'And no, it absolutely wasn't me who took that box.'

'It wasn't?' I gasped.

'No,' he said again. 'It was not. I've no idea who was responsible for that, but it wasn't me. I can understand why you assumed it might be though.'

I was completely taken aback that it wasn't him and wondered who else it might have been. There was no one on my radar. As far as I knew, everyone else was a fan of the festival . . .

'Anyway,' Jason said, when I didn't apologise for mistakenly thinking he was the culprit, 'it's something else I want to talk to you about now.'

'I'm sorry,' I rather bluntly said, 'but it will have to wait, because I really need to get home. Pixie is waiting, and—'

'I just want to say that I'm very sorry for your loss,' he then blurted out, while staring at the table. 'I'm sorry that you were widowed at such a young age and in such a tragic way.'

'You what?' I gasped. 'How did you know about that?'

How had my being the person behind AutumnEverything been bypassed and word about Callum already got out? I looked around to make sure no one was close enough to overhear what Jason had said, just in case it hadn't spread all that far.

'My nephew is a journalist on the paper,' he told me, and my mouth fell open. 'He's writing the story about the festival and how you're the organiser as well as something famous on the internet. I don't understand it. It's all beyond me. But he found out all this other stuff, when he looked you up. Stories about how your husband was . . . drowned, while trying to—'

I put up a hand to stop him retelling me my past. 'I know what happened,' I said quietly.

'Of course,' he said, his gaze darting up to meet mine, 'sorry.'

A brief silence fell between us.

'If it's any comfort, he's only going to write about the

internet thing,' he eventually said. 'He's not going to mention you being a widow.'

'Given that it isn't relevant to the story, I had been hoping that would be the case,' I told him as realisation dawned. 'Though of course, as he'll be mentioning the internet thing, other people will be able to look me up like he has, won't they?'

'Oh, yes,' Jason tutted and his shoulders slumped. 'I didn't think of that. I'm sorry.'

'Two apologies in one sitting,' I pointed out. 'Is that a record?'

He looked at me and smiled and I received yet another surprise. He looked like an entirely different person when he wasn't frowning and scowling and the change in his expression made me momentarily forget the monumental evening I was having.

'I'm actually going to make it three,' he then confessed and his smile disappeared again.

'Why?' I groaned, as it all came rushing back to me. 'What else have you got to apologise for?'

'I didn't come after you just because of the festival,' he said in a rush.

'You didn't?'

'It was the cottage as well.'

'Rowan Cottage?' I frowned. 'My cottage?'

'Yes,' he said, putting his pint down.

'Go on,' I insisted. 'Tell me.'

'You see, I had always hoped it would be *my* cottage,' he explained. 'But when it eventually came up for sale, I couldn't afford it.'

'But why did you want to buy it?' I asked. 'No disrespect, but I can't see you as the roses around the door type.'

When he looked at me that time, there were tears in his eyes and I regretted what I had said because it was suddenly obvious that the impression Jason presented to the world might not be the genuine one.

'You might not believe this,' he said, his Adam's apple bobbing, 'but even I was young and in love once. The girl I was smitten with, Cassy Wicks, loved that cottage. We used to go on bike rides into the Fen just to cycle past it and we'd imagine what we'd do with it if it was ours. I promised her that one day it would be.'

'Oh, Jason,' I whispered, knowing there was going to be a tragedy at the heart of this tale. 'What happened? What happened to Cassy?'

'Cancer took her,' he said, sniffing fiercely. 'The summer we were due to be wed. She was only twenty-one. We both were.'

'Oh god.' I swallowed. 'I'm so sorry.'

'So, I know, you see. I know how it feels and I'm sorry I've made such a nuisance of myself while you've been going through it.'

I could tell he was in earnest. The urgency in his tone and the retelling of his own heartbreak both supported and strengthened his sincere sounding apology.

'Even though it's decades on, I felt jealous that you'd got what I promised Cass we'd one day have,' he rushed on. 'When you got the cottage, well, I felt like I'd failed her.'

'I can understand that,' I told him, after a beat had passed. 'I can understand why you felt that way.'

For a while, I had felt like I'd let Callum down by selling our home, so I knew how much emotional baggage came wrapped up in bricks and mortar.

'Well,' said Jason, roughly rubbing a hand over his eyes. 'That's something, I suppose.'

'But have you been all this time on your own, Jason?' I then gasped, as the empty decades presented themselves. 'Have you truly been on your own for all these years?'

I would have guessed he was nearer to seventy than sixty.

'I have,' he said, sadly. 'And I'll continue to be, too, because who would want a bitter old crock like me? I've spent so long trying to stop things around here from changing so the town will still feel like it did when my girl was alive, that everyone hates me now. I'm going to be alone forever . . .'

So, he objected to what he considered to be the gentrification of Wynbridge because the changes were impacting on the memories he had from when Cassy was alive, not because he thought they didn't genuinely benefit the town.

'That's so sad,' I whispered and he gave me a look. 'What?' I frowned.

'Well, it could be you saying that one day, couldn't it?' he said, suddenly brusque. 'The bit about being alone forever, I mean.'

'Me?' I swallowed.

'Yes,' he said gruffly. 'You, Clementine Bennett. I know the signs and I daresay you've made some pledge to your dearly departed or to yourself that you'll never love again, just like I did. I bet you've said that you'll never let your closed-up heart be warmed by another, haven't you?'

The sentiment could have been poetic had it not pierced my closed-up heart with all the force of a perfectly aimed arrow.

'I . . .' I stuttered. 'I mean . . .'

'Exactly,' he said fiercely. 'I thought as much. Well, don't end up like me, gal. Seeing you, so young and with the weight of this tragedy behind you, has made me realise how young I was when I went through my own heartbreak and how little life I've lived since.'

'I'm sorry you didn't have anyone to help you through it,' I said, setting aside thoughts of my heart and thinking instead of my parents and now my new friends who made life so much more manageable for me.

'I did,' he sighed heavily, 'and I pushed them all away until they left me to my own devices.'

'Well,' I said, 'I haven't done that. I have my family and my new friends and now the autumn festival to keep me on track.'

Callum and I had had friends back in my hometown, all other couples, but we'd lost touch. It had been too painful to see everyone's lives ultimately carrying on while mine had been destroyed.

'So, you're not an entirely lost cause,' he smiled wryly.

'Not now I've been found,' I smiled back, as an idea popped into my head. 'And it's really not too late for you either, Jason. Why don't you start by joining in with the festival?'

I expected him to look aghast, but his smile grew wider.

'It's funny you should suggest that,' he grinned, 'because I've decided to follow your lead with regards to the festival.'

'Oh?'

'I'm going to the library on Sunday to pick up a couple of books that are on the book club list,' he amazed and delighted me by saying. 'And I'm planning to trounce the competition at the pumpkin carving competition later in the month, too.'

My mouth fell open.

'It's time I started living even if I am on my own!'

'I hope this gentleman isn't making a nuisance of himself,' said Jim, who suddenly loomed up.

'Not at all,' I was delighted to be able to tell him. 'We're just discussing the autumn book club reads.'

Jason cracked another smile and Jim moved away wearing a puzzled expression.

'That'll set tongues wagging,' Jason laughed and drained his pint. 'Anyway, I'll leave you to your thoughts. As long as they're not dark ones?'

'They're not,' I smiled. 'But thank you for asking. I don't suppose you'd like to come and see the cottage sometime, would you?'

He looked astonished. 'That's a very generous offer,' he said, 'but I'm sure you've made some changes and I'd rather keep it as I remember it.'

'I understand.' I nodded.

'Though I do hope you've sorted that downstairs bathroom out?' he added, before he walked away. 'Cassy and I always imagined it would be glacial behind that frosted glass in the winter.'

'It's cosy now,' I told him, thinking of my beloved home and the hound who would be waiting to welcome me back into it. 'The whole place is cosy now.'

Chapter 23

When Ash called late that evening to ask how my trip to the café had gone, I took him through all that had been said and after he'd warmly admired me for managing it, I was then eager to tell him the details of the conversation I'd had with Jason in the pub.

'And you'll never guess who I then ran into in The Mermaid.' I knew it was highly probable that I sounded astounded, but that was because I still was.

'Go on.'

'Jason.'

'Oh, no, Clemmie,' Ash groaned. 'He was the last person you needed to see after what you'd just been through. I hope he didn't upset you.'

'No, he didn't,' I was delighted to be able to say. 'Far from it, in fact.'

'What?' Ash asked, no doubt assuming he'd misheard.

It was then that I took a check on myself. Given that I was full of hope that no one was going to be gossiping about me in the coming days, it would have been highly hypocritical of me to tell Ash all that Jason had shared.

'What did he say, Clemmie?' Ash asked.

'He . . .' I falteringly began as I quickly changed tack, 'he told me in no uncertain terms that he wasn't the person who took the ballot box.'

'No way!' Ash gasped, echoing my response. 'Do you think he was telling the truth?'

'Yes,' I said. 'No doubt about it.'

'Well, I never. So, if it wasn't him, then who was it?'

'I've no idea and I daresay we'll never find out now.'

'But even if it wasn't him,' clearly Ash couldn't quite believe that Jason wasn't the culprit, 'I daresay he's still got some mischief up his sleeve. Did he hint at what he has in store for the rest of the festival?'

'Funnily enough, nothing bad, because he's turned over a new leaf.'

It didn't escape my attention that I'd recently said the same thing about Joanne and it had immediately come back to bite me! I hoped the same thing wasn't going to happen with Jason.

'Of course he has,' Ash guffawed.

'No, really,' I told him while hoping I was right. 'I mean it. He has. He's full of regret for his former behaviour now and is going to embrace the festival and even take part.'

'You're having me on!' Ash spluttered. 'You're joking, surely?'

'No,' I said earnestly. 'I'm being deadly serious. He's determined to make amends.'

I could hardly express any doubt when Jason had done nothing to warrant it.

'What else did he say?' Ash asked, sounding suspicious.

'Quite a lot about his private life which almost justified his previous behaviour,' I said. 'But nothing he would want me to share.'

It was more than sad to think that Jason's life had been shaped by a tragedy that occurred in his twenties. In spite of the many decades that had passed since then, I could tell he still felt the impact of it as keenly as if it had happened as recently as the week before.

I thanked my lucky stars that I had been able to process and assimilate my grief and, while I would always live with it, I felt truly blessed to have come so far. Mine and Jason's lives had echoed each other's in their early days, but I had already taken a different path to the solo one he had, until literally just hours ago, continued to walk.

'It sounds to me like you had a proper heart to heart,' Ash said, sounding amazed.

'We did,' I confirmed. 'And knowing how difficult my conversation with Lizzie and Jemma had been, I can imagine it was doubly hard for Jason.'

'I see,' Ash pondered and I could tell he was puzzled, but he didn't ask for more details. 'It's very kind of you to keep what he said to you to yourself, but then I wouldn't expect anything less of you, Clem.'

Those words made me glow.

'That's kind,' I smiled.

'And let's hope,' he then said, 'that when the paper is published on Friday, that everyone else is as respectful of your privacy as you are of Jason's.'

'Time will tell.'

'It certainly will.'

I didn't tell Ash that Jason had said Callum wouldn't be

featured in the article, in case for some reason his nephew had a change of heart and included the details after all.

'Right then,' I said instead, 'I'd better go. There's a little hound here clamouring for my full and undivided attention.'

'All right,' said Ash, 'give her a fuss from me and I'll see you Friday. I'll pick a paper up early and drop it round.'

'That would save me a trip, thank you. We'll see you then.'

'See you Friday.'

Having given Lizzie, Jemma and, most significantly, Joanne the go-ahead to disclose my online identity, I didn't have to wait until Friday to find out if the AutumnEverything revelation was going to have an impact, because those locals who knew me or followed the account, or both, made themselves digitally known to me from early Thursday morning.

I never kept my phone close to hand, but as I pottered about in the cottage, played with Pixie and tidied up my breakfast things, I could hear it pinging away in the next room and when I eventually picked it up, I could immediately see I'd had a flurry of new followers, a dozen or so messages and lots of new comments on my most recent posts. I only had to read the opening words of a couple of the messages to know that people had been looking me up online and that those who had, were now privy to my past.

'I don't suppose it matters what's printed in the paper now, does it, Pixie?' I shrugged as I set the phone aside and picked her up.

I sat with her on my lap and had a think. In the time before I had taken the festival on and ventured into Wynbridge, I had imagined that being outed online would be a huge calamity and that my anxiety would soar to its former heights as a result, but I discovered that wasn't the case. This time around felt different. I had taken an active part in what was happening. I was in a much stronger headspace and consequently, more in control of what I read and responded to and, with that in mind, I carefully composed a post and pinned it.

I thanked everyone for following AutumnEverything, and for their kind words about Callum and their suggestions as to how I could cope. I then explained that I wouldn't be interacting with anyone directly – irrespective of whether they were new or old followers – as so many people had been in touch, and said that I hoped they would all understand.

That was as much as I was willing to do. I would now continue to run the account in the way I always had – without showing my face, Pixie's face, or making any reference to exactly where I lived. Some locals would know that Rowan Cottage was my home, but I hoped they would be respectful enough not to impose.

I felt proud of how I was handling the situation, right up until Mum and Dad video-called and I realised it would have been useful to keep them in the loop before word had got out.

'Clemmie!' Mum practically shouted when I answered. 'What's this post you've just pinned to the top of your account?'

'Yes,' said Dad, as he also wrestled into view. 'Have you pinned it or have you been hacked?'

'It was me,' I told them quickly. 'It's all fine. I haven't been hacked.'

'But this post,' Dad frowned, 'it says an awful lot considering we thought you wanted to keep AutumnEverything anonymous.'

'I did want to keep it anonymous,' I confirmed, 'but someone who visited me at the cottage recognised a jug of flowers I posted and let it slip that I was the account owner.'

'How mean of someone to do that,' Mum tutted.

'They didn't intend to be mean,' I corrected her, thinking of how forlorn Joanne had been when she'd realised what she'd done. 'They just didn't think, but as the news was out and people were already commenting, I thought I should say something.'

'I bet you're being inundated with messages, aren't you?' Dad groaned.

'It's fine,' I said calmly. 'You know I've been down this road before and therefore I'm handling it differently this time. Hence the pinned post. I'm not going to be privately messaging well-meaning strangers this time around.'

Mum and Dad hadn't been privy to the full extent of it, but I recalled how I'd spent literally hours reading every single comment and message I'd received on the previous account, how harrowing it had been and how I had taken it all in. I knew there was every possibility that even more messages were going to pour in now that both new and old followers discovered my identity, but I had no intention of getting sucked into the maelstrom again. Not now I'd so healthily moved on.

'Well, that's good.' Dad nodded.

'I always worry that people will think it's rude if you don't respond,' said Mum, 'but knowing what happened before, I'm pleased you've taken action and you've worded the post so well, if anyone takes offence, it won't be your fault, will it?'

I was surprised to realise that Mum was more aware than I had known that I had spared her and Dad the worst of it before.

'It certainly won't,' I agreed.

'Well,' said Dad, looking happier, 'you do sound like you've got a handle on it.'

'I have,' I told him. 'And I'm determined to carry on with the account in the same way that I've always run it.'

Mum and Dad were both happier when we ended the call and when Ash arrived the next morning with a newspaper hot off the press, I was already feeling content but the feeling was further compounded by the article.

'I am right, aren't I?' Ash asked, as he peered over my shoulder. 'That is it? It's just that little bit there?'

He leant around me to run his finger along a line of print under one of the photos. 'Yes,' I said, 'that's all I can find, anyway.'

I turned around to look at him and he was standing so close, my nose practically met his chest.

'Sorry,' he said, taking a step back.

I turned back to the paper and scanned the page again, just to be sure. The main photograph was of Ash and I standing with the three shopkeepers who had won the 'Best Dressed Window' awards as decided by us, and there was a much smaller one of me with the words – *Clemmie Bennett, Festival Organiser and curator of popular Insta account, @AutumnEverything.*

'Yep,' I said again. 'That's it.'

The journalist, Jason's nephew, had covered what he was supposed to and I was relieved that the festival hadn't been shoved out of the limelight. With so many events still to come, it was paramount to keep pushing its popularity.

I looked up from the paper and turned around to find that Ash was staring at me.

'What?' I frowned.

'You're not regretting telling Lizzie and Jemma about Callum now there's nothing been printed about him, are you?' he asked.

'Absolutely not,' I firmly said. 'And the account has been named anyway, so it was all bound to come out. Besides, my decision to talk to them was about sharing and ensuring I could say what I wanted to before the article was published and then relax into my new life here, remember?'

'Yes,' he said, and his shoulders dropped. 'Yes, I remember. I just wanted to make sure you're really feeling okay about it all.'

'I am,' I confirmed. 'Of course, I would have preferred to keep the account anonymous, but it's done now and I'm sure the messages will soon tail off.'

'Good old foghorn, Joanne,' Ash tutted. 'It couldn't have been anyone but her, could it?'

'Hey,' I said. 'Don't call her that.'

'As I recall,' Ash then laughed, 'you were the one who called her that first.'

'Only once.' I blushed. 'Ages ago and in private, so you can keep that to yourself.'

'What will happen if I don't?' he asked, his blue gaze playfully fixed on mine.

'I'll never offer you another squash pasty again,' I said, and looked away.

'Not even a nibbled edge?' he laughed again.

'Not a nibbled anything,' I said, more loudly. 'Now get out of my way and I'll make us some coffee.'

The room suddenly felt far too small for two people and one dog.

'Come on, Pixie,' he said, ushering her out. 'We know where we're not wanted.'

He only moved as far as the doorframe, which he then leant on, watching me organising drinks. I glanced at the paper again and then, for some reason, felt a rush of tears spring to my eyes and took a shuddering breath.

'Hey,' Ash said. 'What is it?'

He came up behind me again and gently turned me around, taking my hands in his own.

'Relief, I think,' I whispered, as I tried to blink the tears away.

'Relief?'

'Yes.' I swallowed. 'I don't really know why I kept quiet for so long because it's such a relief to be able to openly say Callum's name. I've kept him hidden for such a long time but now I can finally talk about him, if I want to, and it's so freeing. You were right about my time with him being such a big part of who I am, Ash.'

He gave my hands a squeeze then let them go, but didn't move away. 'You loved him very much, didn't you?'

'I did.' I sniffed. 'I still do.'

'He'll always be perfect in your eyes.' Ash smiled.

'Not perfect necessarily,' I said. 'But close to it. We weren't married long enough for the shine to wear off our relationship, but it might have done, in time. Who knows?'

'I do,' Ash said, huskily. 'There's not a man alive who wouldn't shine if he was in a relationship with you, Clemmie.'

'Well,' I smiled, 'that's very kind, but my life's completely changed now and my time to help anyone shine has well and truly passed.'

I got ready to help Lizzie with the lantern-making workshop the next morning and set off to the gallery, with Pixie for moral support and my head held high. I was full of a confidence that I wouldn't have been able to muster even just a few months ago and felt ready for whatever came my way.

'Morning, Joanne,' I said brightly as I crossed the gallery threshold and the bell above the door chimed out.

'Clemmie,' she smiled. 'You're early.'

'I was hoping to catch you alone,' I told her. 'Is Lizzie here?'

'She's just popped next door. Now, about the paper,' she then rushed on. 'I'm so sorry—'

'Never mind about that,' I said, as I pulled her further towards the back of the gallery. 'What I want to know is, have you spoken to Aiden about your concerns over the move yet?'

Before she answered, she pulled me in for a rib-cracking hug, clearly relieved that I wasn't about to bite her head off because AutumnEverything had been mentioned in the article.

'Come on,' I said, breaking free. 'You're wasting time.'

I didn't know if she'd told Lizzie about the reservation she was feeling concerning her imminent move to Germany and we might not get the chance to chat in private again for a while.

'Yes,' she finally said. 'I have talked to him.'

'And?'

'And he admitted that he hadn't been feeling all that certain about the move, either.'

'Really?' I gasped.

'Really,' she repeated. 'He was given the chance to stay in Australia, but didn't take that offer because he assumed I wouldn't want to be living on the other side of the world, so far away from my family.'

'Oh, Joanne,' I groaned. 'So now you've both missed out.'

She shook her head. 'No, we haven't,' she practically squeaked with excitement. 'Because Aiden talked to his boss and . . . he's staying in Oz! And I'm flying out to join him in the new year!'

'Oh, my goodness! That's amazing news!' I applauded and that time, I was the one who hugged her.

'And it's all thanks to you, Clemmie,' she said, her eyes shining when I let her go. 'If I hadn't talked to you, I wouldn't have said anything to him and I don't even want to think about what might have happened then . . .'

The bell above the door rang out as Lizzie walked back in carrying a tray and two drinks.

'Clemmie,' she beamed. 'You're early.'

'That's what I said,' Joanne laughed and had a little jig about.

'You've told her then,' Lizzie guessed and laughed, too.

'I have.' Joanne nodded and bounced again.

I was pleased it was all out in the open and knew there was going to be no controlling her excitement now that she was making a move she could genuinely enthuse about. With any luck she'd be so focused on her own new life, she wouldn't slip back into old habits and even think about anyone else's. Unless she became determined to leave the UK with another match under her belt. I sincerely hoped not!

'It's wonderful news, isn't it?' I smiled at Lizzie, pushing that thought aside.

'The best,' she agreed. 'Though I do feel bad for not noticing anything was wrong when you did, Clemmie.'

Joanne waved Lizzie's upset away. 'I daresay you would have done,' she grinned, 'if I wasn't always being such a pain in the—'

'Now,' Lizzie cut in, 'why don't you pop next door, Clemmie, and pick up a pastry to celebrate? If I'd known you were here, I would have nabbed three.'

'She can have mine,' Joanne offered. 'I'm too excited to eat this morning!'

'Thank you, Joanne,' I smiled. 'And I would rather stay put, if that's okay, because I want to see how a workshop works in its entirety right from the get-go. As I'm still considering your offer, Lizzie, I'd like to help with the setting up and clearing away.'

'Don't forget, you helped with the clearing up last time,' she reminded me.

'Oh, you're right,' I winked. 'So you can do that today, Joanne.'

'Of course,' she said. 'Whatever you say.'

'No, you're all right,' I laughed. 'I'm only teasing.'

'I don't mind,' she smiled. 'I know I have some bridges to mend.'

'You don't actually,' I smiled back. 'Because your gaff last week has been a blessing in disguise.'

'Really?' She blinked.

'Really,' I told her.

'In that case,' she grinned, 'we'll do the clearing up together.'

'Well, before we can even think about clearing up and putting away,' said Lizzie, as she finally put the café tray on a table, 'we need to get it all out and set up. Grab an apron and we'll get going.'

We'd just started arranging everything when Jemma came rushing in to the gallery waving a piece of paper.

'I can't stop because we're rushed off our feet in the café,' she panted, 'but look what I've just found sat on top of the ballot box!'

She thrust the folded piece of paper towards me and I took it.

'Read it,' she urged and I unfolded it. 'I was going to put it in the box, but then realised it wasn't a voting slip.'

I read the few words that had been printed rather than handwritten and gasped.

'What does it say?' Joanne asked.

'"Dear festival organisers,"' I read aloud. '"My mate dared me to take the other voting box for a laugh, but it turned out it wasn't funny and I've been feeling bad ever since. I've got rid of the box, but wanted to say sorry."'

'No way!' Joanne also gasped.

'I don't believe it,' said Lizzie.

'That's what it says,' I told her, turning the paper around so they could all see it.

'So, it was some kids' prank, then?' Lizzie said, shaking her head.

'By the sounds of it,' I said, turning the paper over again. 'And I daresay they've printed this so no one could try and identify their handwriting.'

'That was smart,' said Joanne and we all gave her a look. 'It wasn't good that they took the box obviously, but at least they're feeling bad enough about it to apologise.'

'As they should!' Jemma said, making for the door again.

'No chance you saw who left this, I suppose?' I asked her.

'Not a clue,' she shrugged. 'There have been so many people in and out already this morning, I couldn't tell you. Sorry, my love.'

She rushed off and I looked at the paper again.

'Well, let's hope they've learnt their lesson,' Lizzie tutted. 'And this prankish bad behaviour has been nipped in the bud.'

'I think they must have,' I said. 'Otherwise, they would have just got rid of the box and not said anything. I daresay Joanne's right and it was playing on their mind.'

'Mystery *almost* solved then,' Joanne pointed out. 'And at least now you won't be expecting the box to turn up or wasting time wondering about who took it.'

'I feel so bad for assuming that it was Jason,' I muttered.

'Well, don't,' said Lizzie. 'He gave you enough cause.'

I was just about to say how he'd now made amends, but we were fast running out of time, so I folded the paper up and slipped it into my pocket.

'Right,' said Joanne, rubbing her hands together. 'Let's get this show on the road!'

I hadn't known exactly what the workshop was going to entail, but it was simple enough. The adults were going to decorate glass jars and lanterns with leaves Lizzie had previously collected from the Skylark Farm nature trail and dried and the children were making card lanterns with brightly coloured cellophane woodland motif shapes to create a stained-glass effect.

'I'm going to encourage everyone to use them in the Halloween procession,' Lizzie told me. 'They'll be perfect for that.'

'Oh yes,' I agreed, as I helped set everything out. 'What a wonderful idea. It's the ideal opportunity to include things from one event in another.'

'That's what I thought,' she smiled. 'Joanne, you can work with the children's table today.'

Joanne, for some reason, was reluctant but eventually agreed and headed off to the café to collect the welcome drinks. She looked far less happy than she had when she'd been setting things up and chatting about her move to Australia.

'I don't mind working with the children if Joanne would rather not,' I offered once she'd gone, but Lizzie wouldn't hear of it.

'No,' she said. 'I'm not going to subject you to that and put you off my offer!'

'Subject me to what?' I frowned.

Right on cue, the gallery door was flung open and in marched a tiny terror who Joanne was going to have the pleasure of helping. Rather her than me.

It was a busy morning, so I didn't have time to further think about the note in my pocket. Unsurprisingly, I was the object of some interest, but not too much and most of it centred around AutumnEverything. I wasn't sure if that was because the people present weren't yet aware that I was a widow or if they were too diplomatic to bring it up. I didn't have to wait long to find out . . .

'Clemmie Bennett,' tutted the woman who had been in raptures over AutumnEverything at the felting and decoupage workshop. 'You're a dark horse! All that talk about that magnificent account we were swooning over and you never said a word.'

'Well,' I smiled, as I helped her decide where to paste her selection of leaves, 'at the time, I was trying to keep it a secret.'

'I'm not surprised,' she sighed. 'From everything I've seen online about your husband, I daresay you were worn down with all the attention when he died.'

'I was,' I nodded, as Lizzie rushed around the table to check I was okay.

I realised then that everyone was listening and felt my cheeks flush red.

'And no wonder,' the woman carried on, the volume of her voice rising. 'Well, other than I'm very sorry for your loss, my dear, I won't say a word. Widowed at your age, though. I mean—'

'This is you not saying a word, is it?' came a voice from the other side of the table and I looked across to find the person who had pulled her up, shaking her head. 'I'm sure we're all very sorry for the lass. Now, let's leave her in peace, shall we?'

'Right,' said Lizzie, as she placed a hand on my shoulder and gave it a comforting squeeze. 'Who's ready to start pasting?'

The noise from the other side of the gallery suggested Joanne wasn't making much headway with a couple of the children, so I took the opportunity to head over and give her some moral support. With two adults at the table, and enough attention for everyone, things soon settled down.

'You know what,' I said, popping in a battery operated tealight and holding up the lantern the most vociferous and bossy child had made. 'I think you've made the scariest one out of all of us.'

He looked thrilled about that.

'Can I smash it up and make another one?' he pleaded, making his voice sickly sweet.

'Nope,' I said, with a nod to the clock. 'There's not enough time.'

'Perhaps I'll just tear it up and not have one at all then,' he pouted.

I placed it back in front of him.

'You could,' I shrugged and he went to grab it, 'but then you won't have anything to carry in the Halloween parade, will you? You're going to terrify everyone with these monster shapes.'

He quickly shoved the lantern out of reach and away from temptation.

'You've never made that,' I heard his mum say when she had finished her own lantern and was ready to head off.

He shrugged as if it was nothing, but I could tell he was pleased.

'Thank you,' the woman mouthed to me and Joanne and then took him off for chips from the market as a treat for being good.

'You saved me there,' Joanne said. 'He was testing my patience.'

'I think he'd be enough to test the patience of anyone.'

'You've got a way with kids,' Lizzie said to me.

'That,' I told her, 'was a one off. Beginners' luck. I have no experience of kids.'

'Me neither,' Joanne shuddered. 'Yuck.'

And nor was I ever likely to have, but whereas Joanne might have made a choice about staying child-free, my hand had been forced.

'Well, be that as it may,' said Lizzie, as she wiped her hands down her apron, 'today has been a huge success and you've shone again, Clemmie. You are going to come and work for me, aren't you?'

'I haven't *completely* decided yet,' I told her, 'but I think I've almost got my future all wrapped up.'

'I'm delighted to hear it,' she smiled, warmly.

Chapter 24

It was a classic case of famous last words because the next morning, in the library, Jason threw a grenade into what I had started to envision as my increasingly tidy future and blew the whole *all wrapped up* plan to smithereens.

After the successful workshop and an evening of further pondering, I had decided to accept Lizzie's job offer, but Jason's grenade didn't have anything to do with my future employment. His bomb was far more intimate than that.

'I didn't expect to see you here,' he said rather gruffly, while I waited in line to return a couple of the books I'd previously checked out and somehow managed to find the time to read and enjoy. 'You didn't say you were coming when I said I was.'

Clearly, his social skills still needed some refining, but I was pleased to note his trademark scowl seemed to have been banished.

'Good morning, Jason,' I said, making full use of my manners. I then went to tell him about the note explaining the ballot box mystery, but didn't because I hadn't filled Ash in yet and as deputy, he should know first. 'I didn't mention it, because I wasn't expecting to come. And I'm not staying for the discussion with Kay, because I've promised Pixie a long walk.'

'Oh, right,' he sniffed. 'You're out and about in town though, so you're brazening it out, are you? The mention in the paper, I mean.'

I had known what he meant and flashed him a smile. 'You're smarter than you look,' I quipped.

'Hey,' he objected.

'Yes,' I confirmed. 'I'm brazening it out. I thought if I was seen in public, then my novelty value would soon wane. Though actually,' I added, as I moved up a place in the queue and looked around, 'I don't think my bit of news has caused the stir I thought it might. Barely anyone has said a word, so thank you for whatever influence you had over your nephew, the journalist, who stuck to the window dressing story.'

Jason shook his head.

'Am I wrong?' I frowned. 'About me being newsworthy, I mean?'

'You certainly are,' he told me. 'You're the hot topic all right. It's just that the talking is happening when you're not around to hear it.'

'Oh well,' I sighed. 'I can't control that.'

'And you don't need to worry about it either,' he insisted, 'because everyone is being very kind.'

'I'm not worried,' I truthfully told him, but it was nice to know people were being considerate when they were discussing me.

'So, what are you bringing back then?' Jason asked, as I took the two books out of my bag.

'One non-fiction about the Fens and Milly Johnson, *An Autumn Crush*.'

'I've just picked that up,' he said, showing me his copy of

Milly's well-thumbed book. 'Is it as good as her others? I can't believe I hadn't read this one.'

'Yes,' I said, taken aback but trying not to show it, 'I really enjoyed it. Though *A Spring Affair* is still my favourite from the Four Seasons collection.'

'Mine too,' he agreed. 'I love a good declutter.'

I shook my head. 'You're full of surprises,' I laughed.

'Perhaps I am,' he said as I returned the books, stepped aside and folded up my now-empty tote. 'Though I've never parted with anything of Cassy's when I've been having a clear out. Have you thought any more about what I said in the pub?'

'Which bit?'

He inclined his head to a quieter spot behind some true crime filled shelves and I followed him over to it.

'The bit about not ending up like me,' he said in a low voice.

I looked him up and down.

'You look all right,' I told him, with a smile. 'Especially now you've dropped the mean old man act.'

Unfortunately, he wasn't to be distracted, even though I wanted him to be.

'You know what I'm getting at,' he said and the sadness in his tone made me regret my flippant comment even though it had been intended to lighten the mood.

'I do know,' I said, feeling chastened. 'You don't want me to stay on my own forever, do you?'

'That's it exactly.'

'Even though my heart still belongs to the man I lost,' I reminded him. 'And always will.'

'Perhaps,' he said, eyeing me quizzically.

'No perhaps about it,' I said forcefully. 'Because there isn't another candidate in the universe capable of making it switch allegiance.'

'Loving someone new wouldn't mean forgetting who had gone before, you know,' he batted back. 'It's nothing to do with switching allegiance.'

That ethos sounded like a pot and kettle situation given who was spouting it. He hadn't moved on from his first lost love, so he really had no right to suggest I should. Even if he had inferred that it was something he now regretted.

'Well, that's as maybe,' I said, 'but this heart is not for turning. Or sharing. Which is fine, because no one's about to fall for me.'

Jason snorted so loudly that the librarian at the desk shot him a look.

'Sorry,' he mouthed.

'What was that for?' I tutted.

He looked at me with an expression that was a mixture of bewilderment, confusion and disbelief. It wasn't an easy look to pull off, but he somehow managed it.

'What?' I hissed.

'You don't know, do you?' he then asked in amazement. 'You *really* don't know.'

'Know what?'

He shook his head and blew out a breath. 'Your vet chum, of course.'

'Ash.' I frowned. 'What about him?'

'No wonder the world's in trouble!' Jason grumbled loudly, sounding more like his former rather than his latter self. 'How can you not know?'

'Know what?' I demanded.

'That he's in love with you, you fool.'

I didn't say anything for a moment. I just looked at him and blinked. 'What?' I eventually, and rudely, croaked. My good manners were now completely forgotten.

'He's head over heels in love with you!' Jason said again, as loudly as he dared, without incurring the wrath of the librarian who had moved out from behind the desk and was taking more of an interest in our huddle.

'Don't be so absurd,' I whispered loudly back. 'Of course he's isn't. He's my friend. The best one here that I've got.'

Jason let out another frustrated breath. 'Think about it,' he urged. 'Go on.'

'Well,' I eventually said. 'We did almost kiss once, but—'

'There you are then.'

'But,' I repeated, that time more fiercely, 'that was just the result of some dancing and us getting caught up in the moment. It was nothing to do with love, Jason!'

'Of course it wasn't,' he smiled infuriatingly.

'You're wrong,' I said. 'Completely, utterly and totally wrong.'

'No,' he said mildly. 'I'm not. Tell me, what did he do after this almost kiss the pair of you nearly had?'

I cast my mind back. 'He . . . left,' I said, and Jason raised his eyebrows.

'He ran away, you mean?'

'No,' I said tersely. 'He went to help his family. His nan's had a stroke and he went to help settle her into his mum and dad's place.'

'Of course he did.'

I took a step away. 'I can't listen to you anymore,' I said, feeling a lump forming in my throat as my vision blurred with cross tears. 'You're talking absolute rubbish and by the end of the week, I'll have proved it.'

I stayed angry with Jason and holed up in and around the cottage for the next two days. I took Pixie for her promised walk. In fact, we took a few. They were all long, brisk and furiously paced, and even though they tired Pixie out, they did nothing for me.

However, I did turn my continued bad mood to good use where AutumnEverything was concerned. My irritation made me business-like and helped me to properly draw a line under my pinned post. I felt no guilt about neither reading nor replying to what people had written and normal service on the account was swiftly resumed. I supposed that was the one positive to come from Jason's absurd declaration.

I still couldn't see the wood for the trees where that was concerned and therefore invited Ash, via text, to supper Wednesday evening – the promise of a pasty proved too tempting to resist – and I had a speech rehearsed in which I would tell him what Jason had said and then feel immediately soothed when he laughed and denied it straight after.

The weather on Wednesday took a dreadful downturn and it rained from the moment I opened the cottage curtains and didn't let up for a minute, the entire day. I looked out at it during the rapidly darkening afternoon and hoped it would improve by the weekend. The pumpkin carving competition was happening in the square on Saturday so a dry day would be much appreciated.

When Ash hadn't arrived half an hour after the time we had arranged, and the pasties were rapidly cooling, I called his mobile. I knew he wasn't on call for work, so wouldn't be attending an emergency. Perhaps, I mused, as I rang his number, he'd forgotten our plan. That would be something to tell Jason! If Ash was in love with me – and my pasties – he would have hardly forgotten our arranged evening together, would he?

'Hi,' I said swiftly, when the call connected and went straight to voicemail. 'Just checking in. This pasty is still warm, but it won't be for much longer. Hope you're on your way.'

I hung up and looked at Pixie.

'Did that sound a bit inappropriate?' I asked her and wrinkled my nose. 'This pasty is still warm . . .' I started to say, 'but it won't be for much longer . . .'

Pixie yipped.

'I know,' I huffed, 'Jason has got me second guessing everything now!'

By eight o'clock, a solid hour and a half after our arranged time, there was still no call from or sign of Ash, but the rain was lashing down harder and I'd eaten my supper.

'If he'd broken down,' I told Pixie, as I looked at my phone for the umpteenth time, 'he would have called.'

She laid in front of the fire with her head resting on her paws. I took a quick photo of her because she looked so sweet, then joined her on the carpet for a snuggle.

'Wouldn't he?' I sighed and she licked my cheek.

I was all but resigned to him being a lost cause for the evening, when I decided to call The Mermaid and ask Jeanie if he happened to be there. There had been no reply at the practice and I couldn't think of anywhere else that was open that he might be.

'Oh, hey, Clemmie,' Jeanie said, when Jim, who had answered, handed her the phone. 'What's up?'

'Hi,' I said, feeling suddenly ridiculous to have rung in the first place, but unable to think of an excuse for calling that wasn't the truth.

'Do you want to book the pub for an AutumnEverything photoshoot?' she suggested, with a smile in her tone. 'Because we would be very happy to host you.'

'No, thanks,' I said. 'Not today.'

'Probably just as well,' she yawned, 'because there's no bugger in.'

'Is there not?'

'Barely. The rain has seen them all off. Lightweights.'

'No sign of Ash, then?'

'Ash?' she echoed. 'No, he's not here.'

'Right.'

'I daresay he's down at the river with the rest of them.'

'The river?' I swallowed and sat down heavily.

'Yes,' she said. 'My Tim's down there and I know Will is as well, so Ash has probably gone along to lend a hand, too.'

I knew Tim was a firefighter, but that didn't explain why he, or Will, would be riverside on such a stormy night. Or any night, for that matter.

'Which stretch of the river and to lend a hand with what?' I asked, as my heart started to heavily thud.

'By the bridge on the far side of Blacktop Farm,' she told me. 'There's a horse slipped down the bank and they're trying to get it out. Though how they'll do it when the river's running so fast, I have—'

I don't know what she said next because, feeling sick to

my stomach and with the room starting to swirl, I'd ended the call.

'You stay here,' I said to Pixie as the rain dashed at the windows and I rushed to tug on the oversized waxed coat from the porch. 'I won't be long.'

I'd checked the fire before I set off, but I can't say I paid as much attention to my driving. In fact, I had to slam my brakes on at one point and realised, as I coasted almost sideways across the sodden drove and frighteningly close to the deep dyke that ran alongside it, that I needed to slow down. Slow down and calm down.

As I drove slightly less recklessly, I thought more about what Jason had said. Not that I hadn't considered it over the last few days, but this sudden influx of adrenaline highlighted things I hadn't taken into account before.

In rather less time than it should have taken, I arrived to find a multitude of flashing blue lights in one of the fields that had the treacherous tidal river running alongside it. I couldn't imagine there was a single emergency vehicle anywhere else in the Fens and I did just about muster the wherewithal to make sure I pulled up where my Land Rover wouldn't be blocking the field entrance.

Having been in such a rush, I was suddenly glued to the seat, my knuckles white as I gripped the steering wheel. Through the steamed up windows and the still pouring rain, it was impossible to work out who anyone was among the people toing and froing, but I could just about make out Ash's truck parked next to Will's which had the practice logo emblazoned down the side.

With a force of will I hadn't known I had in me, I climbed out and slammed the door shut. I was soaked in an instant and my Converse, which I hadn't thought to switch for my wellingtons, were no match for the mud. It was a wet, windy and wild night and I roughly wiped my hair out of my face as the coat hood was whipped back and my hair plastered to my head.

'Over here!' I heard someone holler, but it wasn't Ash. 'Quick!'

There were people everywhere, crossing backwards and forwards and dodging around me. I knew I shouldn't be there, but how could I not have come?

'Where's Ash?' I heard Will suddenly bellow and everyone rushed in his direction. His voice was carried to me loud and clear on the wind. 'Has anyone seen Ash?' he shouted urgently again. 'Where is he?'

With much difficulty, I made my way towards the sound of his voice and closer to the riverbank. I wanted to scream into the wind as I struggled to stay upright, but I saved my rapidly draining energy for the tragedy I could feel I was teetering on the brink of. How could this be happening again? How could it be that lightning was going to strike twice?

But then, with just two words . . . it was over.

'I'm here!' I suddenly heard a voice shout back and it unmistakably belonged to Ash. 'I've got the straps! Let's see if we can get her up!'

There was another rush of people towards what I could now see was a mud-covered horse laying on the ground and there, in the midst of the chaos, was Ash. He was soaked to the skin and filthy, but he was alive, he was breathing, he was there.

Noisy, painful sobs that felt literally torn from my lungs filled the air around me, but amongst the wind and tumult, no one heard them and I sank to my knees, grateful for the anonymity as I completely gave way to the all-consuming emotion coursing through me and the acknowledgement that, irrespective of whether or not Ash loved me, I was undeniably in love with him.

I was in love with Ash. I loved him . . .

I don't know how long I was there, but it felt like some time before one of the firefighters' head torches picked me out.

'What the hell?' I heard them shout as they spotted me, sodden and spent, and they rushed over. 'Are you all right?'

I looked up at them knowing I didn't have to worry about the tears coursing down my cheeks because they could easily be explained away as rain.

'Yes,' I said, feeling out of breath and utterly exhausted. 'Yes, I'm fine.'

I'd rarely been less fine, but I could hardly explain.

'Well, you can't sit there, love,' he stated as he unceremoniously pulled me back up and on to my feet. 'Look at the state of you. This isn't your horse we've just pulled out of the river, is it? If it is—'

'No,' I cut him off. 'It's not mine. Is it all right? I only stopped because I was driving by and saw all the lights, then I slipped over.'

'Clearly,' he said, with a look over his shoulder to where the horse was now standing, but shaking all over. 'I think it's going to be okay. We need to trace the owner though, so if you do know anything—'

'I don't,' I said. 'I really don't. And I'm sorry I'm in the way. I should go.'

'Yes,' he said, looking at me again and frowning. 'We'll be clearing the site soon and we don't need onlookers getting in the way.'

'Sorry,' I said, feeling a total nuisance as well as freezing cold, soaking wet and in deep shock.

'I need to get on,' he said. 'You haven't got your car stuck somewhere, have you?'

He sounded exasperated and I felt guilty to have held him up.

'No,' I said. 'It's the Land Rover parked on the verge. I'll go.'

I could tell he was watching me as I slipped my way back across the field and climbed into the cab, then turned the engine over and the heating up to full blast. I waved gingerly as I crept away, knowing the journey home would be driven at a much more sedate pace now that I knew Ash was safe. Now that I knew Ash hadn't rushed into the river to rescue that horse. Now that my life had taken yet another dramatic turn that I hadn't seen coming . . .

Chapter 25

Back at Rowan Cottage, I peeled my clothes off on the doormat and ran myself a deep, hot bath. The water steadily cooled as I lay and stewed, with Pixie watching me from the doorway. It seemed utterly unbelievable that I had fallen in love, but there could be no denying the tumultuous feelings that had been unleashed as a result of the riverside rescue. My reaction and subsequent relief at seeing that Ash was safe from harm ran far deeper than even the firmest of friendships would have warranted.

A sleepless night followed and then another. Ash had messaged to apologise for missing our dinner date and I had sent a suitable reply, but I hadn't suggested a second get-together and Ash hadn't yet pushed for one either. Ultimately, I was as relieved about that as I was about there being a few days' respite from having anything to do for the festival. I needed some peace in which to further think because I had no idea how I was going to free myself from the rigid state of shock I now found myself frozen in.

My life certainly hadn't got any easier as a result of knowing I had fallen in love with Ash, because my heart wasn't free to love him. It was still bound tightly to Callum and the sudden reappearance of the dreadful dreams I hadn't had about his death in months, suggested there was nothing I was going to be able to do to change that.

I felt trapped, flummoxed and guilt-ridden and I remained that way until the Friday morning when, dizzy from lack of sleep, I decided to reclaim the bold course of action I had originally planned for the abandoned supper date in the hope that it might just save my sanity. Having fought for it once before, I considered it worth rescuing again and set the wheels in motion straightaway.

What I still needed to do, just as I had intended to on the storm-filled night, was establish whether Jason had been right. I needed to find out if Ash was in love with me. I had no idea how he was going to respond to the suggestion, but I hoped that focusing on his feelings for a while might offer me some respite from constantly struggling with the shocking ones of mine that had now floated to the surface.

'Come on, Pixie,' I said, picking her up and refusing to overthink what I was about to do. 'It's time for some straight-talking. We're going to the barn.'

I couldn't help thinking that my little friend looked relieved. I daresay she'd had enough of being the only recipient of my rambling and soul-searching to last her a lifetime.

'That's a different truck,' I muttered, when I pulled through the barn gate. 'Do you think Ash has had a change of wheels, Pixie? Perhaps his other one is stuck in that mud-infested field.'

Mention of the field evoked a sudden rush of the sensations I had felt when I had spotted him, safe and sound, heading towards Will the night of the rescue. My shocking lightbulb moment had certainly been a tempestuous one and I wondered then, as I stared blankly at the barn, if I was now doing the right thing. Was he going to laugh at what I was about to ask? Or be offended? Either response could ruin our recently repaired relationship, but which one would I prefer? And which one might help me get a handle on my own emotions?

So much for not overthinking . . .

'Oh, let's just get on with it, shall we?' I said to Pixie.

She gave me another long-suffering look which I read to mean, *I wish you would.*

'Come on then,' I said. 'And if I lose my bottle and don't say anything, at least seeing him again will consolidate my feelings and I'll know what I'm truly up against.'

With my mind made up to use Ash's own *I just happened to be passing* phrase as justification for my randomly dropping by, I unclipped Pixie from her harness and walked up the path to the door. My finger was poised to ring the doorbell when I saw, through the glass door side panel, an internal door open and a woman, wrapped in a rather small towel and with her wet hair snaking over her shoulders, walk out of what I presumed must be the bathroom. She was laughing and said something over her shoulder to whoever she was with. Obviously, I didn't watch for long enough to see who that was.

'Shit,' I muttered, as I picked Pixie up to aid a speedier and hopefully invisible getaway. 'Shit, shit, shit, shit, shit.'

I tiptoed back along the path and launched Pixie on to the passenger seat.

'I'll strap you in, in a minute,' I told her and rushed around to the driver's side, but to no avail.

'Hello!' called the woman from the now open barn door. 'Are you looking for Ash? Only he's—'

'No, no,' I immediately interjected because I absolutely did not need to hear her explanation of where he was. 'I'm not. In fact, I don't know who that is. I've just realised I've got the wrong place. So sorry to have disturbed you.'

I left her looking bewildered as with more speed than grace I reversed the Land Rover back on to the road and shot off.

'Oh well, Pixie,' I said, trying to jolly her as well as myself along. 'That's one thing less for us to have to worry about, isn't it? And at least I know now what I have to do. I'll soon be able to shrug off unrequited love, won't I? Not that I *really* think it was love. More like a silly crush or something.'

Pixie looked flummoxed as a result of being tossed about. And while I should have been feeling relieved that Ash had another woman in his shower and I wasn't going to have to further battle my guilty feelings for him, I wasn't comforted at all. What I actually was, was jealous. I bit my lip to stop myself from crying and sternly told myself that it would soon pass. I just needed to find something else to focus on, like the festival, while I got myself back in check and slotted Ash back into the friendzone he had no idea I'd pulled him out of.

'Ash did tell you that he had room in his life for more than one woman, didn't he?' I said desperately to my canine chum. 'And now we know what he meant, don't we?'

Ash might not turn out be a one-woman man, but I was still a one-man woman and would always remain so.

I headed into town bright and early the next morning, with a slightly forced spring in my step and wearing a slightly strained smile to match it. I had taken my time over my hair, make up and outfit selection – brown low-heeled boots, jeans, a cashmere cream coloured sweater and leaf patterned scarf – and looked the best I could under the circumstances. My emotions were still swirling all over the place if left unchecked for three seconds together, but as long as I didn't run into Ash and his mermaid companion, I thought I'd be fine.

'So, families will be carving and painting their pumpkins in here,' I said, as I swept efficiently through the town hall, with a clipboard and pen in my grasp, 'and adults will be carving outside in the square, once the votes have been cast for the favourite dog outfit.'

The yarn bombers had really gone to town, knitting their selection of autumn outfits for dog owners to pick and dress their pooches in before taking to the catwalk. Or should that have been dogwalk?

I had attempted to turn Pixie into a crocheted pumpkin but just as I had suspected she would, she flatly refused to play ball and was now simply, and begrudgingly, wearing an autumn patterned bandana. I wasn't sure she'd ever forgive me for tying it to her little head, but as the pooch belonging to the festival organiser, it felt important that she should play some part.

'That's it,' said Kathleen, another town local who was as organised as I was and had tweaked the itinerary when some parents told her their children would rather paint than carve their pumpkins. 'Warm drinks and snacks in here and on the market, and judging, for the carving competition after the dogs have been put through their fashionable places, happening at the end of the day.'

'Super,' I nodded, giving another item on my list a big tick. 'And who will be serving the drinks and snacks in here?'

'Only Dorothy, who is the cook from Wynthorpe Hall,' Kathleen told me. 'So, we might need to draft your deputy in to help with that if it gets really busy.'

'No need to bother him with it,' I said breezily. 'I'm here. I can drop Pixie off at the gallery to stay with Lizzie and do it if needs be.'

'Are you sure?'

'Absolutely,' I said as Lizzie herself then rushed in with a tray of paints and brushes.

'More supplies,' she said, then added before she dashed out again, 'and don't forget to cover the tables. It will save time on cleaning up at the end of the day.'

'Already on it,' I told her. 'Right, I'm going to check everything's ready outside.'

It was another cloudy, but thankfully dry day. It would have been wonderful if the sun put in an appearance, but I'd rather have had the cloud than the rain we'd previously been subjected to. Not that I wanted to get sidetracked again thinking about the tumult the earlier weather had unleashed.

'So,' Jason, who was inspecting the large variety of pumpkins available to buy and carve in the competition, said expectantly, as he sidled up.

'So . . .' I said, drawing the word out and looking confused.

'The vet,' he said, a little too loudly for my liking. 'What did he say?'

'Oh, Ash,' I said, moving away from where we could be overheard. 'Nothing.'

'You mean, he denied it?' Jason frowned, as he followed me. 'He actually told you he doesn't have more than friendly feelings for you?'

'I mean, I haven't had the opportunity to talk to him yet, Jason. And actually, I've decided I'm not going to.'

'You're not?' He sounded disappointed.

'I'm not,' I confirmed. 'Because I know for a fact that your deductions about his feelings for me are entirely wrong and I would hate to ruin a beautiful friendship by bringing them up.'

'How do you work that out?'

'Because he's seeing someone else,' I said, grinding the words out. 'And he can't be in love with me if he's seeing someone else, can he? Or if he is in love with me and still seeing someone else, then he's certainly not the guy for me.'

'I thought he wasn't the guy for you, no matter what he felt?' Jason said cleverly.

'You know what I mean,' I tutted. 'Now, let me get on. Why don't you go and select your prize-winning pumpkin? The competition is going to start as soon as the dogs have been judged.'

Pixie and I stood and watched the parading pooches in their array of autumn themed outfits. There were dogs of all sizes, including Bella's spaniel, Tink, strutting their stuff and, for the most part, not looking too mortified. That said, the whippet dressed as a witch didn't look overly impressed with life.

'And the winner is,' shouted the head of the yarn bombing squad, who had counted the show of hands from the large and laughing crowd who had gathered to watch, 'the Yorkshire terrier dressed as a pumpkin!'

'There, Pixie,' I tutted, as the owner claimed their prize. 'That could have been you.'

She didn't look as though she cared either way and scratched at the bandana in another attempt to pull it off.

'I've seen it all now,' Jason said with a wry smile, before he went to claim the pumpkin he wanted to carve.

I watched him walk away thinking that at least the sight of the dogs dressed up had stopped him thinking about the man who looked after a lot of them.

I could then see that Jake and Amber, who were in charge of the pumpkin carving, were getting ready to call everyone together to explain the rules and make a start.

'You haven't seen my deputy, have you?' I asked Joanne, who took Jason's place next to me, once he'd gone off.

I still didn't really want to see Ash, but there was plenty for us to do and we wouldn't have to be together while we did it.

'Jason wasn't giving you a hard time, was he?' Joanne scowled in his direction.

'Absolutely not,' I told her. 'Did you not know he's turned over a new autumn leaf?'

Not only had I still not told Ash that Jemma had found a note about the missing ballot box, I hadn't spread the word about Jason now being a good guy either. My brain, since the night I'd realised I'd fallen for Ash, had been completely distracted and it was time I got it properly back on track.

'Yeah, right!' Joanne snorted, then seeing the look on my face, added, 'You're kidding?'

'I am not.'

'Really?' She was agog.

'Really. He's all for the festival now. Look, he's even joining in with the pumpkin carving. Apparently, he has plans to trounce the competition.'

'I don't believe it.'

'Well, you must,' I told her. 'And you can spread the word about that. He's an entirely different man now.'

'I wonder what's brought that on?' she asked, and I noticed she had turned a little pink as a result of me suggesting she could share the news.

Clearly, she was still feeling guilty about revealing my identity as the person behind AutumnEverything, but I truly didn't mind. Rather than being the nightmare I had once predicted, the revelation had set me free and stopped me being so guarded and preoccupied with putting my foot in it every time I opened my mouth. Being able to simply talk, as opposed to constantly planning what I was going to say, was liberating.

'If Jason wants us to know, I'm sure he'll tell us,' I shrugged, because his story wasn't mine to tell. 'Now, any thoughts on my deputy?'

'Oh, he's not here today,' Joanne then told me casually. 'He's watching the pumpkin field for Amber and Jake. With it being so close to Halloween they didn't want to shut it for the day, so he said he'd take care of it.'

'Well, he might have told me,' I tutted.

Though perhaps he was too preoccupied with other things, or another person, to factor me in to his thoughts now.

'I told him I'd let you know when I saw you,' Joanne then said, which made me feel bad for being stroppy. 'He popped in to the café to pick up some lunch and explained what he was going to be doing then. He also said he's been looking after some horse that got stuck on the riverbank last week. Did you hear about that? It was a full-on drama from what I can make out. It was all over the paper yesterday.'

'Good,' I said. 'That'll take the last of the heat off me.'

'Has it been really bad?' She winced.

'No,' I said, feeling abashed for making more of it than it warranted. 'It's actually been fine. I've barely heard a peep, though I have been told that there's plenty being discussed when I'm not in earshot.'

'That doesn't surprise me,' she said, acknowledging Jemma who was standing in the café doorway and waving a tea towel to get her attention. 'Folk love nothing more than a good gossip.'

She grinned and gave me a nudge as she made the pronouncement, so clearly, she now recognised herself as one of those folk.

'Never mind waving back.' I nudged her in return, with a nod to the café. 'I think it looks like Jemma needs you over there, don't you?'

'I daresay she does,' she smiled. 'She sent me over here to ask you if you wanted me to count the public window display votes.'

'Oh my god!' I choked. 'I'd forgotten all about that.'

'That's not like you.' Joanne frowned. 'We just thought you were a bit pushed for time, not that you'd forgotten completely. What's up?'

'Nothing,' I squeaked. 'It just slipped my mind.'

'So that's a yes to me doing it then, is it?' she further asked. 'And I'm sure Lizzie will be able to quickly print out and frame the certificates if that would be a help.'

'Are you sure that would be okay?' I asked, feeling so bad for forgetting.

'No problem. And if Lizzie's too busy, I'll do it, shall I?'

'Yes, please,' I said meekly. 'If it's not too much hassle. And you know,' I further confessed, 'I still haven't told Ash about the note that was left about the other box yet.'

'That will explain why he was so surprised when Jemma mentioned it.'

I really needed to get my backside in gear before things slipped further out of my control.

'Yes,' I said. 'I suppose it will. Thank her for me, will you, and thank you, Joanne, for counting the votes. I'll come over and get the certificates as soon as I've checked everything's okay in the town hall.'

'No rest for the wicked, is there?' She winked and sashayed off.

I let out a breath and felt my shoulders relax a little. At least I wasn't going to have to face Ash again just yet, but I couldn't believe I'd forgotten about the vote.

'Three cookies and two teas, please.'

'And I'll have that last slice of pumpkin pie and a coffee.'

'Did you expect it to be as busy as this?' I asked Dorothy from Wynthorpe Hall, later in the day and as the orders for snacks and drinks came in thick and fast in the town hall.

I had dropped Pixie – minus the bandana – at the gallery and come along to help. Lizzie was then sorting the certificates I'd forgotten about and, to make amends for my forgetfulness, I was doing my bit as Dorothy's assistant.

'I had a bit of an idea,' she said, as she plated up yet more of Jemma's leaf-shaped ginger and iced biscuits, 'because of how busy it always gets at the festive bake sale.'

I had been told about a whole host of Christmas town traditions now and didn't think I would need to feel worried about not having anything to do once I'd finished curating the autumn festival. Christmas, combined with the job in the gallery, would mean there'd never be a quiet or dull moment.

I had been ready to tell Lizzie that I was going to accept her offer, but since I'd been struck with Cupid's bow, or something resembling it, I'd held back. I was already doing my best to stuff Ash back in the friend box, but until I'd got the lid secure, I wasn't going to make any long-term plans. It was a relief that I hadn't already said yes, but I hoped my feelings would settle soon, because if I couldn't be in the same town as him, I didn't know what action I would have to resort to . . .

'I asked for three cookies and two teas,' said the woman I was serving. 'Not two cookies and three teas.'

'Sorry,' I apologised, making the switch.

'You just can't get the staff!' Dorothy grinned, then seeing my expression, added, 'I'm only joking, you're doing brilliantly. It's full on in here today!'

'It's certainly keeping me on my toes.'

'Hello, you two!' Dorothy then beamed at an elderly gent and younger man who had reached the front of the queue. 'What can I get you? And more importantly, are you here as spectators or are you going to show us how it's done?'

I eyed the pair with interest.

'Have you met Albert and Brodie?' Dorothy asked me.

'No.' I smiled politely. 'I haven't.'

'Well, you're in for a treat,' she gushed. 'This is Clemmie,' she added, by way of introduction.

'The festival organiser,' the elderly gentleman said and doffed his hat.

'And Instagram success story,' the younger man added.

'Both correct,' I said modestly. 'Pleased to meet you.'

'Brodie here,' said Dorothy, indicating the younger man, 'and Albert are famous, too.'

'I'm not famous,' I laughed. 'Well-known perhaps, but not famous.'

'And neither are we,' chuckled Albert.

'Yes, you are,' Dorothy insisted. 'Both of your work is in ridiculously high demand now. When I was in the gallery earlier in the week, I noticed there were red dots on every painting in the place. You can't say you aren't successful.'

'Well, we're getting by,' Brodie smiled.

'Is it your work for sale in the gallery?' I gasped.

'It is,' they said together.

'Oh, my goodness,' I said, feeling starstruck. 'Your paintings are stunning! I was hoping to buy something for myself, but as Dorothy has just said, everything was sold.'

'Well, that's very gratifying. Thank you.'

'I hope you'll be selling more work soon?'

'Next year, perhaps,' Albert said.

'But today, we're here to paint some pumpkins which Amber has asked if she can raffle off at the end of the day,' Brodie explained. 'The proceeds will go towards the fund for the festival next year.'

'Oh, thank you.' I smiled. 'That's so generous of you.'

A few of us had already talked about some of the funds raised from certain events, once expenses had been covered, being donated to a festival fund and I could imagine the celebration in the future becoming even more of an undertaking with money in the pot.

'It will be if anyone is interested in bidding on them.' Albert winked, self-deprecatingly.

I looked around the town hall and realised how much more it had filled up since the two men had arrived.

'Oh, I don't think there'll be a lack of interest,' said Dorothy. 'Here comes Kathleen to get you set up. I'll bring you some tea over.'

'And cake!' Brodie called over his shoulder as Kathleen led them away.

'Well, I never!' I laughed. 'I had no idea Wynbridge was such a hotbed of creativity!'

I was determined that, as it was obvious I wasn't going to have time to decorate my own that day, I would be taking home at least one of their painted pumpkins, whatever the cost. I could already imagine it on my Insta grid. Had Joanne not played her part in outing me, I wouldn't have shared it, but now it didn't matter.

'Oh yes,' said Dorothy. 'We've got all sorts of creative types, here. Hayley will be in later to paint a couple, too. That is, if there's enough to go around.'

'I'm sure Kathleen will have plenty in hand.'

Given the wonderful job Hayley had done creating the branding for the festival, I knew I was going to love whatever she designed, too. It might turn out to be a very expensive day!

'Yes,' Dorothy agreed. 'Kathleen will have enough put by.'

A little while before the carving competition winner was due to be announced I rushed to the gallery to collect the certificates and Pixie and made my way, with Joanne also tagging along, over to the square. The air both inside and out smelt deliciously fresh and sweet and combined with the scent of woodsmoke, it was the season perfectly personified.

'Before you announce the carving competition winners,' I said to Amber who was in a huddle with Jake while they tried to reach a decision, 'would you mind if Joanne announced the second round of shop window winners?'

'Me?' Joanne baulked, and I awkwardly linked the arm holding Pixie's lead through hers so she couldn't escape.

'That's a great idea,' Amber smiled. 'And perfect timing while we've got such a crowd gathered.'

'I can't do it,' Joanne protested.

'Yes, you can,' I said, handing her the microphone Jake had already turned on.

She did, of course, and she made quite a performance of the whole thing, too. The three top placed shops – the boutique in the courtyard being the overall winner, then the gift emporium and finally the baker's – each had a member of staff representing them in the crowd, thanks to some quick thinking by Lizzie, and they graciously received their awards amid much applause.

After that, it was time to find out who had won the pumpkin carving.

The shortlist was announced first and Jason was among them. No mean feat, I realised, when I took in the number of people taking part, along with the wonderful images they'd created. I couldn't see what he had carved, but knew it must have been good. The event had proved to be a popular one. In fact, the whole day had been a success and a distraction for me, too. I had hardly thought about Ash at all.

'Damn,' I muttered, as he established himself front and centre in my head again.

'And the overall winner is . . .' Amber announced and I found myself crossing my fingers, 'Sarah Smythe!'

Not Jason then, but he looked happy enough.

'You did well then,' I praised him as the crowd started to disperse and people carried off their pumpkins.

I could see that some featured traditional scary faces, while others were delicately and precisely carved with more intricate images and designs. I loved them all.

'It's harder than it looks,' he laughed. 'But I made the shortlist and more importantly, it was good fun.'

'It wasn't the winning then, it was the—'

'Oh, I wouldn't go that far,' he said. 'But anyway, I carved this with you in mind. You can have it, if you like.'

He turned his pumpkin around so I could see the front of it and I felt my breath catch.

'It's the cottage,' he said, sounding a little choked himself. 'It's Rowan Cottage.'

'I can see that,' I said tearfully. 'It's stunning, Jason.'

'It might not look exactly like this now, but this is how I remember it.'

'The outside is just the same,' I said, bobbing down to take in the details. 'Right down to the covered porch. It's perfect.'

'Well,' he said, clearing his throat. 'Like I said, you can have it.'

I felt moved to give him a hug, but Jason didn't strike me as the type who would feel comfortable with that, so I settled on heartfelt thanks instead. Looking intensely embarrassed, he insisted on carrying his creation over to the Land Rover, then said a hasty goodbye and headed over to the pub.

I looked at the image and, even though the painted pumpkin auction was still to take place, I decided I wanted to go home. Pixie seemed ready to head off too, and Jason's gift meant I wasn't going away empty-handed. Far from it.

'Can I give you a hand with the clearing up?' I called over to Jake.

'Nope,' he said. 'It's all in hand, Clemmie. You get off if you need to.'

'Sure?'

'Yes,' he said. 'It's been a fantastic day. A total triumph. All I ask is that we do this again next year.'

'For sure,' I said, giving Amber a wave as I opened the Land Rover door.

I hoped I would be around next year to join in, but if I couldn't get my heart to behave soon, I might find myself in danger of closing the door on the world again and that was not a happy thought to end such a wonderful day on.

Chapter 26

The next day, the sun appeared again. The sky was a cheery mix of clear, bright blue and billowing white clouds and, even though I was grateful for the upturn in the weather in time for the hastily created fungal foray in the Skylark Farm woods that the previous rain and damp weather had made possible, it in no way matched my mood.

I had been having a wonderful time at the pumpkin celebration day in town, right up until the moment Ash had popped into my head and then stubbornly refused to walk out again. I knew it was early days for quashing my crush, or whatever it was, but I wished it'd soon pass, so I really could see the wood for the trees again.

And talking of woods and trees . . .

'Clementine,' Molly from Wynthorpe Hall greeted me, when I arrived at the farm on Sunday to take part in the walk. 'I wasn't sure I'd see you today.'

I was primarily attending in my guise as festival organiser who was making amends for her forgetfulness the day before – not that I'd made my slip public and Joanne and Lizzie's help had completely covered it – but I was also there because I was interested in the fungi and it was something I didn't know much about.

'There was no way I was going to miss this,' I told her, making sure I sounded brighter than I felt. 'I'm really looking forward to it. Are you joining in with the walk?'

'Amber has asked me to lead it,' she smiled. 'I'm a bit of an expert.'

I shouldn't have been surprised about that. Of course, a witch would know her fungi!

'Fantastic,' I smiled back. 'And is there much here for us to see? Amber told me the damp weather has helped.'

'Oh yes, it has,' Molly agreed, as she tucked her wild red hair behind her ears. 'There's lots for us to look at. I've already walked the trail and found plenty to admire. Not as much as in the Wynthorpe Hall woods, but enough to hold everyone's interest, I think.'

'Perfect,' I smiled again, as I looked around the yard.

No one else had arrived yet, but then I was early.

'Why don't you go and walk the trail yourself before it gets busy?' Molly suggested. 'I get the feeling you could do with a few minutes of calm.'

My gaze swung back to her and I felt my face flush.

'Take Pixie and make the most of the peace,' she further said. 'I'll let Amber and Jake know you're here.'

'All right.' I nodded, trying not to feel shocked that she had known just what I needed. 'I'll see you in a bit.'

'No rush,' she said and turned towards the farmhouse.

The trail looked rather different in the daylight and I took my time walking the path towards where I knew the seating was. I couldn't stop myself from thinking about my previous visit in the dark with Ash.

We had cleared the air that evening after the awkwardness that followed the Fenview Feast, but everything was muddled again now. As I wandered along, with Pixie sniffing at the fallen leaves, I couldn't help wondering if things might have turned out differently between us if we had kissed that night . . .

Lost in my thoughts, I sat on the bench in the clearing. I didn't take any notice when Pixie pulled on her lead, assuming she'd caught the scent of something she wanted to chase, but when she barked and I heard heavy footfalls I looked up to find Ash rushing to meet us and I had to pay attention then.

'Clemmie,' he puffed, once he'd caught his breath. 'I'm so relieved you're here.'

'You are?' I frowned, taken aback by the seriousness of his tone.

'Yes,' he said, as he took a step closer. 'I am. My god, Clemmie, I've only just found out.'

'Found out what?' I asked as I stood up and Pixie strained towards him.

He looked at me for a moment and swallowed hard. 'About how . . .' he awkwardly started, then pulled off his hat and twisted it in his hands. 'About how Callum . . . died. I've literally just been told.'

I felt my throat go dry.

'*And* that you were at the rescue by the river the other night,' he then continued.

'I see.' I swallowed, feeling myself go hot.

'Tim's just seen your Land Rover parked up and said it was there that night and when I told him it belonged to you, he felt awful. He said he saw you and talked to you, but didn't know it was you and if he had, he would have helped you because he knew what had happened to Callum by then, even though until he just filled me in, I didn't.'

'It was fine,' I lied. I felt incredibly touched that Ash still hadn't typed my name into a search engine. He had doubtless been waiting for me to tell him the details myself, but of course, for one reason and another, I hadn't managed it. It was odd to think that he was one of the last people to know, when really, he should have been the first. 'I didn't need help.'

'But it must have been terrifying—'

'Well, I've had better nights out,' I cut in. 'But I didn't know what I was going to find there when I stopped, did I? I just happened to see the lights and . . .'

'How did you see the lights when you were supposed to be at the cottage waiting for me?' he asked.

'Oh, I had to unexpectedly go out,' I blagged. I wasn't about to confess to being in a panic and trying to track him down. 'Anyway, it doesn't matter now.'

'Of course it matters,' he said, taking another step nearer. 'Had I known you'd been there *and* about Callum's accident, I would have kept you properly informed and come to the cottage to let you know I was okay straight after. You must have been worried.'

'I was when I realised what was going on,' I admitted. 'But then I spotted you with Will and knew you were all right. How's the horse, by the way?'

'Never mind the horse,' Ash said, sounding frustrated.

'Look,' I said. 'I don't want to talk about it, which is why I'm trying to move the conversation on.'

'Okay, sorry,' he said, running a hand through his hair. 'Well, the horse is fine. We're taking her to a local charity next week as no one's claimed her.'

'That's so sad.'

'It could have been a far worse outcome. You saw how the river was raging that night. Sorry,' he then immediately apologised, with a wince. 'That was insensitive.'

'It's fine,' I said. 'Please don't feel like you've got to pussyfoot around me.'

'All right,' he said, his shoulders dropping a little. 'Going forward, I'll try not to.'

He reached out in a way that I recognised as him coming in for a hug and I stepped back, almost tripping over Pixie in my haste.

'What is it?' Ash frowned.

'Nothing,' I whispered.

'Everything is all right between us, isn't it?' He then frowned deeper. 'I know I haven't seen you since before that night, but I messaged and I've been taking care of the horse and working flat out. I promise you though, Clemmie, had I known sooner about Callum, I would have—'

'It's not that,' I cut in.

'What then?'

I looked at him and then at the ground.

'What?' he said again.

I was scared to say the words, but went for it anyway.

'I need to ask you something?' I gulped.

'Go on.'

'Are you,' I said, before I could chicken out, 'in love with me?'

'What?' he laughed, but not in an amused way.

'Are you in love with me?' I asked again. 'Yes or no.'

He squeezed his eyes shut. 'Am I in love with you?' he repeated, when he finally opened them again.

The question sounded ludicrous and if I could have taken the words back, I would have done.

'Yes,' he then said, before I had a chance to apologise for asking. 'Yes, I'm in love with you, Clemmie. Of course I am.'

'That's exactly what I said,' I started to blurt, then realised I'd misunderstood what he'd said and stopped. 'Wait. What?'

'I've been in love with you from the moment you walked into the café the day we met,' he carried on, going for broke himself. 'My world has been turned upside down because of you. My entire being, when we're not together, is consumed by thoughts of you. I've developed a passion for the local birdlife because of you, I've joined Instagram. I've . . . I've done everything I can think of to be near you, knowing I love you, but can never be *properly* near you.'

Pixie started to whine and I picked her up.

'Ash—'

He didn't stop.

'When we first met,' he rushed on, 'I knew you were single and wanted to be, but I clung to the hope that you'd fall for me anyway, right up until the moment . . . right up until the moment that you told me your heart belonged to someone else and, because they had died while you were still in love with them, it always would.'

'Ash—' I interrupted again.

'Then, after the feast, I tried to stay away from you, but that hurt like hell and I realised that if I wasn't careful, I'd lose you as a friend, too. And that would be worse, right? Friends might not be everything, but it's definitely something. Being your friend is a million times better than not having you in my life at all. I can't bear the thought of not having you in my life.'

A sudden and deafening silence followed this emotional outpouring. A part of me wanted to shout out that I felt exactly the same way, but the part of me that could still visualise the woman he'd shared a shower with and the other part that could still feel my wedding band, even though I no longer wore it, won out.

'I have to go,' Ash finally said as he crammed his hat back on his head and after enough time had passed for it to become apparent that I wasn't going to respond.

His voice was strained and not surprisingly, he couldn't meet my eye. He had just poured his heart out to me, confessed everything that Jason, of all people, had noticed and I had given him . . . nothing. If I was in his shoes, I wouldn't have been able to get away fast enough, either, whether I'd already found solace in someone else or not.

'I'm so sorry,' he whispered and with that, he was gone.

It took me some time before I felt ready to leave too, but eventually I made my way back to the yard. There were quite a few vehicles parked up by then, but there was no one in sight and I guessed everyone had made their way to the start of the trail. I sent Amber a quick text apologising for ducking out and drove straight back to the cottage. I'd learn about fungi another day.

The closer I got, the more I hoped I'd find Ash's truck

parked on the side of the road with him waiting for me in it, but the drove was empty and for the first time that autumn, Rowan Cottage felt cold when I turned the key in the lock and walked in.

With the heating turned up and the fire roaring, I sat in my armchair with Pixie on my lap and both of us wrapped in my favourite fleece blanket. I had thought I wanted to know how Ash felt about me, but now that I did and it wasn't the way I had expected, it was no comfort at all. I wasn't sure if I would have felt differently had I not seen his guest at the barn, but what did it matter when my heart was still bound to another?

'Callum,' I said softly. 'Can you help me now?'

I collected the box, filled with his notes and cards, from its spot on the shelf in my wardrobe and carried it down to the sitting room in the hope of finding comfort or inspiration or even both.

I sat cross-legged in front of the wood burner, with Pixie watching from the armchair and lifted the lid. The notes, and their sentiments were as warm and familiar as always, but they offered nothing to help me work through the complications my heart was currently facing. I delved deeper and spread out birthday, Valentine's, Christmas cards and a solitary wedding anniversary card. That was almost my undoing, but I resisted the urge to bundle them away again and carried on searching.

The very last card in the box had a bottle of champagne on the front. Callum had given it to me to celebrate the day we'd successfully bid on and won our broken-down house at the property auction. It was the house we had both wanted, but Callum had doubted we'd be able to secure. I, however, had known without any doubt it was *the one* and in spite of the damning survey, reports and all its associated problems, I fought fiercely for it, we won it and together we had gone on to make it a beautiful home.

'"To my darling, brave, Clemmie,"' I read aloud. '"Thank goodness one of us listens to our heart, rather than our head! Here's to the future and many more adventures following your intuition! With all my love, Callum."'

I sat back and silently read the words again. We might not have had time enough to manage more adventures, but Callum was right, I had always listened to my heart and followed my intuition. In all walks of life, I had been ruled by the feelings I had deep inside, rather than the doubts my head would attempt to scotch those gut feelings with . . . so why was I suppressing them now?

'Ash!' I gasped, as someone suddenly knocked on the door and made me jump.

Given the timing, I assumed that it could only be him, but it wasn't.

'Molly,' I said, feeling both confused and guiltily disappointed to find her standing there. 'Are you okay?'

'I am,' she said. 'But I don't think you are.'

'How did you get here?' I asked, looking over her shoulder.

I remembered she'd mentioned Hayley's driving the day we met at the library, which gave me the impression that she didn't sit behind the wheel herself.

'Hayley was driving me back to the hall from the farm and I asked her to drop me off,' Molly explained.

'I see.'

'She'll be back in a while. I hope that's okay?'

'Of course,' I said, still wondering what the purpose of her unexpected visit was. 'Come in.'

'Thank you.'

After she'd handed me the cloak she was wrapped in, I showed her into the sitting room.

'You have a beautiful home,' she said, looking about her. 'And one of Bella's fairies, I see.'

'That's Aurora,' I told her.

'Dawn.' Molly smiled in her serene way. 'How utterly perfect.'

'That's right. Would you like something to drink?'

'No, thank you,' she declined. 'I was sorry you missed the walk this morning.'

'Yes,' I sighed. 'I'm sorry about that, too, but something . . . came up.'

She looked at me for a moment. 'Clemmie,' she then said more seriously as she sat on the sofa and Pixie slowly sidled along so she was next to her and curled up. 'May I ask what it is that's troubling you?'

I sat in my armchair, rather less elegantly, and realised Callum's cards and notes were still spread about.

'I might be able to help you,' she added kindly. 'If you feel able to let me.'

'Oh, Molly,' I said, giving her a wobbly smile. 'I don't think you can.'

'Let's see, shall we?'

In a move that was very unguarded for me, I then proceeded to tell her how I'd always followed my heart, the card from Callum proving that I was known for it and that I could be brave too, when I needed to be.

'But for some reason,' I swallowed as the words started to

stick, 'I just can't seem to stop letting my head rule things, when it comes to my feelings for . . . Ash.'

Molly didn't seem at all surprised that his name had come up.

'Well,' she said, 'that's because the head is far simpler to work with than the heart and of course, *your* heart, Clemmie, has been battling feelings of disloyalty most likely right from the very first moment you set eyes on Ash.'

'You mean,' I frowned, 'you think I've loved him as long as . . .'

'He's loved you?' she picked up. 'Yes, I do think that.' I was flabbergasted. 'And I do also think that you are now finally listening to your heart again, even if you don't realise it. You'd already started to long before today and these words from Callum here have prompted you further, but you're still not quite there yet.'

'You're right.'

'So, what is it, Clemmie? What's now stopping you telling Ash that you're in love with him and embracing this new dawn?'

We both looked at Aurora again.

'Oh, Molly,' I sadly said. 'There's no point in me telling him now because I know he's seeing someone else. I saw him at the barn, with another woman.'

'No,' Molly gasped. 'No, that's not right. It can't be . . .'

'I saw her with my own eyes,' I sighed. 'And of course I'm not judging, but I can't risk my heart for someone who isn't going to be . . . all in, can I?'

'Ash is all in,' Molly said firmly. 'You need to talk to him.'

'I'm not sure if I can . . .'

'But before you do,' Molly interjected, ignoring the doubt I'd expressed, 'you need to let Callum's hold on your heart go.'

'I still haven't managed to do that, have I?'

'You almost have,' she said, standing up again. 'But not quite.'

According to Molly, autumn was the perfect time for letting go in a big way. Clarifying, she explained, that shedding the feelings that no longer served me and acknowledging that change was both beautiful and necessary would be a huge help going forward. She told me this while encouraging me to write down everything I could think of that I wanted to be free from in preparation for performing a simple fire ritual.

I still didn't know if a relationship with Ash was in my future – Molly assured me that it was, but there was still the issue of the other woman – however, the one thing I was very clear on was that I no longer wanted my life, more specifically, my heart and my potential love life, to continue to be so bound to my past.

I would never forget Callum, but I did now want to love again and I wanted to do it without the associated feelings of guilt and disloyalty that my heart was already nudging me to release. It was time.

Molly and I sat together in front of the wood burner. She said a few words and I repeated them and then I cast my note into the fire. We watched the paper burn and the flames fly up the chimney, taking my former feelings with them.

'There,' she smiled, letting out a long breath. 'How do you feel now?'

'Like a weight has actually lifted.' I smiled in response, as I rolled my shoulders and stretched my neck.

It was true. I did feel very different.

'Well, you needn't sound so surprised,' she laughed in that tinkling way of hers. 'You obviously believed in the magic, otherwise you wouldn't have gone through with the ritual.'

I gave her a sheepish smile.

'You know,' I confessed, 'I was a bit scared of you when we first met.'

'I know,' she simply said.

'But I'm not now.'

'I know that, too,' she grinned and I laughed, just as my phone pinged with a notification.

'Hayley's just pulled up,' I told her once I'd read it.

'Perfect,' she nodded, and said goodbye to Pixie while I collected her cloak. 'Do you know what you're going to do now?'

'I do,' I told her. 'And it's all thanks to you, Molly. Thank you.'

'If you weren't ready,' she told me, 'you wouldn't be going to do it, which means that, actually, it's all down to you.'

Once Molly had gone Pixie and I set off for the barn again. It was getting late, but a corner had been turned and I had no desire to wait a moment longer before I reset my compass on a hopefully new and exciting path.

'Damn,' I muttered, as I pulled on to the drive and my headlights picked out the back of Ash's truck *and* the one belonging to the woman who had been there before.

My heart didn't feel quite so light when I spotted her hugging Ash on the doorstep. I realised that it was the same woman he'd embraced at Skylark Farm and probably in the shower, too.

'Do you think they've noticed us?' I asked Pixie and she barked in confirmation. 'You're right and I'm not bottling it now,' I forthrightly added, then parked and turned off the engine.

While I had been manoeuvring, the woman had walked over, so I had no choice but to open the window because she clearly wanted to say something.

'Hi,' I said.

'Lost again?' she smiled.

'Something like that.'

'No, you're not,' she laughed. 'You're Clemmie, aren't you?'

'Yes,' I confirmed, looking briefly at her. 'Yes, I am.'

She was very pretty.

'I'm Lottie,' she then told me. 'Will's partner.'

I looked at her again, more sharply that time.

'You know, Ash's boss?' She frowned, probably thinking I didn't know who Will was.

'You're Will's partner?' I asked, feeling even more confused, but her next words explained everything.

'Yes,' she said. 'We're in the process of having the bathroom at Cuckoo Cottage remodelled and it's a total nightmare, so we've been showering here while it's being sorted.'

I felt my face flush crimson. 'Oh, right.' I swallowed. 'I see.'

'You've just finished a renovation, haven't you?' she carried on. 'So, you know what it's like. Builders, plumbers and electricians, they promise it'll be a five-day job and five months later you're still living in a building site! We could use the glamping facilities, but it's a bit chilly at this time of year.'

I knew she had vintage caravans to rent on her land and some railway carriages, too, so there were obviously camping style facilities available but as she said, hardly warm to wash in now the summer had long since passed.

'Come on, Lottie!' I heard Will shout and I realised he was

in the driving seat of his truck. 'Otherwise, we'll miss our reservation in town.'

'I'd better go,' Lottie smiled. 'We've got dinner plans and I need to drop my truck at the garage first. It's nice to meet you at last.'

'Likewise,' I said, feeling like an utter fool.

'Do try and talk Ash out of leaving, won't you?' she said, as a parting shot.

'Leaving?' I gasped and Will honked the truck horn, making us both jump.

'Yes, he's on about moving back to Bakewell. Will is devastated.'

I waited until Will, who waved as he went by, and then Lottie had gone, then unclipped Pixie from her harness and climbed out. Ash was still in the open doorway and I felt awkward crossing the drive and walking up the path with him watching me.

'You met Lottie, then?' he asked, when I was close enough to hear him.

'Yes,' I said. 'I'd seen her before, but not to talk to.'

'What, here?'

'It doesn't matter now.' I gulped as I reached him.

'Did you get my note?' he asked, croakily. 'Hello, Pixie.'

'Note?' I frowned, as he let us into the barn ahead of him and then closed the door.

'The one I put through the cottage door.'

'I've just come from the cottage, but I didn't see a note,' I told him, my heart hammering as I looked up into his handsome and familiar face. 'I was with Molly.'

'What, at your place? I didn't realise you knew her well enough to warrant a visit.'

He hadn't looked at me properly since I'd crossed the threshold and I hoped with the whole of my heart, now I knew it had been Lottie and Will in the barn bathroom and not another woman Ash had got cosy with, that he wasn't regretting telling me that he loved me or worse still, had a change of heart and no longer thought he did. Though if Lottie was right, and he was planning to leave, then it was feeling likely that he had.

'Well, I didn't, but I do now,' I rushed to say, all inner poise and former determination to stay calm taking flight. 'Ash, there are things I need to say to you.'

'And there are things I need to say to you, too,' he said, still looking over the top of my head and not giving me a chance to get my words in first. 'To start with, I'm sorry I put you in a difficult position earlier by telling you that I'm in . . . well, you know what I said.'

And clearly, he wasn't about to say it again.

'And secondly, I don't want you worrying about running into me and feeling awkward, because I'm moving back to Bakewell. I can see now, this was the reason why I never found a place of my own and it will be easier for me to go as a result. Will isn't happy, obviously, but you're settled here, Clemmie. You love Rowan Cottage and so I'm leaving to save you further upset. You've had more than enough of that in your life, though upset is hardly the right word, and I don't want to add to it.'

'Right,' I said, standing on tiptoe, so he had no choice but to notice me. 'Finished?'

'I suppose,' he said, looking at me, but only briefly.

'Good.' I nodded. 'Okay, so let's get this straight. You're actually going nowhere, because . . . because I can't bear the thought of losing you now that I've realised I've fallen in love with you, too.'

He looked at me properly then. 'What?' He blinked.

'I'm in love with you, Ash,' I said again and I thought my drumming, but finally properly listened to, heart was going to fly out of my chest.

'You're in love with me?'

'Yes,' I answered, and my knees began to tremble. 'I'm completely and utterly in love with you.'

His gaze flicked to my lips for a fleeting moment and then I didn't have to worry about my knees giving way, because he swept me into his arms and held me close.

'But are you still in love with me?' I asked, wanting to be completely certain before things went any further.

'Of course I am!' he said, twirling me around.

'Oh well, in that case,' I smiled as his mouth dipped tantalisingly close to mine, 'you really had better stay, hadn't you?'

'Yes,' he whispered back, with a smile, 'I think it would be best if I did.'

Our first kiss was long and lingering, seductive and sweet. We were a perfect match, just the right fit and when we eventually drew apart, my heart and my head were as one and I felt both excited and relieved to finally have our love for one another declared and out in the open!

Chapter 27

I mysteriously never did find his note, which Ash told me revealed his plan to leave, and for the next three days, the only time we were apart was overnight and when he was working. With our sincere love for one another finally declared, we had been inseparable and, even though we were taking the most intimate parts of our relationship slowly, we had talked and talked for hours about every aspect of ourselves, including more details about my past as well as Lizzie's exciting job offer and I was beginning to feel that I knew Ash every bit as well as I knew myself.

In fact, I knew him so well and felt so certain that ours was a love that was going to last a lifetime, that I no longer wanted to keep it to myself. We hadn't yet shared the news with our friends in town, but it was Halloween the next day and there was a full-on afternoon and evening of festival events, where we were bound to be spotted together.

As a result, we hatched a plan and happily prepared ourselves for the stir that a well-timed kiss in the square, preferably in front of Joanne, would create.

However, the two people that I most wanted to know about

us first were Mum and Dad and with them set to visit the following weekend, I decided to share the news and give them time to get used to it before they arrived at Rowan Cottage along with the opportunity to air their opinions to one another, whatever those might turn out to be, without being overheard.

'Hello, love.' They both smiled, when I called them straight after Ash had left me on the Friday evening.

He had said he was going early to let me get organised and have a good night's sleep ahead of the imminent busy day, but I knew he'd noticed I was feeling jittery about making the call and thought the earlier in the evening I did it, the better.

'Hello, Mum.' I swallowed. 'Hi, Dad.'

'Look at you, Clemmie,' Dad laughed. 'You're looking wonderful, my love.'

'Am I?'

'Yes,' Mum agreed with Dad. 'You are. I was worried taking this festival on might prove too much for you to manage on your own, but clearly, it's been the making of you. You're positively glowing!'

'Well,' I said, taking up the opening her words offered. 'As you might recall, I haven't done it entirely on my own. I do have a very competent deputy assisting me.'

I could feel the colour starting to rise in my cheeks.

'Ah, yes,' said Dad, with what looked suspiciously like an attempt at waggling his eyebrows, 'Ash, the vet.'

'What are you doing?' I frowned. 'What's with the face, Dad?'

Mum shook her head and gave him a nudge. 'What I think your father is getting at,' she said, 'is that he's seen a photo of the fella on the Facebook festival page and we both think he's a very handsome young man.'

I knew the photo they'd seen. It had been taken in the pumpkin field. Ash looked entirely at home in his muddy wellies and grubby waxed coat and had no idea someone was about to capture the moment he and Jake shared a joke and he burst out laughing. I could have fallen for him on the strength of that one image alone, now that I'd opened my heart far enough to let love in again.

'Oh.' I further blushed. 'I see. Well, yes, you're completely right, Ash is very handsome. Even more handsome close up,' I added, dreamily.

'Exactly how close up?' Dad asked keenly.

I took a deep breath, but didn't then need to grapple to find the right words to tell them because they both guessed.

'You're in love with him, Clemmie!' Mum gushed. She'd never been one to skirt around a situation. 'You're together, aren't you?'

'That's why you look so radiant.' Dad applauded.

'Yes.' I smiled, feeling both ecstatic and still surprised to be saying the words. 'We are together and yes, we are very much in love.'

Mum gasped and her hands flew to her face.

'Are you pleased?' I asked.

Their reactions suggested they were, but I still sought their confirmation.

'Pleased,' Dad tutted. 'That's a feeble word, Clemmie! We're absolutely over the moon, aren't we, love?'

'We are!' Mum cried happily, her hands still cradling her face. 'Oh, my darling, we truly couldn't be happier for you.'

'And I tell you who else will be thrilled, too,' Dad was excited to tell me.

'Who?' I asked.

'Jill and Colin,' he declared.

'Do you really think so?' I gulped.

I had been wondering how Callum's parents were going to feel to know that I'd moved on in a more meaningful way than just moving house.

Dad gave Mum a nudge.

'We've never mentioned it before,' she told me, emboldened by his encouragement, 'but Jill is always asking if you've met someone. And now Colin is coming out of the shadows, he's mentioned it, too. They're going to be so happy for you. We all knew you were too young to be alone and hoped that one day, someone wonderful would come along.'

'Well,' I said, feeling genuinely touched. 'He has. Ash really is truly wonderful and I can't wait for you to meet him next weekend.'

'We're looking forward to that, too,' Dad told me and I realised they weren't going to need time to get used to the idea, after all. 'And if we see Jill or Colin, would you mind if we mentioned it? Or would you rather tell them yourself?'

'Given that the topic has come up between you before, I wouldn't mind you telling them. Unless you think that would be passing the buck?'

'Hardly,' Mum said. 'Let's say, if we see them this week, we'll tell them.'

'And if we don't,' Dad finished up, 'you can let them know after we've visited.'

That felt like a satisfactory plan and knowing how happy Mum and Dad were, I didn't feel at all daunted by the thought of either them, or I, telling Jill and Colin now.

'Sounds good to me,' I therefore said. 'I'll see you next week!'

We signed off feeling excited that we were all going to be together again soon and under such happy circumstances.

'So, they thought I was a good-looking chap, did they?' Ash bragged, the next morning when he arrived in time for breakfast ahead of the Halloween celebrations in town.

He puffed out his chest and looked cock-a-hoop at the thought, which made me giggle.

'They did,' I confirmed as I handed him a plate loaded up with eggs, grilled Skylark Farm bacon, tomatoes and thick slices of buttered toast. 'But I told them the photo was a lucky shot and up close you weren't all that.'

I squealed as he put the plate down and then chased me around the kitchen and sitting room, with a spatula still in my hand and Pixie barking and joining in the fun.

'I didn't! I didn't!' I denied hotly, when he caught me and threatened to tickle me until I retracted the statement.

'As long as you're sure?' he pretended to growl and tickled me anyway.

'I am,' I laughed, pushing him away as I caught my breath and then pulling him back again so I could kiss him. 'I actually said you look even better close to.'

'Well, that's all right then,' he said, kissing me with a passion that left my lips tingling and my appetite at an all-time high.

'Now,' I grinned, 'eat your breakfast before it gets cold. And then perhaps we'll see if we can find a way to work off some of the calories.'

He dropped me in an instant and grabbed his plate and cutlery which made me shake with laughter all over again.

'The compost heap needs turning,' I told him coquettishly once I'd recovered. 'And I could do with more logs bringing in for the fire.'

'Is that really what you had in mind?' he laughed.

'For now.' I winked.

We headed into Wynbridge in plenty of time to check that everything was set up in the town hall for the first of the films that were going to be shown ahead of the Halloween procession. After that, there was going to be another screening and even later a fancy-dress party in the pub which, I'd been told, was Jeanie's forte and an annual event now.

'I'll go and check the procession set up with Tom, shall I?' Ash offered.

'Yes, please,' I said, as I looked over the lists attached to my trusty clipboard. 'And I'll make sure Kathleen and the others have the films the right way around.'

'Oh crikey,' Ash laughed. 'Can you imagine if the two got muddled?'

'Given that the first screening is for tots and the second for teens, it doesn't bear thinking about.' I shuddered, then raced off.

'We'll meet in the square when we're done!' Ash called after me and I waved.

With everything checked, checked and checked again, I walked over to the square and spotted Ash standing alone, with his hands in his pockets. He was wearing a burnt orange and brown chunky knit under his trademark waxed jacket, heavy boots and dark jeans and he looked utterly irresistible. In fact, I wasn't going to resist him. He spotted me coming and bit his lip as I approached which did nothing to temper his appeal.

'Hey, you . . .' he started to say, but I wasn't in the mood for words and I kissed him long and hard without drawing breath.

'Hey yourself,' I smiled up at him when we eventually broke apart.

'I thought we were supposed to kiss when everyone had gathered for the procession?' he said, reminding me of our original plan.

'And so we shall.' I carried on smiling. 'This was just a bonus that I couldn't resist cashing in.'

'Fine by me,' he said, giving me a squeeze and then laughing as he looked over my shoulder.

'What?'

'I just spotted Joanne standing outside the café, with her mouth open so wide she could have easily caught a dozen flies in one gulp,' he told me.

'Well, that was a bit of luck. What's she doing now?' I asked, reluctantly untangling myself from his embrace so I could look, too. 'Oh,' I said. 'She's gone.'

'She's high tailed it back inside again,' he laughed.

'In that case,' I said, holding out my hand, 'let's go over and find out how far she's already spread the word.'

Not far was the answer, because she was engaged in a mild argument with Jason who was then keenly telling everyone who would listen that he had already seen mine and Ash's getting together coming and so it wasn't a surprise at all.

'Well, it was to me,' Joanne pouted and then realised we were standing behind her.

'Absolutely no matchmaking required,' I told her. 'And Jason is telling the truth. He'd worked out that Ash had feelings for me, ages ago.'

'Thank you,' Jason nodded. 'See,' he then added smugly, for Joanne's benefit.

'Close your mouth,' Jemma then told her. 'You're putting customers off their cakes. Congratulations, you two. I'm so happy for you.'

'As am I,' said Jason, as he toasted us with his coffee cup.

'Me too,' said Joanne. 'Though I could have got you together a whole lot quicker than this.'

It obviously hadn't occurred to her that Ash and I had got together when we were meant to or that her former interference could have put a spanner in the works and prevented it ever happening at all.

'Were my eyes deceiving me?' Lizzie then burst in, sending the café bell madly clanging as she looked between us. 'Or did I really just see you two kissing in the square?'

'You did,' I was delighted to be able to tell her as Ash held up our joined hands.

I had always been quite shy about public shows of affection, but our kiss had got the job done and been thoroughly wonderful to boot.

'Oh, that's amazing!' Lizzie grinned and clapped. 'I'm so happy for you both.'

'As are we,' said Ash, as he gave me another quick kiss.

'Yay!' Lizzie cheered again. 'Now I have to go, otherwise I'll have no customers left.'

'And we should go, too,' said Ash, giving my hand a gentle squeeze. 'There's still lots for us to do.'

There wasn't, but I appreciated him pulling us out of the limelight. We could hear the level of chatter rising even before we'd closed the café door.

'Mission accomplished!' he declared, kissing the back of my hand. 'Now, how about some lunch?'

'You can't be hungry already!' I laughed.

'In case you've forgotten, I had a full list of chores to complete before we came out.'

'That's true,' I relented, thinking of the long list of tasks I'd jokingly set him but he'd completed nonetheless. 'Pub then? My treat.'

The novelty of Ash and I being together soon wore off and we were able to enjoy the Halloween procession in town and award more prizes, this time for the best costumes, without too much scrutiny.

The turnout was even better than I could have hoped for and, as a result of helping Lizzie in the gallery, I recognised a few of the lanterns bobbing along the pavements and around the square and even some of the faces behind the scary masks and gaudy make-up.

The central display was full of lit pumpkins and there were strings of lights, too, all with warm orange bulbs. The atmosphere was one of harmony as I handed out sweets to the trick or treaters and felt blessed to live amongst such a wonderful community, especially now Jason had turned out to be a friend, rather than a fiend.

'Are you ready to go?' Ash asked, as lots of people headed back to the town hall for the second film and a few others made for the pub in a fascinating variety of creepy costumes. 'I don't think anyone will notice if we slip away now, do you?'

Even though Jeanie's fancy-dress party in The Mermaid had a thrilling reputation, Ash and I had decided not to attend. Pixie had been alone at the cottage a good long while already and as my beau had plans for a predawn start the next day, he had suggested a very early night.

'I'll pick you up at four,' he told me on the drive home.

'I'll be ready,' I promised.

'And wrap up warm.' I had a good idea of what he had in mind, but didn't want to ruin the surprise. 'And no, we can't take Pixie, but don't worry, because we'll be back before she wakes up and misses us.'

'Are you going to come in?' I asked as he drew up at the gate.

'Not tonight,' he said, leaning across the seat to kiss me goodnight, 'otherwise it won't be worth me going back to the barn.'

'All right,' I said, as I undid my seatbelt. 'I'll see you in the morning, then.'

I still wasn't quite ready to suggest that he didn't have to go home and I wasn't surprised that he hadn't asked. I didn't feel in any way pressured to move our relationship along and I loved him all the more for that. I was still getting used to having him in my heart, so giving him access to my bed wasn't something I was going to rush. That said, if his kisses continued to fill me with such desire it probably wouldn't take as long as I had originally thought . . .

'Oh, my god!' I shouted. 'This is amazing!'

Knowing how much I loved the birds that visited my garden and how keenly I had tracked the migrating geese that traversed the Fenland sky above, Ash had sacrificed my Sunday morning lie-in for an extremely early morning drive out to the north Norfolk coast and a stretch of marshland that seemed rather off the beaten track.

'How many do you think there are?'

'According to the most recent counts,' Ash told me as the air was filled with another intense wave of wing beats and honks, 'well over fifty thousand pink-footed geese, alone.'

'That's incredible!' I gasped.

'And there are other breeds mixed in with them, too.'

'Amazing!'

'I originally planned to come at dusk, when they return to the roost, but the guy who manages this stretch of the marsh is a mate of Will's and he said we could sneak up here, but only at dawn, because this spot isn't open to the public.'

'Well, I really appreciate it,' I told him, reaching for his hand. 'And I don't mind the early start at all. It's a spectacular sight.'

'I'm so pleased you're enjoying it,' he said, pulling me into his side. 'Not every woman would want to get up in the dark and cold and drive all this way to see and hear this.'

'Well,' I said, thinking that what with the gift of my fairy and the bird table and feeders, he already knew me so well, 'fortunately, I'm not every woman.'

'That you're not,' he said huskily as he looked down at me. 'You're utterly unique.'

We were already completely keyed into one another and, as we kissed under the flying flocks who were heading off to their feeding grounds, I found I suddenly didn't want to wait any longer to complete our relationship. It was time.

'Are you ready to go home?' Ash asked me, as the clamour of hungry geese started to die down and the sky grew lighter.

'Yes,' I said, my words filled with far more meaning than he could yet comprehend, 'I'm ready.'

Chapter 28

By the time November fifth, the day of the bonfire party on the edge of town, rather than at Wynthorpe Hall as I'd been told was usual, dawned, my life had changed beyond all recognition when compared to what it had been the year before. Then, I hadn't had so much as a sparkler to celebrate the day with, whereas now, I felt like I had an entire box of fireworks at my disposal.

I had completed the cottage renovation, I had a whole host of new friends, including perfect Pixie, I had organised and was overseeing the inaugural Wynbridge Autumn Festival, there was a new job on my horizon, my Insta account was still thriving and, most surprisingly of all, I had healed my heart enough to open it again and let love in.

What a phenomenal and transformative few months I had created! The intention I had pinned to Aurora's skirt had been about being brave enough to continue to walk the path I had started out on, but now it felt like I had sprinted miles along it.

Ash had been initially tentative about my suggestion that we should move our relationship forward when we arrived home after the trip to see the geese, but once I had convinced him that I was ready for the upgrade, he was both delighted and willing to acquiesce.

Very willing . . . and kind and tender, too, and then increasingly passionate. I was thrilled he wasn't down to work that day, or the next, and we could commit to getting to intimately know one another without any disturbance of any kind. It was certainly time pleasurably spent, even if Pixie was inclined to sulk that she had limited opportunity to snooze upstairs.

'Hello, you two!' Jake grinned when he and Amber spotted us holding hands at the party that evening. 'We heard a rumour that you were a couple now. What fantastic news!'

'Very discreet, Jake!' said Amber, as she rolled her eyes. 'But he's right,' she then said to us both. 'We're really happy for you.'

'Thank you.' I smiled as Ash pulled me close.

'And I'm sorry to dash off,' she then tutted, 'but I really need to round the kids up before they're full of sugar! Come on, Jake.'

'Actually,' he said, refusing to budge, 'I was just going to ask Ash if he might have a spare minute to give me a hand with the bonfire? I'm in charge of it and could do with a deputy.'

'Oh, he makes an excellent deputy,' I laughed.

'Come on then, Ash,' Jake also laughed.

'Do you mind?' Ash asked me, before making a move.

'Not at all,' I said, letting him go. 'I've just spotted Lizzie and I need to have a word with her, so I'll see you in a minute.'

He gave me a quick kiss, then went off with Jake and I headed over to Lizzie.

'Hello, you three,' I greeted her, Dorothy from Wynthorpe Hall and Jemma as they continued to set up a table which was already groaning with hot dogs, jacket potatoes and toffee apples. It was all proper bonfire night fare and my tummy growled in anticipation of enjoying it. 'Have you got a second, Lizzie?'

'For you,' she said, 'I might even have two.'

We walked a little distance away from the rapidly filling space around the towering bonfire that was still to be lit. The recumbent, straw-stuffed Guy had now been launched on, but not made it right to the top and looked to be in danger of sliding down.

'I know it's taken me an age to come back to you,' I told my new friend while my heart thumped hard in my chest, 'and I'm sorry about that.'

'With everything you had to organise for the festival,' she said, guessing it was her job offer that I wanted to talk about, 'you know I told you I was in no rush for an answer. And that was before you had everything extra going on in your private life, too!' she added.

'I know.' I smiled. 'It feels like an age since you offered me the job, but I do want it. I definitely want to accept it and I can start as soon as you need me to. Even before Joanne leaves, if you like. That is, assuming you still want me . . .'

'Oh, Clemmie,' she said, giving me the hugest, tightest hug. 'Of course I still want you! I can't tell you how excited I am! I'm thrilled! We're going to have the best fun.'

'Yes,' I said, smiling broadly. 'I think we are.'

'And between you and me,' she giggled, 'I already knew you were going to say yes after the lantern workshop.'

'You did?'

'Of course I did! And if you really can start before Joanne

leaves, then I could do with a hand in the run-up to Christmas. The workshops are all fully booked now, thanks to some extra interest as a result of the autumn festival, which,' she added, after taking a breath, 'everyone will definitely want you to organise again next year, if you're up for it?'

'Yes, to both!' I said, feeling excited about each of the opportunities that had come my way. 'With a whole year to get organised and funds already in the pot to grow it, the festival will be even bigger next year and I might even consider having a strategy in place by then to use AutumnEverything to help further spread the word.'

'I'm even happier now,' Lizzie beamed.

'I'm happy too,' I laughed. 'And I have to admit, and there were times when I never thought I'd feel this, that I am now so grateful that you stopped by the cottage that day and subsequently goaded me into taking the festival on.'

'I think goaded is a rather strong word,' she protested. 'Though I did sense that you weren't quite so impressed with me in the early days.'

'I really wasn't,' I laughed along with her. 'But then I met Joanne and realised meeting her first would have been so much worse!'

'I heard that!' said a singsong voice behind us.

'I know you did,' I said, turning around. 'You were meant to, Joanne.'

She stuck her tongue out and we all laughed. 'But you know what, Clemmie,' she then said, 'if Moses has been looking down on what you've achieved during these last couple of months, then I know he'll be feeling that the festival and its future is in the safest of hands.'

'Oh, Joanne,' said Lizzie, sounding choked.

I felt moved by her kind words, too, but a deafening squeak from a loudhailer cut the emotional moment off and started a couple of children crying. Jake's voice then boomed out, telling us it was time to light the bonfire and the sobs quickly turned to cheers. As the flames rapidly rose to the top of the stack, Lizzie and Joanne went to help with the food and I spotted Ash making his way towards me with two onion packed hotdogs.

'So,' he smiled. 'Did you miss me?'

'Of course I did,' I grinned. 'Is one of those for me?'

'They're both for you if you'll tell me you love me again.'

'I love you, again,' I laughed and he handed both over.

'Idiot!' I giggled, handing one back.

He took a huge bite out of his to claim it and I followed suit and tucked into mine.

'How come,' I said, once I'd swallowed a few mouthfuls and wiped most of the ketchup from my chin, 'they taste so much better outdoors?'

'I dunno,' Ash shrugged. 'Everything does though, doesn't it?'

I stood on tiptoe and kissed him, ketchup and all.

'Oh yeah,' I said. 'You're right. It does.'

I looked beyond the bonfire and spotted Molly watching us and smiling serenely. Given the number of people at the party, I was surprised she was there, but it was definitely her. I waved and she inclined her head and raised what looked like a silver chalice, rather than the recyclable paper cups the rest of us were drinking from.

'Who are you waving at?' Ash asked.

'Molly,' I said, with a nod, but when I looked again, she'd gone. 'Oh, she's disappeared.'

'Oh, well,' said Ash. 'I'm sure she'll pop up again when you least expect her to.' I knew he was right. 'Now, toffee apple first or a sparkler?'

'Um,' I said, screwing up the paper napkin my hotdog had been served in. 'Sparkler, I think.'

We wrote each other's names and drew love hearts in the dark as the full moon came into view. It was an incredibly romantic evening and the loving feeling continued when Ash drove us back to Rowan Cottage and accepted my offer to stay the night again.

'Don't go,' I said, reaching across where Pixie was asleep between us, very early the next morning and as he made a move to get up. 'I don't want you to leave.'

'I was just going to make us breakfast in bed,' he said, as he softly brushed my hair away from my face, 'but if you'd rather I—'

'No, no,' I said, then pushed him out. 'You carry on. Breakfast in bed would be wonderful.'

'That's what I thought,' he laughed. 'Come on, Pixie,' he added as he pulled on a pair of boxers. 'You can help.'

She opened her eyes, stretched and reluctantly jumped off the bed and followed him.

'There's smoked salmon in the fridge if you fancy going fancy!' I called after him.

I must have dozed off again and it was just a few minutes later, that I was startlingly woken by what sounded like my father's voice. I sat bolt upright and stock still and cocked an ear. With Pixie yapping, it was hard to make anything out clearly and I was just about to snuggle back down on the assumption that I must have been dreaming, when I heard

Mum shouting a greeting up the stairs. Her voice was followed by the sound of footsteps and Ash burst back into the bedroom still in his boxers, looking red faced and sounding out of breath.

'Your parents are here,' he puffed, reaching for his jeans and pulling the hoodie he had taken to keeping at the cottage over his head.

'But they're not coming until tomorrow!' I protested, as I flung back the duvet.

'Oh well, in that case,' he laughed, as he rushed out again, 'would you like me to tell them they're a figment of my imagination, or would you rather do it?'

By the time I had pulled on my dressing gown and descended, Dad and Ash had ferried in a multitude of bags and were chatting as if they'd known each other forever and Mum was making a pot of tea with Pixie neatly tucked under one arm. Had I not been feeling so shocked, it would have been a charming scene.

'Clemmie!' Dad shouted, when he spotted me in the doorway. 'At last!'

He rushed across the room and pulled me into his arms.

'Oh, Dad,' I gulped, tears springing up, because in spite of the unexpected nature of his and Mum's arrival, it was wonderful to see them both. 'It's so good to see you.'

'We thought we'd surprise you,' Mum chimed in, handing Pixie to Dad when he let me go and squeezing me tight herself.

'Oh, you've certainly done that,' I told her. 'Mission very definitely accomplished.'

'You were right, love,' said Dad, nodding at Ash. 'He is even better close to.'

'Dad!' I flushed and Ash shook his head.

'I apologise for my previous state of undress,' Ash said, holding up his hands. 'Had I thought, I would have got dressed before I opened the cottage door.'

'No need to stand on ceremony with us, lad,' Dad chuckled.

'Though next time, we'll telephone in advance,' Mum laughed, too.

'We'd been parked up a few minutes, wondering whether to knock or ring,' Dad elaborated. 'Then this fella opened the door to pick up the milk and, well, you know the rest.'

'Yes,' I said. 'I do, and as you're here, shall I introduce you properly?'

'Bit late for that,' Mum pointed out, with a wry smile.

'But we wouldn't say no to a bite of breakfast,' Dad requested, with a nod to the smoked salmon and eggs Ash had already got out.

The meal that followed, with us all crowded around my little table and Pixie balanced on Mum's knee, which was usually strictly forbidden, was the polar opposite of what I had envisaged would occur after my night with Ash, but it was the jolliest way I'd eaten in the cottage so far and it was wonderful that we were all together at last.

Chapter 29

With Mum and Dad unexpectedly in residence at Rowan Cottage a full twenty-four hours earlier than planned, Ash and I had limited opportunity for further alone time that day. I did, however, manage to make a trip down to the barn in the evening on the pretext of finalising plans for the festival's grand finale which was unbelievably happening the next day. We didn't do all that much planning, but along with the kissing, we did have a good giggle about Mum and Dad's impromptu arrival and the subsequent farce that had ensued!

'I was supposed to be on call tomorrow,' Ash told me, as I got ready to leave, 'but Will has switched things to be available himself.'

'That's brilliant,' I smiled. 'So we can have the whole day together.'

I was pleased about that. As excited as I was about the festival's big finish, I was feeling rather emotional about it, too. So much in my life had changed since I had taken it on and along with acknowledging that, I wanted to enjoy every last second and not get too teary. With Ash by my side, I knew I would be able to achieve both.

'We can,' he confirmed. 'Though not the night, of course. I think it would be a bit of a squeeze at the cottage with all four of us staying there, plus Pixie.'

'You're right,' I agreed. 'But perhaps I could sneak back here again for a while at some point,' I suggested, replicating my father's wriggling eyebrows.

'As tempting as that sounds,' Ash laughed, 'your parents will be gone again before you know it, so I think you should make the most of having them with you.'

'I know that really,' I said, as I pulled him close, 'but I want to make the most of having you, too.'

'Well,' he said, lowering his lips to mine and igniting another spark of desire. 'You've got me forever, so there's plenty of time for us, Clemmie. I'm going nowhere.'

The spark was sadly snuffed as a lump formed in my throat and the memory of hearing words similar to those whispered to me before forced its way in. I tried to swallow the recollection away and smile, but I knew the result was rather wobbly.

'Sorry,' I said, still trying to shake the emotion off.

Ash took my hand and led me back to the sofa where he sat me down. He then looked at me seriously and I wondered what was coming.

'I need to ask you to do something for me, Clemmie,' he began softly. 'Is that okay?'

'Of course.'

With my hand still in his, he looked deep into my eyes.

'I know,' he said, after a beat had passed, 'that you must be feeling scared and all kinds of vulnerable and that memories of conversations you had with Callum and the loving words you spoke to one another must be springing up all over the place now we're together.'

Tears filled my eyes and there was nothing I could do to halt their progress as they streamed slowly down my face.

'And I don't want you to suppress any of that, okay?' Ash continued. 'Trying to pretend that those words were never said or even that you don't think about Callum anymore, would be exhausting, so please, don't do that.'

I nodded as more tears came.

'I want you to know that I am fully aware that Callum will always have a place in your heart, that a part of you will always be attached to him and that you'll always love him. I would never ask you to switch him out for me. There's room for both of us, okay?'

'Okay,' I whispered.

'And I also want you to, but only if you want to, tell me when the tough days will be, birthdays, anniversaries, all of it. What you've experienced has shaped you, Clemmie, and I would be a pretty crap partner if I didn't acknowledge that.'

I looked into his eyes and wondered what I'd done to deserve such a magnificent man entering my life.

'My god, Ash,' I sobbed. 'How did you get to be so amazing?'

'I'm not amazing,' he said, drawing me to him. 'I just want to have the best possible life with you and be the very best person for you, that I can be.'

'Well,' I sniffed, 'in my book, that does make you amazing.'

I knew my eyes were still red and puffy when I arrived home and seeing the look that passed between Mum and Dad when I walked in, I also knew I needed to explain why I had been crying. Mum shed a tear when I told her and Dad was misty-eyed, too.

'He's a keeper, Clem,' Dad said, squeezing my hand.

'He certainly is,' I agreed, while Mum blew her nose.

'That was a truly genuine heart to heart,' Mum sniffed.

'It was,' I agreed.

'And you know,' Dad then smiled wryly, 'we knew you hadn't really gone to see him to talk about tomorrow.'

'How did you work that out?' I gasped.

'You left your clipboard and notebook here,' Dad said, with a nod to the table.

'I'm an idiot,' I laughed. 'Now, shall I put the kettle on?'

Mum and Dad shared another look and Dad nodded.

'What is it?' I asked.

'Well,' said Mum, as she reached down the side of the chair for her handbag, 'as we're traversing emotional territory, it feels like the ideal time to give you this.'

She pulled out a letter and held it out for me to take.

'It's from Jill and Colin,' Dad said unnecessarily because I recognised Jill's handwriting. 'I saw Colin a couple of days ago and told him your lovely news, and that evening, this was posted through the door.'

I turned it over and started to open it.

'You don't have to read it now,' Mum rushed to say.

'I want to,' I told her. 'Like you said, we're navigating emotional territory, so . . .'

'As long as you're sure?' Dad asked.

'I am,' I told him.

I pulled out the single sheet of notepaper and took a deep breath.

'"Our dearest, Clemmie,"' I slowly and steadily read aloud. '"This is without doubt one of the happiest letters I have written in a very long time."'

I felt Dad move closer to where Mum was sitting and kept my eyes on the paper.

'"Your wonderful news has given us so much joy and we want you to know that we're absolutely delighted for you. We have always hoped that you would find love again and now that you finally have, we couldn't be any happier. You were such a wonderful wife to Callum."' At this point my voice started to wobble and I had to take another breath. '"And we know that you would have his heartfelt blessing. We're sending you and Ash all the love in the world with these words and hope that you'll keep in touch. With love, Jill and Colin."'

'They're right,' Mum said, her words catching as I handed her the note. 'You were a wonderful wife to Callum.'

'And you do deserve so much happiness,' swallowed Dad.

'I definitely will keep in touch,' I responded, 'and perhaps one day, we'll all meet again.'

'I'm sure they'd love that,' said Dad, as Mum passed him the letter. 'Now, how about you put this somewhere safe, my love?'

'I have just the place,' I said, thinking of the box in the wardrobe.

'And I'll go and put the kettle on,' Dad offered.

'My goodness,' Mum smiled. 'Wonders will never cease!'

We all laughed and the mood, even though it hadn't felt particularly sombre, lifted back to what it had happily been when they arrived.

*

The next day, the last day of the first Wynbridge Autumn Festival, dawned sunny and cold. It was perfect weather for spending the day outside and celebrating the season. Especially when there were such wonderful shops and the pub and café to warm up in. Every spot on the market was filled and I made a point of introducing Mum to Bella because I knew she'd love her fairies as much as I did. Dad found a friend in Jason and while Ash and I showed Mum further around the town, they went off to the pub for a lunchtime pint.

'You're looking rosy,' I laughed, when Dad came to find us just ahead of the time when Lizzie and I would be making our 'farewell to the festival' speech.

I had been terrified by the prospect of public speaking the day we launched, but looking around the town that day, seeing it so beautifully dressed thanks to the efforts of the whole community and recognising so many friendly and familiar faces, I wasn't fazed at all.

'I only had one pint,' Dad grinned. 'But it was some guest ale, and I think it was a little on the strong side.'

'In that case,' said Mum, 'I'll definitely be driving us back.'

Ash, Pixie and I had come to town in the Land Rover, but Mum said it was too high for her to climb in and out of so she and Dad had followed on behind in their car.

'So,' said Lizzie, as she came over to join us. 'Are you ready, Clemmie?'

'I am,' I told her, still carrying the air of confidence I wouldn't have thought possible just a few weeks ago. 'But first, can I introduce you to my mum and dad?'

'You certainly can,' she smiled.

'So, we've you to thank for getting Clemmie involved with all this, have we?' Dad asked, his voice carrying further than usual because of the lunchtime tipple, once I'd said her name.

'Not really,' Lizzie laughed. 'It's me and everyone else in town who has to thank Clemmie for taking it on. Had she not put herself forward,' I gasped at that, 'after some mild encouragement,' she then added sheepishly, 'the festival would never have happened.'

'And that would have been a tragedy,' said Ash. 'I honestly don't know how you've managed to pull it all off in such a short amount of time, Clem.'

I felt myself turning warm under his and Lizzie's praise and loosened my scarf.

'I've pulled it off because everyone was so willing to pitch in,' I pointed out. 'Everyone who could offer to do something has and of course, I've had the best deputy in the business to help me every step of the way.'

Ash wouldn't accept that.

'I haven't been able to do as much as I would have liked,' he shrugged.

'You've done loads,' I reassured him. 'But don't worry, if you're feeling like there's more you could have done, you'll get your chance next year.'

He laughed at that and Dad nudged him, but I wasn't joking and Ash knew it.

'Are you going to announce next year's festival today?' Lizzie then asked, as we were beckoned towards the stage which had been set up again.

I handed Mum my bag and followed Lizzie up the steps. 'Absolutely,' I told her. 'No time like the present!'

Between us we carefully and methodically went through the list I'd drawn up, making sure we thanked everyone who had contributed in any way to the festival, including Moses Talbot who had originally come up with the idea and finally we reminded the crowd of everything we'd been able to offer as a result of the generous input and donations. As we reeled it all off, I couldn't pick out what I'd enjoyed the most.

The variety of events had ensured there had been something to appeal to everyone and I promised that next year the festival would be even bigger and the planning would start a whole lot earlier. That raised a few laughs.

'And now,' I announced, stepping to one side, 'it's time for Jake and Amber to auction off the magnificent pumpkins which have formed the main part of the wonderful displays here in the square! A percentage of the money raised will be added to the festival fund, so thank you both very much for donating that!'

'Well,' said Lizzie, as she took the microphone from me. 'It's *almost* time for the pumpkin auction. There's still one more person to thank.'

I checked my notes, but couldn't see that we'd missed anyone. I looked into the crowd and I couldn't see Ash either. I had hoped he might have been able to give me a clue.

'Before the auction gets under way,' Lizzie said, looking at me, 'we need to thank you, Clemmie!'

Her declaration was met with many cheers and much applause and I felt myself turn the colour of a beetroot.

'It was nothing!' I tried to shout, but my words were drowned out.

'She's trying to say it was nothing,' Lizzie tutted, 'but we know it was a lot and as a token of our appreciation, we'd like to give you these flowers, my darling . . .'

At this point, Joanne appeared at the side of the stage with another vast autumn bouquet.

'Oh, my goodness!' I laughed, as I took it from her and became completely hidden from sight which made everyone laugh. 'Thank you, everyone,' I said emotionally into the microphone that Lizzie was holding in front of my face, or where she thought my face was. 'I've had the best time organising the festival and I can't wait to do it all again *and*,' I added keenly, 'I want to thank you all most sincerely, for making me feel so welcome in Wynbridge!'

Another cheer went up and afterwards, as the crowd got ready for the pumpkin auction, Ash took the flowers from me because they weighed even more than the first bouquet Joanne had given me. I had almost got through the speech without tears, but a few had escaped.

'Are you okay?' Ash asked kindly.

'I think so,' I nodded, as I patted my face with a tissue and thanked my lucky stars that I'd opted for waterproof mascara.

'I know you're not just thinking about the festival today,' Ash continued. 'You've done so much in the last few weeks—'

'Please don't,' I cut in, with a smile. 'I love you dearly for understanding that, but if you talk about it now, you're going to properly set me off.'

'Fair enough,' he smiled back and I kissed his cheek.

'Right,' I said, as I took a deep breath. 'What now?'

'Well, there's another present for you back at the cottage,' he told me as he shifted the weight of the flowers from one arm to the other. 'Shall we go and find it?'

'Is there?' I laughed. 'Well, I don't know where you've hidden it because I didn't notice anything this morning.'

'All will be revealed . . .' he said mysteriously, and I wondered if he was offering me the chance to unwrap him.

If that was the case, I wasn't going to feel quite so guilty for slipping away for a little while, but then I remembered Mum and Dad.

'And don't worry about your parents,' Ash then said, having read my mind, 'Joanne has taken them over to the café where Jemma's giving them an early afternoon tea.'

'I'm not sure how I feel about Joanne talking to Mum and Dad,' I grimaced. 'But then I suppose, given that all of my secrets have now been revealed, she can't do too much damage . . .'

'Best not to think about it in case you've forgotten something,' Ash laughed. 'You can get the low-down from her later. Come on.'

Back at Rowan Cottage, Pixie was thrilled to see us and, while Ash tended to whatever it was that he'd somehow hidden outside, I propped the bouquet of flowers in the kitchen sink to arrange later and promised her I'd take her to town with us when we went back again.

'It's not exactly where it needs to be,' Ash told me as he led me outside having made me promise not to open my eyes until he said I could. 'But if I'd put it where I think you're going to want it, you definitely would have seen it before now.'

'Where was it before?' I asked, as I tripped along.

'In your shed,' he confessed, as he steadied me. 'Your dad helped me put it in there the other day when you and your mum were looking at something online and then he hid the key in case you went in and fell over it.'

'You sneaky pair!' I laughed.

'I hope you're going to like it—'

'I'm sure I'll love it,' I said. 'Whatever it is. Now can I please open my eyes?'

'Go on then.'

It took me a moment to take it in.

'Oh, Ash!' I gasped in shock. 'Did you make this?'

'I did,' he said, looking even more proud than when he'd constructed the bird table and feeders. 'It's a bit wonky in a couple of places, but—'

'It's perfect!' I quickly cut him off and rushed over to where he'd positioned the quirkiest henhouse, which he had also painted to match his other projects. 'I love it!' I told him as I clapped my hands and took in the details.

'It's not too much?' he asked, inclining his head to the roof which even had a little chimney and ornately cut barge boards.

'It's perfect,' I said again, as I skipped back to him and threw my arms around him. 'It matches Rowan Cottage to a T and we can spend the winter setting it up and making a massive run ahead of getting the hens in the spring. Thank you so much!'

He picked me up and twirled me around.

'I was thinking I could make Pixie a kennel next,' he suggested as he put me down. She barked at the sound of her name. 'Just for laying in when you're in the garden.'

'I think she'd like that,' I smiled up at him.

'And would you like it?' he breathlessly asked as he looked intently down at me.

'I'd love it,' I told him. 'But then, you already know, I love everything you do and everything about you, Ash.'

He kissed me for the longest time and if possible, I felt myself falling fathoms deeper for him.

'I'm not entirely sure you know everything about me yet,' he smiled, 'but I'm very much looking forward to you finding out.'

'Yes,' I laughed, as I squeezed him tight. 'I'm looking forward to that, too.'

I kissed him that time and then he let me go, picked up my darling Pixie and carried her along the path and over to the cottage, stroking the top of her head as he went. As he turned back to see if I'd followed him, he was framed perfectly in the doorway and seeing him standing there, with my four-legged friend nestled in his arms, I felt that at long last, not only had I processed my past, but I was ready to embrace my future. I had a wonderful home, fabulous friends and now, the perfect partner, too.

Everything I wanted, even though it had only been recently that I realised I did, was all wrapped up.

'I don't think anyone will miss us if we don't head straight back,' Ash said, with a smile I found more than a little seductive.

'No,' I said, rushing along the path to reach him. 'I don't suppose they will.'

I urged him across the threshold and firmly closed the door behind us. Our return to the festival finale could wait a little longer.

Acknowledgements

As always, there are a vast number of people I want to thank for helping me along the creative path while writing this book.

Firstly, my wonderful editor, Clare Hey, who asked if I would consider telling an autumn story back in October 2025. I immediately knew that Wynbridge, the pumpkin capital of the Fens, would be the perfect setting and the entire plot came together during a week with the Famous Five on our annual writing retreat. I don't think I've ever found a character and her story so fast. It was an amazing experience!

And while I'm thinking about that incredibly creative week, I want to thank Clare and Des Marchant, too. I'm not going to say why, because it isn't my tale to tell but it is a wonderfully romantic one.

I consider myself truly blessed to have a whole host of family and friends to call on when I need to talk 'at' them about a plot tangle or a minxy character. Huge thanks to Lia, Mum, Dad, Storm (my cat), Claire, Sue and The Famous Five, to name just a very few.

Thanks also to the whole team at Simon & Schuster and my wonderful agent, Amanda Preston. Not only have you helped me write this book in record time, you've also made this milestone year, celebrating publishing twenty books in ten years, so memorable and I'm forever grateful for that. What larks! Can you believe this is the twenty-first?

And last, but by no means least, thank you, readers, Swainettes, bloggers, librarians, content creators, book buyers and event organisers who champion my books both here in the UK and far beyond.

Wishing you all an awesome autumn and, until the next time we meet, may your bookshelves – whether virtual or real – be filled with fabulous fiction!

H x

About the Author

Heidi Swain lives in Norfolk. She is passionate about gardening and the countryside, and collects vintage paraphernalia. *All Wrapped Up* is her twenty-first novel.

You can follow Heidi on X or Instagram @Heidi_Swain or visit her website: heidiswain.co.uk